Praise for *A True Cowboy Christmas*

"Readers willing to brave the emotional turmoil like a frigid winter day will be rewarded at the very end with Christmas warmth and love." —*Booklist*

"Get yourself a cowboy for Christmas this year!"
—*Entertainment Weekly*

"Crews hits the mark by concentrating on personal development and internal struggles, minimizing outside drama. The story flows smoothly, is loaded with charming characters, and is full of wit. These mature, thoughtful, caring protagonists will win the heart of any romance fan."
—*Publishers Weekly* (starred review)

"Full of emotion, humor, and small-town charm. Caitlin Crews delivers everything I want in a cowboy!"
—Maisey Yates, *New York Times* bestselling author of *Claim Me, Cowboy*

"Caitlin Crews writes cowboys you'll swoon over, heroines you'll root for, and families that will grip your heart."
—Nicole Helm, author of *Cowboy SEAL Redemption*

Also by
Caitlin Crews

A TRUE COWBOY CHRISTMAS

COLD HEART, WARM COWBOY

The
Last Real
Cowboy

CAITLIN CREWS

St. Martin's Paperbacks

This is a work of fiction. All of the characters, organizations, and events portrayed in this novel are either products of the author's imagination or are used fictitiously.

First published in the United States by St. Martin's Paperbacks, an imprint of St. Martin's Publishing Group.

THE LAST REAL COWBOY

Copyright © 2020 by Caitlin Crews.

For information, address St. Martin's Publishing Group, 120 Broadway, New York, NY 10271.

www.stmartins.com

ISBN: 978-1-250-29527-9

Our books may be purchased in bulk for promotional, educational, or business use. Please contact your local bookseller or the Macmillan Corporate and Premium Sales Department at 1-800-221-7945, ext. 5442, or by email at MacmillanSpecialMarkets@macmillan.com.

Printed in the United States of America

St. Martin's Paperbacks edition / February 2020

10 9 8 7 6 5 4 3 2 1

If you've ever felt you didn't fit where you were planted, this book is for you.

Acknowledgments

I'm in awe of Monique Patterson, Mara Delgado-Sanchez, Natalie Tsay, DJ Smyter, and the rest of the team at St. Martin's—especially the *wildly talented* art department that keeps gifting me with these glorious covers—for all their hard work getting these stories into shape and these books out into the world!

Christa Soulé Désir has copyedited all three Cold River Ranch books, which means her reactions are not only the first I get to see—but she also cleans everything up so no one knows *how many* sentences I start with the word AND. A hero, in other words, who I can never thank enough!

I would be lost without the incomparable Holly Root, who handles everything, including me, with enviable good humor.

I feel grateful and lucky every day to have Nicole Helm and Maisey Yates as friends and readers, but they both went above and beyond on this book when I had to tackle some tricky revisions and needed even more guidance than usual. Thanks seem inadequate, so I will have to make it up some other way. I suspect sugar will be involved.

I'm deeply thankful, as ever, that the wonderful Jane Porter is willing to read my terrible drafts and always, always helps me change them for the better.

And none of this would possible without Jeff, my favorite.

Or without you, my marvelous readers!

Brady Everett was the insufferable, patronizing, sadly all-too-gorgeous bane of Amanda Kittredge's existence.

Because he was completely oblivious to it. Or rather, to her.

Cold River, Colorado, holiday potlucks were always the same, which could be a good thing, like the reliable appearance of Janine Winthrop's curry chicken salad from Labor Day to New Year's and back again.

Amanda found the sameness comforting, especially when she was hungry. But today, it all felt crushing in a way that made her want to upend her twenty-two years of polite behavior—along with the buffet table set out in the yard of the Everett ranch house to take advantage of the perfect early September weather.

And if she did, it would be Brady's fault.

She was standing in line to get some of that chicken salad, along with far too much cornbread, and he'd taken it upon himself to load her plate for her because he had possession of the serving spoon. Not as if he were being a gentleman, which might have been okay, but like he thought she required assistance to scoop up chicken salad.

Unfortunately, she'd seen that look on his face before. Polite yet distant. It was the kind of look he aimed at geriatrics and preteens.

Then he made it worse. Because he tried to be nice.

"How's school?" he asked. Polite smile in place, the way it had been when he'd asked Whitney Morrow about her recent hip replacement while helping himself to her signature shepherd's pie.

"School?"

He didn't hear the astonishment in her voice. Clearly. "Having a good year?"

Amanda was not in college. If she'd gone to college like Brady had, she would have been the first in her family to go. That meant that even Brady, the Everett brother who'd moved to Denver rather than staying at the ranch like Gray, or riding bulls like Ty, would have heard.

More to the point, she would have graduated already.

With a mixture of horror and despair that his polite smile only made worse, she realized he probably meant high school.

Brady Everett thought she was in *high school*.

"Fun fact, I actually graduated from Cold River High." Her jaw hurt from holding on to her own polite potluck smile when what she wanted to do was start flipping tables. "When I was eighteen. Which was over four years ago."

He blinked, indicating he did not know that. He was her older brother Riley's best friend, had known Amanda her entire life, was actually looking straight at her right this very minute, and he *didn't know* she wasn't *in high school*.

"Huh," he said. Still polite. Still distant. Then he smiled the same way. "Good job."

"*Good job?*" she repeated, painfully aware that her voice got way too squeaky. With outrage.

But Brady didn't notice. He was too busy turning his maddeningly broad and sculpted back on her as he carried on down the buffet table. Making polite and patronizing conversation all the way.

She did not flip the table in front of her, an act of will-power and sacrifice she thought deserved a standing ovation or two. Nor did she throw things at him, and not only because it would be a pity to ruin that national treasure of a T-shirt he wore that made his shoulders look like poetry. But also because despite what he seemed to think, she really wasn't in high school.

Amanda wasn't sure when she'd started noticing Brady, since he was a solid ten years older than she was, but now she couldn't stop. He was undeniably, unfairly gorgeous. He'd actually *been places* when most people around here thought a drive over the mountains to Aspen was a huge undertaking. And unlike every other person in this town, he wasn't the slightest bit afraid of her brothers.

Because Amanda was twenty-two years old and she considered herself not *entirely* hideous, but she had been on exactly three dates. In her entire life. Two homecoming dances and her senior prom. And her four older brothers had ruined all three occasions.

Now that her oldest brother, Zack, was the sheriff, her brothers would probably use his job as an excuse to throw any man foolish enough to try to date her straight into a jail cell. Jensen had all that EMT training to help with his firefighting, but also, he'd said once—to Amanda's prom date—that he knew exactly how to both hurt a person and bring him back for more. Add in Riley's reputation as the most dangerous of the brothers plus Connor's wildcard temper, and it made a man who *wasn't* intimidated by them all the more intriguing.

It made him magic.

Also, those shoulders. Not to mention the dark green eyes that made her belly flip.

Maybe she was a masochist, because when she'd piled her plate high with enough food to feed three of her, all of which she intended to eat merrily, she didn't go and find a seat near her mother or her friends. Or even with Abby Everett, who Amanda viewed as a surrogate big sister as well as her boss at the coffee shop in town—and who was almost the guest of honor at the Labor Day potluck today. The real guest of honor being her cute little newborn baby boy, Bart, who she'd just had with Brady's oldest brother, the forbidding Gray. Who looked more besotted than forbidding today as he gazed at his wife and son.

Instead, she headed for the table where Brady sat with Riley and Connor.

Because if Amanda let a few infantilizing comments wreck her day, she would never get out of bed in this town, where she was universally seen as forever twelve. Amanda headed for the empty chair next to Brady.

"By the way, congratulations, Uncle Brady," she said breezily, as if she was continuing their buffet conversation. "Bart is adorable."

"He's already an uncle," Riley growled. Because Riley always growled, as if the words themselves offended him as he spoke them. All the words.

"Remember Becca?" Connor asked in that lazy voice he used when he was being a jerk, which was basically all the time. "Pretty sure she made Brady an uncle sixteen years ago."

Becca was Gray's daughter from his first, unhappy marriage that had ended tragically more than ten years ago. Amanda had babysat her, for God's sake. But she didn't bother to snap back at either one of her brothers, because Brady was smiling at her.

Not that polite, buffet line smile. A real smile.

And for a moment, the Labor Day afternoon seemed a whole lot sunnier than before.

"Looks like we're keeping him," Brady said genially, nodding over in the general direction of Abby and his brother and baby Bart.

Amanda knew he smiled at everyone in exactly this same way. He would smile at a tree or a horse just like this, but beggars couldn't be choosers, as her grandmother liked to tell her. Regularly. She basked in Brady's smile anyway, as if it were hers. As if *he* ever could be hers.

She would add it to her personal collection of Brady moments, like that conversation they'd had when he'd been a little bit drunk at his brother Ty and sister-in-law Hannah's retying the knot ceremony last week, and she could have sworn he'd noticed she wasn't a child any longer. If only for a moment or two, right here in this same yard.

Something she didn't need to be thinking about around her brothers.

The youngest of her older brothers, Connor, was kicked back in his chair and staring at her, all six feet of him obnoxious. A mere eight years older than Amanda, he was the closest to her in age, which sometimes made them friends.

"The kids' table is over by the porch, monkey," he said.

So, not friends today.

What struck Amanda—hard—was that he wasn't being mean. He wasn't teasing her or trying to get in a dig, for a change. He didn't even have that lazy note in his voice that indicated he was deliberately being jerky.

Connor was legitimately directing his twenty-two year old sister to the kids' table. He was being *helpful*.

She snuck a look at Riley, but what Connor was saying was so unobjectionable, so *normal* to him, that Riley didn't appear to be paying the slightest bit of attention. He was glaring across the yard instead, no doubt because his ex-wife, Rae—one of Abby Everett's two best friends—was over there, cluttering up his line of sight the way people did in small towns whether you wanted to see them or not.

As usual, no one was here to save her from the *helpfulness*.

And Brady might think Amanda was in high school, but he still wasn't as messed up in the head as all of her irritating brothers. He should know better, but instead, he kept on smiling. He looked perfectly polite again. And as distant as if she were grouchy old Lucinda Early with another complaint.

Amanda was having a Brady moment, and *he* clearly thought there was absolutely nothing wrong or weird about shunting her off to sit with a selection of loud toddlers, feral ten-year-olds, and a couple of actual surly teenagers.

Assuming she recovered from this indignity, she would never forgive him. She would never forgive any of them.

"The kids' table," she repeated. Flatly. "Where . . . the actual children are."

Riley shifted his attention back to the conversation at hand and frowned at her.

"Right by the porch." He sounded like he was trying to be helpful too. Or at least kind, which somehow made it worse. "I saw Becca over there."

If they'd been home on the Bar K, their family ranch north of the Everett spread, Amanda might have lost it. Not that losing it would help. It would only lead to comments about *ladylike behavior* and *why are you so* emotional *all the time,* but maybe she would have felt better.

Sadly, they weren't at home. This was a party, half the town was here, and Brady Everett was smiling at her. More importantly, her mother would not be pleased if Amanda caused a scene in public. Ellie Kittredge had been forced to accept that she couldn't control the behavior of her four sometimes rowdy sons. Or, if the whispers Amanda had ignored her whole life were true, of her husband. She accordingly placed all her expectations for acceptable behavior on her only daughter, whether Amanda felt like being *appropriate* or not.

Amanda turned around without a word, leaving her brothers and beautiful, oblivious Brady Everett behind. She did not walk around to the front of the ranch house to find a place to sit with teenage Becca and the rest of the actual, honest-to-God children. She headed inside instead, because she needed to do something with her plate of chicken salad and cornbread, which now felt like a concrete block in her hands.

It was funny when an everyday thing turned into a revelation. Amanda had probably been treated like a child a hundred times yesterday too.

But here, now, *today*—she'd had enough.

Yet she still smiled at everyone she passed, because it was a reflex. It was one more way she was invisible right here in the middle of her life. Always and ever *that little Kittredge girl.* Always a child to everyone, no matter how old she was. She kept thinking she would magically reach a certain age and everyone would wake up and collectively notice that she wasn't twelve any longer. She'd thought turning eighteen would do it. Graduating high school. Making her own money, getting promoted, all the things other adults around here did.

But it hadn't worked.

On her twenty-first birthday, when she'd gone into the nice, respectable bar in town instead of the seedier and therefore more intriguing one, all of her brothers had been there. Ready and waiting. They had allowed her one and a half drinks, absolutely no fraternization with anyone male they hadn't already vetted or intimidated, and then Zack had driven her home much too early in the sheriff's department-issued Bronco he'd already had as a deputy.

She understood now, like a lightning strike to the head, that it wasn't going to change.

It was never, ever going to change.

She was going to be fifty-seven years old and still living, dateless, in her parents' house. Her brothers would still swarm around her like living armor every time she tried to have a life. She would become one of the fixtures of this town, a part of the spinster scenery like that Harriet Barnett with all the cats or the fearsome Miss Martina Patrick, and would be forced to start appearing at parties like this one with her own signature potluck dish. Would she try a variation of her mother's potato salad? Strike out the way the younger women always did and appear with strange dishes related to whatever diets they were on that no one wanted to touch—and then surrender to the inevitable taco cups or brownies? Or lose her head completely and attempt to compete with old Martha Douglas's glorious pies?

"You are going to wither away and die, a husk of a woman, still treated like a child when you're actually seventy-eight and fighting senility," she told herself. Out loud.

Luckily, there was no one else in the Everett kitchen to hear her dire prediction.

And who was she kidding? If anyone had been there, they would have agreed. Then patted her on the head and told her to *go play*.

Amanda tossed her paper plate into the trash can and listened as it made a thudding sound, like a drum.

Like her own death knell.

Not that she was being dramatic.

Then again, was she? Because Amanda knew every single person at this gathering. And with the exception of Hannah, Ty Everett's rodeo queen wife who was only a few years older than she was, each and every one of them treated her like a precocious toddler. And would likely continue to do so, forever and ever, amen.

Amanda kept waiting for things to change. For the people around her to change. For *someone* to notice she wasn't a kid any longer.

And maybe ask her on a date too, while they were at it.

But *the kids' table* incident today made it clear that no one in Cold River was going to notice her on their own. Ever.

She was going to have to go ahead and change her life herself.

Later that week, Amanda sat in her normal place at the usual Sunday dinner that Ellie had insisted on as long as anyone could remember.

She almost lost her nerve.

But it was already done. She reminded herself that her brothers were the main reason the rest of the town saw her as an infant. All four of them had their own spreads out here on Kittredge land. Which meant that if Amanda went and lived somewhere else, she could kill two birds with one stone. She could have a private life, unsupervised by any of her brothers. And that very act of independence might send the message that she really was all grown up, of legal drinking age, and more than ready to live her own freaking life at last.

It wouldn't matter if they were convinced or not, because she would be off living said freaking life.

No time like the present, she urged herself, suddenly uncomfortably warm.

"I'm moving out," she announced into the quiet that fell as everyone around the table tucked into the typically huge meal that Ellie had made.

There was a small, charged silence.

Then, to Amanda's astonishment, everyone kept right on eating.

She set down her fork and looked around the table. Her brothers and her father were all big men. And Ellie always looked bigger than she was, because a woman had to have a presence to order five big, strong men around the way she did. At the moment, the six of them looked like a wall.

They were her family. Amanda loved them, she really did. Even if, right now, she wanted to throw things at each and every one of them.

She waited, but they kept on eating.

Riley stirred, and Amanda tensed. "Pass the bread?" he asked.

"Here you go," Ellie said and passed it.

Then everyone got back to quietly eating.

Amanda had another unpleasant revelation. She'd spent the week since Labor Day taking steps to change her life, and marveling at how easy it was once she'd made the decision to do it. She'd also spent a lot of time wondering why she hadn't done this before. Why she'd waited.

Now she knew. It was this wall of silent disapproval. Normally she wilted in the face of it because her role in her family was very clear. She was here to mend things, the way she had her parents' marriage as their later-in-life baby, or so the stories went. She was supposed to keep everyone happy, not make things worse. She was glue, and glue stayed put by definition.

Maybe it's time to make yourself happy, she told herself sternly, in case she was tempted to let this go.

Not that she could. She'd gone ahead and done a thing she couldn't easily take back. Deliberately. So she *couldn't* wilt.

"The silent treatment isn't going to change the fact that I signed a lease on an apartment in town," Amanda said tranquilly. "I'm moving in next week."

That broke the wall into pieces. Loud pieces.

"Like hell you are," Jensen said with a laugh.

"Language," Ellie snapped at him.

"An apartment?" Zack gave her that assessing sheriff's look of his. "What apartment building?"

"You don't mean by yourself, do you?" Connor demanded. "That can't be safe."

Riley glared. "You already have somewhere to live. Why do you need an apartment?"

But Amanda watched her father, a man of precious few words. Donovan wasted none of them now. All he did was look down the length of the table toward Ellie, communicated something to her with one of their unreadable glances, then set his utensils down on his plate.

The sound rang in Amanda like judgment. Her stomach twisted into a knot, but she refused to show it. She could cry about it later. In her own place, with a lock on the door and none of her family around to see it and tell her she was being childish.

"There aren't that many apartments in town," Zack said. He shook his head. "And none of them are places I'd want my baby sister visiting, much less living."

"Good thing it's not up to you, then, isn't it?" Amanda replied.

Very, very calmly.

Because one thing she knew all too well. If she showed the slightest bit of emotion, or temper, or anything at all but aggressive coolness under fire, they would dismiss her. Instantly. There was no crying in baseball, as Connor liked to say when there was no baseball of any kind taking place, and there was certainly no crying in the Kittredge family.

"Where is this apartment?" Ellie asked from her end of the table, matching Amanda's calm tone.

Amanda couldn't read the expression on her mother's face. It could go either way, she knew. Ellie was nothing if not a mystery, especially to her own children.

"Up above the Coyote," Amanda said.

Then she braced herself, because the Coyote was the seedier of the two bars in town. It favored simplicity and dim lighting over the craft beers, live music, and ever-expanding menu options offered in the more respectable Broken Wheel Saloon on Main Street. The Coyote was where the bikers who came through in the summers liked to drink the road away, and Zack had once said he headed over to the Coyote at closing time whether or not he'd been called, because there was always a fight to break up.

The explosion here at Sunday dinner was instantaneous. And loud.

All four of her brothers started talking over one another, each registering their varying degrees of dismay. There was no point fighting with them, so Amanda sat back in her chair, folded her arms, and waited.

"That's absolutely no place for decent girl to go, much less live," Zack thundered.

Amanda was tempted to inform him that she was old enough and decent enough to vote, thank you, then lie and tell him she'd voted for his opponent in the sheriff's race.

"You can't live there," Riley kept saying. At her. And when she didn't respond, he threw it out to the rest of the table. "She can't live there."

Jensen let out another laugh. "This must be a joke."

"Come on, monkey," Connor said in disgust from beside her. "This is ridiculous. If you want your own place, we can fix up one of the outbuildings. You can have all the independence you want."

"But without actually, you know, having any," Amanda pointed out.

"You can have independence without putting yourself in danger," Zack argued.

"What's ridiculous is that all of you are talking to me like I asked for your permission," Amanda said into the lull. She looked around at each of her brothers in turn. "I didn't."

Jensen turned to their father. "Obviously we don't want Amanda in that kind of situation. You know the kind of people who hang around the Coyote."

"You mean . . . you?" Amanda asked.

All of her brothers stared at her as if she'd grown seven heads.

She smiled.

"I didn't ask Mom and Dad either," Amanda told them, matter-of-factly, pleased that she sounded so certain when her stomach was still in a tangle. "Because I know this will come as a big surprise to everyone, but I'm not twelve. I'm twenty-two. I can afford rent, and I certainly don't need anyone's permission to pay it."

"How can you afford rent?" Riley demanded. "You work in a coffee shop."

"It's called savings, thank you," Amanda replied, then pulled herself back before she got *too* testy. "And I'm not an idiot. I have a new part-time job too. Just to make sure I'm covered."

That wasn't the only reason. But she wasn't going to get into that part of things with them. If she told them how she planned to spice up her social life, they would make one of the outbuildings into a prison cell and toss the key. The way they'd locked her in her room so she couldn't go to her sophomore dance with a boy they didn't like. Jerks, all of them.

"That sounds like a reasonable plan, Amanda," Ellie said quietly from her end of the table, still expressionless.

Amanda had to blink away the heat in her eyes at the unexpected show of support. From such an unlikely source.

But she knew she wasn't done. Not yet.

"Where did you get a part-time job when you already work full-time in the coffeehouse?" Zack asked suspiciously. Or maybe this was him in full interrogation mode.

Amanda decided that since this was happening, and they were all being idiots, she might as well enjoy it.

"Didn't I tell you?" she asked brightly. And smiled wider. "It's how I got the apartment. The Coyote needs a new bartender."

Then she sat back and enjoyed the show.

2

Brady Everett parked his truck in the gravel lot on the wrong side of the river, then headed into the Coyote to find himself some trouble. The more trouble, the better.

Because there was only so much family time he could take.

He liked to think he'd come to terms with his return to his hometown of Cold River, though it hadn't been his choice. Left to his own devices, he still would have been enjoying his life down in Denver, far away from this place he'd always been in such a hurry to leave. But when his father had died last Halloween, Brady and his brother Ty had promised their older brother, Gray, that they would stay and work the ranch for a year. With Gray, not against him. That had been the deal the three of them made, out in the snow on a bitter Christmas Eve not far from the old man's grave.

Only Gray could wander over to the farmhouse next door one morning not long after their father's funeral, announce he thought their pretty neighbor should marry him, and have that all work out for him—now complete with a baby. Even Ty had produced a wife and kid out of thin air, in typical showy, dramatic Ty style. These days,

Ty was looking to build on the family land, which was a good indication he wasn't planning to vote for selling. That meant Brady alone wanted to shift the albatross this land had been around all their necks since they were born and give them all a chance at a real life instead of working the land until it killed them. The way it had their father and grandfather in turn.

But his brothers didn't treat him like what he was: the only member of the family with any actual business experience. And the only one with real perspective. Gray had been working this land since they were kids. Ty had spent his entire adult life trying to sit on the back of a pissed-off bull. Brady was the only one who'd gone out into the actual world.

A strike against him in Gray's opinion.

Most of the time, Brady rolled with it. He could do anything for year. But some nights, like tonight, he found he had enough of his older brothers and the domestic bliss they'd rustled up for themselves since Amos had died.

Brady wasn't domestic. He wasn't much into bliss either. But there was a particular kind of temporary happiness he was only too happy to indulge in, and he'd had the early morning ranch work hangovers to prove it.

Ty had once claimed that Gray wanted to be a country song, but he'd meant one of the old-school ones about honor and steadfastness and the cowboy way. Brady liked to think that in certain parts of Cold River, like the Coyote late at night, he was the other staple of the country genre. The kind where mamas were warned against him. Songs about women and whiskey and a whole lot of sin.

He was more than ready to get his own sin on when

he walked inside the Coyote and took a moment to let his eyes adjust to the dim lighting, carefully calculated to make sure bad decisions had a place to hide. He expected the rowdy pack of bikers clustered around the pool table. He wasn't surprised to see the same set of long-faced locals bellied up to the bar—there for the whiskey, not the company. And it wouldn't be the Coyote without the shouting over the music, the too-intense laughter, and the dark booths filled with disreputable types tossing back alcohol like they were in a competition.

What Brady was not expecting was little Amanda Kittredge.

Behind the scarred, sticky bar and framed by all that classy, flashing neon.

"What the hell are you doing here?" he barked, scowling over the bar at her.

She stared right back. "What does it look like I'm doing?"

"It looks like you're tending bar here, which is impossible. Obviously."

The look she leveled at him then was not friendly. Worse, she did something with her body, shifted it somehow, to put her hands on her hips. And it was suddenly terrifyingly hard to remember that she was *Riley Kittredge's kid sister.*

Because little Amanda Kittredge was not dressed for church. She was dressed the way the female bartenders here were always dressed, but she was *little Amanda Kittredge*, for God's sake. Her hair was in a high ponytail that was too thick, too long, and too much like honey. She was wearing a whole lot of makeup that did things to her eyes, which he had not until this moment known or cared were a hazel that looked gold, somehow.

He told himself she looked like a kid playing dress-up, but only if she was dressing up as a hot barmaid. She had on skintight jeans tucked into cowboy boots that made him feel like a pervert. And she was wearing a scandalously tight tank top that clung to her body and made a meal of her—

He was not looking at her chest. *He was not.*

Though it was possible *he* was having a heart attack.

"Does that mean you don't want to order a drink?" she asked, an edge to her usually sweet voice.

The whole tank top situation did not resolve itself. And no matter how many times he chanted *little Amanda Kittredge*, it didn't help.

Because for a minute there, he didn't see little Amanda the way he always had. Always underfoot, her hair in braids and a sunburned nose, climbing on and off the back of those horses her family bred. He didn't see the skinned knees or the dirty jeans that had marked her as a horse girl. Horse girls were a particular kind of tomboy, indistinguishable from one another in skinny packs, who hung around horses and related to them better than people.

For a moment, all he saw was a full-grown woman who filled out her tank top a little too well. And her hair was too blond, with just enough falling down here and there to make a man's fingers itch to get in there and pull out the rest.

He tried to slam that door closed. On his own face, if necessary. He tried to lock it up and pretend it hadn't happened.

His body objected, so he ignored that too.

"Whiskey," he croaked out.

Then the horror continued, because when she wheeled

around to get him his drink, he got a good look at her long, lean legs packed into tight denim and that curvy—

Brady didn't actually punch himself in the face, to get a jump on what Riley and his brothers would do if they ever suspected Brady's thoughts had strayed in this direction. He just thought about it. A lot.

Pull it together, Everett, he ordered himself.

And when *little Amanda Kittredge* turned back around and slid him his drink, he threw some bills on the bar, managed a nod, and then got the hell away from her before he disgraced himself further. He didn't usually like to venture back into the questionable booths on the other side of the pool table, all of them filled with drama of one sort or another, but he obviously couldn't stay at the bar. Or near the bar.

He sat by himself, scowled to discourage any social overtures, even though that was why he'd come here, and was nursing his whiskey straight on toward philosophical.

Until the door swung open and three of Amanda's brothers walked in.

All of them except Zack, which made sense. The sheriff couldn't hang out in a place like the Coyote. It was bad for business. Both his and theirs.

Jensen and Connor shouldered up to the bar, looking grim and pissed. Given that Brady's own reaction to Amanda had been completely inappropriate, he understood their concern.

But all he did was smile when Riley slid into the booth opposite Brady, like he didn't have a care in the world. And certainly hadn't been ogling Amanda's butt in tight jeans like every other red-blooded man in this joint.

"Have you seen anyone mess with her?" Riley asked, not bothering with any niceties.

That suited Brady fine. He and Riley had grown up together. They'd played football together in high school. Then Riley had stayed here to work on the family ranch and marry his high school sweetheart while Brady had gone off to college. They had less in common every time they saw each other, but that only made them like each other more as the years passed. When Riley's marriage with Rae had busted up, he'd come down to stay with Brady in Denver for a while, until he got his head back on straight enough to carry on.

Tonight, Brady was glad their friendship didn't require a whole lot of talking. No chance, then, that he'd accidentally say something he really shouldn't about what his best friend's little sister was wearing.

"What is she doing here?" he asked, mildly enough, with no mention of that freaking tank top.

Riley shook his head, his dark gaze moving restlessly from one questionable character to the next in the dim lighting. The jukebox swung from country to rock as over at the pool table, two gentlemen who clearly belonged to a couple of the Harleys parked outside disagreed about something that had the rest of their friends moving to pull them apart.

But this was the Coyote, where a man minded his own business unless he wanted a bloody nose for his trouble. Or worse, a broken bottle over the head.

"I have no idea what she's doing," Riley muttered. "She showed up at Sunday dinner and announced she was moving out. And when everyone freaked out, she laughed. We all told her we wouldn't help her do something so dumb, and she didn't care. She moved herself and then told us not to visit her. Can you believe that?"

Brady looked over toward the bar with new interest, though he shouldn't have. If the look on Amanda's face was anything to go by, she was not pleased that two of her brothers were now standing there, intimidating the other patrons. He looked at her face and only her face. He did not look any lower. Then he swung his gaze back to Riley.

"I know you all like to do it up commune style over there at the Bar K," he drawled. "But it's actually normal not to want to live with your family. You know that, right?"

"We have thousands of acres, and we each have our own spread," Riley replied. "We're not exactly living in one another's pockets. How is an apartment over the Coyote better than the land?"

"You're talking to a man who spent the last ten months living in his parents' house," Brady pointed out. He didn't touch the land part because his opinions on albatrosses and generations of needless toil were not exactly welcome around here. Certainly not by people who'd given their lives over to said albatrosses and needless toil. "An apartment over the Coyote sounds pretty good right about now, especially with the new baby in the house. Do you know how *loud* babies are?"

A hint of a smile moved around on Riley's mouth, which was the equivalent of full-scale laughter from him. "That's why I've never wanted any."

"It's getting a little crowded." Brady shrugged. "But I only have a few months left. I'm assuming your sister has to be of legal age if she's working behind the bar here."

He raised his brows at Riley, who frowned. "She's twenty-two."

Brady tapped his glass. "Ten years ago, there's no way I would have spent a summer in my parents' house. Much less lived there forever with no end in sight. And neither did you, if I remember it right."

"It's different," Riley grunted. He jerked his chin at Amanda as she served drinks farther down the bar, ignoring her brothers as they hulked there on one end, sending evil looks at anyone who spoke to her. "I was married. Just look at her. She's like Snow White. And Brady, the people who spend time in a place like this are not Disney dwarves."

Brady did not want to look at Amanda. Because no matter how he chanted to himself that he should be seeing scraggly braids and dirt on her cheeks, like she was still about seven years old, he didn't.

No, he really didn't.

He decided he needed to stop drinking whiskey before he forgot his amiable nature. So when Jensen ambled their way with enough beers to go around, he took one gratefully.

"It might surprise you to learn that our baby sister is not that psyched we're here," Jensen said, nodding to Brady as he took a seat. "She's getting downright salty."

"She can be as salty as she wants," Riley muttered. "I don't like how any of these degenerates are looking at her."

Brady made sure his gaze was on his beer. He'd never felt more like a degenerate, and less like getting his sin on, in his entire life.

"I don't think any Cold River locals will be dumb

enough to do anything," Jensen said, a certain gleam in his eyes that reminded Brady that while Riley had a reputation as the most dangerous of the brothers, Jensen had always been a force to be reckoned with. The man played with forest fires for fun, for God's sake. Some people might call that a death wish, but either way, Brady felt sorry for the poor fool who might put himself in Jensen's crosshairs.

"Brady figures Amanda wants a little privacy," Riley said, tipping his beer bottle Brady's way. "After all, none of us stayed in the big house with Mom and Dad as long as she has."

Jensen took his time taking a pull from his beer. Then he shifted his arresting gaze to Brady, and let it sit there a while.

Instantly, Brady felt like an awkward kid again. Jensen was four years older than Riley, and therefore Brady, and he'd been off doing *man things* while the two of them were still figuring out what being a man even meant. Brady had been pretty clear that he was going to do whatever his father hadn't, but that still left a lot of road to cover. Jensen had always seemed to understand every curve in that road.

Brady couldn't say he liked revisiting that old sensation now. He already had two older brothers. It irritated him that for all intents and purposes, he might as well have two more in the form of Jensen and Zack Kittredge. With the added bonus of not being a blood relative, so if they had the slightest notion he'd noticed their sister's backside at all, they'd tear him limb from limb. Happily.

"You sound like our mother," Jensen said. He sounded disgusted. "I can't for the life of me recall the last time Ellie Kittredge had a positive thing to say about anything, and yet there she was, not only supportive, but helping Amanda pack."

"Female solidarity?" Brady ventured.

Riley shook his head. "I didn't think that was something Mom did."

"If Amanda wanted to move out of the big house, there are a lot of ways she could have done it that make more sense in this," Jensen said, as if he was arguing his case to the table. Clearly the actual recipient of this argument had been less receptive. "I don't like where this is headed. Feels like trouble."

"It's already trouble," Riley muttered darkly, glaring around into all the Coyote's shadows.

Connor appeared then, dropping into the booth as well. Brady was walled in by overly large Kittredges, all of them with a mood on. Something that would not have boded well on any night, but was particularly dangerous in the current circumstances. That being their baby sister behind the bar of the Coyote, looking like she belonged there.

"That tank top is indecent," Connor said hotly. "I told her so."

Brady was going to be dreaming about that tank top for the rest of his natural life, but he didn't have time to scrub his face clean of any hint he might be thinking such suicidal things because Amanda came storming up to the booth herself.

Brady focused on the center of her forehead. Nothing else, God help him.

"There's nothing indecent about this tank top, Connor," she snapped at her brother, pitching her voice so it could be heard perfectly well over the music. "Unless what you're trying to tell me is that every girl you've ever dated was something a whole lot worse than indecent. I think we all remember the time Missy Minton showed up at the church picnic with her shirt cut down to here."

Brady, trapped in the booth by three scowling Kittredges, did not need the visual she provided. She poked her finger directly into the area of her body that he was absolutely not looking at. Certainly not that low down, where he could see the upper edge of the bra she was wearing—

Or he could have seen it, lacy and blue, had he been looking there. Which he wasn't. Because he wanted to live through the night.

"Missy was a misunderstood being of great generosity," Connor said piously. "She liked to share. She was that good."

Amanda rolled her eyes, her hands settling on her hips again. Brady could not understand what was happening to him. Why was he suddenly so *aware* of her? All those curves must have been there this whole time—a vaguely disquieting notion—but he'd never noticed them before. He'd never noticed *her* before, really. Not as anything more than one more facet of Cold River that he forgot about when he went down to Denver. Hadn't he seen her at that Labor Day thing Abby and Hannah had wanted to throw out at the ranch to celebrate the many Everett family changes over the past year? He racked his brain and came up with a vague memory of her smiling at something. Gray's new baby, if he had to guess.

He certainly couldn't remember her *hips*.

Maybe it was because she was here. Put a girl into a den of iniquity and it didn't matter if she was sweet. She was here. That made her fair game.

Her brothers had a point.

"Listen up, idiots," Amanda said, her gaze hot but her

voice controlled. Brady shouldn't have been offended that she was including him in that, even though he was clearly acting like a grade A fool tonight. "It's not me who's going to throw you out of here if you don't stop it. Harry takes a very dim view of men who harass his bartenders."

They all looked over at Harry Ahearn, the grizzled owner of the Coyote, who sat on his stool at one end of the bar, kept his shotgun within reach, and had no qualms whatsoever about shooting up his own ceiling to shut down a fight.

"We're not harassing you," Connor threw back at her. "We're trying to protect you."

"From yourself, apparently," Brady chimed in, because she was glaring at him too.

For some reason, that made Amanda's eyes blaze. All that hazel lit into liquid gold, and something in him kicked. Hard.

"You're not family." She sounded like he'd sunk a knife in her back. "You have no excuse."

Riley made a scoffing sound. "Brady might as well be family. He's known you since you were born. Mom made us learn how to change your diapers together."

Brady really could not have said why he . . . didn't like that. At all. Especially because it was true.

Amanda looked like she was on the verge of homicide. It reminded Brady that she was, in fact, a Kittredge. Just like her hotheaded, rabble-rousing brothers.

"I respect the jobs all of you do," she said. She shifted her gaze to Brady. "I would respect what you do, but no one knows what that is."

"Oh, ouch," Connor said lazily, and pretended to wince. "Burn."

Brady would have died before admitting that it felt like a burn too.

Amanda was still talking. "I don't show up to your places of business, acting like a fool, with no other purpose than to harass you. Do I?"

"Amanda," Jensen began, a conciliatory note in his voice.

But she held up her hands. "All I ask is that you give me the same respect you would give anyone else. This is my job. I don't care if you like it. But if you come in here, it better be to have a drink and get rowdy like everybody else. If you can't handle that, you can head over the river to the Broken Wheel, eat some truffle fries, and stay away from me altogether."

She didn't wait for anyone to reply. She glared at them all, then turned on her heel and stormed off.

Brady absolutely, positively, did not watch her as she walked away.

Sometime later, when the Kittredges decided they'd better go before Amanda really lost her cool and encouraged Harry to get trigger happy, Brady left with them.

He walked out into the cool night, high up here where fall was already gathering in the mountains, and couldn't help but think he was dodging a bullet.

That didn't make much sense, but then, it was a feeling he was getting used to after almost a whole year back here, neck-deep in family dynamics whether he liked it or not. His own family and everyone else's family too, because that's how small the town was.

"I don't like this," Connor muttered as he headed for his truck.

"Not one bit," Jensen agreed.

Brady nodded goodbye to Riley, then swung into his

own truck. He needed to head home because mornings came ugly-early on a ranch, but he didn't move. He sat there, staring out the windows at the night sky, thick with stars above and the gentle lights of downtown Cold River, such as it was, shining on the other side of the river.

Down in Denver, he had a life. Friends. Business associates. People at his gym. He'd come home for holidays here and there because that was what sons did. That was what his friends who'd grown up elsewhere did, and Brady had learned early that it was easier to pretend his family was like other families. It was better not to talk about Amos's rages. His drinking. The many times he'd flipped the kitchen table and broken it, until they'd taken down an old barn door and made it into a table he couldn't break. Or that will and testament he'd liked to shuffle around with, marking and remarking it in red pen every time someone made him mad—which was always.

Brady had always been good at pretending.

Still, he'd put his entire life on hold when Gray had asked. Sometimes he liked to work up a head of steam about that, usually after Gray dismissed yet another one of his ideas or suggestions, but out here in his truck, with his hometown sparkling in the night, he didn't bother to lie to himself.

It hadn't been a hard decision to stay here. He'd been waiting his whole life for his family to ask for his help. To indicate, in any way at all, that he could be useful. Helpful. A part of things.

The truth was, he'd come running.

Brady watched the Kittredges drive out and a new truck filled with Coyote customers roll in, but he still didn't start his engine. He stayed where he was.

He was closer to his brothers now than he'd ever been before, but he couldn't say that was all that close. He knew as much about the two of them as he always had. Neither one of them knew the first thing about him. He'd watched first Gray, then Ty, come to grips with themselves, and on some level he envied that. Marriage certainly wasn't for Brady, after growing up in the shrapnel of his parents' nasty, bitter relationship. To say nothing of Gray's first marriage, which had failed long before Cristina had crashed her car that terrible night.

"No, thank you," he muttered to himself. Out loud in the cab of his truck.

But watching his brothers get their comeuppance from their wives, while satisfying, wasn't why he was here.

Gray wanted them all to work the land, he'd said. He wanted them to experience their birthright hands-on. But Brady knew what Gray really wanted was for them all to come around to Gray's way of thinking. To ranch the way they'd always ranched, generation after generation of Everetts stretching back to the pioneer days.

It never ceased to amaze Brady that a man whose life depended so heavily on Mother Nature's unpredictable moods could be so devoutly disinterested in change. But that was Gray—more mountain-like than the Rockies all around him. Amos had sneered and called him a martyr. Brady thought he was a pain. And proud of it.

But he couldn't help wondering, after spending an evening with a front-row seat to another family's dynamics, if what he really wanted was for his older brother to take him seriously. Just once.

"Why not get out a tiny violin and play it?" he asked himself darkly. *Boo freaking hoo.*

A movement out of the corner of his eye caught at him, and he turned. The last thing he needed was to see Amanda again, coming out from the side door of the building, hauling a garbage bag toward the waiting dumpster. Brady had been unable to control his unwanted reaction to her inside a crowded bar. He certainly didn't need to see what further foolishness the dark might bring.

He didn't mean to move, but there he was, pushing the door of his truck open. Then he climbed out. And stood there.

Amanda threw her garbage bag up over the lip of the dumpster on the side of the building, then wiped her hands on the black apron she wore around her waist.

The night was dark, but the neon the Coyote used on its signs inside and out flashed pink across the parking lot and made her skin seemed to glow as she regarded him. A little too steadily for his taste.

"Did they leave you behind?" Then she sighed. "Wait. Are you babysitting me?"

"I'm not much of a babysitter."

"Really? And here I thought you and Riley spent all your free time changing my diapers."

It was bad enough he was talking to her in a dark parking lot when there was no one else around. But then he compounded the error by drifting closer.

"Yeah, that was one time, and I think your mother was proving a point. It put me off babies for life."

"That was probably her goal. She's mysterious, but if you stare long enough, there's usually a kind of sense buried there somewhere."

He didn't tell her there'd been a time he'd wished strange, unreadable Ellie had been his mother instead of angry Bettina, who'd walked out on Amos and left her three sons behind without a second thought. Or a backward glance. Ellie was frosty, but she was *there*.

"I'm not babysitting you," he said.

Then something changed in the air, or in him. Or maybe it had changed earlier, and he was still reeling around, playing catch-up.

He didn't know why he'd gotten out of his truck, but he had. And she seemed to be waiting for something, standing there in the pink light with her eyes much too wide for his peace of mind.

Brady wasn't sure he'd ever really seen her. Not until tonight. Not until he'd walked into this dive, expecting to see a pretty girl behind the bar because Harry always had at least one.

And he had, but it was *her*.

He couldn't seem to come back from that.

"You know what it's like out there," Amanda said, her complicated gold eyes mysterious and shadowed. And a problem. "You escaped."

He would have used that exact same word himself, and had, but he didn't like the way she said it. "I went to college. It's not really an escape. Just a different path."

"A path that took you away from here. Isn't that what everybody claims they want?"

"Not everybody." He found himself smiling. "You know better than that, Amanda. The Kittredges, Everetts, and Douglases founded this place. Mostly, we don't go anywhere. We sink ourselves into the ground, like roots."

Amanda laughed. "Those roots are getting gnarled. Now that Abby Douglas took it upon herself to become

Abby Everett, uniting two proud families in one fell swoop, we're basically all a big knot."

"Everybody claims there was no historical intermingling. But I've always had my doubts."

"My grandmother keeps the family Bible in her front room. She's written down every known Kittredge going back five generations, and no, there are no other Cold River founding families in there. I've looked."

"It always seemed funny to me," Brady said, and the weirdness of before—that strange compulsion—loosened its grip on him. He could breathe again. "Families are like countries unto themselves out here. It's not like that in the city."

"We're not related, Brady," she said, and there was a different note in her voice, then. It reminded him, again, that she wasn't the little girl who'd tagged around after the rest of them. She was a woman. And for all he probably knew half the names in that family Bible her grandmother kept, it occurred to him that he didn't know her at all. "You're not one of my brothers. If you haven't noticed, I have enough brothers already. I don't need any more."

"I know I'm not your brother," he gritted out, gruffly, and everything felt strange again.

And worse this time. Suddenly the pink from the neon light seemed too bright, and he had the notion it revealed too many things on his own face that he couldn't control. Because he didn't know what they were.

"Good," Amanda said.

And with a look his way that would make her brothers take turns killing him, she turned around again and headed back for the bar door.

But this time, for an odd moment out here in the dark where no one could see, Brady stopped pretending.

He watched little Amanda Kittredge until the door slammed shut behind her.

Loud enough to snap him out of it.

And horrify him.

So deep and wide, he figured he'd need a bottle or two of the hard stuff to wash it out.

3

"Rough night?"

Ty sounded far too entertained for approximately five in the morning, which meant Brady would rather die right there in the dirt outside the barn than admit he was anything but 100 percent.

"Never better, brother," he drawled, even forcing a grin as they walked back toward the ranch house after their early morning rounds of tending to the animals. A month ago, the summer sun would already have been peering over the eastern mountains, but now it was September. It was still dark. Brady hoped it concealed the worst of the drinking he'd done when he'd come back to the ranch last night and holed up in his bedroom—the bedroom that had been his father's, not that he liked to draw parallels between himself and Amos—and tried his best to pretend the entire evening at the Coyote had never happened.

A common reaction to nights at the Coyote, sure. But never before had his best friend's little sister claimed a starring role in Brady's regrets.

"Real convincing," Ty replied, sounding even more

amused than before. "That might work better if you weren't so bleary-eyed."

"Since when did you become a morning person? I seem to recall you stumbling your way to the barn not so long ago."

Brady knew things had changed for Ty. He'd lived through those changes himself, right here. But it still took him by surprise when instead of hiding behind a sharp-edged grin and an answer that sounded considered when it was actually evasive, Ty laughed.

"I've never been a morning person," he said. "Can't say that's changed. Though there's a lot to recommend an early morning with Hannah before Jack wakes up."

Ty and Hannah were newlyweds, in a sense. They'd married about two years ago, in secret. Then Ty had gotten stomped by a bull and forgotten all about it. The wedding they'd had a week or so back had celebrated no more secrets and no more hiding. Now they were honeymooners with a one-year-old son. As far as Brady could tell, they both seemed to like the unconventionality of it all. Then again, what else could you expect from rodeo people?

"You mean the quiet moments of contemplation and prayer each morning, of course," Brady deadpanned.

Ty smirked. "God comes up a lot, as a matter of fact."

Brady rolled his eyes. Ty laughed at his own joke, then pushed his way inside the ranch house to the kitchen, letting out a blast of heat and light and the scent of bacon.

It was hard for Brady to keep telling himself he wanted nothing to do with this place when something like that could wallop him the way it did. The smell of bacon in the air reminded him of the few good moments in his childhood. It was morning on the ranch, through and through.

He stayed outside, breathing in the last of the night and that fresh, crisp breeze that came straight down from the mountains. Horses and dirt, green things and far-off snow, plus coffee and bacon. Home.

These days, home was a lot more welcoming that it ever had been while Brady was growing up.

He could see his two sisters-in-law bustling around the kitchen through the windows, not talking at this hour, but clearly working together in a way no one in his family ever had in his memory. It made something kick in him, like the scent of bacon, warm in the dark. Like another kind of homecoming.

Brady had always liked Abby. She'd only been a year or so behind Brady in school. She'd also been their closest neighbor, a few miles away in the old Douglas farmhouse where her grandmother had raised her and still lived. Abby had been widely known for her decency and practicality at age twelve—learned at her equally no-nonsense grandmother's knee, everyone agreed. This morning, she had baby Bart strapped to her chest as she cooked up the farmhouse breakfast she liked to make each day before she sent Gray out into the fields.

Hannah, on the other hand, Brady had disliked on sight when she'd turned up earlier in the summer. He'd wanted to know where she'd been when Ty was in the hospital, recovering from his injuries. What kind of wife left her husband hurt and alone?

But he'd come around on Hannah too, and there was no arguing with the fact that once Ty got his memory back—after a memorable, if foolish, eight seconds on the back of the bull that had stomped him two years earlier—he was happier with Hannah and their son than Brady had ever seen him.

Happiness was going around. Like homecomings.

Brady turned around, there at the bottom of the steps that led into the kitchen where his brothers' happiness babbled in toddler-speak and smelled like bacon and love, and took in the land.

The albatross. The ancient history of the Everett family in dirt and crops and cattle, stretching out across hundreds of acres. This land had been a torment and a teacher, a paradise and a prison. It still was.

Amos had made them work along beside him when they were kids, learning the family business one tough chore at a time. He'd punished any hint of weakness. Severely. Gray had taken to it early, and by the time they'd all gotten to high school, their roles had been firmly laid out before them. The same way the ranch was laid out. The ranch house here, the corral there, and the barns and outbuildings close enough that rope could be laid out between them should the weather get so bad it threatened visibility. Farther out, the old family graveyard hunkered like a threat next to the cold river full of snowmelt that had given the ranch and the town and the whole freaking area its name.

Everything here felt preordained, especially family positions. Gray was the responsible one. Ty was the charming one. And Brady was the eternal pain in the butt.

Sometimes Amos had upgraded that to *the smart one*, but that wasn't a compliment.

Brady could remember being ten or so, raising a pig for the FFA and feeling like the man he'd always thought he'd become as he cared for that pig. He'd fed it, grown it, then taken it to market. Back then, he'd never questioned that he would stay here, another Everett in the shadow of these mountains, eking out the same existence so many of his ancestors had. Eight years later, he'd taken the free ride to the University of Colorado at Boulder he'd won with those smarts Amos sneered at, driven himself out of these mountains in the rickety old truck he'd bought with his own money, and had never planned to return for more than a brief visit.

These days, he felt strung out somewhere between those two visions of his future. And he'd never been much of a tightrope walker. When his father had raged, Brady had done his best to fade into the walls around him.

He'd spent years telling himself that was why no one could see him. And still couldn't.

But it was too early in the morning—and he had too much of a headache—to dig around in the swamp of his family memories. He concentrated on the view instead.

The sun was taking its time these days, sending glimmers of hope over the mountains in streaks of gold and red. Fall was already coming, and every hint of crispness brought with it the promise of winter right behind it. There was already snow on the highest peaks, and this was Colorado. There could as easily be a blizzard tomorrow as a gorgeous summer day. Both, maybe.

His grandmother had always liked that kind of contradictory weather. She'd called it a fox's wedding when it rained while the sun was shining.

Which for some reason made him think about Amanda Kittredge.

In that tank top of doom.

Brady had all of that sitting on him, uneasily, when

he saw Gray's headlights coming back in from his initial run up through the fields to check on the stock and the fences.

He waited as his brother parked in the yard, then swung out of his truck. People claimed the Everett brothers favored one another, but Brady had never thought so. Gray looked the way he always did, like he was chipped from the same granite that made mountains around here. And Ty had always seemed to shine a little brighter.

"Don't tell me you're lurking out here to come at me with another one of your multilevel marketing schemes." Gray didn't raise his voice in the slightest as he walked toward the ranch house, but still, it echoed. "If you start talking about leggings or skin care products, I can't promise I won't snap."

All thoughts of happy homes and granite faded into the usual kick of irritation that colored every interaction Brady had with his oldest brother. "When have I ever tried to involve you in a multilevel marketing scheme? Or any scheme at all?"

"Llama farms. Hemp milk latte nonsense. Whatever, I'm not interested."

"Again with the llamas." Brady shook his head, wondering if one of these days, he'd grind his back teeth down to dust. "I was watching the sunrise, actually. But it's good to know you really don't listen to a single word I say about anything."

There was a time when a comment like that would have gotten a sharp rebuke from Gray, but not this morning. He didn't look like he was carrying all four hundred acres of the ranch right there on his shoulders any longer. He only looked amused.

It wasn't much better.

"I'll tell you what I tell Becca, Brady. You want to be treated like an adult, then act like one."

In the split second Brady took to wrestle with his temper, he knew three things. One, Gray wanted him to lose it, whether he would admit it or not. It would prove every point he'd ever made about Brady still being a kid. Two, it was unwise to imagine that because Gray was mellowing about some things now that he had a new wife and baby, that meant he was in any way mellow overall.

And three, Amos had done his job too well.

Brady didn't know what he was going to have to do to get Gray to treat him—not like an equal. That was impossible to imagine when a person had as much faith in his own authority as Gray did. But as his associate. As his brother.

"Does your sixteen-year-old daughter have ideas for the diversification of the family's ranching assets with respective business plans?" Brady asked, aware there was an edge in his voice. It was better than all that gravel and spleen. "I can't wait to see them. I've always said she was the brightest of all my nieces."

Gray did that thing where he didn't actually smile, but still, the smirk came right on through. "It's too early for this. You never wanted any part of this life. You don't now. Diversification isn't going to fix that problem."

They'd been having some or other version of this argument for ten months. Brady couldn't decide if that was better or worse than the previous entire lifetime in which they hadn't talked about anything. Nothing real, anyway.

"I have a degree in evolutionary biology. I always wanted to be a rancher, Gray. Just not a poor one."

Gray's face took on that familiar, forbidding cast. "I didn't realize I had a cash flow problem."

"Does any ranch not have a cash flow problem?"

"We're fine. The ranch is fine. There aren't bankers trying to take a bite out of us, at present, anyway. The only people concerned with my bottom line are the realtors and property developers you sicced on us."

Brady wasn't going to touch that one. He'd considered the calls he'd made to developers and realtors after Amos had died due diligence. Gray viewed it as a betrayal.

"The fundamental problem with any kind of agricultural lifestyle is that you're always one or two bad seasons away from disaster," Brady said instead, keeping his voice neutral. "You might not remember those bad years when we were kids, but I do."

"I remember them. I'm older than you."

"Really? Weird. You should probably bring that up constantly and use it as some kind of weapon. Just to switch things up."

"You're hilarious, Denver."

"Diversification means no one season can take you down," Brady said patiently. "No more and no less. Whatever feelings you have about llama hemp farms or skin care marketing schemes, or progress, in general, or the fact it's me telling you this and what could I possibly know about anything, that's the simple truth."

"Stop ambushing me, Brady." Gray's voice was hard. "I want my breakfast. And then we have fences to mend."

He didn't wait for Brady to reply, because Gray Everett waited for no man. And he wasn't into metaphors either. He meant the literal fences Brady sometimes thought he went out and knocked down himself to keep them busy with the repairs. Gray shouldered his way into the house, leaving Brady outside with nothing but the late-rising September sun for company.

That and the specter of Amanda Kittredge's tank top, his hangover, and the usual mix of frustration and temper that marked almost every interaction he had with his family members when the topic was the ranch.

"Welcome home, idiot," he muttered to himself, the way he'd done a lot these last ten months. "You gave up your entire life to help out, and this is your reward."

The worst part, always, was that it still surprised him.

The question he couldn't seem to answer was what he could do to change this same old conversation when that was the heart of the matter right there. Brady thought change was the future. Gray thought it was the enemy.

And as long as Gray kept thinking it was the enemy, he was bound and determined to think Brady was too.

Much later in the day, as the afternoon began to roll toward a golden finish, Brady was driving along yet another stretch of fencing way off in one of the upper pastures. He tensed when he saw a pickup coming from the other direction, expecting it to be Gray. No doubt out to issue more orders and make it clear how unimpressed he was with whatever Brady might be doing.

But it wasn't Gray. It wasn't even Ty, who did a great many of the same things Gray did, but with a lot more smirk and sarcasm to spice things up.

Brady recognized Riley's truck some distance off and ignored the resurgence of that headache in his temples. He aimed his pickup in his friend's direction, both of them bumping over the long, dry riverbed that marked one of the boundaries between Everett and Kittredge land.

Back in the late 1800s, there'd been a twenty-year feud between the two families as they'd wrestled over this particular stretch of land out here, where there was nothing but sky above and mountains all around. Each family claimed the other had taken the first shot. There'd been bad feelings for years. But then, or so the story went, Buck Everett and Caleb Kittredge had walked off into the higher elevations one summer night as enemies and surprised everyone by coming back down both alive . . . and friends.

The two families had been more or less on the same page ever since.

Something that would change in a heartbeat if Riley had the faintest notion that Brady had even noticed his sister's tank top. . . . or had felt the need to stick around and talk to her. Alone. Much less go on home and numb himself against any further thoughts concerning her.

"Nice day," Riley said when they drew up next to each other, window to window with only the fence between them.

"Not bad," Brady agreed.

It had taken him years down in Boulder, then Denver proper, to understand that when city folks talked about the weather, it was small talk. But it was never small talk out here. Or never only small talk. Out here, people made their living from soil and beast, weather and hope. Out here, a simple change in the weather could herald doom. A heavy rain could cause flooding. A drought could wreck the crops. Wind could destroy whatever it found in its path, and an early frost could destroy a year's careful farming. A storm could drive wild things out of their usual habitats and into the middle of a carefully tended herd.

And if you were friends with your neighbors, the way

most folks around here were in some or other fashion, that meant you'd be called to help salvage what was left.

A nice day was a blessing—a reprieve, a wish—all around.

"I couldn't tell which one of you was angrier last night," Brady heard himself say. "The three of you. Or her."

For the first time since he'd come home for Christmas and stayed on, it occurred to him that maybe his brothers weren't entirely wrong about him.

You can't help yourself, can you? Ty had asked him after another round or two with Gray the other night after an otherwise perfectly pleasant dinner. *You have to stir it up.*

That was something Brady was going to have to think about. Later. Assuming Riley, who'd known him his entire life, couldn't read his unfortunate thoughts about Amanda all over his face.

Riley shoved his cowboy hat back from low on his brow, his dark eyes grim. "She has no idea what she's doing. She doesn't think she's sheltered, but she is. She always has been."

Any doubts Brady might have had about whether or not he liked to stir things up disappeared then, because he was smiling blandly at his friend instead of commiserating. "I would have thought that the fact she wanted to move out in the first place means she knows exactly how sheltered she is."

Then he felt guilty because Riley didn't react like it was a challenge. He only shrugged. "Amanda thinks none of us sympathize with what it's like to be her age. We all remember how much we thought we knew. And how adult we thought we were."

Brady considered it an act of supreme self-sacrifice not to mention Riley's wedding occurred when he was younger than Amanda was now. Much less what became of his marriage.

Riley was still talking. "Her problem is, she's too much like our mother. Offer her a helping hand and chances are, she'll mistake it for a fist. Every time."

"Looking on the bright side, a fist will come in handy down at the Coyote."

A little curve appeared in the corner of Riley's mouth. "I sure do appreciate you putting out these fires instead of starting them."

"My pleasure."

"But that's why you're perfect."

"That's what I've been telling everyone for years. I'm tickled you noticed."

Riley ignored that. "Amanda obviously can't handle having her brothers in there."

"Can Amanda not handle it?" Brady thought she'd handled it fine. "Or is it Harry and his gun that's more concerning?"

"Either way, you're the perfect plan B."

"Plan B?"

But even as he asked the question, Brady had an inkling he wasn't going to like the answer.

"Just keep an eye on her," Riley said. "She trusts you. More than us, anyway."

"Keep an eye on her? Babysit her, you mean."

"Call it whatever you want. It will be great to know that even if we're not there, you will be. You're in the Coyote all the time, anyway."

Something Riley knew because he was too. But Brady had that tank top on the brain. And more, that odd moment alone in the dark. He had definitely not been filled up to unwieldiness with notions of *babysitting*.

His gut twisted at that, because it felt like more of the same old thing. The way Gray talked down to him, so kneejerk and dismissive. The way Riley was acting like Brady couldn't possibly be a threat to his sister the way he thought every other man alive was. Brady was tempted to get a complex about whether or not he'd actually blended into the wall when he was a kid after all.

But what could he say? *Sorry, buddy, but your sister is too surprisingly hot for me to babysit. Did you really look at that tank top?*

Not if he wanted to remain friends with Riley. Or stay alive.

So he tried to look as unthreatening as Riley clearly believed he was. Toothless and soft.

"I did change her diaper," he drawled. "What's a little babysitting on top of it?"

His oldest, best friend smiled. As far as Riley ever smiled, that was. Then he nodded once, like they'd shaken hands on it. "I knew I could count on you."

Which only made Brady feel worse.

They talked about nothing in particular for a few more minutes, and then Riley drove off, kicking up dirt as he went. Leaving Brady to sit there in a dried-up riverbed, on his own beneath the mocking sky and mountains that saw too much for his peace of mind, trying to convince himself that he was no liar.

That he could do what Riley wanted him to do and watch over little Amanda Kittredge like she was a member of his family. Like she was his baby sister too.

Because until last night, if he thought of her at all, that's exactly how he would have described her.

"No problem," he said, out loud to the fence. The dried-up sediment beneath his wheels. The watchful sky. "No problem at all."

One way or another, he'd get back there. To that place where Amanda was safely in the sister-he-never-had zone, no tank tops or strange moments, and certainly no *ideas* that required a whiskey chaser to erase from his head. He would get back there if he had to beat himself up. And if he had to beat up every last fool in the Coyote who imagined he could get a piece of his best friend's baby sister, so be it. He would.

Brady would do this. He vowed it, then and there.

Because he had no other choice.

4

Amanda's new apartment was small, smelled forlorn, and had fallen far short of her standards of cleanliness when she'd taken possession of it. Someone had swept it. Maybe.

The first thing she did was clean the place. When she was done, the wood floors gleamed. And the windows, initially grimy with years' worth of buildup and a great many other things she didn't want to identify, sparkled as they let the late-summer light pour in.

With all the light dancing everywhere, and the smell of lemons and elbow grease instead of sadness and neglect, the apartment no longer felt cramped. It felt cozy. A place that could actually be a home.

Even if it was lodged there on top of the most notorious building in the whole of the Longhorn Valley.

The Coyote owed at least part of its disreputable reputation to its location, down by the river but across from the town proper. Back in the gold rush days, the Coyote had been one of a number of buildings that constituted the town's red-light district. When a few concerned citizens—the historical record suggested they were less hopped up on righteousness than looking to avoid paying off their debts—set fire to the infamous bordello next door, the rest of the buildings on this side of the river burned down with it. But the Coyote stood tall.

The building remained empty until the early 1900s, when it was finally sold and repaired. It had existed as a watering hole of one sort or another ever since. These days, its location provided its clientele with the same privacy this side of the river always had. Visitors could drive in from out of town and turn down the riverside road before anyone saw them. Residents could show up for a dark night of debauchery without necessarily advertising their intentions up and down the length of Main Street.

Amanda liked being a part of so much history, especially because it was all so scandalous. She particularly liked the fact that anyone lucky enough to be living in the apartments above the bar had views of the river, the bridge that crossed it, and the whole of pretty little Cold River nestled there outside her windows. From the two church steeples to the Grand Hotel, with the mountains rising up behind like an embrace. Or a warning. As this was Colorado and those were the Rockies, usually both at once.

She loved it.

When Amanda had left her parents' house, she'd taken nothing with her she couldn't fit into her tiny hatchback. But by the end of her first week in her new apartment, she'd assembled a delightfully ragtag assortment of furniture that didn't go together at all and yet somehow worked together beautifully, thanks to friends and the local flea market.

By the time Connor showed up to drive her out to Sunday dinner the following week—obviously so he could spy on her new place and report back—she was proud of the whole thing. She'd done it. She'd moved out. She had a key on her keychain that unlocked a door to a space that was only hers.

Not a hand-me-down. Not up for debate. Not something she had to share whether she wanted to or not. *Hers.*

Amanda really didn't see that getting old any time soon.

"Wow," Connor said, leaning against one of her beautifully clean walls just inside the door. With a typically jerky sort of expression on his face. "Really, monkey? You look like you're living in a garage sale."

"I don't recall asking for your opinion." Amanda shoved him back out into the hall. She slammed her door shut behind her, then locked it. *Her* door. *Her* lock. "And you want to know why? Because I've seen where you live. It looks like a hunting magazine threw up all over your cabin."

"If you mean, it looks like a man lives there, sure."

"You're not invited into my home, Connor. Ever."

He treated her to an eye roll. "Okay."

"Anything that works on vampires should work on annoying brothers too."

"Should I be concerned that you're talking about vampires?" He stopped at the top of the metal staircase out back, then stuck his face much too close to hers. "Are you on drugs?"

"I'm not on drugs." Her throat actually hurt, then, from not screaming at him. "But I'm taking my own car."

Because she wouldn't put it past any of them to "accidentally" strand her on the Bar K when she had to be at work, claiming they couldn't possibly make the thirty-minute drive into town for whatever reason. And then ignoring her protests, the way they liked to do.

"Your stubbornness is going to get you in trouble," Zack growled at her over her mother's mashed potatoes a little while later, more sheriff than big brother.

"Has yours?" she replied sweetly.

He glared. She smiled.

Amanda enjoyed confounding her brothers, who all acted like her wanting a life was a deep, personal betrayal. For once, she enjoyed not giving in because it was easier, or to smooth things over.

But she was honest enough to admit to herself when she was out of their clutches, away from their commentary, and driving too fast on the county road toward town that she probably would have caved already if it hadn't been for Miss Martina Patrick, the first and foremost of Cold River's small but notable spinster population.

Miss Patrick was the cautionary tale Amanda and her friends had told one another while they were growing up, unlike the much younger Harriet Barnett, who had made more recent cat and life choices. Miss Patrick was the longest serving secretary in Cold River High's history. And if the yearbooks Amanda's friend Katrina Hastings had dug up in the town library when she'd been supposed to be working at the B&B were any indication, she grew more ferociously pursed-mouthed every year. She lived alone in a tiny house in town, not far from the high school that she referred to as the center of her existence, from which she delighted in calling in parking violations to the sheriff's office. She had an indeterminate number of cats. She doted on the high school's crotchety old principal, cared for her elderly mother, and deeply disapproved of all the students in the school—an enduring opinion she was never too shy to share with any of them. And their parents. And anyone else who didn't run off before she could bend their ear about the sad state of American youth.

Every nightmare Amanda had ever had about finding herself an old, burned-out husk of a woman was about Miss Patrick and her infamous bitterness. About turning into Miss Patrick whether she liked it or not.

Perhaps sensing that Amanda was weakening in the face of so much brotherly disapproval, Kat rolled out the big guns while she helped Amanda arrange things in her apartment one night.

"You should absolutely move back home," she said, innocently washing dishes that didn't need to be washed while Amanda wrestled with shelf liners she didn't think her kitchen cabinets needed. But her mother had pressed a roll of them on her as if it was the Holy Grail, so of course, Amanda was going to use them. Ellie was the type who would check. "Once you do, it should only take another few years for the early stages of Miss Patrick-ism begin to show."

"You're a terrible person."

"You know what I mean. A sudden collection of cats and too-shiny purses. And also the uncontrollable need to make unsolicited comments and moral judgments about other women's clothing. To them."

"A terrible person, Kat, and a worse friend."

"After that, it's the kind of disease that picks up speed, but don't worry. I think it's painless. Next thing you know, you'll start doing that *thing* with your mouth."

Kat demonstrated, but she was laughing too hard to mimic Miss Patrick as perfectly as she usually did. And had been doing since they'd started high school.

Amanda tried not to laugh. "For all you know, Miss Patrick's mouth came that way."

Kat slapped the faucet off and wiped at her forehead, leaving a trail of bubbles behind. She looked up at Amanda, balanced there on the counter as she wrestled the unnecessary shelf liner into place.

She was still laughing, but her gaze was serious. "Miss Patrick isn't something that *just happens*. No one's born that mean, Amanda. It's a choice. Just like this apartment is a choice."

A choice Amanda knew her friend would make in a heartbeat if she could, and likely would, when her long-term boyfriend finally got back from the navy and made good on all his promises. She knew that was why Kat looked more sad than serious, even though she was still smiling.

"If you let other people dictate your life," Kat asked softly, "how can you ever be sure you're the one living it?"

Later that night, Amanda served drinks at the Coyote, found various ways to smile for tips while discouraging hands on her body, and found herself searching every dim corner for one particular broad-shouldered cowboy.

But Brady wasn't there.

She shivered every time she thought about the conversation they'd had out behind the bar. Despite all the moving, cleaning, and nesting, she'd thought about it a lot. She'd waited her whole life for him to actually *see* her, and she could have sworn that he did—even if it was next to the garbage.

There was probably a message in that.

She was thinking happily about messages and Brady's deliciously raspy drawl, when a couple of women she knew came in, draped more in laughter and cigarette smoke than clothes. They settled themselves at the bar, midway through a typically too-loud and inappropriate conversation. They did the same thing in the coffee-house. Kathleen Gillespie and Tracie Jakes had been some years ahead of her in school and had always fancied themselves far too sophisticated to talk to younger girls like Amanda, but because this was Cold River, Amanda knew their stories anyway.

Amanda had always admired them. Because she cared too much about what other people thought, while doubting such concerns had ever plagued either one of the women sitting in front of her, both of them as dangerously pretty as they'd been when they were terrorizing the boys in high school.

Tracie narrowed her eyes at Amanda when she came to take their drink order. "You're that little Kittredge girl."

"I'm afraid so."

"Your brothers let you work here? Really?"

A question Amanda had already gotten too often, and always in that same scandalized tone. She'd learned to smile innocently. "I didn't actually ask them."

"If you're a Kittredge, you know Brady Everett," Kathleen said from the stool beside her friend. If she personally recognized Amanda, she didn't show it. She swiveled to peer into the rest of the dimly lit, crowded bar instead. "Has he been here yet tonight?"

Amanda turned about seventeen different shades of red at the sound of his name, but neither woman was paying attention to her, both too busy scanning the crowd.

"No," she managed to say, when they turned back to her. "I haven't seen him around."

Tracie and Kathleen looked at each other and laughed.

As if they had deep, intimate, extremely personal knowledge of Brady. Something a whole lot more than a few words next to a dumpster.

Amanda couldn't serve them their drinks and escape to the other end of the bar fast enough.

Wake up, idiot, she snapped at herself as she angrily wiped down a spill that didn't need even half the attention she lavished on it. *Whatever happened, it was only a Brady moment for* you.

Because Brady might—*might*—have seen her as something other than a child for thirty strange seconds out there in the dark. But that certainly wasn't the same as seeing her as an actual woman. No one seemed to be able to make that leap.

Tracie and Kathleen, on the other hand, had barely been girls when they'd been in high school. They'd always been like this, advanced beyond their years and ripe with all the feminine secrets no one had ever taught Amanda. If *they* were waiting around for Brady to turn up, why would he ever bother to look past them to someone like Amanda?

He wouldn't. *He won't.*

That was when she decided it was high time she found herself a man who didn't know she was a Kittredge, didn't know a single one of her brothers, or better yet, didn't care.

Not to keep. Just to *try.* Because clearly, she needed to learn things. She needed to have as many experiences as she could while she could. She needed to try being more like Tracie and Kathleen and see where that got her. She needed to hurry up and throw herself into these things before she looked in the mirror one morning and saw Miss Patrick looking back at her.

She lifted a hand to her mouth to check for unconscious pursing and thankfully found her lips in their normal shape. Even so, she had the sinking sensation that it was already too late.

It's only too late when you give up, her mother liked to say.

Amanda might not know what she was doing, exactly, but she wasn't giving up. She refused to give up.

When she was done with her shift at eleven, there were still a few hours before closing, and Amanda decided there was no time like the present to keep turning over this new leaf. She dipped into the bathroom to freshen up and practice that sultry, knowing look she'd seen Tracie and Kathleen fling around earlier. They obviously knew what they were doing, since they were both currently giggling in the corner with two men Amanda vaguely recognized as paid hands from Cold River Ranch.

"There's no reason you too can't flirt with a paid hand," she told her reflection brightly. "Or anyone else."

She pulled her hair out of the ponytail she kept it in to work, tousled it, and then gave herself permission to flirt outrageously. With . . . whoever. It was only flirting, right? She could do that. She was sure she could do that. She'd always been a quick learner.

Amanda flung open the door, threw herself into the hall mid-pep talk, and then stopped dead.

Because Brady was standing there, blocking the door that opened into the main part of the bar. And taking up far too much of what air there was in this back hallway that led out to the dumpster of oddly charged moments.

Amanda tried to be surreptitious as she reached down and pinched herself viciously on the thigh. She needed to make sure she hadn't tripped and smacked her head in the bathroom and was even now crumpled in a sticky corner, dreaming she could conjure up Brady Everett at will.

Ouch.

He was apparently real. And he looked edgy tonight in a way the knots in her belly told her was dangerous. Very, very dangerous.

His dark gaze dragged over her, and she could feel it like another sharp pinch. It was almost as if he were running rough hands from the low-cut T-shirt she wore down over her jeans, then back up to linger on her hair where it fell over her shoulders.

His mouth tightened, and *he* didn't look pursed-mouthed. He looked grim.

And delicious.

Ridiculously delicious, in fact, all *shoulders* and that tall, lean body of his that he'd packed into nothing more exciting than a black T-shirt and jeans.

And yet looking at him was like surrendering to a roller coaster ride, only Amanda had no desire whatsoever to close her eyes.

He was a little too much cowboy tonight, which should have seemed a bit funny when he was the Everett brother who'd gone off to live in the city. But there wasn't the faintest hint of city slicker around him. Especially with that pissed-off look on his face and the scowl he wore.

Which for reasons Amanda couldn't begin to fathom, he was aiming straight at her.

"My shift is over," she said, as if he'd asked.

She would have thought that was obvious. She'd gotten rid of her apron, let her hair down, and leaned in hard to her favorite lip gloss. But he was still scowling at her.

"That means you should be going home. To bed." In case she might have been tempted to imagine that was some kind of surly invitation, he kept going. "Don't you have to work at Abby's coffeehouse in the morning? You need your sleep."

"I'm sorry, you're going to have to catch me up." Amanda tilted her head slightly to one side as she gazed up at him, trying to puzzle out that grim look he wore. "Since when have you given the slightest bit of thought to my schedule? Or even known that I had a schedule, for that matter? Or, while we're on the subject, the fact that I even exist?"

He looked affronted. "I know you exist."

"Right, right. Diapers, brothers, blah blah blah. That's all been true for twenty-two years. Why am I now suddenly subject to dramatic silences in parking lots, and this . . . looming thing in the hallway of a bar?"

She thought for a moment a muscle in his jaw flexed, but the light back here was weak, and she was sure she was mistaken.

"There's a door at the end of this hallway, leading out back," Brady told her, his voice hard. "Out back, where there is also a private staircase that leads directly to your new apartment. There's no need for you to walk back into the bar."

"No need whatsoever. Other than the fact I want to, it's none of your business, and I'll go wherever I please."

He smiled, then. "You can try."

She was not mistaking the challenging way he looked at her.

Something simmered in his dark gaze. It filled the space between them, like a visible humming. Amanda could feel it sinking into her, making her heavy. Misshapen. Twisted into knots that made her ache, though she barely understood what they were.

She had felt it a few nights ago too. Out in the dark, when the very fact that she'd been dealing with the garbage and standing next to a dumpster should have ruined the whole moment. The most Brady moment of all Brady moments up to that point. The stuff of fantasies, even. That she should appear and he should be waiting there. And then get out of his truck. And then *stand there*, with only the stars as witness—

But her wishful thinking was out of control. She had already decided to stop the madness, hadn't she? Crushes were crushes. They made fools out of people, but that was all. Like that depressing part of *Love, Actually* with the sad coworkers who couldn't get it together. Or the way everyone in town had always known that poor, sweet Abby Douglas had mooned over Gray Everett for most of her life. That had worked out for Abby, eventually, but Amanda couldn't think of much worse than being thought of as *poor, sweet Amanda Kittredge*. Being known as *little Amanda Kittredge* was bad enough. She didn't want to moon. And she didn't want to miss out on her life and find herself stuck up on a shelf like Harriet Barnett part two, then straight on into Miss Patrick's domain of mean, pursed lips and the mockery of high school students.

Her brothers hadn't restrained themselves from having social lives. Neither had Brady. Why should Amanda?

The more she thought about how overprotective they all were, particularly in contrast to even the least scandalous rumors she'd heard about them, the more filled with self-righteous indignation she became.

Brady made it all worse.

"I thought it was your brother Ty who got hit in the head," she said coolly now. "But apparently head injuries are going around the family."

"The door's behind you." His dark eyes glinted. "And you can turn around and walk through it without talking."

Amanda wanted to scream, and almost did, loud and long and strictly for her own benefit, because no way would anyone inside the bar hear her over the music. But she didn't. Her brothers could rant and rave about anything they liked, and at worst, it was called *venting*. If Amanda did it? She was out of control. Someone was bound to ask her, in some convoluted way or another, if it was *that time of the month*.

Jerks, all of them.

So she only crooked an eyebrow in her best approximation of her own enigmatic mother, folded her arms over her chest, and did not give in to the urge to let her temper get the best of her.

"No one's asked you to speak, as I recall," she said, and he wasn't the only one who could toss out a cowboy drawl when necessary. "And yet here you are, shooting off your mouth like it's your job. When guess what, Brady? It's not your job. *I* am not your job."

"You have three seconds to make a decision." Brady's voice was as implacable as that expression on his face. And something in her . . . fluttered. Amanda assured herself it was more temper, but it wasn't. She knew full well, it wasn't. "You can turn around and walk outside of your own volition. Or I can throw you over my shoulder and take you outside myself. I don't care which."

"You've lost your mind."

"One."

"Have you forgotten who you're talking to? I have four big brothers already, Brady. None of them are you. And none of them would dare *throw me over their shoulder.* You won't either."

He looked bored. "Two."

"You should also know that Riley taught me how to fight before I could walk. Just tossing that out there so you have all the facts."

"Three," he said, a different light in his gaze that reminded her his eyes were that deep, dark green, and she wanted to stand her ground. She really did.

But he stood upright, then, shockingly fast when he'd been lazing there in the hallway as if he could lounge about like that until dawn.

Amanda understood in a searing split second that if he did what he'd said he would—and he looked like he couldn't wait to toss her around like a bale of hay— something in her would . . . die, maybe. It would change her from whoever she was now into a woman Brady Everett carried out of a bar, kicking and screaming if necessary, and her problem wasn't that she would be ashamed of that spectacle.

Her problem was that if he did that, she would know.

She would *know* what it was like to have his hands on her instead of only imagining it—and how could she possibly carry on with what she needed to do to kickstart this life of hers if she knew that?

Riley really had taught her to fight. But Zack had taught her strategy, and the most important lesson of all: when it was wiser to retreat.

Amanda turned on her heel and actually dove for the back door before Brady could take matters into his own hands. But that didn't keep her from *imagining* that he had.

There was no getting those images out of her head.

When she burst out into the night, the chill of the September dark was a welcome slap. She wanted to press her hands to her cheeks to see if they felt as red against her palms as they did against the cold air, but she didn't dare. She didn't want to draw attention to the things her body was doing. Not when Brady was here to witness it.

The shoes she'd worn tonight were entirely too high, and much too ridiculous for rural Colorado. Her toes had gone numb about four minutes into her shift, and she was slightly worried she'd caused permanent nerve damage, but whatever, she was doing a thing.

A thing she deeply regretted when she lost her footing in the gravel out back.

She braced herself, fully expecting to go facedown. A humiliating end to an already mortifying encounter—

But instead, she felt a strong hand wrap around her elbow. And then hold her there in front of him, so even though she didn't quite have her balance, he did.

The shirt she was wearing wasn't another one of those tank tops that her brothers had found so appalling, but it was probably worse, because it was cut even lower. Harry preferred his girls to show some skin. Not to mention the push-up bra she'd never dared wear before, in case the unavoidable evidence that she had breasts caused her brothers to topple over instantly from a series of cardiac arrests. And then what would happen to the ranch?

Amanda had thought her brothers' reactions were completely over-the-top when they'd come into the Coyote and tried to intimidate her and anyone unlucky enough to be standing near her.

Until now.

Because Brady's hand was on her bare arm, and in

order to keep her upright, he'd swung her around to face him. And that gaze of his glittered beneath the floodlights that poured over the both of them until suddenly, Amanda felt naked.

Completely and utterly naked.

Her lungs twisted themselves into some kind of ball, then lodged themselves in the back of her throat.

Right along with her heart.

"Maybe don't wear shoes like that," Brady bit out, seemingly without moving his mouth.

"What do you have against my shoes?"

"You're going to break your neck in them. You almost did."

"They're not hiking boots, Brady. Their function is not to race up the side of a mountain like a goat. You're supposed to stand around in them, looking impractical." She almost said *edible*, but thought better of it at the last second and frowned at him instead. "How can a grown man not know this?"

"You're not an impractical girl."

"One, I'm not a girl. And I wouldn't mind people calling me a girl, but they're never doing it for good reasons. They're doing it to keep me in my place, and guess what? I already know how old I am. I don't need to be reminded of it every three seconds."

"Was there a number two? Or just a long, annoying number one?"

She glared at him. "And two, you have no idea what kind of girl I am."

"Pretty sure we've already covered this."

"There are a lot of people I've known my entire life since we all live here in the great and glorious Longhorn

Valley. We all went to Cold River High. We all shop in the same stores. We not only grew up together, our parents grew up together, and their parents before them. We can all sit around and play 'pin the baby on the family tree' until we go blue in the face."

"That's not a game anyone plays. Or is that what happens at all those baby showers?"

"You might think this means I know everything there is to know about every last person in this valley. I don't. Why? Because knowing a collection of facts about a person isn't the same thing as knowing them. I know a lot of facts about you, for example." She started ticking things off on one hand. "High school quarterback who ran off to the city, turning his back on his family like so many do these days, and only came back when there was a will—"

"What are you doing, Amanda?"

It was the quiet way he asked it that got to her. It cut right through the indignation, and that was a shame. Because the self-righteousness had sure helped her feel puffed up and strong. Capable of dressing down Brady Everett to her heart's content.

The quietness was something else. And that look on his face, a wary sort of concern that made her want to . . . cry, maybe. *Something.*

"At the moment," she said, annoyed that it felt so fraught when it shouldn't, when it likely didn't feel like much of anything to *him,* "I'm standing outside a bar I would rather be drinking in. Because it was that or find myself bodily removed by a person who, to the best of my knowledge, is not employed by Harry in any capacity. Certainly not as a bouncer."

"Pretty sure you know that's not what I mean."

She felt cold, suddenly, and she hoped that meant that her cheeks were less red. But then she flushed all over again, because he was still gripping her arm.

There was nothing the least bit cold about Brady's hand.

Amanda glanced down at the place where he touched her, where his strong fingers wrapped around her upper arm, and felt shy when she lifted her gaze to his again.

That dark, glinting thing in his eyes took her breath. Again. But he dropped his hand.

And she discovered how unsteady she could feel on her own two feet.

"I understand," Brady said, and the shyness fell away, because he sounded much too friendly. *Aggressively genial*, even.

Amanda wanted to kill him. That was the same voice, overbright and pointedly helpful, that he'd used in the buffet line. Carefully calibrated to charm elderly women with hearing issues. Or misbehaving toddlers.

He even cracked a smile to go with it. "Everyone feels rebellious from time to time. I only have two older brothers, and I couldn't wait to get away from them when I was eighteen. Put some distance between me and them. You know."

"I'm not eighteen."

He spread his hands open, another exaggerated show of how *friendly* he was that made her teeth hurt. "All I'm saying is that I get the need for independence. I support it."

"I didn't ask for your support. But thanks, I guess."

"You want to be smart about it, Amanda. That's all."

"Maybe I don't want to be smart. Maybe I'd like to

take a big old swan dive into stupid, selfish behavior that turns into stories I'll tell for the next two decades. Like every other person alive."

"So, have a few adventures. Smartly."

"Right. And when you were in your rebellious phase, did you sit around figuring out how you could do it *smartly*?"

He muttered something, raking a hand through his hair. Unlike some cowboys who only looked good from beneath a Stetson, Brady just . . . looked good. All the time.

It was so unfair.

"The Coyote is a rough dive of a bar, and you know it," he said after a moment, dark and impatient. "I'm sure that's why you decided to work here, since you're such a rebel all of a sudden. But there's a big difference between working behind the bar, with Harry sitting there two inches away from his shotgun, and frequenting the place as a patron."

"Yes, the difference being that in one part of that scenario, I'm at work. And in the other, I'm enjoying a few drinks and who knows? Maybe making new friends."

"You can make new friends in town. At the saloon."

"I didn't ask for your permission." Amanda shook her head at him. "What's gotten into you?"

"I'm concerned about you," he said, but she thought he sounded strained. And something flashed over his face as he looked down at her. "You're like a sister to me."

Oddly enough, that was what flipped a switch in her. Of all the things he'd said. Of all the threats, the slights. *That* was what spun her too far. That she was *like a sister* to him.

Amanda surged forward and poked him right in the chest.

She didn't know which one of them was more surprised, so she did it again.

"I'm not your sister, Brady. We're not even friends. The only thing you know about me is who my brothers are. I can't imagine why you think that means you can interfere in my life."

There was that arrested look in his dark eyes. That faintly astonished expression on his face, too arrogant by half, that only made him look that much more gorgeously, insufferably male. And there was something like granite along the fine line of his jaw.

"Tough," he said.

So she poked him once more, harder.

"Here's an idea, Brady. You stay out of my life, and I'll return the favor and stay out of yours."

"Yeah," he said, barely more than a mutter. "That's not going to happen."

He took the finger she was poking into his chest in one hand, and then he was too close. He was looking down at her, something dark and tense between them that made her breath catch.

For a moment he looked—for a moment she could have sworn he almost—

But instead, he dropped her finger. Worse, he stepped away.

Amanda had to work much too hard to keep herself from crying, then. Actually crying, whether from frustration or that *ache*, she didn't know. But it was so ridiculous that it triggered another, blessed wave of temper.

And *that* was why she hauled off and punched Brady Everett in his insufferable, too-hard, wholly obnoxious chest.

Just the way Riley had taught her.

5

Brady stared down at Amanda in disbelief.

He couldn't remember the last time someone had punched him. It had probably been a family member— and long, long ago.

He had certainly never been punched by a woman.

Much less so hard.

"Do you expect that to hurt me?" he growled at her. "Because news flash, Amanda. All you've managed to do is piss me off."

He fully believed that Riley had taught her to fight. He also believed he would rather die than admit to her she'd landed that punch well enough to get his attention. He might have been in the running for the position of Most Apparently Unthreatening and Toothless Man in the Longhorn Valley, despite the work he'd put in after hours in this very bar, but he did have *some* pride.

"If I were trying to hurt you, I would have aimed else-where," she told him loftily, like she thought she was a badass out here in those ridiculous shoes and with all that smoky stuff around her eyes that made them gleam straight gold. "Believe me."

Brady had to take a moment. He forced himself to

breathe. Because no way could he react to this the way everything inside him was telling him he should. He'd threatened to pick her up and throw her over his shoulder, and the notion still held a lot of appeal, but he thought better of it.

He made himself think better of it.

Because at the moment, he couldn't really think of anything he would rather do than get his hands on her. Which led straight to all kinds of badness.

Not that Brady could think of any examples just then.

He forced himself to think about Riley. His best friend. Her brother, who had taught her how to throw the punch she'd landed. And who would kill Brady with his own two hands if Brady looked at his baby sister the wrong way.

But none of that seemed to really penetrate.

Not when Amanda's hair was tousled like that, begging for a man's hands to mess it up some more. Or those shoes, God help him. Ridiculous, yes, but they did things to her body, throwing her into shapes a skinny little horse girl, all tomboy and dirt, should never, ever make in the presence of a man like him.

Or any man at all.

That part got through to him, which was a blessing. Because he needed to stop before he did something he couldn't take back.

If he concentrated on the impractical shoes, teetering out here in the gravel like a sexy suicide attempt, he could pretend that low-cut T-shirt—plastered to her curves enough to make him bite his own tongue—wasn't burned into his brain. Possibly forever.

"What if it wasn't me out here?" he asked her, focusing on the shoes. "What if it was someone else?"

"Hello. That was the entire point. I want it to be someone else. *Anyone* else. You're the one who forced me to come out here, fleeing threats all the way, when what I wanted was to head into the bar and get a drink. To start."

"Don't you know better than to wear shoes like that?" Brady demanded, keeping himself on topic. And away from images of Amanda all smoky and sexy, swinging her hips up to the bar. In the Coyote. Where invitations and expectations turned into regrets at the speed of a single shot, tossed back neat. "You can't run. You could barely walk out that door. You would have taken a header if I hadn't caught you."

"If it weren't you, Brady, I would have introduced you to the real purpose of wickedly high heels."

"Stripper poles?"

She looked disappointed. Or disgusted. Maybe both.

"I would have happily sliced open your shin. Or slammed a heel into your groin. I'm not actually a complete idiot. My brothers taught me enough hand-to-hand combat to make me the slightest bit dangerous."

She sounded bloodthirsty enough to make him wince. But she was about as dangerous as his hat.

"Landing a punch on someone who's standing there, letting you punch him, isn't the same as hand-to-hand combat. It isn't combat at all. Most people wouldn't actually *let* you punch them."

Amanda sniffed. "Says the man who got punched."

"I'm actually on your side here." Though that was waning by the second. "I think independence is a good thing. I don't think every kid born on a ranch needs to dive in headfirst to the family business because it's there.

I'll wave that flag up and down Main Street. But you do have to be smart about it, Amanda."

"Oh, terrific. Now the guy who thinks he *let* me punch him is debating my intelligence."

"It's not a debate. If you can't take care of yourself—and one punch I did nothing to block is not taking care of yourself—you shouldn't put yourself in positions like this."

She folded her arms and shifted her weight in a way that made his gaze drop to follow her hips—

Brady jerked his eyes back up. Immediately. Because he was not here to ogle her hips in those astonishingly tight jeans.

Amanda did not look appropriately grateful for his counsel, Brady couldn't help but notice. She looked mulish and annoyed.

"This is the Coyote, Amanda," he said, trying to sound more friendly. More *brotherly*. "It's not a theme park dressed up to look like a dive bar. It really is a dive bar. That's not the cast of a TV show in there—those are real bikers."

She scowled at him, which did nothing to make her less upsettingly attractive. Quite the opposite. She looked cute.

Way too cute.

"When you went off to college, did every single person in your life sit you down and lecture you on how to handle yourself?"

"I don't really see what my going to college has to do with you working in a place like this."

"Just answer the question."

Brady stared back at her, aware his jaw was rigid in a

way that made him think of Gray. And that should have appalled him, because he prided himself on not being as uptight or intractable as his oldest brother—ever. But it didn't seem to make a difference, out here in the dark, with this maddening woman—*girl,* he reminded himself harshly, *she is still only a girl*—because with every breath, she seemed to burrow deeper and deeper beneath his skin.

He rubbed a hand over his jaw and sure enough, he was doing that granite thing. Maybe someday he'd find that funny, but not tonight.

"What, do you think they threw me a party?" he asked, his voice a low scrape. "My father laughed in my face. That was it. Parental pep talk achieved."

She frowned. "What do you mean, he laughed in your face?"

Brady couldn't think of a single reason he'd introduced this topic. And having done so, because he'd obviously lost all control tonight, he really should have backed away. Talked about something else. Or avoided all of this altogether, because it wasn't his business, she wasn't his responsibility, and he didn't owe Riley anything—

But that wasn't true. Brady would have said Riley was like a brother to him, but he had brothers. And unlike his actual blood relatives, Riley had never spent years at a time treating Brady like a whiny, surly adolescent. Even when they'd both actually been whiny, surly adolescents cursed with raging hormones, bottomless appetites, and nothing but football games to save them from themselves.

Riley had walked through that fire with Brady. More than that, he'd brought Brady home with him like a stray. His parents might not have been in the running for a

Norman Rockwell painting, but their quiet acceptance of Brady had seemed like heaven after a steady diet of Amos all his life. The Kittredges had whole meals without breaking anything or shouting insults at one another.

It was a miracle.

Riley had given Brady that miracle. The least Brady could do was perform a very small favor, relatively speaking, in return.

"You knew my father," he reminded Amanda now. "Does it really surprise you that he wasn't exactly sweetness and light?"

"Not at all. He could get in a knock-down, drag-out fight in an empty room."

"And usually did."

"But why would he *laugh*?"

Something about that caught at him. The way she asked the question, so genuinely *baffled*. It made a part of him that he would have said he'd long since buried, out there in the family plot with nothing but the frigid river for company . . . ache.

"Because that's what he did." He didn't say that in a particularly self-pitying way. It was a simple fact. "He used to ride Gray hard about living up to his responsibilities. He loved to fight with Ty and call him names. But me? He didn't bother fighting. He laughed."

Brady didn't understand what she was doing when she swayed toward him, then. Not until she reached over and put her hand on his arm. He stared down at it, uncomprehending.

Because he could feel that touch move through him, and it wasn't as simple as heat. As want or need. All things he navigated easily and well, and without ever giving over too much of himself.

But Amanda's hand was soft and strong at once. Her nails were painted something sparkly and absurd that reminded him of the fairy princess getup she'd worn when she was very small and her brothers had carried her around like a football.

That should have horrified him, like everything else, but it didn't. Instead, it got tangled up with the sweetness and warmth of her hand on his forearm. Pretty but capable, like the ranch-bred woman she was, instead of the soft uselessness he'd gotten used to down in Denver.

Another thought he didn't need to have.

Especially not when she was gazing up at him, and everything was golden and much too solemn.

"I'm sorry," she said. Short, sweet, and to the point.

She was holding onto him, making things kick around inside him that he desperately needed to ignore. But worse, she kept *gazing* at him like that. As if she could see him.

Really see him.

The Brady who was trying to help her, out behind the Coyote, sure. But also that eighteen-year-old kid he'd been. The one who'd tried to mask his pride and wonder at his own achievement, sitting there at the family table one night with his acceptance letter and scholarship details burning a hole in his pocket. He'd tried to keep the smile out of his voice when he'd told his father. He'd tried his best to tamp down any faint whiff of excess pride.

He wanted to show his father what he could do. He'd been *so sure* that a full-ride scholarship—making him the first Everett to go to college, ever—was something even Amos would be forced to respect. Like when Ty had started winning rodeo prizes. Amos liked to call Ty a punk to his face, but he sure did like bragging on Ty's stats when he wasn't around.

Brady had been convinced this was his shot.

But then, he'd always been an idiot.

You want a round of applause, boy? Amos had asked, with a snort.

Brady hadn't looked over to see what Gray's reaction was that night. Gray liked to keep his head down at dinner, as much to avoid Amos as to pretend he didn't see his first wife's growing unhappiness. Or maybe to play with cute little toddler Becca. And Brady had tried to model himself after his stoic, quiet oldest brother, but he never quite made it there.

It didn't matter anyway. Amos had taken one look at him and cackled in delight.

Looks like you do, he'd drawled.

Then he'd laughed. Laughed and laughed, until he had tears rolling down his weathered face and his complete and utter derision was thick enough to wrap the whole valley in a layer of fog.

We have hundreds of acres here that need tending, Amos had hooted when he could speak through all that vicious hilarity. *What kind of coward signs up for four more years of books instead?*

Sometimes, Brady thought even now, he could hear that laughter echoing around and around inside of him. That and the word *coward*.

Sometimes, he thought he wore those things in place of the tattoos everyone else his age seemed to have. That they were as visible to the naked eye.

He would have said he'd gotten used to it years ago. But the idea of Amanda seeing those things made something in him twist into a hard little knot.

"Why are we talking about this?" Brady asked, aware his voice was harsher than it should have been. That it, too, was telling her things she didn't need to know. "Do you really want to hear more stories about life with Amos Everett? Everybody thinks they want to hear what it was really like. Or they think they already know. But they don't. They really, really don't."

"I do." And again, she disarmed him. It was her hand. Or the look on her face that told him she would happily stand out here in the dark all night long if necessary. If that was what he wanted. If it would help. What was he supposed to do with that? "He always seemed like such a bitter, twisted old man."

"He was. If there was a drop of happiness around, he'd stomp it out before it could leave a mark. It was his mission in life."

"Can you imagine that? Taking pride in being broken?"

Brady could feel something swell in him, then. The urge to say something scornful. Mocking. Harsh, anyway, to wash away the softness in her. The softness she was beaming around her like a spotlight when there should have been nothing out here but the accidental light from the bar, and far off, the uninterested stars.

The need to cut this moment into jagged pieces he could understand welled up inside him, almost like a sob.

As if Amos had been in him all along. Just waiting to come out, dark and mean.

But Brady didn't *sob*. Amos had beaten that out of him too.

And there was her hand. On his arm, in the dark. Warmer by the second, but still capable. Still deceptively tough. He should shake her off—

But he didn't.

For another long, endless, deep personal betrayal of a moment, he didn't.

Because he liked her hand on him. He liked her touch. He liked her voice, soft and urgent in the dark. He liked the way she tipped her face back, so she could look him in the eye, hitting him with all that smoky gold heat. He liked her attention.

He liked all of it, and he hated himself for that, but the hate didn't make it go away.

It was yet another hint that he was more like Amos than he'd ever imagined. Too bitter and yet entirely too interested in the promise of a soft voice—no matter that she was forbidden.

Ty had been gone and Gray had been involved in his own stuff while Brady was finishing high school, so Brady had been the only one around with an up close and personal view of Amos's last live-in girlfriend, Karen, of the messy marital status and a thirst for the bottle to match Amos's.

Their brawls should have put Brady off women for life.

It certainly should have taught him better than to get himself unnecessarily tangled up with a woman who could only cause him trouble.

Particularly this one.

He moved away, hoping it didn't look like he was reacting to her hand on him. When he was.

It was her fault. Because none of this would have been happening if she hadn't started working at the Coyote, of all the dank and dirty places. If she hadn't showed up in that freaking tank top. If she wasn't compounding that error tonight, with the shirt she was wearing that made it physically painful not to stare at her breasts in pure male appreciation.

God help him.

Because Brady was going to need a little divine intervention if he didn't want the Kittredge brothers to bury him out there on their ranch where no one would ever find him. Not even the vultures.

"What do you know about broken?" he asked her, far too gruffly. But he couldn't stop himself, even when he saw her jolt at his change in tone. "You're a fetus."

"Wow. A *fetus*. Really?"

"I know how old you are, Amanda. And even if I hadn't helped babysit you when you were a kid, the fact remains that you've lived a ridiculously sheltered life."

"I'm not sure that a person with a college degree and a one-third stake in one of the county's wealthiest cattle ranches ought to be lecturing me—a coffee server and brand-new bartender—on my sheltered upbringing," she drawled. A hit he had not been expecting. Because it landed hard. "But you go on ahead, Brady. Don't let me get in the way of more male posturing I didn't ask for."

"You don't know what you're asking for," he bit out, because that was the point. Surely he could focus on the actual point for five seconds, no matter how many other points she scored off him when he hadn't expected her to swing. Repeatedly. "You're careening around in a bad situation, miraculously unharmed. For the moment. How long can you expect that miracle to last?"

"Let me guess. You think the Coyote is a dark alley and my skirt is too short."

"I don't care what you wear." And he was deeply disconcerted to discover that even as he said that, it was not, in fact, true. On any level. "I would defend anything you wore, anywhere you wanted to wear it. But when I was finished defending it, Amanda, I might ask you what you were thinking. Because there's a certain expectation about the kind of woman who wants to tend bar in a place like this. And wearing shirts that require half of your bra to hang out is as good as announcing you're one of them."

"Thank you, Brady." Then she laughed at him. Actually laughed. Right at him. "I'm aware of the reputation of the average Coyote barmaid. Which is why I wanted to work here, not in a kindergarten."

"What are you talking about?"

Amanda flung her arms wide, the kind of theatrical, dramatic gesture that both reminded him how young and uncynical she was, and made him want things he couldn't allow himself to acknowledge.

Desperately.

She made him *desperate*.

"You and every last one of my brothers keep storming around ranting at me about all the mistakes you think I'm going to make. Well, guess what? I *want* to make them. All of them."

"No. You don't."

"You got to go off to college and figure it all out for yourself. Riley had a starter marriage. Just to pick two examples at random. I want to make my own mistakes, Brady, whatever that looks like."

"Regret isn't just a word, Amanda. You should remember that. Anyone who tells you that you only regret the things you didn't do is lucky. And obviously hasn't made a real mistake."

"What do you regret?" she fired at him.

The way this evening was going, he really should have expected that.

"That's the thing about regret," he gritted out, because the things he regretted weren't decent topics of conversation under the best of circumstances. Which this wasn't. "It's not something you particularly want to discuss. It's something you live with, like arthritis, that you pretend isn't there until it flares up again."

Amanda studied him for a whole lot longer than he liked. Until he started to feel a little too itchy because of it.

"It's easy for you to say things like that in retrospect," she said quietly. "As you look back on all the mistakes, big and small, you made in the privacy of the life you were allowed to have. I don't need to be protected from my own decisions."

He wanted to put his hands on her, because he was apparently an animal like his father. He rubbed them over his own face instead and reminded himself that unlike Amos, he could choose to be better. He could and would.

"You've got to be kidding me." He glowered at her and told himself to think about diapers. Princess outfits. But instead, there was only Amanda. "You need a leash. And a collar with a bell on it."

He immediately regretted saying that. Because it conjured up all kinds of images that were not helpful. But she only scoffed at him, obviously free and clear of any upsetting imagery involving collars and leashes and . . . what was *wrong* with him?

"When you were my age, you'd graduated from college. I bet it didn't occur to you that you were anything less than an adult. But somehow, I'm supposed to accept the fact that everybody in my life wants to treat me like a dim-witted ten-year-old."

"You should take it as a compliment, little girl," Brady

seethed at her, not sure which one of them he was more pissed at. "You have a lot of people in your life who want to protect you. Not everybody does."

For another long moment, there was nothing between them but all that tension. The dark. Her smoky, gold eyes, too considering and much too intelligent to give a smart man any peace. Brady's awareness of how hard his heart was beating. And how, if he didn't know better, he would have chalked up his body's reaction to something other than temper.

Diapers, you idiot, he shouted at himself.

"Like I said some time ago, you should go on up to your apartment, lock yourself in, and get some rest," he said, quietly and carefully. "Don't you have a shift over at the coffeehouse in the morning? Early?"

"Your concern over how much beauty sleep I get is commendable. Really." She shrugged with an exaggerated lack of concern. "But I could open the coffeehouse in my sleep. And will, if necessary. Tonight, I'm going to walk right back into the bar and make some new friends. And I'm not asking you for your opinion on that, Brady. I'm telling you what's going to happen, so you can resign yourself to reality."

"The only place you're going is to bed." He glared at her. "Alone."

"Maybe. Maybe not. You don't know. And guess what? It's none of your business either way."

She braced herself, glaring at him like she expected him to *do* something. And the crazy thing was, he kind of expected it too. An electric wire ran down the center of him, and it was on fire. Lit up and buzzing and making him feel like a complete stranger.

A stranger who couldn't think of a single reason why,

if Amanda Kittredge was out here looking for trouble, he couldn't be the one to provide it.

But he kept his hands to himself.

Somehow.

"You're not going back in the bar," he said, his voice flat now. Granite and fury, like Gray when he was giving orders. "I'll stand right here and watch you walk up to your apartment, like a gentleman. But if you go for the bar door, so help me, I will cart you up those stairs and lock you in myself."

"I think you're full of it." She tossed that at him like she was throwing knives. A skill he expected Jensen might have gone ahead and taught her, now that he considered it. "What do you think my brothers would say if they discovered that *anyone* was manhandling me? Even if it was you? I get that you're not afraid of them like everyone else in the entire state of Colorado. But are you actively suicidal?"

"Your brothers would thank me," Brady told her, with a grin that felt like a threat on his own mouth. "They'd call me a hero and throw me a party."

"You wish."

"Why do you think I'm here?"

For the first time, Amanda looked uncertain. Something on her face changed, making her look entirely too vulnerable, suddenly, for his peace of mind.

It was exactly what he should have wanted.

There was absolutely no reason on earth he should have felt like such an ass.

"I should have realized." Her voice was *too* quiet, then. He found himself missing that strange defiance of hers that had enraged him all of three seconds before.

"Of course that's why you suddenly care what I do. You're my guard dog, aren't you?"

"I'm not sure I would consider myself a *guard dog*. A concerned friend, maybe."

Amanda gazed up him for a long, surprisingly un-comfortable moment, making no effort to hide the vul-nerability on her face. Making no move to hide anything at all.

It was excruciating.

"A concerned friend," she said quietly. "But not *my* friend."

Then she left Brady to work out why that got to him the way it did.

It was like she'd actually started throwing knives and had sunk one deep into his chest when he knew she hadn't. All she did was turn and slowly, carefully, noisily make her way up those stairs toward her apartment.

Step by tottery step on her ridiculous heels.

It gave him ample opportunity not only to question why he felt so unnerved by her, but to contemplate that backside of hers, swinging this way and that like she was trying to hypnotize him.

Long after the door slammed behind her, Brady stayed where he was, grappling with the unwelcome no-tion that like it or not, she already had.

He was hypnotized, all right. And he needed to wake up.

6

A few days later, Amanda was wiping down tables in Cold River Coffee, brooding over her failed attempts to kickstart her social life, when she looked up to find Hannah Everett walking toward her.

Sauntering, more like. Because former rodeo queen Hannah never walked when a strut would do.

Amanda straightened. She was suddenly and pointedly aware of the fact that *she* was wearing her work uniform of a T-shirt and jeans with the usual stains from a day's work, complete with a messy bun.

"You're staring at me like I picked up an extra head on the way through that door," Hannah drawled as she approached, with that Georgia accent of hers that made a meal out of every syllable. Listening to her talk was like chugging molasses.

"Just one head," Amanda replied, because she was used to the pangs of jealousy she got every time she was near Hannah. It made her painfully aware of the fact she still looked like the half-feral tomboy she'd been as a girl. "One head with perfect blond curls, gorgeous blue eyes, and that's not even getting into the whole rhinestone situation everywhere else."

Hannah grinned, not the least bit uncomfortable with praise. Amanda admired that as much as the curls. Maybe more. What would her life be like if she didn't want to sink through the nearest floorboard and die any time someone looked like they might say something nice or kind to her?

"I always tell myself I'm not going to be flashy for once," Hannah said as she ambled even closer. "But I can't help myself. I'm a magpie, plain and simple. If it shines, I want to wear it. With everything else I have that also shines, and then look at that, I'm a big old walking glare."

She dropped onto the low couch with a bit of theatrical flourish. Then she pulled a fat paperback out of her bag. Amanda leaned against the sofa's wide arm, because it was nearing the end of her shift on this fall afternoon and the coffeehouse was pleasantly quiet. There were a couple of teenagers handling things behind the counter, the way Amanda had when she'd been their age. She could take a minute to herself.

It also wasn't the worst thing to remember that as much as she wanted to shake up her life, there were parts of it she loved as is. Like sweet afternoons in this pretty place, all brick walls and cheerful tables, a giant book-case and couches set up around a fireplace. The sound of Noah, the owner and chef, slamming pots around in the kitchen. The occasional roar of the espresso machine. And the music playing softly on the speakers.

"Mama and Aunt Bit have finally settled into their cute new house," Hannah said in her chatty way that made Amanda imagine they were neighbors leaning over a picket fence somewhere.

They had been actual neighbors all summer, but there

was no direct road from the Everett ranch house to her parents'. It was about ten miles as the crow flew, occasionally dangerous on the dirt lanes here and there, and longer still by circuitous county road. And there were no picket fences to mark the transitions between Everett and Kittredge land. Just historical squabbles, fencing to keep the cattle contained, and the odd old river or seasonal creek.

"It's on a sweet little street, barely five minutes away from this very coffeehouse. They love it." Hannah sighed happily. "And now that they're settled, they've demanded their usual time with Jack. Who am I to refuse?"

"Is it weird not to live with them anymore?" Amanda asked.

Hannah had spent the first part of her marriage to Ty thinking that he didn't want any part of her or their baby. She'd accordingly lived back in her Georgia hometown in the house where she'd grown up with her mother and her aunt, who'd moved here not long after she had this summer.

Hannah laughed. "Whether it's weird or isn't weird, Ty was of the opinion that I could continue to live in the same house with my mother and her sister, or I could be married to him. But not both."

"I can't say I blame him on that."

Hannah's grin said she didn't blame him either. "And now I get this lovely afternoon to myself while my mama gets her grandmother on. I'm going to read a book and drink coffee, and then I'm going to go home and meet my husband when he comes in from doing something appropriately manly out there on the range like a true cowboy. Everybody wins."

The first time she'd seen Hannah, Amanda had been

having dinner with Kat under the watchful eye of her brothers at the Broken Wheel Saloon. Hannah had sauntered in, all rodeo queen curls and that swagger, and had clearly had the otherwise unapproachable bull rider Ty wrapped around her little finger in seconds. Amanda—and most of the town—had been in awe.

But Amanda and Hannah were friends because Amanda had also seen her less certain and a whole lot more vulnerable the next morning.

"Was it hard?" Amanda asked now.

"Was what hard?"

"All of it. Everybody thinking your life is going to be one thing, and then it's another. But they still think they get a vote."

"In my case, they often did get a vote. If you mean the rodeo."

"I moved out of my parents' house," Amanda blurted out.

Hannah's grin widened. "Oh, I heard. I approve. You told me you were going to blow everything up, didn't you?"

"I don't really consider getting an apartment any kind of a bomb." Amanda smiled, though it felt thin. "It's a reasonable life choice, I would have said. But it turns out, everybody else thinks it's a declaration of war."

"If I've learned anything this summer," Hannah said after a moment, as if she was picking her words carefully, "it's that you can only be responsible for the fires you set. You're not required to make everybody else's raging wildfire your responsibility. No matter how much they might act like you should get out there with your bucket and a hose and get to work."

"Okay, but I wish that everybody wasn't treating me

like a pyromaniac when all I did was light a tiny little match."

When Hannah laughed at that, a too-knowing look on her face, Amanda found herself flushing.

"Are you sure part of you doesn't like it?" Hannah asked lightly. "Because I'll tell you something, sugar. When *I* walk into a room, I expect to get noticed. Or I wouldn't bother."

"Well, sure. But you're . . . you."

"I like to make an entrance. I'm at peace with that."

"The rhinestones help."

Hannah looked down at what was, for her, a restrained outfit. That still meant she glittered. "Rhinestones, in my opinion, help with everything. But you don't have to wear a rodeo queen costume to make an entrance. And I'm not saying that you want that much attention anyway. What I'm saying is, if you do? Own it."

"That sounds like excellent rodeo queen advice, but I make coffee. And now tend bar. Both are less about making entrances than getting the orders right in a timely fashion."

Hannah lounged there on the couch, the very picture of a woman at ease. Except for one manicured finger that *tap tap tapped* against the bright cover of her book. "Did I tell you that Ty and I are thinking of opening a little rodeo academy? He could train up some new bull riders, I could train up some queens, and really, I can't think of a better use of all the years we spent on the circuit."

"That's a great idea."

"The question is whether or not I can handle all the mamas who think their precious little daughter is *just right* for a crown when she can't sit a horse or answer the simplest question."

"In any battle between a proud mama and you, Hannah, I'm putting my money on you—the woman who tamed *Ty Everett*, which anyone in Cold River would have told you was impossible."

Hannah laughed at that, but there was an undercurrent in it that made Amanda sit a little straighter. There was a joy in it, sure. But there was also something so *knowing* that Amanda had no doubt had to do with things like sex and connection, love and intimacy.

Amanda was fed up with not *knowing*.

"I'll give you a little preview for free." Hannah's blue gaze was very direct, then. "You don't win over a crowd by second-guessing yourself. Crowds feed on confidence, period. So when I advise someone to start making an entrance, what I mean is that once you do, people start to expect it. They think there *should* be fanfare when you enter a room, because you're in complete control of yourself and everything around you. Fewer accusations of pyromania that way, is all I'm saying."

"It's a lot easier to be in complete control when you don't have a gang of obnoxious cowboys coming out of the woodwork to tell you how every decision you make about your life is wrong."

Hannah reached over and patted her on the leg. "Don't I know it."

"All I want is a life," Amanda said.

It felt like she'd said that or some version of it approximately eighty million times today already. And every day.

"You already have a life," Hannah drawled. "You just don't like yours very much."

"I wouldn't say that." Amanda looked around the coffeehouse, every inch of which she knew as if she'd

built this place with her own two hands. "I've been working here since high school. And it's great. But people have
already started telling me that I'm following in Abby's
footsteps."

"There are worse footsteps."

Amanda liked that Hannah and Abby, openly sisters-
in-law now, got along. But that didn't change *her* life. "I
love Abby. I always have. My brothers have been bossing
me around since I was born, and then I started working
here and finally found myself the perfect older sister."

Abby had coached Amanda through all the things
Amanda had been too intimidated to talk over with her
own mother. Because Ellie was excellent at giving chilly
instructions about how one ought to behave, but she
wasn't a safe space to talk about high school concerns.
Or boys, God forbid. Or really any of the kinds of private, mysterious girl things that didn't seem to touch Ellie
at all.

Amanda had always had Abby for that.

But she didn't want to *be* Abby.

"These days it looks like a happy ending was always
lurking there, just out of sight," she said. "But I remember how it actually was."

"How what was?"

"Abby," Amanda said. "Her life. Everyone used to
cluck sympathetically about how *single* she was. Then
sometimes they switched it up and made a big deal out of
telling her how *capable* she was too."

Hannah looked mystified. "Is that an insult?"

"You might as well compare her to an orthopedic
shoe." Amanda shook her head. "I don't mind telling you
that I want, desperately, to be pretty much anything but
an orthopedic shoe."

"There's nothing *wrong* with being capable," Hannah said carefully. "It's better than the alternative, surely."

"But it's not a compliment, is it? If someone walked up to you and smiled sadly, then told you they were *just tickled* that you were *so capable* . . . ?"

"I see your point."

"I like knowing that orthopedic shoes *exist*, Hannah. But I don't want my life to be supportive footwear. I want it to be . . ." She waved her hand at Hannah and all her flash and sparkle. "Rhinestones. Bright and fun, totally unnecessary, and yet what outfit is complete without them?"

"I haven't found one yet."

"Exactly."

"Mind you," Hannah said with a laugh, "not everybody on this earth appreciates shiny things. I don't understand this point of view myself, but it's tragically true. However, you are not required to tolerate their commentary on it. Remember that."

Amanda was feeling a whole lot better about things when her shift ended a little while later. She left Hannah to the coffeehouse and her book, and set off down Main Street. It was an achingly perfect September afternoon. A bright blue sky above, setting off the Colorado mountains. Crisp weather, just this side of a little cold snap. She could almost sense the coming sharpness in the air, waiting to happen.

It had been so nice when she'd woken up that she'd decided to walk to work this morning, taking advantage of the fact that she *could* walk to work. Living in town gave her a new take on Cold River and the Longhorn Valley, both of which she would have said she knew inside and out. She'd been born here and had lived here all her life, after all.

But she hadn't lived *here*, she'd lived a thirty-to-forty-five-minute drive out in the far reaches of the valley. And that was in good weather.

She remembered the nights she'd stayed over at Kat's house in her early high school years, because by the time she was finished with work or extracurriculars, not to mention any homework, it didn't make sense to drive all the way back out to the ranch with someone who would have to turn around and drive her back too early the next morning.

Amanda had always understood her family's connection to the land. The ranch. She felt it like the blood in her veins. Her grandparents had built themselves a smaller house on the property when they'd decided they were old enough to be done with the day-to-day running of things, and there was no greater happiness on this earth than walking across that crisp meadow on weekend mornings, profoundly aware of the great expanse of Kittredge land all around her. Nothing but mountains, horses, and what those who shared her name had been fighting for long before she'd been born.

All that Colorado sky, bright and beautiful, and the demanding earth below.

But at the same time, she had envied Kat her town life, and not only because there was no chance Kat's family would find themselves cut off from town for a week if the winter decided to throw a big fit. There were also no chores in the barn every morning.

And it was amazing how decadent it felt to simply walk wherever she wanted to go.

But she felt significantly less rhapsodic about walking today when the door to Capricorn Books swung open, a woman barreled out, and Amanda found herself face-to-face with Rae Trujillo, her former sister-in-law.

Or as she was known around the Kittredge dinner table on the few occasions the family talked about her or acknowledged she both existed and had once been married to Riley, *her*.

"Oh." Rae looked as taken back as Amanda felt. "Amanda. Hi."

"Hi," Amanda replied.

Then they stared at each other.

Amanda felt torn, the way she always did. She'd loved Rae. Adored her. Abby had been a big sister to her, and a confidante, but Rae had been her sister in fact. She and Riley had started dating in high school, and Amanda had been so deeply invested in their relationship and their subsequent marriage that she'd treated them the way other girls treated their celebrity crushes.

Their divorce had flattened her, and there had been no discussing it. Not in the Kittredge house. Once it was clear it was over, it was as if Rae no longer existed.

All these years later, Amanda didn't know whether she was supposed to cry when she saw Rae, or angrily defend her brother's honor. Not that she would do either. But this was a small town. Every interaction was packed full of all the things everybody knew, but didn't say. All that history and rumor crammed into a perfectly polite *hi*.

"I hear you moved out," Rae said, and Amanda both admired how easily conversational she sounded and was deeply offended by it at the same time. Because nothing could ever be simple or straightforward. There was too much history, even if none of it was hers.

"Seemed like the right time."

"Your brothers must not have liked that *at all*," Rae said with that big laugh of hers. It was the most genuine sound Amanda had heard her make in the presence of a Kittredge in years.

Rae's laugh was bright and infectious and merry, and Amanda hated that she couldn't enjoy it anymore. Instead, she wanted to leap in and defend her idiot brothers, when she would have knocked their heads together right now if she could. She certainly couldn't stand here and listen to Rae Trujillo talk badly about them, even if it was only by inference. And still, beneath all of that, there was the same old grief that Rae had been family and now wasn't, and there was nothing but this weird no-man's-land between them forevermore.

"We're family," she found herself saying. But she smiled to take the sting out of her gruff tone. "We protect our own."

When Rae smiled again, it wasn't sad. Not quite. But it wasn't filled with any of that infectious merriment either.

"Don't I know it," she said quietly. "It's nice to see you, Amanda."

They both smiled politely and moved along. But Amanda found herself scowling as she kept walking down Main Street and headed for the river.

Interactions like that were exactly why she often thought longingly of picking up and moving to a big city. Any big city, she didn't care. Just somewhere she could go where no one would know she was. Where she could walk down a street and not be assaulted by feelings that weren't even hers.

It wasn't *her* marriage that had broken up.

Rae had never been anything but nice and sweet and sisterly to Amanda. Even if Amanda did live in an anonymous big city, she suspected she would still feel profoundly unforgiving of the woman who'd broken her big brother's heart—whether Riley chose to put it that way or not.

But she wouldn't have to run into her on the street.

When a truck idled beside her as she left the pretty brick buildings behind her and followed the road as it wound down to the river, she sighed. Then she rearranged her features into something more welcoming as she turned, expecting it would be one of her brothers. Or a neighbor. Or any one of her friends' parents, or parents' friends, who took it upon themselves to comment on the behavior of any child they happened to have known growing up.

But it was none of those people.

It was Brady.

"Get in," he ordered her.

"Why?" But even as she asked the question, she remembered what Hannah had said earlier. And she smiled at him before he could answer her. "I'm walking because I want to walk, but thank you."

If confidence was all that mattered, well, Amanda could certainly fake that, or she never would have survived a single family meal. And would even now be locked away in her old bedroom in her parents' house, forbidden from participating in her own life because it made her brothers so uncomfortable.

"You have to get in," Brady replied, his voice as calm as his dark gaze was . . . not. "Lucinda Early just drove by and slowed down to take a closer look. You know what a gossip she is. What kind of reputation would I have left if I let that little Kittredge girl walk back to her scandalous apartment when I could have given her a ride?" He looked in his rearview mirror. "She pulled over. I think she might be filming us."

Amanda wanted to throw a temper tantrum. But that would only prove that everything people were saying about her was true, wouldn't it? Besides, Brady wasn't wrong about Lucinda Early. The older woman was, as Ellie liked to say when she found Christian kindness a challenge, an opportunity to practice grace.

She stared at Brady a moment, irritated. Then she looked up the street toward town, and sure enough, Lucinda Early's car was idling on the shoulder. She was likely already on the phone, calling Ellie to ask her if she knew her daughter was wandering aimlessly by the side of the road and *hitchhiking* too.

Amanda surrendered. She climbed into Brady's passenger seat and tried to pretend that everything wasn't different now, as he started to drive. Because she'd ridden in his truck before. They were neighbors, and he was her brother's best friend. He'd driven her more times than she could count.

There was absolutely no reason this should feel any different than those times. But it did.

She told herself it was because he wasn't driving her back out to her childhood home. He was driving her down to the river, then across to her very own, private apartment. Where, if she wanted, she could invite him in. For coffee, the way they did on TV shows, and no one would be around to loom intimidatingly or ask aggressive questions.

Or even know about it.

Amanda had already had enough coffee to float away on today. But when Brady pulled up behind the Coyote, delivering her to those same steps where they'd stood and argued a few nights back, she thought about rhinestones. And shine. About controlling what flashed, and what didn't.

When Brady threw the truck into park, she swiveled in her seat, smiled at him, and even batted her lashes.

Because why not make an entrance when she could?

"You want to come up for coffee?" she asked him.

Then watched, fascinated, as Brady went volcanic.

7

"What did you ask me?" Brady demanded, because his blood was roaring in his ears and he'd obviously misheard her.

He must have misheard her.

"Do. You." Amanda drew each word out, as if he were very, very dim. And possibly hard of hearing. "Want. To come up. To my apartment. With me." And then she smiled, much too sweetly for his peace of mind. Or his blood pressure. "For coffee?"

Maybe she really liked coffee. She worked at the coffeehouse. Maybe she thought she was issuing a perfectly innocent invitation.

But even as he tried to tell himself that, her body language told him something else. Because she was twisted around in the passenger seat to face him. One leg was crossed over the other, and she was twirling a hank of her honey-colored hair around and around one finger.

The look in her eyes was pure evil.

"For coffee," he repeated. "You are inviting me up for coffee."

"Sure." More twirling. "Or whatever."

"Are you out of your freaking mind?"

It wasn't until the echo of his words careened around inside the cab of his truck that he could admit that yes, he'd added a little more volume than necessary.

But all Amanda did was make a *tsking* sound. "No need to get all worked up about it, Brady. A simple *yes* or *no* will do the trick."

"What do you think you're doing?"

She lifted one shoulder, then dropped it, never shifting her come-hither gaze from his. "I like coffee."

He thought he might crack his own steering wheel in half.

"You don't invite men up to your apartment, Amanda. If you do, you have to know what kind of invitation they're going to think it is. Do you?"

"You know what kind of invitation it is." She batted her eyelashes at him, which should have been laughable. And yet Brady wasn't laughing. "Coffee. Haven't I already said that?"

He found himself rubbing his hands over his face, the way he seemed to do a lot around her. He was also praying for deliverance. Both at the same time, and neither helped.

"It's three o'clock in the afternoon. Why are you inviting anyone anywhere?"

"This is the problem," she complained, dropping the hair-twirling part of her act. Though she didn't sit back. Or revert to an easily ignored ten-year-old the way he wanted her to. "You have a dirty mind."

Brady stared at her. "I do. Because I'm a grown man. And normally, when I'm issued invitations to other people's apartments, it's because they also have dirty minds. Because they are grown women."

"Did you think when you picked me up that you were scooping up a preschooler? That I was toddling down the road to nursery school?"

"Pretty much," he snapped.

Amanda smiled at him, even sweeter than before, and a whole lot more problematic. "Then what are you getting so upset about? It's only coffee." Her smile widened. "Unless it's not. To you."

Everything inside Brady went still.

The afternoon sun caught at her, flooding the cab of the truck. Amanda was dressed in a regular old T-shirt that wasn't scandalous in any way. And a pair of jeans that couldn't be the same ones she wore to work in the bar because they were looser.

But it didn't really matter, because he knew now. He knew what she looked like in tight clothes. He knew she had curves, and he'd seen her hips sway. He'd seen her twirl her hair around her finger, and he'd seen the flirtation in her eyes. And he couldn't figure out how to unknow any of those things.

There was a breeze coming off the river and into the rolled-down windows of the truck. There was a hint of snow in it, because this was the time of year when the mountains whispered premonitions to the people down below.

Any way he looked at it, Amanda was a problem and her presence in his truck spelled foreboding.

He would show her the error of her ways, then get out of here. It was the only rational way to handle this. Her.

"Okay," Brady said instead, not shifting his gaze from hers. And not aware he'd even said anything until he heard his own voice.

"Okay?"

Brady nodded his head toward the stairs. "Let's go. Coffee."

He had the distinct satisfaction of watching Amanda go from sultry to purely startled.

He liked that far more than he should have.

And not only because this was an excellent opportunity to impart a lesson. But because he was tired of being considered unthreatening. Undemanding. The local equivalent of a Labrador retriever, according to his family and hers. It wasn't that he wanted the people he loved most to cringe around in fear of him, but a little respect wouldn't go amiss.

He could start teaching that lesson right here.

Brady waited, but all Amanda did was stare back at him, her eyes wider than before and filled with more wariness than flirtation.

"Weird," he drawled as the silence spun out between them. "If I didn't know better, I might think you were suffering from second thoughts here."

"I have coffee all the time."

But she still didn't move.

The stillness inside Brady seemed to bloom a bit. Then take root. He studied her for a moment. Then did nothing more than lift a brow.

And watched Amanda flush.

He wondered if she'd been flushing like that out in the dark where he couldn't see it. He certainly hoped so. It made him feel a lot better about the riot going on in him.

For a moment, for one little second, he didn't beat himself up for any of it. There would be ample time for that later. For a moment, a breath, he let himself enjoy the tension between them. The breeze and the heat on her cheeks. A pretty woman in his truck and a blue sky above.

Amanda blew out a breath. And when she moved, she moved quickly. She threw open the truck's door, jumped out, and then headed for the stairs. She took the metal steps two at a time, and Brady followed. Much more sedately, because he was enjoying the view. And appreciating how fast she moved, because it told him all kinds of things about the energy crackling through her.

He didn't have it in him to pretend it wasn't buzzing around in him too. That didn't mean he would act on it.

Amanda unlocked the outer door at the top of the stairs, and Brady followed her into the small, narrow hallway inside. There was a window down on the other end, thankfully, or it would have been dim and much too close. There were two doors that opened into the hallway on opposite sides, and it took Brady a moment to remember that he'd been in the other one. And Amanda's too, come to think of it, because these were the apartments the Coyote bartenders used.

He waited until Amanda fumbled with her deadbolt at least three times and then, bright red in the face, shoved her door open and led him inside.

"Nice to see you put a new coat of paint on the place," he said cheerfully, as he looked around.

Then got to watch, like it was his own, personal show, as Amanda processed that information. What he was telling her. What it meant.

He would have said it was impossible, but her face got even redder. Then she scowled, though he only got a glimpse of it before she turned her back on him and moved farther into the apartment.

"I hardly recognize the place," he drawled when she'd retreated to the other side of the island in the kitchen portion of the living room, and stood there as if she thought it was a wall. A fortress. "It's actually pretty."

"Yes, Brady." Amanda sounded impatient. But he was staring straight at her while the afternoon sun poured in those big windows that looked out toward town, and he could see she was more rattled than she sounded. "Message received. You want me to know that you've spent lots of time in these apartments. I get it. What's the word for a male slut?"

He laughed at that, to his own surprise. "There isn't one."

"And I'm betting you don't think that's a problem."

"I can't say that I believe in sluts, as a general concept," Brady said merrily. "It's an ugly little word to describe one of life's most glorious gifts."

"You mean sex."

"I mean a person—"

"A woman."

"An individual who likes sex. A lot of sex. I, personally, consider the enjoyment of sex cause for celebration. Not condemnation."

Amanda blinked. "Do people not enjoy sex?"

Brady tipped his head slightly to one side while that question spun around in him. It suggested that Amanda had never experienced bad sex, or even indifferent sex, which was cause for a whole different level of celebration.

But then he remembered who she was. And who her brothers were, more to the point. And he couldn't quite make himself believe that little Amanda Kittredge had been out there indulging in any kind of sex at all—not bone-melting, life-altering good sex, run-of-the-mill, functional sex, or even the bad sex Brady had never experienced—with four angry bodyguards always lurking around her. He feared for his own life when he was with her, and he wasn't some pimply high school kid.

He would be very surprised if she'd ever gotten naked with anyone.

But the alternative was that Amanda was . . . untouched. Innocent.

Something shifted inside him. He had the uncomfortable feeling that it was a tectonic plate.

But Brady wasn't here to indulge in his own earthquakes. He was here to cause them.

"Some folks don't enjoy anything," he told her. "Even sex."

He'd thumbed his hat off at the door, and now he tossed it onto her counter and ran his hand through his hair. She was even prettier as the light fell through the windows, making her look like she was made of golden honey.

His mouth watered. He ignored it.

"Are you going to make me coffee?" he asked while she stayed where she was on the other side of the kitchen island and gaped at him. "Or do you want a keep the focus on sex?"

Amanda jolted, and there was color high on her cheeks again. And there was something deeply wrong with him that he couldn't think of anything he wanted to do more than reach over and run his finger over the curve of her cheek to feel all that silky heat himself.

Brady ignored that too.

She jerked into action. She pulled a bag of ground espresso from her freezer. Then she spooned it into the silver espresso maker on her stove. Once she set it on the gas flame of her stovetop, she busied herself rummaging around for mugs in her cupboard. When she found a couple, she went back to the refrigerator to lift a carton of heavy cream from inside.

"What?" she demanded defensively, when he only stared back at her. "I don't like fake things."

"Noted."

She slammed the carton down on the counter with enough force to make a dollop of cream spill over.

"Lite this, fat-free that, low fat, low whatever." She wrinkled her nose. "I think it's going to kill us all. We ate real food out on the ranch. I still do."

"Amanda."

"People feed their farm animals better than they feed themselves. If I wouldn't put it in one of our horses, why would I put in me?"

"Easy, killer," Brady drawled. "Who are you talking to? I grew up ten miles away from you. Frankenstein food is not my thing."

Amanda didn't look remotely mollified, but the espresso maker made noise behind her, indicating the coffee was ready. She took longer than strictly necessary to turn around and handle it.

Brady watched in a silence that felt thicker by the second as she poured espresso into two mugs, then topped each one up with a dollop of heavy cream. She slid one mug in front of him, keeping one closer to her.

"You don't normally take sugar," she said. "But I have some if you want it."

There was a strange note in her voice, like she didn't want him to know that she was aware of how he took his coffee. Which, again, was a little pinprick of information he didn't quite need.

Because he would expect a person who must have

made him more coffee drinks than he could count, over the years, to know how he took it. But a completely neutral barista would hardly have feelings about that, would she?

Sure enough, when all he did was regard her steadily by way of reply, that pink flush bloomed again on her cheekbones.

"You blush a lot," he pointed out.

Amanda tilted her chin up fractionally. "It's an uncontrollable reaction when in the presence of so much foolishness."

"What foolishness is that?"

He didn't reach for the coffee she'd made. And not reaching for her seemed like an act of supreme self-sacrifice. Instead, he braced his hands on the countertop, because she was doing something similar across from him.

"I think you know, Brady." But she wasn't sounding quite as sure of herself at the moment. "There's been a lot of looming. A lot of threats and dire pronouncements. I think we can tie it all up in a bow and call it pure foolishness, don't you?"

"You're the one who invited me up." He smirked. "For coffee."

"You said you wanted some."

"Is that really what you were offering, Amanda? Because I don't think it was. And I think you know it."

"I distinctly remember telling you I liked coffee."

But her voice was a little bit breathier than before. And when Brady straightened from the counter, then took his time rounding the island toward her, her jaw didn't exactly drop. Instead, her lips parted, and her eyes began to look a little bit glassy.

"I—I . . . I don't—"

"Now, sweetheart, you spent a lot of time ranting at

me about how grown-up you are," he said, almost like he pitied her. He didn't. "Are you really going to tell me that I misunderstood you down there in my truck?"

She kept turning as he came around the corner, keeping her body pointed toward him. That suited Brady fine. He waited until they were face-to-face, and then he moved even closer, trapping her with her back to the counter while he caged her between his arms.

For a long moment he did nothing but listen to her fight to breathe.

This close, he could smell her soap on her skin. And mint in her hair. And he could smell coffee too, but then he'd always had a deep appreciation for the rich, thick scent of it.

The pulse in her neck was going wild. She looked jittery and hopped up, but he knew it was something far more intense than caffeine. He could feel it too.

"I've been up in these apartments a time or two, I don't mind telling you," he said, and with his hands on the counter he had to lower his head toward hers. So he did. "But it hasn't been for coffee. In fact, Amanda, I believe you're the first woman to actually make me a cup of coffee outside of a coffee shop in a good long while."

"I can't help it," she said weakly, and he liked how greedy her voice was, then. How shaky. "It's literally my job."

"And that's why you invited me up here?" he asked, his voice a low, lazy rumble. "To do your job?"

"To be honest," she said, and then swallowed so he could hear it, "I didn't think you'd come."

"No?"

"No. I thought you'd rant at me some more about walking on the street, crossing without a crossing guard, not maintaining a buddy system, or any number of other things that apply to kindergartners that you somehow think also apply to me. Then I thought you'd growl something and drive off in a cloud of dust. After telling me that you might as well be my older brother a few thousand more times."

"You've made it a point to remind me that you're not my sister."

Amanda arched her back to keep looking him in the eye. And her body brushed against his while she did it, costing him more than he wanted to admit. He had to fight to keep his expression impassive, but she didn't do the same. Instead, she made a shuddery little sound, and then, worse, he could see goose bumps prickle to life down the line of her neck.

And once again he was . . . desperate.

He told himself to ignore it.

"I'm not your sister, Brady." Her eyes searched his. "I never was."

Brady couldn't decide if he was furious or filled with something far more dangerous than temper. That place inside himself where he stayed so still, so watchful, seemed to grow wider. Ravenous.

He couldn't keep himself from following where it led. Not for one second more. He shifted, pressing himself against her while he smoothed back her hair. Then he held her face in his.

He didn't let himself think about how natural it all felt.

Her hands came up too, and Brady could feel them on his abdomen. He hoped she wasn't pretending to herself that she wasn't affected by this, when he could feel her shaking.

For a moment, he didn't bother to hide. He gazed down at her, intense straight through and wild with it, buffeted by seismic changes he refused to name.

He let her see all of that, and then he dropped his head even closer.

"Brady—" she started, though it was more like a squeak.

He took a thumb and dragged it over her lips. Back and forth, over and over, to make them both crazy.

"I'm not one of your older brothers," he told her, his voice going gravelly. "And if you want to play these games of yours, you need to remember that I'm an adult. Not a kid."

She blinked, and then her eyes flashed liquid gold as her gaze went defiant. "Right back at you."

Brady knew he needed to teach her a lesson. One she wouldn't forget.

So he kissed her.

He could have kissed her sweetly. He could have eased in.

If he'd thought about the fact that this was *Amanda Kittredge*, he might have. Assuming the thought didn't kill him first.

But this was a lesson, and he wasn't here to be sweet.

He kissed her like she was a girl in a bar. Like she'd invited a man she barely knew up to her apartment on the flimsiest of excuses. He kissed her like a one-night stand, deep and hot and carnal.

There was every chance in the world that Amanda had never been kissed before, so he didn't waste time pretending he was a safe, domesticated boy.

He kissed her like a man. Need and hunger and expectation, with every stroke of his tongue against hers.

She made a noise in the back of her throat, but he couldn't tell if she was startled or greedy. So he kissed her until he could tell the difference.

He knew when her hands smoothed out against his abdomen, then dug in. He knew when her tongue met his.

And for a blistering moment, it was all earthquakes and appetite, so he ran with it. He hauled her up against him, up off the floor until he could set her on the counter. Then he moved between her legs. He pulled her flush against him and didn't protect her from his arousal. Or the force of his hunger.

But it wasn't until he slid his hand down her back to grip the sweet curve of her hip that she finally made a noise and wrenched her mouth from his.

"I—I can't—"

"You can't what?" he asked her pitilessly.

"I can't—I mean, I've never—"

She blew out a long, shuddering breath. Brady understood she had no idea of the picture she made. Her hair, tousled and wild, and her lips damp and faintly swollen from his.

He didn't understand the tenderness in him, then. When the whole point of this had been to overwhelm her. He didn't understand why he wanted to hold her, pull her head to his chest, soothe her.

He didn't understand any of this magic, only that Amanda was making a mess of him.

But that didn't matter. What mattered was that he cleaned up her mess.

"Riley is my best friend in this world," he gritted out. "And I'm pretty fond of the rest of them too. That's what you have going for you when things get too intense between us. I know them, they know me, and because of that, I know you too. But what happens if it's some other guy? One of those men you think you're going to pick up downstairs? They won't know a single thing about you except the invitation."

"So what?"

He could feel the growl inside him. "What if you change your mind, and he doesn't want that, Amanda? What's your plan, then?"

"Just because someone likes to drink in the Coyote doesn't make him a monster, Brady. You should know. You drink there all the time."

"And you can tell the difference. With all your vast experience with men, you can tell if you're looking at a good guy or bad mistake waiting to happen. Are you sure, Amanda? And what are you prepared to risk if you're wrong?"

She pushed at him, looking panicky, so he didn't move. He was proving his point. One beat, then another, and all he did was wait. Only when she pushed again did he move to the side. She pulled her legs together, then slid off the counter and onto the floor.

Amanda caught herself with one hand on the kitchen island, letting him know without another word how unsteady she was. It was one more detail he filed away, vowing that he wasn't going to look at it. And if he did, it would be much later. Alone. Somewhere his shame wouldn't choke him.

"Is that what this was?" she asked softly. Uncertainly. "You wanted to teach me a lesson?"

"Did you learn something?"

Brady hated himself when a look of misery washed

over her face. And he wondered why, if hurting other people felt like this, his father had committed himself to it with such gusto. He couldn't get his head around it.

But this wasn't the time or the place to examine his Amos issues. Or to wonder how he'd picked up so many of the old man's ways when he'd been so sure he wouldn't. That he couldn't. That he'd gone ahead and built a life somewhere else to prevent it.

"I'm going to go wash off this day," Amanda said, still in that small, shaky voice that made his bones ache like an old man's must. "And that's not an invitation, Brady."

She didn't look at him again. She wrapped her arms around her middle, ducked her head, and headed off across the room toward her bedroom.

Leaving him there with nothing but his hat on the counter and a stone deep in his belly, chock-full of all that regret he'd warned her she didn't want to experience. He didn't much care for it either.

Brady heard her shower go on and tortured himself for a while, imagining those curves he'd felt pressed flush against his chest, finally bared to his view. And better still, covered in water and soap and—

"Enough," he muttered.

At himself. At this situation. At innocent Amanda, who tasted like sin and redemption and who had already ruined him without even trying.

He let himself out of her apartment and took the stairs too fast, throwing himself into his truck. But no matter how much dust and gravel he kicked up behind him as he pulled away, he had the feeling his Amanda Kittredge problem was only just beginning.

8

"It's the last weekend of September, Uncle Brady," Becca said over breakfast a week or so later, staring at Brady as if he'd transformed before her very eyes from her uncle into a fire-breathing dragon. Or a clown. "This is Cold River. In the Longhorn Valley, Colorado, right here in these United States. All of this taken together can only mean one thing."

"Come on now, Denver," Ty drawled in a chiding sort of way.

Ty was kicked back in his normal place at the big kitchen table in the ranch house, holding a sleeping Jack against his chest. He had one hand on his son's back. And yet he managed to look as smirky as he ever did.

"Do the math, college boy," Gray chimed in gruffly, though there was a hint of a curve in the corner of his stern mouth.

Because it wasn't a morning at Cold River Ranch unless his brothers were riding him.

Brady closed his laptop with a decisive click and made himself smile. "This might come as a shock, but none of that actually helps. I still don't know what it is you all think I should be excited about this weekend. That October's coming?"

"Uncle Brady." Becca said that like she despaired of him, and when he only stared back at her, she sighed even louder. "Homecoming and the Harvest Festival, of course. It's *always* the last weekend in September."

Brady loved his niece, often more than he loved his annoying brothers, so all he did was smile at her. "Of course. Silly me. I don't know what I was thinking."

"Seems to me you'd have better recall," Ty drawled over the top of Jack's head, his dark eyes merry. Or malicious. With Ty, there wasn't much difference. "You were on the homecoming court two years running, as I remember it. I would have thought you'd slap that right on the top of your resume."

"Sure," Brady agreed. "Because in the corporate world, what really matters is whether or not you went to a dance in high school."

"It's not just a dance," Abby piped in from next to Gray, sounding deadly serious—though she bit back her own smile. "Don't you remember? It's an entire week of celebrations, though most of those are in the high school. On game day, which I know you remember because you won every homecoming game you played, there's a little parade through town. Leading straight into the Longhorn Valley Harvest Festival all weekend. Becca isn't wrong. These are *staples* of life here in Cold River."

"I do love me a festival," Hannah drawled, from her spot next to Ty where she could keep a hand on him and on Jack, if she liked. And she often liked.

Brady looked around the table at the various grinning members of his family. He couldn't decide if this was an elaborate practical joke or if they had all woken up this morning significantly more interested in meaningless nonsense than they ever had been before.

"Um. Great." He would have preferred to study his stock portfolio, but he tried to do the opposite of things Amos would have done. That meant concentrating on the things that were important to others. The image of his father scribbling away at his ever-changing will right here at this repurposed table would haunt him forever. "I can't say I have any personal feelings about festivals one way or the other."

"The Harvest Festival is the last big town event before winter," Abby told him. Bart was in a sling across her chest, only the top of his head and his chubby legs showing. "All the shops stay open, and people come in from out of town to have themselves a little fall getaway. The Grand Hotel does a booming business, the restaurants tell themselves lies about how they'll make it through the low season, and the high school kids have the homecoming dance. If we're lucky, it doesn't snow for at least a few more weeks. If we're not, well, we get an early winter wonderland and do the whole thing anyway."

"This is the first time in years that you've been home on homecoming weekend," Becca said. Intensely.

"That is . . . true," Brady agreed.

"I already told the school you'll be in the parade."

"The what?" Brady rubbed a hand over his face, wondering why it was only around his family—and if he was honest, a certain other member of the wider Cold River community, though this was certainly not the time to think about Amanda Kittredge—that he felt so sucker punched all the time. He didn't like the sensation. "I'm not a parade kind of person."

"Becca is on the student council homecoming committee this year," Abby said mildly, kissing the top of the baby's head. Almost as if she was telling Bart that information.

"I haven't been much of a parade person *historically*," Brady corrected himself without missing a beat. He smiled at his niece. "But I'd be happy to change that for you. I need to stay on top as favorite uncle."

Next to him, Ty hooted. "Favorite uncle? You lost that crown a long time ago, son."

Becca beamed, and Brady was no more immune to that smile than anyone else sitting at the old barn door that made their table. Because he remembered all too well the many years when the only smiling Becca had done had been forced. Faked. She'd been a kid who thought she had to act middle-aged. It could only be a good thing that Becca was interested in regular old teenage things. Because that meant she was doing what she was supposed to do, not what she thought she *should* do.

You could take a lesson from your niece, a voice in him commented.

But Brady was getting real good at ignoring those obnoxious little voices. Since they never said a thing he wanted to hear.

After breakfast was finished, the various members of the Everett clan launched themselves into the main part of their day. Abby and Hannah set off toward town with the kids and Becca in tow. Ty went off to tinker with one of the farm vehicles that had been acting up, because he had a way with machines and thought he could save them having to shell out cash for an expensive part.

Gray went into his office to make a few calls before they headed out into the fields, so Brady cracked his laptop open again. He'd taken an indefinite leave of absence from his firm, but he still liked to check in with his partners and keep a close eye on all the various financial balls he kept in the air.

He also liked to read the paper, out here in the hinterland, too far from town for anything like a daily paper delivery. He liked to remind himself there was more to the world than this ranch house, something he had fervently believed when he was growing up here. Or hoped, anyway. Now he knew it for sure. And he didn't want to sink back down under the surface of that particular swamp again.

Some mornings, the act of reading a few headlines felt like a revolution.

When he glanced up sometime later, he found Gray standing there in the doorway that led into the living room. He was leaning against the doorjamb, studying Brady in that way he had. As if, by his reckoning, Brady was a different species.

"Counting your money?" Gray drawled.

Brady was almost certain he was kidding. That this was Gray's version of joking around, as stone-faced as ever, but maybe with a little less gravel in his voice.

But it didn't really matter when his joking around was in no way different from all the other times, when he wasn't joking around at all and said much the same thing.

Or maybe, another little voice inside him needled him, *you've been waiting for an opportunity to vent your spleen ever since you found it necessary to kiss Amanda Kittredge.*

He was not thinking about that.

He was only thinking about that.

Either way, it was easy to scowl at his brother.

"You say that like it's a bad thing to have money," he said, employing his own drawl, in case it was a competition. "And I get it. I do. You're nobly allergic to the idea of profit."

"I make a profit."

"I'm tired of having this argument with you." Brady took his time standing up from his seat, because he really was determined not to have the same fight. Ten months in and he was exhausted by it. "But I should congratulate you, big brother. You might be the first rancher in history who has no interest in expanding his profit margins. What's your secret? Can you see into the future? You know exactly how everything's going to go, so no need to worry about it?"

"You're tired of having this argument, yet here you are. Having this argument."

"I sure am glad that one of us inherited Dad's ability to act like a brick wall," Brady said. "Particularly when no brick wall is needed."

It was below the belt. He knew that. Then again, it was also true.

Gray stared at him, his face the grim stone that Brady was most familiar with. "Comparing me to Dad isn't going to make me change my mind. About anything."

"Because nothing could possibly make you change your mind, I know." Brady shrugged. "You make up your mind, and it might as well be a brand-new mountain range. Immovable. Impassable. You're perfectly happy to stand in exactly the same place for the next three hundred years, simply because you can. Or because you decided to once upon a time."

"I came in here to thank you for agreeing to do that

homecoming thing for Becca." Gray's dark eyes glittered, though his voice stayed calm. "But we both know you only did it as a personal favor to her. You may have grown up here, but you shrugged that off a long time ago. It's not like you have a connection to Cold River. Or the high school. Or this ranch."

"You have no idea what I have a connection to or don't," Brady replied, his voice harsher than necessary, but he couldn't do anything about that. "Because you never ask."

"I don't have to ask. Your absence does all the talking for you."

Brady understood, maybe for the first time in his life, why a person might do something like flip a table. Would that get through to Gray? Would it make a big enough statement?

But he refused to become Amos, no matter how seductive it seemed while he was in a temper. There were some slippery slopes a man couldn't climb back up.

"My absence?" he demanded. "I've been right here, busting my ass next to yours, for the past ten months. You might have to revise your story, Gray. And then what? What will the excuse be?"

"The ranch is not here to fuel your get-rich-quick schemes," Gray said, all granite and disapproval.

That was how he always sounded when he was talking to Brady, and Brady hated the fact that it still got to him. With the exception of his college scholarship, he'd given up on getting Amos's approval early. But here he was, still wishing he could turn Gray around. And it ate at him that he cared.

"Is this what it's going to be like forever?" Gray was still a wall standing there in the door. "Do I have to worry that if you come up with bad hand at a poker table one night, you'll gamble the ranch away?"

Brady did not make his hands into fists. Or use them. "Why would I bet the ranch?"

"Why would you do anything?" Gray pushed away from the doorjamb and moved farther into the kitchen, swiping up his Stetson from the counter. "This has been illuminating, as always. But if you don't mind, I thought maybe we could work on the land we still have. Until you sell it out from under me."

"If I wanted to play poker, Gray," Brady said, trying to keep his temper out of his voice, and failing, "I would cash in with some of that actual money you hate so much. Because I don't need the ranch to get rich. I'm good."

"I'm happy for you."

Gray headed out the door without a backward glance. Brady shouldn't have been surprised. That was Gray. And if this had been any other part of his life, any business meeting in the normal course of events, he would have shrugged it off. Because he would never have tolerated a corporate contact who treated him that way.

But this wasn't business. It was his family.

He could admit he was more frayed around the edges than usual today.

How could he possibly have let that happen with Amanda? And not merely *let that happen*. Who was he kidding? He was the one who'd made it happen. She was so innocent, she had legitimately asked him up to her apartment for coffee. She'd actually gone ahead and *made them coffee*.

He was the one who'd made the moves.

Brady was thoroughly disgusted with himself.

The result was, he couldn't seem to put his usual effort and energy into pretending he was less bothered by his brothers than he was. Well. Ty stirred the pot when the mood took him, because he found it all entertaining. It was Gray who drove Brady around the bend.

Brady was following him out into the yard before he had time to think it through.

Out in the yard, the sun was starting to contemplate its duties over to the east. The sky was bluing its way out of the night, kicking off the heavy fall shadows and the frosty temperature.

Maybe Brady had finally had enough.

"You don't want to talk about diversification, fine," he said to his brother's back. He didn't yell. He didn't have to yell. "You don't want to talk about any ideas I have. You demanded that I promise you a year, and I'm delivering that, but you don't want to give me anything in return."

Gray turned slowly. The sun poked over the eastern ridge in earnest as he faced Brady, making him look like some kind of holy relic. "I'm giving you room and board."

"I own one-third of this land and that house. I'm giving myself room and board, Gray. And in case you missed it, I'm the one who put my life on hold."

"You want to do this? Fine. I'm tired of hearing about how you had to walk away from your great life. I'm tired of hearing about all your sacrifices."

"Why? You want to hang up on that cross all by yourself?"

"This should be your life," Gray thundered. "This is

my life. It looks like it's Ty's life these days too. It was good enough for generations of Everetts, and it's good enough for us. Why is nothing good enough for you?"

Brady was aware the sounds from over by the garage had stopped. If he turned his head, he was sure he would see Ty over there, listening in on this latest confrontation. But he stayed focused on Gray.

"It's not a question of whether or not it's good enough for me. It's a question of that sacrifice you don't want to hear about. This is your life, like you said. There's no sacrifice for you to be here, is there? And Ty's rodeo career is over. Looks like the ranch is a good solution for him too. Out of the three of us, I'm the only one who gave up something to spend this year here."

"Well, shoot," came Ty's drawl. Inevitably. "And here I am without my violin."

Brady gave him a one-fingered salute without looking in his direction. He kept his gaze trained on Gray. And kept going, since he'd started.

"I don't want a violin. I don't need any sympathy. I could have said no, and believe me, I know it." He shook his head. "But just once, Gray, it would be nice if you would acknowledge that you're asking more of me than you're asking of anyone else. Including yourself."

He watched something flicker on his oldest brother's face. He braced himself, because a year ago, Gray would not have accepted that. He would have laughed in Brady's face with that call to violence in his dark eyes.

But today, he only studied Brady for another too-long moment.

"Okay," he said. Eventually. "I acknowledge that you had to give up your life in Denver for the family. Is that really it, Brady? That's what you need?"

"I can go find that violin," Ty offered from the garage. "It's no trouble."

This time, Brady glared in his direction too.

"If you two wanted to go to college, you could have," he said quietly. But intensely enough one of Ty's rodeo horses over in the corral nickered quietly.

Predictably, both Gray and Ty let out big laughs at that.

"That's a hard pass from me, baby brother," Ty said when he was done howling. "I barely made it through high school. I'm about as good behind the desk as you are on the back of a bull."

"I thought about college for maybe three seconds," Gray added darkly. "But what I know is land and cattle. And I don't need to sit in the classroom for that."

"Then stop giving me a hard time because I did go." Brady belted that out like jab.

Over by the garage, Ty looked to the ground. But Gray kept his gaze steady.

"I don't mind that you went to college," he said. "You were always smart like that. It made sense for you to go. What I mind is that you never seem to connect the life you live now with what gave it to you."

"You mean my hard work?"

"I mean, this land. The cattle. The ranch, Brady. It supports all of us, you included. You treat it like a weight around your neck, dragging you down with every step." His jaw tightened. "It isn't just Dad's folly or the family legacy. It's our future. All the book learning in the world, and you can't get that through your head."

"I'm not the one the land drags down, Gray," Brady objected. "You spent a decade here, trapped."

"I might have been trapped in my circumstances,"

Gray conceded. "But never by the ranch. The ranch is what saved me. You'll forgive me if I can't handle the level of disrespect you throw at it day and night."

Back in the days when he'd been so good at keeping his cool, back before he'd put his mouth on little Amanda Kittredge and knocked his whole world sideways and spinning, Brady would not have gone toe-to-toe with Gray. He would have sucked it up the way he always did. He and Gray had skirmishes, but Brady always backed down rather than take it too far.

Right now was a great time to do just that.

But he'd already messed up his life. Sooner or later, Riley would find out, and it would all get worse. So why not make it universal?

"I don't disrespect the ranch," he threw at Gray instead of biting his tongue. "If I did, I certainly wouldn't have spent the better part of a year working it, would I? I wouldn't have come back at all, not even for holidays while Dad was alive."

"I'd believe that you respected something about this place if you'd done anything to help before I asked it of you," Gray retorted. "Dad had to die for you to remember where you came from. I figure soon as your year's up, you'll forget again as fast as you can. You already did it once. Why not again?"

"I never forgot a thing." Brady didn't shout. Not exactly, but he could hear his own voice echo back at him. "It's not my fault Dad didn't care that I got my degree in a useful subject. Just like it's not my fault that I went out there and made money for the express purpose of sinking it into the ranch, and he wouldn't take it."

For a moment, it seemed like the rising sun was making all that noise. Racketing around, tangled up in all those old, bright resentments Brady would have sworn he'd long since stopped carrying around.

But one moment led into the next, and he realized the noise was in him. His head, his chest.

And the astounded look on Gray's face didn't help.

"What are you talking about? Ty sent home some of his winnings from time to time. But you—" Gray shook his head. "Never a penny. Dad was terrible about paying off its debts, but he recorded every cent that ever came in."

"He wouldn't take it."

It never changed, the kick of that. The bitterness. If he listened closely, he could still hear the old man's drunk cackle.

I'd rather put myself out of my own misery than take a penny from a jumped-up egghead like you, Amos had said. *A man deserves to lose a ranch if the only way he can keep it is by taking charity from a son so ungrateful, he put it in his rearview mirror and left it in the dust.*

"That doesn't make sense." Gray adjusted his hat on his head, shooting a look over toward Ty, then back to Brady. "Obviously Dad took a distinct pleasure in being mean, but this isn't family stuff. This is money."

"My money," Brady said from between clenched teeth. "And like everything that has to do with me, he preferred to ignore it."

"Maybe he didn't understand—" Ty began.

"He understood. I sent him checks. And he returned each and every one of them, ripped up into little pieces."

It was gratifying on some level to watch his older brothers stare at each other as if they'd never heard of such a thing. As if they couldn't imagine it.

"Brady," Gray began.

"Maybe it's time you ask yourself not just what Dad

did to you, but what he did to me," Brady suggested. "Ty, you could ask yourself why it was that Dad watched every single one of your rides, could quote your stats, and even went so far as to visit you in the hospital after your accident. All of which would surely take a whole lot more effort than attending a Cold River High football game. But he never attended one of mine."

He shot his gaze back to Gray. "You were here, Gray. And I get it, you had a lot of stuff going on. Cristina, Becca as a baby, I understand. But you sat here, night after night, and watched him scribble down names into that will of his. Scratching them out, writing them back in. You listened while he told us what each and every person he bothered to mention had done to him. And he was terrible to the two of you, everybody knows that. But me? He acted like I didn't exist."

Brady found he didn't have a lot to say after that, and even less he wanted to hear.

He stalked off to his truck, slammed his way into it, and spent the rest of his day taking out his aggression whaling on fence posts. And when the day was done, he didn't stick around for the usual Everett family dinner. He showered in the room he'd taken in the main house because it had a private entrance—and because, maybe foolishly, he'd imagined that staying in the main house would make him feel more connected to his family, even if the room was tainted with Amos's ghost—and he headed back into town.

Not to the Coyote. That would have been his normal preference, given the mood he was in. But in the week or so since he'd made the vast mistake of kissing Amanda, his preferences had shifted.

Because he couldn't possibly go back to the Coyote

while she was working there. And given that Harry didn't exactly post his staffing information on the front door of the place, it meant Brady was out of luck unless he wanted to take his chances. Or start sticking his head in, spotting Amanda, and running away like a pathetic kid.

He'd been opting for the Broken Wheel Saloon instead. But all the reasons the Broken Wheel would have been a far more appropriate place for Amanda to work made it less satisfying for Brady. The Broken Wheel was a family place. Folks brought their kids in for dinner, and it was only after 8 p.m. or so that things shifted over into more of a nighttime scene. But even that lacked the edges and surefire entertainment of a night at the Coyote.

The Broken Wheel Saloon, right there on Main Street, was not a place a man went for a palate-cleansing hookup. Not unless he wanted all the gossipy old ladies in town to be plotting out wedding announcements and baby showers before dawn.

He shuddered at the thought.

Tonight, Brady got himself a beer from Tessa Winthrop behind the bar and ambled over to the table where Riley was sitting with Connor, Jensen, and a bunch of other friends and neighbors. Including Matias Trujillo, who wasn't too long back from the service—and was also Riley's ex-brother-in-law.

How do you handle that? Brady had asked, back when he'd first come home. *Isn't it awkward?*

Everything is awkward in a small town, Riley had said darkly. *It's just a question of degrees.*

Brady reminded himself of that as the Kittredge brothers gazed back at him. He got to marinate in his own form of awkwardness, tinged with the knowledge that if they had any idea he'd had his hands on their baby sister, they'd kill him right here on the saloon floor.

"Guess what?" he asked.

"Is this a knock-knock joke?" Jensen asked in a drawl. "I'm a firefighter. I don't wait for someone to open the door; I kick it down."

"I'm a marine," Matias replied. "I'll take your kick and raise it a battalion or two."

Jensen rolled his eyes. "You would."

"The only girl I love has made a special homecoming request of me," Brady announced, pulling out a chair and dropping into it. "And I do not have it in me to deny my niece a single thing her heart desires. Even if what it desires is my presence at that egregious homecoming parade."

"The parade of faded glory." Riley raised his beer bottle. "Good luck with that, brother."

"I'm not your brother, praise the Lord." Brady smiled blandly. "But I am your former quarterback and team captain, and I'm ordering you to do this with me."

"You know that's not a thing. It doesn't last past the actual team." Riley nodded toward Jensen and Matias. "If it did, Matias could order Jensen around to his heart's content."

"Don't I already?" Mattias asked.

Jensen smirked. "You try."

"It's not a thing," Riley insisted. "And also, no. I've avoided that parade for years. I see no reason to stop now."

"No problem," Brady drawled. "I'll just tell my sixteen-year-old niece, the one who's always idolized all of you, that each and every one of you is too afraid to walk down a street."

And that was how, when Brady surrendered himself to the humiliation of walking in the hometown parade that weekend, he could at least take comfort in the fact that he had company.

Surly, furious company, sure. But company all the same.

Then they figured they might as well stay for the game, and Brady found himself looking around the stands at all the beaming, cheering parents. All the fathers who'd come out on this Friday night to watch their sons throw balls around. All the proud smiles and extra-loud shouts.

That was the funny thing about bitterness, wasn't it? Poke at it, and it wasn't bitter at all. It was nothing more than a wish for sweetness that was never fulfilled and sat there like an ache instead.

It occurred to him—while the marching band played, the crowd cheered, and Cold River High School looked like the setting of some perfect little American dream—that he'd figured out pretty early on that he was never going to get anything he wanted from Amos. It was why he'd spent so much time at the Kittredge house. It was why he'd played his heart out on the football field, killed himself in the classroom, and told himself the only thing he ever cared about was getting away. Even after he'd done it.

But he would have to have been made of stone like Gray not to understand, as he sat there as a grown man in the football bleachers, that the hollow thing inside him wasn't because he looked down on any of this. He'd been telling himself that lie for so long that he'd stopped questioning it. It wasn't that he hated this place. It was that he'd missed out on it.

Even when he'd been right here, doing it, he'd missed out on it.

If he didn't belong in his own family—something his father had made abundantly clear—then how did he belong anywhere? All the lights of the big city and what he'd built down there was commotion, not connection.

He knew that too, though it was another thing he'd stopped looking at directly.

Brady had always considered himself a simple man. He liked the fuss of a high school football game, like anyone else. It was even better on the stands than it had been on the field, because there was no pressure. He didn't miss quarterbacking.

What he missed was what he'd never had. The idea that his father could be up here, cheering him on. The idea that he could care enough about anything Brady did—about Brady himself—to show up.

If he squinted, he could almost see a version of his father here, like a phantom limb.

Brady knew plenty of folks down in the city who would be only too happy to tell him how stupid they thought it was to care about a high school football game. In or out of high school.

But it wasn't the game that got people out. It was the community. The sense of being part of something bigger than their own lives. That by identifying themselves as a Cowboy like the boys on the field, they felt like one for a while. It was no more than a few fall nights every year, scattered in against the coming darkness, but it felt like a talisman.

Tonight, it felt like one more ache.

Brady shouted something about hitting the head to Matias, who nodded. Then he picked his way down through the crowd. He did his neighborly part, nodding and smiling, as he climbed down to the ground. Even as he waited in line for the facilities.

On his way back, he stopped for a moment down at the bottom of the stands, letting the memories of his time here wash over him. Down in Denver, high school seemed like it had happened to someone else. It still did, but now it also felt like a movie, maybe. One he'd watched recently, so he could pick up the nuances.

After ten months back in town, he recognized a lot of the faces in the stands. He would have sworn up and down that familiarity was the sort of thing he wanted to get away from. But tonight, here in all the bright lights and noise of the homecoming football game, he could admit there was a part of him that liked it.

Home was home, after all. No matter how complicated.

When he caught a movement out of the corner of his eye, he turned his head, saw Amanda, and liked that even more.

The very fact of her, picking her way beneath the stands. She was laughing uproariously while she and her friend Kat linked their arms together and navigated their way beneath all those stamping feet. And it walloped him.

He had to check to see if he'd actually ended up on the ground.

Her friend veered off, heading for the bathrooms. Amanda kept walking, and only as she drew closer did she look up.

If she felt a similar wallop when she saw him, she didn't show it. Her eyes sparkled. Her laughter turned into something else, some kind of too-hot smile, and he should have turned tail and run for it. He knew that.

Two of her brothers were sitting in the stands above him. He'd come with them. Her other two brothers were at large. Connor could be anywhere. Zack was almost certainly in this same crowd and could appear at any moment, flashing his badge.

Though his badge would be the least of Brady's worries.

Brady needed to get away from her before anyone saw them. Before anyone saw *her* and that look on her face that was broadcasting the fact that they'd kissed.

But he couldn't seem to move as she came closer.

"I've been looking for you," she announced, reckless and careless as she rocked to a stop beside him.

They weren't exactly hidden. Still, he could have backed up a step or two to put more space between them, and he didn't do that either.

It was as if he wanted to be caught. As if he wanted to cause himself trouble. Maybe he really was like his father, in all his self-destructive glory.

What an unpleasant thought.

"I'm the last person you should be looking for," he told her, his tone dark and oppressive, as if that could get the message through her thick head.

It did not.

He knew that because she swayed closer, one hand on one of the metal supports that kept the stands up, and the other out in front of her as if she planned to rest it on him.

Which would be as good as her signing his death warrant.

But he still didn't move back.

He would never know why it suddenly occurred to her

to be cautious. But instead of touching him, she let her hand drop.

It was a funny thing, how much he hated that. How much it turned out he wanted her hand on him, no matter the price.

Brady would have preferred not to know that about himself.

"I've come to a decision," Amanda said, with the tone of someone sharing a delicious secret. "And involves you."

"Does it involve you needing a ride to a nunnery?"

That smile of hers should have been illegal. "It does not."

"It should."

"It's been a while since you came into the Coyote," she said.

"Has it? I haven't noticed. You shouldn't have noticed either."

Amanda rolled her eyes. "Okay. Whatever. I think you might be right. That is possibly not the best place to try to meet someone."

Brady felt light-headed. "*Meet someone?* Why would you even . . ." He dragged a hand over his face. "You know what? This is not my business."

"It is your business," she said, and it was her earnestness that got to him. She looked like she could be talking to him about buying Girl Scout cookies, for God's sake. "That's the whole point, Brady. You can probably tell that I don't know anything about . . . well, anything."

That flush of hers was going to kill him. Maybe it did, because having actually died already was the only explanation for why he was still standing there, frozen solid, as if he couldn't move. He should have been halfway back to the ranch by now.

"We're not talking about that," he gritted out. Clearly not dead. "We're pretending that never happened."

She wrinkled up her nose, like he was being silly. "I don't want to forget about it." And again, that smile. Little Amanda Kittredge was going to kill him with a smile. "Brady. I want it to be you."

He was pretty sure he really did die, then. Of a heart attack that felt a lot like a sledgehammer to the chest.

"I don't know what you're talking about."

He couldn't have sounded as mean and forbidding as he wanted, because she moved closer. Then she pressed her fingertips so gently against his chest that he shouldn't have been able to feel them at all.

But he did.

Like she was beaming light and sensation directly into all the places he ached.

"I want it to be you, Brady," Amanda said, shining gold eyes and that impossible smile. "I want you to teach me everything there is to know."

When he only stared back at her, possibly dead, that flush of hers deepened.

But it didn't stop her. Amanda smiled wider. "About sex."

9

Amanda didn't know what she expected from Brady.

Okay, maybe she did. Maybe she thought her announcement—more of an invitation, really—would inspire a little enthusiasm. Maybe not cartwheels. But a smile, possibly. *Something* to show he'd heard what she said and wasn't standing there, trying not to laugh at her. Or actively repulsed.

It had occurred to her that a person who'd never really been kissed before should probably figure out whether or not she'd done it right before leaping into offers of sex, but caution was Old Amanda's game. New Amanda was all about leaping in first and seeing what happened.

Old Amanda had gone into her shower to hide from that kiss. New Amanda had come out wanting more.

Tonight, Brady stared down at her with an expression she couldn't decode. For what felt like a lifetime to Amanda. Maybe several lifetimes, and while he wasn't laughing at her, he wasn't jumping for joy either.

She wanted to say something. Make it into a joke, maybe. Do something—anything—to divert attention from the fact she'd asked him to have sex with her.

But having thrown that out there, she couldn't make her vocal cords produce a single other sound. Not one.

A thousand lifetimes later, Brady simply turned on his heel and walked away, back into the Friday night football crowd. A crowd that was kicking it up even more than usual, because it was homecoming weekend.

Amanda was tempted to feel slighted.

Maybe a whole lot more than simply *slighted*.

But when she emerged from beneath the stands, she got swept up in the crowd, and the marching band, and it got inside her ribs. It made her feel like dancing when she should have felt more like curling up in the fetal position somewhere.

She should have felt deflated. But all she could think about was that look on his face. That gorgeous, incredulous face of his. And he hadn't said anything, but all she could seem to feel was exhilaration. And before she knew it, Kat found her standing at the fence at one end of the field, clapping along and cheering her heart out.

"You really don't look like someone who's done with the small-town experience," Kat said over the noise and music, grinning widely.

"When did I say I was done with it?" Amanda thought of those lifetimes beneath the bleachers, nothing but Brady's gaze on hers, far better than any touch. Far more intense. "I want to expand it a little bit, that's all. Complicate it. Change it up."

"I can't tell if that means you want to move to California, dye your hair purple, or truly live dangerously and bring a microwave dinner to the next potluck."

"I want to complicate my life," Amanda said dryly. "Not end it."

"Some people think complicating their life means going

to a different service at the same church on a Sunday," Kat said loftily.

"I'm a twenty-two-year-old woman," Amanda said, gesturing grandly with one arm, like the homecoming queen she'd never been.

Kat laughed. "Thank you. I'm aware. As I am also a twenty-two-year-old woman. One who's known you since birth."

"You're a twenty-two-year-old woman who's actually been in a relationship. You're in one now. I'm not. And everything I've read and watched or even heard about in passing tells me that as a twenty-two-year-old single woman, I should be out there." She gestured at the crowd again, though she didn't quite mean out there on the football field. "Living it up."

"You're talking about sex."

"I'm talking about one-night stands, Kat. Morning-afters. Walks of shame and awkward silences when you run into last night's hookup in the grocery store line. These things, I'm told, are the spice of life."

"Told by who?"

"The internet, mostly."

"Shame and awkwardness have never appealed to me, personally," Kat said. Diplomatically, for her.

"That's the thing, isn't it? We don't know if they're more appealing than they sound. Because we've never actually experienced any of them ourselves."

Kat made a face. "I haven't experienced being set on fire. Or a root canal. But I feel pretty sure I wouldn't enjoy either one."

Amanda shrugged. "You always seem to think that making out with Brandon is fun. Why wouldn't making out—and more—in general also be fun?"

"Brandon has been deployed so long, I can't really remember making out with him. Or even what he looks like in real life."

Amanda bumped her shoulder against her friend's. "You remember."

Kat smiled, and neither one of them mentioned that her smile was more and more brittle these days. "The difference is that I've known Brandon since we were kids. We got together in the seventh grade. I don't get the impression you're actually talking about a relationship."

Amanda thought about brooding, overwhelming, gloriously too-much-for-her-to-handle Brady Everett. She remembered his mouth on hers. She hadn't slept well since he'd left her apartment that afternoon. It was like he'd flipped a switch in her, and her body was still in the grip of a brand-new, breathtaking electrical current. Even now.

"Relationships are great if it happens that way," Amanda said with the great confidence of a person who had only ever had a deep relationship with her horse. "But what I'm talking about is *experience*."

"Terrific," Kat replied. She turned her head and regarded Amanda so steadily, it made Amanda's stomach twist. "But you know that kind of experience is a surefire way to end up wishing you had less, right?"

Amanda leaned over and kissed her best and oldest friend on her cheek, grinning when Kat batted her away.

"I know," she said, her voice hidden beneath the sound of the crowd so only Kat could hear her. "I really do. That's what I want."

She was still thinking about experience and regret and wishes later that night, curled up in her apartment while the usual Friday night party in the Coyote raged on

below. Weekend nights were major nights for tips, she'd
learned, and that meant the older, more seasoned bartenders covered the shifts. Brand-new girls like Amanda
were relegated to the off-hours.

Amanda didn't mind. If it weren't for the pounding music from the jukebox below, the raucous sound
of drunken laughter, and the way her windows rattled
slightly every time the heavy outdoor slammed, she
would have called it an idyllic evening.

She was coming up on a month of living on her own,
the best spontaneous decision she'd ever made. And she
still couldn't quite believe she'd pulled it off. That she
got to call this apartment home and newly experience
this little town she would have said she already knew
too well. Even if she did have to pay attention when she
got into the car because if she wasn't careful, she'd drive
halfway to the Bar K without thinking.

Amanda tucked her feet beneath her, resting her
book on the wide arm of her chair. It was already cooling down considerably at night, so she'd pulled on heavy
socks. And she was contemplating wrapping herself in
the quilt her mother had brought by on one of her visits.

You're giving me Grandma's quilt? she'd asked in surprise, when she'd opened the door to find Ellie there with
the quilt in question in her arms. Instead of on the bed in
what had once been Riley and Connor's room in the big
house, and now had become a guest room.

Why not your grandmother's quilt? Ellie had asked
coolly.

Because it's yours.

Ellie had smiled, though even that was reserved. Distant and untouchable, just like her.

Amanda, she'd said briskly. *It's a quilt. Anything else*

attached to it is your own nostalgia. Memories. You get to decide how much weight they have.

Maybe that was her mother's typically roundabout way of saying it was their secret that she was quietly outfitting her daughter with all the things Amanda hadn't taken with her when she'd left. Ellie wasn't the type for a grand gesture, after all. She preferred quiet acts of rebellion instead.

Amanda had waited her whole life to have secrets. Her brothers all had their share. That was obvious in all the silences and sideways glances. But Amanda's life had always been the family's open book. Everyone got to read along. Everyone had a say.

But now she had her own space, her own home. And best of all, her own secrets at last.

She had a new job, though she couldn't say she liked bartending in the Coyote, exactly. It was more that she liked the challenge of it. The funny feeling she got low in her belly at the rough clientele. The things she now knew about folks she'd known all her life, but not in the context of their late-night adventures on the wrong side of the river.

She'd kissed Brady Everett. And it had been far, far better than even her wildest imaginings. Then she'd gone ahead and asked him for everything else she wanted. It almost didn't matter what happened next.

Almost, she thought, wriggling a little in her chair as all those Brady-specific sensations wound around and around inside.

Maybe it wasn't surprising that when she took herself off to bed some time later, with the brand-new earplugs she'd bought to combat the late-night revelry below, she dreamed of dark green eyes. Quarterback shoulders. And that brooding, intense look he'd trained on her beneath the homecoming bleachers, as if she was as much of a problem to him as he was to her.

God help her, but she wanted to be his problem.

"If you had it to do over again, would you do it all the same way?" Amanda asked Abby the next day.

They were sitting together in the back office of Cold River Coffee, recapping what had already happened over the course of a long Saturday during the Harvest Festival. And also taking a break from said festival. The coffeehouse had been jumping since opening, and this was the first time Abby had come in to work a full shift since she'd had the baby.

"That wasn't really a shift." Abby gazed down at Bart, currently sound asleep in the little bassinet she brought with her. "It was more of a test run. I wanted to see if it was even possible to work with him around. That's why I scheduled you for the same time."

"And it went great. Everyone loves him already. He's better than ordering coffee. Everyone cooed at him instead."

Abby laughed. "Maybe a regular cup of coffee. Not those monstrously sweet things you like to drink. People are pretty clear they want their fix."

"I like sugar." Amanda grinned. "But I meant . . . all of this. Getting married. Bart. The whole Gray situation."

Abby regarded her steadily for a moment, the way she always did, because she listened. Really listened, instead of ranting on about her opinions or what everyone else ought to do, like Amanda's brothers.

"What's funny to me is that we've been married for

almost a year now," Abby said, one hand on the sleeping infant's deliciously round belly. "We already have a son. We're as happy as I know how to be, if currently sleep-deprived. And yet the only thing anybody remembers is that I mooned around after Gray for a thousand years."

"So you would change it."

"The mooning? Or the marriage?"

"Any of it." Amanda busied herself with a sudden, intense study of her fingernails. Which were not beauti-fully manicured to a high shine like Hannah's. Amanda's nails were cut short, because as much as it turned out she might like to make an entrance upon occasion, the rest of the time she had to work. Her hands had to *do things.* "What if instead of mooning around after him, you'd dated other people instead?"

Again, a long look from Abby. "Is there someone you want to date?"

"I've never been on a date in my life." Amanda forced her lips to curve, though it wasn't exactly a smile. "Only closely chaperoned dances in high school. Because who would dare ask me out? They would have to contend with the brother death squad. It's easier all around to . . . not."

"I would have told you that all I wanted was to go on a date," Abby said. "That was true. I did. My problem was that I was only ever interested in one person, which would have made going on dates with other people chal-lenging."

"Everybody knew how you felt about Gray. That's why you never went out with anyone else."

"Also no one asked," Abby said dryly. "My friends would tell you things could have happened if I were looking, but I really only ever saw Gray. So I'm lucky it all worked out the way it did. Because otherwise, I was right on track to becoming Cold River's very own vestal virgin."

"I don't want to be a virgin," Amanda blurted out, from the very depths of her soul. Because the back office had always been a safe space for such confessions. "Vestal or otherwise."

"I can't blame you there," Abby said in her typically calm, matter-of-fact way. "I'm not going to lie to you and pretend that sex isn't amazing, because it is." She concentrated on the bassinet a little more fiercely than before, but Amanda could see the faint color in her cheeks. "Do you have someone in mind to help you out with that?"

That last question was slightly more deliberately bland than the rest, and Amanda smiled, because that was the big sister coming out in Abby. It made Amanda feel safe. Protected. But that didn't mean Amanda planned to announce she'd kissed her older boss's even older brother-in-law. She was starting a new life. She didn't want to end it before it got good.

"Not really," she lied.

She reminded herself she was a woman with secrets now. That meant she couldn't go sharing them with anyone, or they wouldn't be secrets any longer. And that, too, made her feel somehow safe and sultry at once.

Abby nodded sagely. "You must have too many prospects to count."

"I think some people have prospects, and then other people are me," Amanda said quietly. Matter-of-factly, because she might have been making grand gestures at the football game, but she'd also been thinking about this for a long time. Or she never would have moved off the ranch. "And if I don't make my own prospects, it's never going to happen. It's not only my brothers who treat me like a child. Everybody does. I don't want to be the town's vestal virgin, or even a legendary spinster like Miss Patrick, but both those things are infinitely preferable to being treated like a kid. Forever."

"I understand that." The baby made a small sound, and Abby moved her hand in a soft circle on her son's chubby belly. His mouth moved, but he stilled. "And I know a lot of people have a lot of strong opinions about what you should do. Or not do. But it doesn't matter what anyone else thinks. I know it feels like it does, but in the end, the only opinion that really matters is yours."

"You don't regret anything, then?"

"I don't." Abby got a dreamy sort of look on her face. "But I was terrified to tell Gray how inexperienced I was. I thought it was embarrassing. Or that I would do the wrong thing. And it was fine." Her eyes danced, then. "It was so much more than fine, I don't have the words to describe it."

"You married him, though," Amanda said. "I think maybe the protocol is different if it's more of a casual thing."

Some part of her expected Abby to clutch at the pearls she wasn't wearing. Instead, she smiled. "In my head, I wanted to be the sort of person who had a great many casual things. Instead, I read about them. But it's not as hard as you think it is to talk about stuff. Especially if you know the person. Not that I experienced the alternative, of course."

Amanda tried to imagine sitting around having an in-depth discussion with Brady about the intricacies of sex. Or even about that kiss, rather than simply blundering in and out of moments that left her spinning for days. She felt herself ignite at the notion, and it was a wildfire this time. It was a slow, steady, calamitous burn that unfurled from the deepest part of her and sent licks of flame dancing along her limbs.

She hoped Abby couldn't see it all over her.

"I know what it's like to have everyone think of you one way when you want so desperately to be thought of in a different way altogether," Abby said in her same quiet way, no hint of judgment in her voice. "What I found out is that, sure, there are always going to be people who can't let go of whatever image they had of you. But most people in Cold River want you to be happy. Whatever that looks like."

"I believe you," Amanda said after a moment, when she thought she could speak without giving away that fire inside of her. But her cheeks were still too hot when she lifted her gaze to Abby's. "My trouble is, there are four particular citizens of Cold River who do not want me happy. They want me in a box. And if that box holds me exactly like this for the rest of my life, they will be delighted."

"Too bad it's not up to them." Abby's gaze was steady. "I don't think there's ever anything wrong with asking for what you want, Amanda. I wish I had, and a whole lot sooner."

"Unless, of course, you don't get it," Amanda said, thinking of that unreadable, too-intense look Brady had fixed on her. There in her apartment, and beneath the bleachers at the football game last night too.

She tried not to shiver.

"Sure," Abby replied, with a small smile. "But what if you do?"

When the baby started fussing, Amanda shooed Abby out the door with him. Then she spent the next few hours handling the coffeehouse paperwork and the usual back-log of calls. Anything that made a dent. She meant to leave, but she got sucked back into the late-afternoon rush, made even more crowded than usual thanks to the Harvest Festival still going on outside.

By the time she actually left, dusk had already settled in. She pushed her way out the back door of the coffee-house, smiling as she heard the music and sounds of general merriment floating over the back of the brick buildings that fronted onto Main Street. She figured she might as well go home, shower off a day of coffee, and then come back into town on foot so she could enjoy the live bands at the Broken Wheel. Or maybe do a little shopping in the boutiques that would stay open tonight until late.

She was congratulating herself on the perfect evening ahead of her as she made her way out to her car, parked in the lot behind the coffee shop.

Until a shadow detached itself from a nearby tree.

Her stomach dropped. Her heart kicked up.

Then it all got worse, or better, because it was Brady.

He looked like part of the night itself. Dark hat, a Henley and jeans, all of it forcing her to pay too much at-tention to that *chest* of his that she'd felt beneath her fin-gers. She didn't know how she was supposed to handle herself.

There had been twenty-two years of imagining—and now she *knew*. She knew what his mouth tasted like, and how it moved on hers. And it was nothing like fairy tales or Disney movies. It was raw and physical, wet and hot. Under the bleachers, surrounded by so much noise, she'd forgotten that. A little.

She'd lost it in all that commotion.

But now they were all by themselves in the dark. Everyone they knew and everything in Cold River was on the other side of the stout row of brick buildings, standing there, cheek by cheek, like a wall. And Amanda had known this from the start. She could never go back.

She could never be a girl who didn't know those things. His taste. His touch. The scrape of his cheek against her jaw. The precise scent of the exact place where his neck met his shoulder.

Amanda had no idea how she was supposed to just . . . *talk* to him.

For a moment there, with only the far-off stars as witness, she panicked. She wondered if she'd lost her voice altogether.

"Is this your new game?" Brady growled at her. "You wander around asking random men to teach you about sex?"

He sounded so outraged, so thoroughly disgruntled, that the panic in her eased a little. Or shifted until it joined up with the heat within her, then bloomed into something new.

She felt an ache low in her belly, and what she would have called fear if it hadn't felt so much like flying.

"I wouldn't call you random, Brady," she said. With a bit of a drawl. "You did change my diapers, after all."

He muttered a curse. "This isn't something that can happen. Ever."

But her eyes were adjusting to the dark. She could see the tense, taut line of his jaw. And if she wasn't mistaken, that particular glitter in his dark eyes that appeared to be wired directly to the slippery place between her legs.

"I've thought a lot about what I want," she told him, venturing closer.

"God help us all."

She ignored that. Virtuously. "That kiss was clarifying."

"That kiss scared you half to death."

"Only half." She nodded at him. "And showing up in the dark like this doesn't make you any less scary, by the way."

She stopped by the hood of her car, maybe three feet away from where he stood. And she couldn't help but imagine that he'd been leaning against that tree for hours. That he'd only straightened when she'd come out the back door of the coffeehouse. If that wasn't what happened, she didn't want to know.

"You think I don't know what it's like to be your age, but I do," Brady said, low and dark. "I remember. You want to get out there and grab hold of everything the world has to offer, and you should."

"I like to sing 'Wide Open Spaces' at the top of my lungs like the next girl," Amanda replied. "But Colorado is filled with a whole lot of open space. And I like Cold River. Unlike some people, I didn't race on out of here twenty seconds after graduating from high school. This is home. I like home."

He made a dismissive noise. "It's easy to think you love a place when you've never been anywhere else."

"That's why I made you an offer." She kept her voice as bright as if she'd offered him a pastry, not herself. She remembered what Abby had said about talking things through. "I've been a virgin with no sexual experience for quite some time now. I like it fine. It's comfortable. But how can I know whether or not I prefer abstinence if I don't experiment a little? Just to make sure."

Brady actually laughed. "You think you're going to debate me into having sex with you?"

"It's a rational argument." She leaned against the hood of her car and grinned at him. "All I ever hear are claims that if I was a little more rational, I might actually get what I want."

"And what happens if I say no?" Something changed, there beneath the tree that would have hidden them from view, had anyone been watching tonight. Though Amanda found she didn't have it in her to care too much if they were. "Are you going to run out and find someone else?"

Her instinct was to respond from the gut with a sharp no. To tell him that she'd had any number of offers at the Coyote and hadn't felt compelled to take anyone up on any of them.

But there was something else in her, kicking around, hot and bright and connected to that pulsing heat between her legs. She *knew things* about him now. And that meant she knew things about herself too.

A month ago, she would never have smirked the way she did then, or shifted her body so that it emphasized her curves.

"This is Cold River, Brady," she drawled, watching his gaze move over her curves and take its time finding her eyes again. "There's no shortage of cowboys."

She didn't see him move, but he must have. Because suddenly he was close enough to cup her cheek. And he held her there, though there was no tenderness in it. Or nothing so simple as tenderness. There was torment in his gaze and what looked like denial flattening his mouth.

But then his thumb moved, a small scrape over her cheekbone and she understood. That this was the truth. This pulsing, exultant sensation, like their own, secret heartbeat.

"I can't have you wandering around the valley, propositioning cowboys anytime you feel like it," he rumbled, his voice as much inside her chest as in her ears. "It might cause a riot."

It was hard to focus on anything but the hypnotizing sweep of his callused thumb against her cheek, but Amanda tried. "Can't you?"

"Your brother asked me to look out for you. I should have known it would mean something like this."

"Poor Brady," she murmured sadly, though there wasn't a shred of sadness inside her. "Do you have to take one for the team?"

"You're going to be the death of me, Amanda."

"I hope not." She tipped her head back, swaying closer to him. "If you died, I'd be right back where I started, wouldn't I?"

He took possession of her other cheek, and then he held her there. A breath away from his mouth. From another kiss. From all those things that swirled inside of her, looking for a way out. Looking for *him*.

Amanda melted.

The entire Cold River High School marching band could have paraded around them, then, and she doubted she would have noticed. There was only him. Only Brady. His hands on her face and that hot gleam in his eyes.

"Let's you and me get real clear about the rules," he said, after a whole lifetime of that shuddering excitement.

"Why do you get to make the rules? This is my thing, not yours."

"You made it my thing, Amanda. Suck it up." He

waited until she inclined her head slightly. "No one knows. Ever. Not your friends, definitely not Abby, and never, ever your brothers. I'm going to need you to agree with me. Out loud."

"I agree with you." And she shuddered again at the sheer deliciousness of the situation. And the possibility that it was actually happening. That she was here in the dark making bargains with Brady Everett for sex. *For sex.* She was finally going to have sex. *With him.* She was glad he was holding her, because otherwise she might have fallen over. "Nobody knows but us."

"And as long as this goes on, as long as it's you and me, it's only you and me."

"I already told you I'm a virgin," she said, laughing. "Do you really think you're going to crack open that door and I'm going to come storming out like I'm on a mission to make up for lost time?"

"This isn't a debate about expectations, little girl." There was something dark and particularly, marvelously male about the way he said it. "We're agreeing to terms."

"I agree; no one else." She couldn't let that settle in her. It made her knees feel weak. "You have to agree that if you get all weird, you can't just snap your fingers and be done with me. No ghosting. You have to actually talk about it. With me. Like I'm a grown adult woman and not your best friend's little sister."

"Except you are my best friend's little sister."

"I want you to teach me, Brady, not condescend to me. Do you think you can handle that?"

His mouth crooked up in one corner. "Do you?"

"I'll need you to agree out loud, thank you."

"I agree," he said.

Then there was nothing but his hands on her face, the things they'd agreed to, and all that heat kicking around between them.

Oh my God, she shrieked inside. *Is this actually happening?*

"Okay," Brady said after a long, drugged sort of moment. Or maybe only Amanda felt that way. Maybe he had conversations like this every day. "Okay, then. We have rules."

Amanda was . . . jangly. Tangled up inside, filled with anticipation, and panic, and straight-up terror—all mixed up together with excitement and that *trembling.* She'd never wanted anything as much as this. She didn't know if she could survive it.

But all Brady did, after a last, long look, was drop his hands. Then step back.

There was a roaring in her ears. "You have to be kidding me. That's not it, is it?"

"It's going to be hard to keep a secret if we're making out behind the coffeehouse, Amanda. This is still Cold River."

She blinked. "Is this what people mean when they talk about someone being a tease?"

He let out another one of those laughs, as if she'd punched him again.

"You're killing me." It sounded like he was talking through clenched teeth. "Get in the truck."

She wasn't following him. "The truck? You mean your truck?"

Then, before she could puzzle that out, he was advancing on her. She made an embarrassing squeaking sound as he got directly into her space, crowding her there against the side of her car. He hooked one arm around her back, then hauled her up against him, so every part of the front of her was pressed tightly against the front of him.

She was pretty sure she flatlined.

But when she didn't *actually* die again, she felt everything.

Everything.

His hard chest against her breasts, which felt deliciously swollen tonight. His belly, flat and enticing, pressed tight against her. And that hard ridge even lower down that made her . . . dizzy.

"Yes," he said, his mouth too close to hers, "my truck. You're going to get in it. Your car is here, and anyone who sees it will imagine you're out at the Harvest Festival, wandering around with everyone else. They certainly won't expect you to be with me. I'm going find us a nice big space with your name on it, and then you and I are going to have a little lesson in attitude readjustment."

She wiggled a little in his hold, but only so she could get closer. And then melt into him all over again. "Why do I need to adjust my attitude? It feels fine from this angle."

He muttered another curse, and it took him a very long time to set her back down on her feet. Then he jerked his head toward his pickup, and Amanda had to order herself not to run around to the passenger side in what could only be called indecent haste.

Surely a lady would be less obvious.

But Amanda had never been much of a lady. She'd always smelled too much like her beloved horses for that.

She jumped into the truck, and found herself grinning like a fool when he slid in behind the steering wheel.

"You're enjoying yourself, aren't you?" He sounded

disgruntled, but she was looking at him. She could see that smile he was trying to hide.

"I've always wanted a secret," she told him, and then slid down on the bench seat, so no one could possibly see her. She rested her head on Brady's hard thigh and looked up the wall of his perfect body, sighing happily, because this was happening. This was really happening. "I'm so glad it's you."

10

Brady had ample time to think about what kind of man he was on the drive out of town.

Amanda was sprawled out across his bench seat, her head on his thigh and the hair she'd tugged out of its ponytail spilling all over his lap like honey. Like a pool of sunlight even though it was dark outside.

He was only human, no matter what lies he told himself about his character or his abilities from time to time. She kept laughing like this was all some grand adventure, and he didn't know what else he was supposed to *do*.

He took a bunch of back roads, the better to avoid the center of town, any Harvest Festival shenanigans, and all the citizens of Cold River who knew both of them. And as he drove, he mounted a rousing defense of his own actions as if he were standing up in a Kittredge tribunal.

She'd said she would find someone else, hadn't she? Brady believed her. She'd moved out of the family home against her brothers' wishes and was still working at the Coyote, despite outcry on all sides. She'd punched him, for God's sake. The smart move was obviously not to doubt Amanda.

But all the defenses in the world didn't matter. If he didn't want to do this, he wouldn't be doing it.

That was the part that should have made him feel queasy. Riddled with self-loathing. He tried his best to get there.

But her head was in his lap, and she was singing along to the country song on the radio, and when she looked up at him, Brady didn't feel like Gray's endlessly disappointing baby brother. Or Ty's annoying tagalong.

He didn't feel like the one Amos had ignored, the one Bettina hadn't stuck around to raise. Amanda didn't study him the way everyone else in this town did, gearing up to make snide remarks about his life down in Denver, his degree, or what they assumed he must think of himself because of those things. She didn't look at him like she was angling for the ranch—or as if she cared about the ranch at all, because why would she? She was a Kittredge. She had her own.

She looked at him like he was just . . . him.

Just a man.

A man she obviously liked—and it was intoxicating.

If he had ever wanted anyone this much, he couldn't remember it.

He drove out over the hill and into the wider valley filled with fields and cattle, pastures and horses. The old Douglas orchards and Grandma Kittredge's goats. Three founding families and the land they'd claimed while the west was still wild, then held through everything that came after. One stubborn, hardy generation after the next. But instead of heading for the ranch house or the Kittredge main house, he took one of the sneaky little dirt roads that cut through the fields but didn't appear on any official maps. He stayed far away from the main county roads, winding his way down to his favorite spot by the river.

It wasn't until he saw the rock that he liked to think of as his real parent that it occurred to him to question why he'd brought her *here*. This was rural Colorado. There were a million places to go where no one could see them—so why the one spot that was shrouded in a haze of his old memories?

But by that time, it was too late to change course.

He parked where he always did, down where the trees that lined the river would make his truck impossible to see until you were on top of it—not that anyone had ever come out this way in all the years he'd come here. Amanda sat up, shoving that thick spill of honey back from her face. He cut his headlights, and she made an impressed noise as she looked around.

"Is this where you took all your girlfriends in high school?"

"The point of dating the quarterback was to be seen, Amanda." Brady spread his arm out along the back of the seat and settled in, grinning at her when she turned to him again. "I took them up on the hill, where everybody else was. This spot was always just for me."

"Just for you?"

It sounded like an idle question, but then she fixed that gaze of hers on him, and he didn't get why she was the only one in this whole valley who seemed to really *see* him. Who *wanted* to see him. And who wasn't rushing to push her version of him at him.

He had the odd notion that she would sit there forever, waiting to see what he'd say. And why that felt a lot like her arms around him, he couldn't have said. Only that it did.

It was why he actually answered her honestly.

"I spent a lot of time at your parents' house, but I couldn't spend every night there. So sometimes, when I couldn't stay there and I didn't want to be home, I came here." He nodded at the dark fields that stretched out in every direction, studded here and there with trees and the odd rock that was too big to move. "It's too deep into Everett land to be public. And too far away from the ranch house to run into anyone in my family."

"Perfect for when you had to get away, then," Amanda said, and it was the lack of pity in her voice that tugged at him. "I've heard a few stories about your father being less than awful at times, long ago, but I never knew him that way. He was always mean to me. He must have been terrible to you."

She was being matter-of-fact. Brisk, even.

"He didn't smack me around or anything," Brady heard himself say, when this was a subject he barely talked about with his brothers, much less anyone else. "Ty got it a lot worse."

Amanda didn't look away. "There are a lot of ways to be terrible."

"And my father knew them all."

Her gaze remained so kind and steady that his ribs hurt.

Brady had to remind himself why they were out here in the dark of a September night, and it wasn't to reminisce about his father. Or even his adolescent attempts at independence for a night here and there.

"In other words, this place is perfect for our purposes," he said gruffly.

Amanda straightened at that, as if she'd also forgotten why they were here. Brady didn't know whether to be oddly touched by that, or insulted.

"Right." She cleared her throat. "Sex. Let's get to it."

He watched, amused and something like tender despite himself, while she reached for the hem of her shirt. Then tugged it up like she meant to tear it off, right that minute.

"Slow down, killer," he drawled. "There's a process here. An art, if you will."

"That's definitely not the feedback I've gotten from a lifetime of cultural sources. Everyone's pretty clear that the whole 'doing it in a car' thing is less than ideal."

"That's what makes it so much fun. My advice? Embrace the frustration."

He reached over and traced the line of her neck, down to the collar of her T-shirt and back. Idly. Easily. He felt the way she trembled. He saw her swallow, hard.

"I . . . don't actually know what that means," she whispered.

God, she made him ache. Everywhere. Inside and out.

"Don't worry," he promised her. "You will."

There was still the possibility that he could call things off. Brady didn't *have to* do any of this. There was no gun to his head. There was nothing around for miles. There was the river, the trees, the September night—and a thousand excellent reasons to extract himself from this mess before he made it much, much worse.

But he didn't do the right thing. He noted it and ignored it.

Then he reached over, got his hands on her, and pulled Amanda into his lap.

"Brady." Her voice was barely a wisp of sound. And she was shifting around on his thighs in a way that made his eyes want to cross. "You really should know . . . I . . . I'm afraid I won't do this right."

"There is no right or wrong." He kept his gaze steady, no matter how much he wanted to react to all her artless wriggling. "There's only us and what works. Okay? If you don't like something, tell me. That's it. That's all you have to remember to do."

She pulled in a breath, then let it out, unevenly. "I can do that."

Brady settled back against the seat, holding her and letting her get comfortable. Letting her find her seat like the cowgirl she was.

He could feel her relax, inch by inch. And when she finally slid her arms around his neck, he figured she was doing fine.

"We're not having sex tonight," he told her.

"What?" Amanda tensed again, but this time, it was clearly from outrage. Not uncertainty. "The entire purpose of being in this truck is to have sex."

"I'm getting that this is going to be hard for you because you seem to take so much pleasure in being impetuous." He shook his head at her. "But you're not in control of this, Amanda. I am."

"I'm not sure I signed up to be controlled."

"You don't know what you signed up for. That's the problem. And that's why I'm telling you."

"But . . ."

She never finished her sentence, or uttered more than that single, plaintive word.

Because he slid a hand around to the back of her head, then guided her mouth to his.

Maybe it was because he'd set the boundaries already. Maybe it was just Amanda. Whatever it was, there was no rush. No drive to get somewhere. He kissed her lazily, thoroughly.

He kissed her as if he could spend all night doing nothing but learning what she liked. What she loved. And what made her squirm in his lap, testing his restraint.

Brady had told her he would control this, but that word didn't seem to have much to do with an arm full of Amanda Kittredge. Because whatever his plans, she wasn't content to simply be kissed.

She experimented. She moved closer, then away. She let her hands roam where they liked. And when she got really excited, she moved so she could straddle him there on the bench seat and rock herself against him.

God help him, but it cost him something to hold himself in check. Especially when it felt so good.

Because the other key thing about Amanda Kittredge was that she was magic. Sheer magic, pouring through him. Light and heat.

Her hair fell like a curtain around them, smelling like lilac and mint. And when he was on the edge of breaking, he traced his hands down the length of her back instead. He found the hem of that T-shirt she'd so desperately wanted to remove before, and then found his way beneath it.

Her skin was softer than should have been possible, warm and sleek.

She pulled her mouth from his, her breath sawing in and out while she stared down at him. Her eyes were wide and dark gold with need. He could feel that same need inside him, pulsing through him.

He waited for her to call it off, but she didn't say a word as he traced a pattern up her back. Then he slid his palms around to her front to fill his hands with her breasts.

Amanda moaned and pressed herself against him. And

Brady prayed for strength as he played with her through the lacy bra she wore, making her moan even louder.

When he took her mouth again, everything got . . . slippery.

As if he'd suddenly found himself too drunk to stand. Spinning and sliding, overflowing with lust and need, and the sheer perfection of Amanda in his hands and in his mouth at once.

He moved his thumbs over her and felt the friction surge through her, like a wave. She arched her back to get more and ground herself into his lap, rocking against him until he thought she might actually break him. He'd love every second of it.

But he held on. Somehow.

Brady took the kiss deeper. He toyed with her, gently teasing her until the noises she made were as heedless as they were addictive.

And he thought, *Just a little more. Just a little further.*

He kept going. There could have been a gun to his head, and he still wouldn't have stopped. Not when she was such a glorious thing to behold. Flushed and greedy and so beautiful, it hurt.

It only took another moment or so, though it felt to him like he lived and died a thousand times by then.

Amanda stiffened. Then she tore her mouth from his, tossing her head back and riding him even harder. It was almost too much. It was almost the end of him, but he held on—

She let out a glad, shocked cry that he knew he would carry inside him forever.

It almost sent him spinning out over that same edge with her.

She slumped down against him—his reckless, beautiful girl. Brady murmured something encouraging, one hand holding her head to his shoulder as if he was at ease.

While everything inside him screamed for his own release.

He spent some time and the better part of his willpower fighting it back.

Brady stared out the front window at the stars above and the moon that rose over the fields, bathing them and the river in its silvery glow.

He chanted statistics. He willed himself to calm down. And meanwhile, Amanda panted in a boneless heap in his arms and made him so wild for her, he wasn't sure he'd recover.

Approximately twelve million years later, when he'd remade himself into the image of the monk he'd never been a hundred times over, she lifted her head.

"Um." She was still flushed. She looked dazed. "Wow."

Brady wasn't sure he could speak. He didn't try. He ran his thumb beneath her eyes, catching the faintest bit of moisture, and stopped himself from doing something weird, like tasting it. What was wrong with him?

"Are you sure you don't want to have sex?" Amanda asked. She wriggled against him again, in case he'd forgotten that the hardest part of him was wedged there where she was hottest and softest. He really hadn't. "Because it feels like you do."

The torture of the last little while was worth it, then. Because it allowed him to lift a lofty brow and stare at her as if he'd never been so insulted. "I'm a grown man, Amanda. I can control myself."

She shifted against him, experimentally, and smiled. "But do you want to?"

Brady laughed. He threw open his door, tugging her

off his lap and swinging her to the ground outside. He liked that she had to reach out and grab the door to keep her balance. That meant it wasn't just him.

He tried not to wince as he climbed out after her. He reached into the back seat to pull out the blanket he kept there, then he took her hand, tugging her behind him. The moon lit the way to the wide, flat stone he'd treated like a second home when he was a teenager. He sat on the rock where it jutted out over the rushing river, then he pulled Amanda down on his lap. Then he took care to tuck the blanket around her so she would stay warm.

He could feel her heart pounding wildly. She held her breath, then let it out shakily.

Brady didn't say anything. He sat there and let the river rush along at their feet.

"Brady—"

"Watch the moon," he told her, gently enough, because he was acting like her armchair and that too-incisive gaze of hers wasn't directed at him. Plus, he liked the heat of her, the soft weight against his chest. "Enjoy it."

He thought she might argue, but instead, she sighed again. Then she settled against him. And she . . . fit. Like she'd been made to lie back beneath fall skies and let him keep her warm.

Brady wished, suddenly, that he could go back in time and tell the lonely, angry kid who'd sat out here alone so many nights that he would be okay. That he would be more than okay in more ways than he could imagine. And better still, he would come back here one night with the prettiest girl in Cold River and change the way he felt about this rock forever.

But that felt a little more momentous than anything

he'd had planned for the evening—or his year back home—so he kept it to himself.

"When are you leaving?" Amanda asked.

Because apparently she was also psychic.

Brady frowned at the moon he'd told her to enjoy. "Are you in a rush see me go?"

"Not at all." She sounded tranquil and unbothered, and he didn't know how to feel about that when he was still wound tight enough to explode. "The rumor around town has always been that you only agreed to stay a year. Isn't that next month?"

"I'm glad everyone in town is so concerned about a promise I made my brothers."

"Welcome home, cowboy. Maybe you forgot that everyone in the Longhorn Valley is concerned about everyone else, forever and ever, amen."

Brady wanted to work up a little righteous indignation to go along with that, but he couldn't get there. Because for a man who'd gotten very little in the way of satisfaction tonight, he was in a remarkably good mood. "Next month marks a year since my father died. But I didn't make any promises about staying here until Christmas."

"Oh." There was a curious note in her voice. He almost turned her around so he could try to read her expression, but decided against it. Because he didn't think he wanted her reading him. "I could have sworn you were leaving by Halloween."

"A common misconception."

One he'd had himself, in fact. Until he'd said something about leaving at Halloween last spring, and Gray had said something typically brusque about the promises of bankers always being worthless. That Brady was actually not a banker in the classic sense, and would certainly never call himself one, didn't matter. Not when Gray wanted to get a dig in.

"And what will you do once Christmas comes?" She tucked her chin deeper into the blanket and settled a little more against him. He had no idea why it felt so good. "You must be impatient to get back to your real life."

Brady would have said the same thing himself. And had, often, to whoever would listen. But there was something about Amanda saying it that scraped at him.

"I figured we'd sell the ranch." And he heard her little intake of breath. The usual horror people from around here always showed at the very idea that anyone would sell land. Ever. No matter how desperate they were. "We all agreed we'd vote on what to do after a year, but Gray's always been against selling. And Ty hasn't said anything, but the fact that he's building Hannah a house makes his vote pretty clear."

"Do you think they'll buy you out?"

Not for the first time tonight, he was struck by how matter-of-fact she sounded. Far more levelheaded and clear-eyed than the twenty-two-year-olds he'd known in his time. Or than he'd been himself.

He was reminded once again that Amanda wasn't an overserved college coed, giggling her way through another happily blurred Saturday night. She'd spent her whole life in the company of some of the valley's most esteemed ranchers. And that was just her family.

If he knew anything about ranch people, it was that they kept their idealism and their sentimentality tucked away, down deep, where a tough winter or a suddenly ill animal couldn't touch them. They expressed their dreams through hard work and their commitment to a future they might never see themselves.

And when it came time to talk about selling up, after the gasps of horror, they tended to get straight to the point. Because otherwise, there was nothing but whatever shattered sentimentality and dreams remained, and who wanted to talk about that? Of course Amanda wanted to know if they were talking about buyouts. Not only because there must have been similar conversations around her dinner table, but because the Kittredges were their neighbors. They'd be the most likely first offer if the Everetts had to sell.

How had he spent all this time concentrating on her age and her choice of second job, and so little time reflecting on the fact that Amanda was a Kittredge? She had Longhorn Valley ranch blood in her veins, same as him.

Brady only realized he hadn't answered her when Amanda shifted again.

"I guess a better question, and one my grandparents always ask us, is what would you do if you could do anything? If there were no other factors. No brothers, no will, nothing. If all that Everett land was yours to use as you like. Every time they've asked us that, we've all always answered the same thing. We like the Bar K as it is. My brothers work it because they believe in it. I fully support it. But I like that they ask the question." And he thought he could sense her smile. "It makes it feel less like an obligation and more like a choice."

"I always thought I'd stay here," Brady found himself telling her. Because she was magic, and this rock felt like home, and he could whisper these truths to the top of her head. He could tell them to the dark and the moon and the faint scent of mint in her hair, and it didn't feel like he was exposing himself. "I expected to come back after college and get right back into it."

"Why didn't you?"

Such a simple question. And a simple answer, too, though *simple* wasn't how it felt.

"Amos didn't want me back." Brady had said versions of that before. But he'd never said it so baldly, and not to someone like Amanda, who knew. She knew his family. She'd known his father. More than that, her family had been in this valley as long as his, and she knew all the intricacies of that. All the layers and complications. All the reasons none of this was *simple*. "He was actively opposed to the idea, in fact. He wouldn't take my money. He wouldn't use my labor. And if it were up to him, he took care to tell me, he would have cut me off altogether. Even from the holidays. He made sure I knew he only let me come home, then, because it would have been harder to explain why I didn't."

Someday, Brady liked to tell himself, he wouldn't talk about his father at all. And if he did, it wouldn't taste like ash on his tongue. But he still wasn't there.

"He could have cut you out of his will," Amanda said levelly. "He didn't. Maybe there was more going on, deep down inside. I don't know. Is it possible that mean old Amos Everett had layers?"

Brady laughed. "I've thought about that a lot. *A lot.* Because it doesn't make sense that he would give me, or any of us, a gift. That wasn't his style." He blew out a breath, amazed that he was actually talking about this. "But then I realized, it wasn't a gift. Of course it wasn't a gift. That will was the perfect punishment."

He expected Amanda to argue that, but she didn't. She

only waited, her head tipped back so if he had wanted to, he could have rested his chin on the top of her head and held her there. Like they were puzzle pieces, snapped together at last.

He told himself the image was disturbing. He told himself that was why he didn't do it.

"Obviously the ranch should have gone to Gray," he said. "But Dad didn't leave it to Gray alone. Because how better to punish Gray than to make him share the land he'd given his life to with the brothers who'd left it?"

Brady stared at the moon, remembering all the other times he'd sat right here. All the different moons he'd watched rise and set. And he couldn't decide if it made him feel sad or oddly connected, despite himself, that he was still sitting here trying to figure out Amos.

"Meanwhile, Ty got famous. But then he was broken. And the last thing he'd ever want to do was come back and have to face the possibility that he was no better than where he started. Amos left a third to him to force that, obviously."

"And you? How is this punishing you?" But Amanda made a noise. "Because you want to sell and sharing it means you can't?"

"Because I wanted to come home, and he wouldn't let me," Brady said quietly, because he really had thought about this. And he really did know his father. "Because he knew I would never want to come back like this, looking like I'm riding on a dead man's coattails. Especially after he spent all these years making sure Gray thought as little of me as possible. Once again, it's a punishment."

She tilted her head up, and he could feel her breath against the underside of his jaw. It shouldn't have comforted him.

"Amos is dead, Brady," she said quietly. "He can't punish you from beyond the grave. Only you can do that."

She settled against him so sweetly, so easily, that Brady was sure she had no idea she'd ripped him wide open. That she might as well have torn him into tiny pieces, then tossed what remained into the river below.

He stayed where he was because he couldn't move. He was amazed that his heart still beat. Stunned that his lungs still took in breath. He stared straight ahead at the river because he was afraid that if he so much as moved a muscle, she would know. She would see.

And then he had no idea what might become of him.

"What about you?" he asked, when he could keep his voice even. When there was no trace whatsoever of that body blow she'd landed on him. "Are you going to tend bar forever?"

Amanda laughed. "I thought I was going to like bartending a whole lot more than I do."

"What's not to like?" Brady asked dryly. "Nothing's better than crowds of drunk people, wandering hands, and cleaning up all manner of sticky substances."

He didn't hear her laugh again, but he could feel her body shake with it. "In a lot of ways, it's not really any different from working in coffee. Except for the clientele. And the state of the bathrooms."

"Especially at the Coyote."

"If there had been apartments available over the public library, I would have happily worked there." He felt her shoulders rise, then fall. "Oh well."

"That doesn't make it sound like something you plan to do for the rest of your life."

Not that he cared. He was making conversation. Because why should he care?

"People around here are constantly doing something they don't plan to do for the rest of their lives, and then oops. Look at that. They end up doing it anyway."

"I don't think that's a Cold River thing. That's a life thing."

"There are only so many things to do here," Amanda said.

"Didn't you grow up breeding quarter horses? You could do it in your sleep."

"I probably could. But I know, personally, the five best quarter horse breeders and trainers in Colorado. And therefore the world. And I'm related to all of them. So sure, I know a lot about horses, but is that enough to spend my life working with them by default? I don't know."

"You've worked in the coffeehouse a long time. Maybe it's time to make that less a job you do and more a career."

"I love Cold River Coffee. I do. It's like a home to me." Amanda sighed. "But Noah is the owner and the chef. And Abby is the manager. And I don't see either one of them switching that up anytime soon. Where does that leave me?"

She considered for a moment, then added, "I mean, Noah is single. And he's not bad to look at. Women are always hanging around, ordering food they don't actually want, just to watch him cook it."

Something hot and prickly swept over Brady, then. It took him a moment to recognize it for what it was. Not a sudden attack of nocturnal fire ants, but pure, unadulterated rage.

"You can't date Noah Connelly." His voice was flat.

"Because he's so grumpy all the time?" Amanda sniffed. "Or because he's my boss?"

"Pick one."

Brady was surprised at his own reaction, to put it mildly. And deeply, wildly glad that she couldn't see the expression on his face.

"Anyway, I'm not planning to buy the coffeehouse from Noah, even if he were selling it, which he's not. And I'm certainly not planning to put Abby out of a job." Amanda laughed. "Even if I wanted to, no one would ever accept me as Abby's replacement. Not for at least another thirty years."

"You don't want to ranch. You don't want to tend bar, something I'm betting your brothers don't know, or they'd be less bent out of shape about this whole Coyote experiment. And you also don't want to keep working at Cold River Coffee forever." He found himself holding her tighter and could have sworn he hadn't meant to do that. "Answer your own question. What do you want to do?"

"The thing I keep coming back to is that everybody who wants to stay here and do something different has to be creative about it," Amanda said as she sank against him. "Obviously there are a million depressing ways to stay. To end up here. But if you want a good life, and you want it to be meaningful and fulfilling—and you don't want to take part in the family enterprise, whatever that is—you have to make your own. You have to cobble it together from whatever pieces you've been given."

"Are you going to start talking about crafting? Because my experience there is that crafting is a conversation you can better have alone. And should."

"People call it crafting because they need a special merit badge to do the same thing their grandmothers have done since the dawn of time." Amanda's voice was tart. "Some of us just knit. And make the occasional ornament."

"If you say so."

"If I could do anything," Amanda said grandly, "I would open a farm stand."

Brady took that in. "I'll admit, I didn't see that coming."

"Not an actual stand. More a shop." Her voice got dreamy. "I would source everything from the community, and make it a celebration of Cold River. Flowers from the Trujillos. Beef from the Everetts. Horse rides and lessons with my brothers. And that's just off the top of my head. There are so many people here working a job and then doing what they actually love around it. Wouldn't it be great to have a place where they could make money from that? A place that's right here, where the rest of us can support each other locally and the tourists can come and really get a sense of what Cold River has to offer."

"Look at you." And he wanted to look at her, almost more than he wanted to breathe. But Brady had the very real sense that if he turned her around his arms, all the boundaries he'd set and all the promises he'd made—to himself and to her—would blow away in the fall wind. "You might as well be a Cold River ambassador."

She made him wish he could see this place the same way she did.

"It would be like a farmers' market, but a building," she said. "It could be open all year-round and bring a little money in for everybody. The more people make a little money, the less desperate it is around here in the middle of February. And the more likely people are happy. I don't know about you, Brady, but I like happy people."

"I want to like happy people," Brady said, only half joking. "But I can't trust them."

She was the one who turned then, flipping over to her knees and kneeling there before him, the blanket around her shoulders like a cape. He could feel that wind, kicking up as the night wore on.

Or maybe it was just her—pretty Amanda with her hair down and that wicked fire making her eyes pure gold.

"There has been *so much* talking," she said, a smile curling the corner of her lips. "It has to be time for more kissing now, doesn't it?"

"I thought we decided I was in control."

"You decided that, Brady. But you can be in control of kissing. Now, if you want."

Brady couldn't have named the things he wanted. There were too many. They were like a howl inside him, loud and long, and every last one of them centered on this woman and her innocence and how deep inside him she was already, without even trying.

He'd told himself so many lies in the truck on the way out here. He'd been so sure he would stay removed. Interested, but distant, the way he always was.

But there was nothing about Amanda that didn't get to him. Not one thing.

He pulled her toward him, toppling her off balance and catching her against his chest. Then he indulged himself, rolling her over. He kept her on that blanket instead of the rock, but this time with him on top.

That was a mistake.

A catastrophic mistake.

Brady might as well have doused himself in gasoline and then danced around the bonfire, hoping for the best.

But he couldn't seem to stop.

This time, he kissed her without holding anything back. He poured it all into her, every ache, every surprise, every odd moment of this night and his own reactions. He kissed the impossibility of her, and how much he wanted her.

But this was Amanda, so she rose up against him and poured herself right back into him.

She was the one who got her hands up beneath his shirt, streaking along his flesh and moaning her appreciation. She was the one who figured out how to hook her legs around his, holding him right where he wanted to go, and rolling her hips to experiment with that snug, mind-blowing fit.

She really would be the death of him. Brady understood that fully.

And still he kissed her, recklessly.

Ruinously.

It was only when he found his hands moving restlessly at her waistband, dipping a bit beneath it, that he finally yanked himself back to reality.

Brady was not taking Amanda Kittredge's virginity on an old blanket a few feet away from his truck. An upgrade from the front seat of his truck, to be sure. But still. No.

He tore his mouth from hers. With a strength he didn't know he had, he forced himself to get up. To climb to his feet, scrape his hands over his face, and remind himself that he was not having sex. Not tonight.

Even if it killed him; not tonight.

He was going to pay for this, eventually. There was no doubt about that, no way around it. But since he knew that going in, there was no excuse for doing it shabbily.

If there was ever a time in a man's life when it was all or nothing, it was now. It was this.

It was her.

"Did you change your mind?" Amanda asked in a low, husky voice, still splayed out there on his blanket in total abandon. Brady couldn't decide if it was because she really was that free of shame and self-judgment, or if—and this knocked around inside of him like a wrecking ball—she simply trusted him that much. "I swear to God, if you changed your mind, I will kill you myself. With my very own hands. Here and now."

"I should change my mind. I should be locked up."

She pushed herself up on one elbow and scowled at him. "For what, Brady? Adulting in the presence of another adult? A shocking sin, I think we can all agree."

"I haven't changed my mind. About anything. Remember, I told you we weren't having sex tonight. I also told you frustration was part of the deal. Did you think I was kidding?"

"I *hoped* you were kidding."

She sounded so delightfully cranky, it made him smile.

Brady held out his hand, and Amanda stared at it with suspicion. But she took it, and that made him smile even wider as he tugged her up from the rock and onto her feet.

"Come on, killer," he said. "I'm taking you home."

11

Amanda would have cartwheeled into Sunday dinner the next day, complete with sparklers and a unicorn horn, had she not feared her entire family would disown her on the spot. And worse, know instantly what had happened last night.

Which wasn't even everything she'd *wanted* to have happen. But still.

It really, truly happened.

She had to keep telling herself that in the spaces between bouts of giddiness. She had to keep reminding herself that no, she actually hadn't dreamed the whole thing.

Instead of throwing herself her own parade, she drove out to the Bar K sedately. She parked her car in its usual place beneath the big bur oak by the barn, and took her time climbing out. Then she stood by her sturdy little hatchback, listening to the engine mutter as it settled down. And once it was done, she tipped her head back and listened to the quiet.

The ranch was always sleepy on Sundays. Her family took their day of rest seriously, though when it came to ranching, that never meant an actual day off. There were cows to milk and eggs to collect. And all the horses that always needed attention. It was strange not to be a part of those things any longer. Not to be a part of the cycles that had dictated the rhythm of her days for as long as she could remember.

She shook that off. Or tried. Meanwhile, that giddy bubble was still lodged in her chest, making her feel silly and obvious in a way she was afraid would be all too visible.

"You need to get it together," she told herself sternly.

Across the meadow, she could see her grandparents' house at the far edge with dogwood trees in the back and the big maple in front. There was smoke coming from their chimney, a sign they weren't planning to join the rest of the family for Sunday dinner this week. If they had been, there'd have been no smoke, and if she'd waited another few minutes, she would have seen them start across the meadow.

Amanda was a little early, so she set off toward her grandparents' house instead of her parents', loving the kick of the breeze as it rushed down from the mountains. It had that fall edginess to it, stirring things up as it danced over the land and wound through the trees. She hunched down a little into the wool sweater she wore, and could feel the chilly undertone of the breeze making her cheeks glow as she walked.

Her grandparents' house was neat outside and tidy within. They kept goats in the back, maintained a lush vegetable garden the goats were forever breaking into, and spent fine evenings sitting out on their porch with its view of the mountains, the valley, and the line of aspen trees that marked the north arm of the river. When

Amanda had been small, her grandparents had kept working dogs, but the lazy old mutt who greeted her in their front yard had never worked a day in his life. He lifted one silky ear in greeting, but didn't get to his feet. That would take energy.

Amanda let herself in the porch door that was always too well-oiled to squeak, followed the sound of the radio in the back, and found her grandparents where they always were on Sunday afternoons when they planned to stay in. Grandma was bustling around the kitchen, still in her church clothes. Grandpa was sitting in his chair, listening to the radio with the TV on, but muted, so he could also watch the game.

For a moment, before either one of them looked up, Amanda got to bask in them. In the sameness of this quiet, comfortable scene that when she was very small, she'd seen play out in the kitchen over at the ranch house too. The house smelled the way it was supposed to, like the lemon soap Grandma liked to use to clean her floors, the yeasty smell of newly baked bread, and flowers. Always flowers.

"Happy Sunday," Amanda singsonged, and then it was a rush of hugs and smiles, and exclamations from her grandmother about how her old heart wasn't what it had been and sneaking up on her was a risky proposition.

"Your heart is fine, Janet," Grandpa said from his chair.

Grandma rolled her eyes. She returned to the potato salad she was making and eyed Amanda over the bowl as she stirred. In that way she had that made Amanda stand up straighter and wish she'd worn something a little nicer than her best jeans and a sweater.

"I didn't see you in church this morning," Grandma noted. "I hope that fancy town life hasn't gone to your head, Amanda. You need to remember who you are."

Grandpa made a harrumphing sort of sound. "She's here, isn't she? Seems she remembers just fine."

Amanda laughed. It was funny how criticism from her grandparents never struck her the same way it would have if it had come from her brothers. "I had an early shift at the coffeehouse, Grandma. I haven't forgotten anything."

"I know your generation loves its scandals," Grandma continued while the wooden spoon she used made its own percussion against the side of her metal bowl. "In my day, I'd have been afraid that working in that bar would send a terrible message."

"Maybe I want to send a terrible message."

Grandma made a *tsking* sound. "I can understand the urge, I suppose." Another long look that made Amanda want to squirm, and told her that Janet Kittredge in no way wanted to send a terrible message of any kind and never had. "But the trouble with sending out such messages is that you never can take them back. They're out there, for good or bad, forever."

"Janet. Amanda doesn't need a lecture." Grandpa's voice was gruff. "Besides, when has a lecture ever worked on you? Why would you think one might work on anyone else?"

"I love a lecture," Amanda assured them both. "Who doesn't?"

Grandma was still muttering under her breath when Amanda left a little while later to walk with her grandfather back toward the ranch house. She tried to imagine what it was like for him, having passed on the bulk of the responsibility to his son, presumably so he could simply enjoy his time. Travel a bit in the fifth wheel they kept in its own barn. Visit friends and family in a way they'd never been able to do when they'd had to make sure the ranch was running and the livestock were fed.

Today, she found herself thinking about Brady as she walked. This land either beat men down, like Amos Everett, or it made them tougher. Stronger. She could picture Brady like her grandfather, weathered and worn in all the right ways, but without that bitterness that crept into some men over time. And with that gleam in his eyes that always made him seem like a much younger man.

Her heart tripped over itself.

"I always loved living with my family," Grandpa said, after a while. After Amanda had assumed this would be one of the times he simply walked and didn't say much. "But the time comes when a person has to claim their own space."

"Is that what you and Grandma did?"

"When you're used to taking care of people, it's hard to stop. Even if they want you to. It's in the blood, you see. And there's no getting it out. That's a kinder way of saying we found it hard to mind our business, you understand."

Amanda grinned. "It's better to move, then?"

His mouth crooked in the corner. Every inch of him looked like a pure Colorado cowboy, down to the hat he'd stuck on his head as he'd exited the house and those old cowboy boots on his feet. But Amanda knew that Daniel Kittredge was a true cowboy in the best sense of the term, straight down into his bones. He was honest to a fault. His word was his bond. He loved his family, his land, and his horses. He took pride in his country. And he thought life wasn't worth living without good neighbors.

Her brothers all wanted to be him. Amanda simply adored him.

"Absence really does make the heart grow fonder, Amanda," Daniel said now. "And it also helps remind people who needs looking after and who is capable of doing it all on their own. Sometimes folks need an object lesson."

"What about you, Grandpa?" she asked. She held her breath as she studied his face. "Are you worried about me working in a bar?"

"That's your grandmother's department," he replied. His eyes gleamed. "Me, personally, I figure I taught you how to shoot a gun. I expect you can take care of yourself."

Amanda took that as his blessing.

She was feeling pretty buoyant when she kissed him on his cheek, then made her way toward the big house again. She didn't look closely at the collection of trucks in the yard that told her that her brothers were in from the fields and their own houses, because she was too busy making herself breathe deep to get the giddy out. She went in the side door, ducking past the pegs bristling with coats and the boots lined up against the wall to slip into the downstairs bathroom. She washed her hands, studied her face to make sure there was no lingering evidence of how she'd spent last night, and only then did she walk farther into the house. With a big smile on her face that froze in place when she saw Brady sitting in the living room, watching the game with her brothers and father.

On the one hand, it could have been any Sunday from back when he'd been in high school and really had spent too much of his time here. On the other, it wasn't years ago. It was today. The day after the night he'd had his hands on her breasts, his mouth all over hers, and she'd rocked and rocked until she'd—

Brady hadn't reacted to the sight of her in the doorway, but when she stood there, frozen, that arrogant brow of his rose.

She got the warning loud and clear.

"You're almost late, monkey," Connor said lazily from the couch, oblivious. "And we have company today. Mom might actually let you help in the kitchen."

"Why don't *you* help in the kitchen?" she shot back.

To her surprise, Connor actually got up. He made a face at her, then herded her back into the ranch house kitchen as if everything were normal.

As if anything could be normal ever again.

My God, she thought. *Did I really want a walk of shame? What would this be like if we'd actually had sex?*

But she didn't exactly want that in her head either.

So she was thrilled when her mother put her to work setting the big dining room table while Connor handled drinks and platters, because it was far, far better than the riot inside her.

It was the most excruciating family dinner of Amanda's life.

Previously, she would have sworn up and down that nothing could be more gruesome than, say, Riley's announcement that his marriage was over. Or the time her brothers had felt she truly needed to know that she had been her parents' marital olive branch, and had started telling awful stories from the dark years before she was born. Amanda would have welcomed either of those painful conversations today.

Amanda had to fight to keep from squirming in her seat. She kept surreptitiously checking her temperature because she felt too hot, then too cold. Too prickly. Too uncomfortable. Too close to bursting, too *something*. She sat in her usual place, which meant Brady was directly across from her, and she couldn't *look* at him. What if everything that happened was all over her face? What if she turned bright red again and everyone could *see* what he'd done with his *hands*—

For a whiteout sort of moment, Amanda thought she might faint.

Maybe breathe, she ordered herself.

She picked at her food, not sure how she could force herself to eat. And yet all too aware that if she didn't eat, that would inspire commentary from all sides.

Amanda felt like she was coming out of her own skin.

None of this was helped by the fact that Brady was fine.

Aggressively, obnoxiously fine. So fine, and so normal, and so evidently unfazed by last night that if Amanda hadn't remembered it so vividly, she might have doubted it had happened at all. He laughed with Jensen. He traded mild, brotherly insults with Riley. He cleared his plate and had seconds.

Then she passed him the potatoes while he was too busy telling a tall tale about his fishing prowess to even glance at her, and she started to dream about possibly killing him. With her own barely used fork.

But by the time dinner wrapped up and she'd finished pitching in with the dishes, she felt oddly . . . flat.

"You aren't rushing back into town for a change," her mother observed when Amanda finally returned to the living room with everyone else. And, instead of making her excuses and racing for her car, she sat on the arm of her mother's chair.

Where she absolutely was not keeping an eye on Brady and all the fun he was having hanging out with her brothers like she didn't exist.

"I have a late shift tonight." Amanda wrenched her gaze away from Brady and focused on her mother. "At the bar."

"I didn't think the coffeehouse had started staying open nights all of a sudden," Ellie said in that sedately chiding way of hers that always felt like a sharp slap.

Maybe it was her mother's superpower. No matter what happened around her, Ellie Kittredge remained unruffled. She was always the eye of every storm—a dampening, cooling influence on everything around her. And given all the rumors and stories about the state of the Kittredge marriage before Amanda had been born, not to mention the current state of all her brothers' lives and loves, it was often only Ellie's unflappability that kept a lid on things.

A lesson Amanda would do well to take to heart. Especially on a day like today, when it took every scrap of self-control and fear and paranoia and hope inside her not to start screaming right here in the middle of living room.

"I think I'm going to go for a ride," she told her mother. "It's been too long."

Ellie didn't look up from the button she was sewing on to one of Donovan's shirts. "There are riding clothes for you in the closet. And make it a nice, long one, if you can. Cinnamon gets lonely."

That felt like a slap too, but Amanda kind of liked it. Because her mother getting on her to take better care of the horse that had always been unofficially Amanda's felt good. Right. It snapped the world back into place, so it spun the way it should on the same old axis. What had happened with Brady was the oddity. He was the thing that didn't make any sense.

Maybe it wasn't the worst thing in the world to take a moment, while he was acting as if he didn't know she was in the same room, to remind herself who *she* was.

Amanda changed into a battered pair of jeans and better boots. And when she went back outside again, breathing deep in the crisp afternoon air felt like a revelation.

She wasn't sure she'd taken a full breath since she'd walked into the living room and seen Brady sitting there.

It was a perfect late Sunday afternoon. The air was cool, but the sky was blue and the sun was that deep gold of nearly October. There was snow in the mountains, and the scent of it, every now and again, cut through the richer scents of horses and hay, dirt and pine trees. Amanda liked the dirt beneath her feet. She liked the way her boots felt against the rich earth, solid and strong, as she made her way into the barn.

As a girl, she'd always found September sad, as it was when the ranch conducted its second big sale of the year. Folks came from all over the country—and some came from outside the country—to bid on the Bar K's horses. Some came to watch the horses in action, then order what they needed to breed their mares with Bar K's stud, or get on the waiting list for the various other services the Bar K offered. Over time, Amanda had grown more practical.

A soft heart is only going to hurt you, Ellie had told

ten-year-old Amanda when she'd found her sobbing over the sale of a gelding. *You have to love hard, Amanda. You have to expect it will hurt and let yourself love any-way. Or you'll never survive.*

"She meant as a rancher," Amanda muttered to herself as she ducked into the barn. But she stopped inside the door, letting her eyes adjust.

She'd always *thought* Ellie meant as a rancher. But if one scandalous and secret night with Brady had taught her anything, maybe it was that Ellie's advice was something Amanda should view with a wider lens.

Inside the barn, it was okay to have a softer heart. The horses who stayed here weren't part of the Bar K breeding program—or not any longer. They were old family friends.

Cinnamon was Amanda's best friend. The chestnut mare tossed her head when she saw Amanda approach, then wasted no time complaining that it had been too long.

"I know, I know," Amanda murmured as she went into the stall and said her hellos, kissing the horse on the white blaze that marked her smooth face. "I've been a terrible friend."

Cinnamon agreed. Loudly.

Amanda had grown up with horses everywhere. Horse talk, horse breeders, and good, old-fashioned horse people inside her family and out. She'd learned how to ride almost before she could walk, or so her brothers liked to claim. And they'd accordingly taught their baby sister tricks better suited to the circus, mostly to horrify their mother.

It hadn't been until Amanda found herself talking to the tourists and townsfolk who sometimes came out for lessons or trail rides that she realized how lucky she was to have grown up like this. She'd fallen off horses so many times when she was little that it didn't scare her anymore. She didn't worry about being stepped on. Or kicked. Or nipped, even, or any of the other things people who didn't know horses worried about.

But there was a difference between being comfortable with horses in general and being in love with a particular horse. And Cinnamon had been a steady, dependable friend for most of Amanda's life. She couldn't explain it, not even to Kat.

There was something about riding out with nothing between her and her horse but trust. On days like today, when Amanda wanted to connect with herself and her mount, she didn't bother with a saddle. She and Cinnamon had been communicating for some fifteen years. The minute she slid into place on Cinnamon's back outside the barn, everything made sense.

It had always been that way. Amanda had always been so conscious of the fact that she was different from her brothers. Younger, a girl, more coddled and more ignored at once. But she and Cinnamon would ride out toward the mountains, and she'd find a way to open up her heart again no matter how battered it felt. No matter what mood she was in when she left, a good, long ride set her right again

Today, they galloped. They went flat out, moving like liquid, like they were both wild.

Until they were.

When they were far enough out there, so deep into the land it almost felt like getting lost, they slowed down again. They found one of the many offshoots of the river that laced this part of the property. Cinnamon drank while Amanda rolled up her borrowed jeans and stuck her feet in, then waited for them to go numb.

This time of year, it only took a few moments.

She splashed some water on her face, shuddering at the chill of it, but she liked the way it felt afterward. Pinpricks of sensation climbing all over her body. A lot like an echo of the night before.

Thinking of Brady as another part of the elements, like snowmelt on a sunny day, helped.

Then she sat, on a different rock on the bank of a different offshoot of the same river, and she let herself feel all that nervous energy that had been clattering around in her all day. She didn't try to tamp it down or pretend it wasn't there.

Surrounded by this land that her ancestors had fought and died to keep, she knew she would never spend too long in town. She flexed her bare toes against the cold rock and felt the sun and the hint of coming snow on her face. It was fun to try on a different life for a while, but she'd been born out here in the Colorado dirt. There was only so much asphalt and brick she could take.

Something she had no intention of sharing with her brothers, because they'd pack her up and haul her out of her apartment before she got the sentence out.

But even that struck her as funny, out here where any emotions she might have, or any problems that might feel consuming back home, seemed as insubstantial as the breeze. Scented with this or that, but still just a breeze. Not the immense, towering Rockies. Not the mighty river or all its many tributaries that kept the fields green. Out here, the elements were all that mattered, and because of that, the things that kicked around inside of her seemed to matter less. Or matter differently.

It had always worked. Amanda figured it always would.

Whatever magic it was, by the time she rode Cinnamon back home, she was calm again.

Calm, but not dead.

Because that same sort of cold water prickle took her over when she looked up from brushing Cinnamon down to find Brady watching her, his back up against the wall across from Cinnamon's stall.

"I always forget what a great rider you are," he said, an odd note in his voice.

"I'm surprised you're aware that I know how to ride a horse at all."

"Everyone knows how to ride a horse around here. But you're something else."

"That's what happens when you have four older brothers who think it's fun to teach you dangerous tricks when your parents aren't around." She slid him a glance. "Like a circus animal."

Brady's voice was even enough, though his dark green gaze was intense. "Why aren't you doing something with that instead of serving drinks night and day? Or dreaming about farm stands?"

Amanda finished up what she was doing. She patted Cinnamon's sturdy flank and got a nudge in return, then she made her way out of the stall. She looked around, expecting to find any or all of her brothers looming around, but there was only Brady.

Only Brady. All alone out here.

Maybe she wasn't as calm as she'd imagined.

"I love horses," she told him. "I love Cinnamon in particular. But I don't want to fill my head with breeding schedules. Gelding. Training. I want to enjoy her."

"They're not mutually exclusive."

"Maybe not, but they complicate each other. The other option would be performing in some way, and I don't want to do that either." She shrugged. "I'm not like your brother Ty. I like interacting with people, not entertaining them."

He looked almost startled, but then his gaze dropped, and she wondered if she'd imagined it.

"Everybody assumed when you moved into town that it was some kind of crisis. That you were flailing, the way people sometimes do." There was amusement, and a different sort of heat, in his gaze when it met hers again. "But you weren't, were you?"

"It was a sudden decision. But it was a serious one." She smiled. "You're just caught up on the sex part."

"You could say that, yes."

"People always think that other people's decisions are rash and reckless. That doesn't mean they are."

She was outside the stall then, with Brady still propped up against the wall. She was listening for any hints that her brothers might be headed this way. Any faint noise that might indicate someone could show up in the middle of this conversation and draw the wrong conclusions.

Or the right conclusions.

Meanwhile, she was much too *aware* of him.

She was aware of him in a way she hadn't realized a person could be aware of another. Everything about him had a different meaning to her now. His height, because she liked the way she had to tip her head back to meet his gaze. And she loved the way he'd sprawled over her on that rock last night, that deliciously long body of his pressing her down into the stone.

She knew the touch of his hands now. Her breasts felt swollen simply because he was there and might at any moment touch her again. She hoped.

It seemed wondrous and strange that there was distance between them now when Amanda knew it would be so easy to throw herself forward, directly into him, so she could feel the strength of his chest or taste his mouth once more.

She'd been walking around half-asleep her whole life. And now she was wide awake. She could sense the tension of this, the bright, taut space between them. And she understood in a flash that the whole world must be filled with pockets of awareness, just like this. These invisible dances of surrender and denial playing out between people. Everywhere.

It was like discovering a brand-new color.

"Don't look at me like that," Brady ordered her, his voice low and dark.

"I told you," she said, but she hardly sounded like herself. She was too calm. Too sure, maybe, because she could feel so much. His intent. His desire and hers. And that enduring heat between them. "I'm not a performer. I would find it hard, to pick a random example, to show up at your family dinner and ignore you completely."

"What was the alternative?"

He shook his head, leaning there against the wall, except Amanda no longer believed he was unmoved. On the contrary. She had the distinct impression he kept his arms crossed like that to make sure he kept his hands to himself.

That knowledge felt like a light switching on, blazing bright. It felt like joy. It bubbled up inside her like its own hot spring, and it didn't matter, anymore, that she wasn't touching him when she wanted to. Because this was almost better.

Her body knew the truth. As awake as she felt, her body had rocketed straight on into alertness. She felt taut and hot everywhere, and between her legs, she melted.

"We agreed to keep the secret," Brady said.

Amanda shrugged. "I hope that means you have a good explanation at the ready as to why you're suddenly so interested in my horseback riding skills. Should anyone ask."

"Riley told me to keep an eye on you."

"Today?"

"In general."

She smiled. "I sure do appreciate you adhering to the very letter of the law, Brady."

"I ran into your mother yesterday in town." Brady, she noted, did not sound calm. That only made her more so. "I meant to tell you that last night, but I forgot."

"Oh? Why did you forget?"

His dark look made her laugh. "She reminded me I hadn't been to Sunday dinner here in a long time. So here I am. I guess the timing could have been better."

"The timing was perfect."

She moved toward him, then, because she could. Because she wanted to, and she couldn't think of a single good reason not to. He looked like a cowboy should on a Sunday, in a crisp button-down shirt tucked into his jeans and his good boots nice and shiny. A Stetson on his head and a clean-shaven jaw.

It made a girl want to break out in appreciative country songs or a celebratory two-step.

"Careful," he said in a low voice, but he did nothing to stop her when she came even closer, then melted against him. "Any member of your family could come in here at any time."

"Then we'd better give them an eyeful," Amanda murmured, her gaze trained on his mouth.

This was also new. Reckless and thrilling. She surged up on her toes and pressed her mouth to his.

He did nothing to help her, and that made it hotter. Better. She kissed him, and then she tilted her jaw, opened her mouth, and took the kiss deeper.

She felt it when he made a dark, male noise in the back of his throat. Then he took control. His hand snaked around to her lower back, then pulled her tight against him.

Everything was breathless. Everything was heat and need.

Everything was perfect.

When he set her away from him again some time later, she wasn't the only one who was having trouble breathing.

"If your brothers kill me today, Amanda," he said, with the kind of exaggerated, intense patience that she could feel like a shiver all through her, "you're going to have to find some other cowboy to experiment on. Is that what you want?"

"I thought we agreed it was only us."

"You'd obviously be released from that in the event of my death. Though I guess that would be a moot point, because after they finished killing me, you can bet your brothers would lock you up tight in the nearest convent."

"They probably would have done that years ago if we were Catholic." Amanda smiled sunnily. "Oh well."

Brady studied her for a long moment, that same current hot and bright between them. That particular light making his dark eyes even greener. Then he reached up and tipped his hat to her, in a manner that should have looked silly and old-fashioned.

But it didn't. It really, really didn't.

"I'll be seeing you around," he said.

A threat and a promise, and she found them both equally delicious.

"Or," she said, as he turned to go, "you could take my number. You know, like a normal person. Then we could contact each other instead of waiting for my mother to issue Sunday dinner invitations. Just throwing that out there."

He looked back over his shoulder at her, and Amanda sighed.

"Oh, right. My mistake. After all that speechifying last night, you still want to pretend this is some kind of accident."

Brady didn't say anything, but he didn't have to. That muscle in his jaw told her everything she needed to know.

Amanda held out her hand. And kept holding it out while his eyes darkened and that muscle tightened. But finally, he fished his phone out of his pocket and handed it to her.

"Don't worry," she murmured. "This will only hurt for a second." She entered herself into his contacts, but made a considering sound while she did it. "I suppose I really shouldn't put my name, should I? What if you're sitting at a table and the phone rings, and one of my brothers—"

"I'm glad you think this is funny, Amanda. Really. It's all fun and games until your own execution, I guess."

"I know." She typed something. "Perfect."

She called herself, and when her phone buzzed in her

pocket, she entered his number into her contacts. Meanwhile, Brady was staring down at his screen.

He lifted his gaze to hers. "'Jailbait Jones'?"

"It felt appropriate."

"You're not jailbait. Not even close to jailbait."

She smirked at him. "That's what I keep trying to tell you."

He plucked her phone out of her hand, then, and she thought the little laugh he let out was reluctant. But real. It warmed her straight through.

Just like that dark look he shot her. "'Gramps'?"

"I thought that was why this had to be such a big secret. Because once I was in diapers but you weren't and blah blah blah."

"I'm ten years older than you."

"I know how old you are. Cradle robber."

Brady shook his head, that muscle in his jaw as hard as granite. "It turns out your brothers were right to be worried, because look at what's happening. Every minute you spend near me, you lose a little more of your innocence."

"It's mine," she replied. "If I want to lose it or hold it close to me forever, that's my choice. Not theirs. And frankly? Not yours either."

This time, when he walked away, she let him go.

Because this time, she knew he'd be back.

12

"Are you finished sulking, Denver?" Ty asked a couple of days later, throwing the question out there like it wasn't insulting. Complete with one of his big, wide, rodeo smiles that dared Brady to take offense.

Guaranteeing that Brady would rather die than indicate he was in any way offended.

"Am I sulking?" He treated his brother to a genial grin of his own, there in the late-morning light that was losing its battle with the cold wind rushing down from the mountains. "I thought we were out here repairing fences."

They'd been at it all morning. Gray had ridden out with the foreman and paid hands to handle an irrigation issue, leaving Ty and Brady to wrestle with the fencing that had gone down overnight. Worse than usual today, thanks to a little rainstorm that had spooked the herd into all kinds of shenanigans.

Brady liked to complain about the fences. They were always going down for various reasons, which meant he was always putting them back up, but the truth was, he liked the work. It was hard enough that he could work up a sweat, repetitive enough that he both couldn't think too much or too little, and left him pleasantly tired when done.

Too bad about the company.

"You've been wanting to get all that stuff the other day off your chest for a long while, I imagine," Ty said, with less drawl than usual. It usually meant he was being serious. Brady straightened, wiped at his forehead, and eyed his older brother warily. "It was good you did. But all this storming around and giving everyone the silent treatment for days is kind of taking the legs out from under the argument, don't you think?"

"When Gray chooses not to talk about something, it inspires people to start comparing him to John Wayne. Has it been sulking all this time?"

"And when I'm quiet, you all think I'm a raging alcoholic neck-deep in a bottle," Ty countered. He shrugged. "Welcome to your family, little brother. Suck it up."

The fence they were working on was fully repaired, tragically. Brady had no choice but to swipe his bottle of water from the cab of the truck and then stand there. And take it.

Always taking it. What would happen, he wondered then—out in the fields with nothing for miles but the cut of the wind and the two of them with the same old resentments between them like stones—if he just . . . stopped?

"I'm not storming around, and I'm not sulking." He sounded more patient than Ty deserved. "And I'm really tired of having to explain myself every three seconds. I have a better idea, since we're having this heart-to-heart. Why don't you tell me when you decided you didn't want to sell? And why you're waiting for me to come to that conclusion on my own rather than stepping up and telling me yourself?"

Ty was lounging against the side of the truck in his usual imitation of something boneless. Brady had always considered that position Ty at his most dangerous, so he was surprised when Ty nodded. "That's fair."

"Because I can't help noticing that for all the carrying on about *college boy* this and *Denver* that, I'm still the only one who's been completely open and transparent about my motivations."

For the ranch, he modified. To himself. Because the murkiness that was everything involving Amanda was . . . not something he planned to think about. Deliberately, anyway.

"Gray's still pissed off that I talked to some land developers and realtors to get a sense of what we were sitting on here," he continued, "but the point is, he knows I did that. I didn't sneak around."

"I said, fair enough." Ty shook his head. "That wasn't an invitation to start lecturing me."

"Do we need invitations to lecture each other? My bad. I thought that was a brotherly prerogative."

Ty's grin was lazy, but real. "That's an *older* brother's prerogative, Brady. Come on. This stuff rolls downhill. Always downhill. You should be used to it by now."

Despite himself, Brady had to bite back a laugh.

"It's not that I didn't talk to you about my decision," Ty said after a moment. He wasn't looking at Brady anymore. He was looking out over the upper pasture they were in at the moment, at all the rolling fields, the trees, the mountains. All the fencing they'd put in and would fix, again and again and again, as long as Everetts ran cattle on this land. And as long as cattle did what cattle do. "I didn't actually make a decision. I didn't talk about it with anyone."

"You're building a house. Here. That seems like a decision."

Ty nodded, and as much as Brady wanted to marinate in his righteous indignation, he knew his brother really hadn't spent much time considering what he was doing. Or viewing it as *a decision*. He'd been busy getting his wife, his son, and his memory back. It was hard to blame him for holding on tight to what he'd almost lost.

"My whole life, the only home I ever had was my trailer." Ty met Brady's gaze. "This was no home for me. I'm not sure I would have ever used that word to describe it."

"I always tried not to."

"Believe me, I get that. I drove around from show to show, I took care of my horses, and that was all I needed. I never thought that would change. I never wanted that to change."

"Until Hannah."

"Until Hannah." Ty laughed. "I would have sworn up and down I'd never fall in love with anybody. Instead, I've had the good fortune to fall in love with that woman twice. And when Hannah looks around at this land, she sees its history. Our legacy and Jack's future. Most of all, a home. And if that's what she wants, that's what I'm going to give her."

There were so many things Brady could have said to that. He could have reminded his brother how quickly he'd left at eighteen. How many years he'd spent in the rodeo and the many times he'd vowed he would never, ever come back to this place. Much less stay here, like all their ancestors had done. Growing up, Gray had been the committed one. Ty and Brady had been the ones to roll their eyes, mutter through their chores, and vow they would never end up like this.

But he didn't say any of that.

Because the thing they'd all had in common as kids

was that they'd been unhappy. Desperately, hopelessly unhappy. Gray had stayed and had his own issues around that, but Brady and Ty had gotten out. And Brady knew that even though they'd chosen different paths to follow, he and Ty had left for the same reasons.

This had never, ever been any kind of a home. This was where they were from, that was all. And maybe the land haunted them, packed deep with the sweat and tears, blood and bone, of the men and women who had come before them. But that didn't make it *home*.

It had taken Hannah coming here and loving Ty as much as he deserved—and far more than anyone else ever had, especially their parents—for him to find his home on the ranch. Brady had watched it happen. He liked to think he'd even helped the two of them along at a crucial moment.

The difference between him and his older brothers was that he didn't have it in him to fight their happiness. It was too hard won. Or he cared about it too much, maybe, after everything they'd gone through.

Not that he said this to Ty.

"You have to do what you have to do," he said instead.

"Thank you for your rousing support."

"And I know you'll understand I have to do the same."

"Whatever that means, Amos Junior," Ty drawled, and Brady had to take that one on the chin, because he'd once called Ty that too. It turned out karma smarted as much as everyone said it did. "And while we're talking about Dad and the things I disliked about him, the fact he always claimed his situation was forced on him has to be the top of the list. Have you ever noticed that it's always the people who make the worst choices who claim they never had a choice to begin with?"

Brady sighed. "I know I have a choice. That's the point I'm trying to make."

Ty leaned back against the side of his truck again, getting his boneless on. "You talk a good game, Denver, but I don't see it. We both shot our mouths off about never darkening Dad's door again, but here we were. Every holiday, like clockwork. And I was the one who was drunk. You came back enough, and sober, that it's hard to imagine some part of you didn't like it."

"I came back because that's what you're supposed to do."

"Yeah, I'm not buying that." Ty laughed. "Maybe at first, you wanted to show up to prove that it didn't matter if Dad supported you or not. I respect that. But after college? Why would you bother?"

"You're acting like I commuted to school every day while living at home; I didn't. And by the end there, I came home pretty much only for Christmas."

"That's what I'm getting at," Ty said, his gaze steady in that way that still took Brady by surprise. Because it wasn't an act. It wasn't Rodeo Ty at all. "You came home. You like to talk about selling, Brady, but I don't believe that's what you want. Not really. And if this is home to you too, even after all these years, maybe it's time you admitted that."

Ty ended the conversation there, getting the last word the way he liked to do by climbing in the truck and cranking up the country music. Brady pretended to shrug the whole thing off—the best weapon he had when trying to infuriate his older brothers.

As the day wore on, he thought about what Ty had said a whole lot more than he wanted to. And his phone was burning a hole in his pocket, because it took a lot of energy to avoid thinking about someone as hard as he was. He felt scraped raw with all the things he refused to name. Or admit existed in the first place.

After the day's work was wrapped up with only a few unexpected crises along the way—meaning it was a decent, almost boring day at the ranch—he took a hot shower. And he took the opportunity to question his motives as he got dressed again in his bedroom.

Amos's bedroom, to be more precise.

The proper ranch house master bedroom was upstairs, currently occupied by Gray and Abby. Growing up, Amos had lived up there, first with Brady's mother Bettina, and then with each successive wife or woman foolish enough to give him a chance. But in his later years, his habit of drinking himself blind and falling down the narrow stairs had become more medically imprudent than simply a sad statement on his life choices. Amos had redone the back bedroom and claimed it was because he wanted more privacy. The reality was that it was on the main floor and so when he fell down, he wouldn't have to risk breaking his neck on the stairs.

As Brady sat there, staring around at all the hardwood and the absence of any decoration on the walls, it occurred to him that choosing to live here this year was as much an act of penance as anything else.

Oh sure, he told himself and anyone who would listen that he'd decided to stay in the main house rather than one of the bunkhouses because he wanted to connect with his family. But it was easy enough to show up for meals from one of the outbuildings, the way Ty had all year. Because the rest of the time, Brady was sitting here in a room where a mean old drunk had calcified, stewed in his own hatefulness, and then, one fine morning almost a year ago, had gone out to the barn and died alone.

Maybe not the best plan. Not for a person who claimed he didn't want to follow in his father's footsteps, anyway.

There were no specific traces of Amos here, because they'd long since gotten rid of his clothes and personal effects. What few such things there'd been. Amos had been anything but sentimental.

Still, Brady couldn't pretend the walls weren't stained with the residue Amos had left behind. Sometimes, like tonight, he was sure he could hear the old man laughing derisively.

You're real smart, boy, Amos had said once, clearly using the word smart as an insult. *But the land don't care. And your brain can't feed the cows. When it comes right down to it, you don't have what it takes.*

It was easier to tell himself he didn't care if he had it or didn't have it, down in Denver. In Denver, he was good at his job. He'd always had a thing for math, and working with financial markets came easily. It was like doing puzzles all day long. What wasn't fun about that?

Brady had built up an excellent life over the years. He made friends easily, because he worked hard and played hard. He was used to being liked.

But none of that mattered when he was back here. Back home.

This year had already been too long. These days, when he went back down to Denver to handle things he couldn't from afar, it was Denver that no longer seem to fit. And it turned out, he got more from prickly, irritating conversations with his brothers than he did from happy, frictionless parties in the city.

And he was still sitting here, in an empty bedroom, trying to come to terms with a dead man. He could definitely hear Amos cackling with malicious glee.

Maybe he shouldn't be so surprised that he couldn't seem to stay away from Amanda. He was clearly not right in the head. He could hear his dead father *laughing*, for God's sake.

He headed down the hall toward the kitchen, passing the office where Amos had always holed himself up, and now Gray sat in the evenings, handling the endless paperwork. Abby usually sat in the office with him, these days with baby Bart, and it was a different house with the two of them in there, talking, laughing, and living out their happy life together. None of the stark, tense silences that had reigned when Amos had been locked away in there. Usually drinking himself into yet another rage.

The ghost of Amos might still have a grip on Brady, but not this house. Not anymore. There were different noises now. Ty and Hannah's Jack, squealing and laughing. The sound of little Bart crying, and then being soothed.

"You're just in time!" Becca cried when Brady walked into the kitchen, making it hard to feel as out of place as he always had here. "I made an experimental pasta . . . thing."

"That sounds appetizing."

His niece made a face at him, then returned her attention to the stove. Brady had come to think of the kitchen as Abby's domain, but things had shifted around now that Bart was here. He could hear the low murmur of female voices over the sounds of small humans from the other room, and figured Hannah and Abby were out there . . . mothering.

That, too, was a big difference from his childhood. His parents had never taken their responsibilities seriously. If they thought about them at all. Brady couldn't remember the last time he'd spoken to his own mother, something he felt a vague, enduring anger about—though he had no intention of changing anything. Bettina was the one who'd abandoned her children. He didn't think it was his responsibility to track her down to ask why.

Though he could admit it bothered him that Ty, apparently, had seen her over the years.

He shoved that aside and let Becca put him to work in the kitchen. He got the table ready for the usual big family dinner, then helped plate up sizable portions of the big, gooey pasta dish she'd made.

"Thank you for the parade," Becca said as they carried plates and serving dishes to the table. "It was the biggest returning alum presence in years."

"Is that a good thing?"

She wrinkled her nose at him. "Of course it's a good thing. People like to see returning heroes."

"You don't know this yet, but there's nothing heroic about a washed-up high school star. People don't like seeing the old high school quarterback because they think he's a hero." Brady laughed. "It's because they want to see how low he's fallen."

"Good Lord, sugar," came Hannah's drawl. His sister-in-law sauntered in from the other room, a babbling Jack on her hip and her trademark mascara making her eyes smoky. She set the toddler down in his high chair, but her gaze was on Brady. "That's breathtakingly cynical, even for you."

"Is it? Or is it the simple truth?"

"Sometimes," Hannah said, in a voice that sounded

awfully close to the one Ty had used on him earlier, "a parade is just a parade."

The rest of the family trickled in, and they all took their places. Brady hadn't felt particularly cynical before Hannah had called him that, but now it felt like pure discontent, clawing at him from the inside out.

The more settled his brothers became, the happier they seemed, the more restless Brady felt. No matter how much he supported their happiness. Philosophically.

When he was younger, the only cure for restlessness had been getting away from this place. And maybe it didn't make sense that he'd had the same reaction to Amos's reign of terror back then as he did now to his brothers' growing contentment . . . but that didn't change the edginess in him. And these days, he couldn't go and blow off steam the way he had in the past. There was Amanda now.

He thought of her, then, though he shouldn't have. The way she'd stopped in the entrance to her parents' living room and stared at him as if she'd been struck over the head. To his way of thinking, she might as well have taken out a megaphone and announced to her entire family what was going on between them. He couldn't believe no one had noticed.

Every time she'd looked at him, he could feel the heat. He'd left the house with every intention of getting in his truck and driving away, because walking into that barn and talking with her was asking for trouble. It was begging all four of her brothers to get suspicious.

It was plain dumb.

But he'd seen her gallop back in from the fields, bareback and beautiful, as if she and her horse were one.

He might dress himself up like a city boy from time to time, but at heart, he was all country. He wasn't built to do anything but marvel at a girl on her horse, her hair blown back and her body low, lithe, powerful, and as perfect as the scenery.

He been so disconcerted, and so struck, that he'd been standing inside the barn watching her brush down her horse and murmur sweet nothings before he knew it.

Basically daring her family to catch him.

But the funny thing was, sitting here around the battered old barn door that was the Everett family table, thinking about Amanda seemed to take away that restless edginess inside him.

It wasn't only when he was touching her. Just looking at her did the trick. He'd been a little keyed up about going to the Kittredge Sunday dinner, but the moment he'd seen her, it had gone away. He'd worried about her brothers figuring out what had happened between them, but the mess in *him* just . . . eased.

There was something about the way the light hit her, he thought. Neon lights at the Coyote or the late September sun. There was something in the way she smiled. There was even something about the way she sat across from him at a crowded table, obviously going out of her way not to look at him directly.

Brady didn't understand how she could turn him on and make him feel oddly soothed all at the same time, two things he would have said didn't go together. Or why he was leaning in deeper to that guaranteed disaster, every time, when if he was really as smart as he'd always thought he was, he'd run in the other direction.

Like his life depended on it. Because it did.

He was so busy turning that conundrum over and over in his head that it took him too long to realize Gray was talking to him.

"Already planning your next trip to the city?" Gray asked, and in case Brady was tempted to tell himself that this was another instance of his big brother joking around, he saw Abby cut her husband an exasperated look.

Clearly not joking, then.

"It doesn't require that much planning," Brady drawled. "Mostly I just get in my car and go. But I guess that might seem overwhelming to a man who doesn't like to leave Longhorn County."

He expected Gray to get terse. Stern and harsh. But instead, he could have sworn that his older brother's eyes gleamed in what might have been amusement. On someone else.

It was confronting to admit that he almost preferred it when they were all wholeheartedly at one another's throats. It was less confusing, in its way.

"It's hard to leave the land," Gray said, leaning back in his chair in a way that set alarms to ringing inside Brady. He cut a glance Ty's way, and that made it worse. Because Ty was sprawled back in his chair, one arm draped over Hannah, and that big old grin of his flashing wide.

Terrific.

"Again," Brady said, all drawl and bravado, "it's really not that hard. You just drive away. With or without a cloud of dust, depending on how dramatic you're feeling at the time."

"That's easy enough to do when you know someone else is tending your land, I imagine," Gray said, evenly. "It's lucky for you that I don't leave this valley much. In fact, the only night I've spent away from this ranch that I can recall was my wedding night a year ago."

"Thank you, Gray," Brady said, grinning to take the

sting out of it. Or some sting. "I think we all know that you're the responsible one. Since birth."

"I didn't know you'd ever tried to help." Gray's gaze was steady and his voice direct. "I'm sorry. The truth is, I should have known there was more to the story than Dad ever told. Because there always is."

"Amen," Ty chimed in.

Brady stared back at his oldest brother, feeling the usual mix of resentment, frustration, and helpless admiration that characterized all interactions with Gray.

This was a classic example. How was he supposed to stay outraged at a person who looked him in the eye and apologized for something that wasn't his fault?

"Don't apologize for Dad," Brady managed to say. "We'll be here all night."

"All night, all month, and straight on into the next millennium," Ty agreed. "And that would still be nothing more than a good start."

"You were right to take a piece out of me," Gray continued. He nodded decisively. "I deserved it."

Becca's eyes went wide. She swallowed, then put her silverware down on her plate. Carefully.

"You're freaking out your daughter," Brady told him. "And me. I appreciate the apology, but you know what they say about gift horses."

"I'm not the mouthy one in this scenario," Gray replied, with a little curve in the corner of his mouth. And this time, Brady didn't have to look at Abby, the human barometer, to determine that was Gray's newly discovered lighthearted side making an appearance.

"Ty and I have been talking," Gray continued. "And no, before you get your nose all out of joint, not behind your back. We're not hiding anything from you."

"That's real convincing."

"Easy there, Denver," Ty said, amiably enough. "You don't have to fight everyone. Maybe save it for people who are actually attacking you."

"Sage advice from a man who, until a couple of months ago, was engaged in a desperate cage fight against every last thing in the known universe."

But Ty only laughed. "I'm the voice of experience, baby brother. You should listen. Do as I say, not as I did."

"Everybody does as you say and not as you do, sugar," Hannah drawled from beside him. "That's not exactly advice. More like common sense."

Brady didn't catch the look Ty threw his wife, but Hannah sure did. And she laughed, though her face looked more flushed than it had before.

"I figure I've been going about this the wrong way," Gray said, taking control of the table again. "The fact is, I expected you to bail months ago."

"I didn't realize I had a reputation as a man who goes back on his word." Brady barely kept his tone civil. And he had to all but bite his own tongue to keep from sounding defensive. "I can't wait to see where the rest of this conversation is going."

"You've been after me to diversify for a year, more or less." Gray sat back in his chair with his arms crossed, looking like the Marlboro Man and some kind of judge all rolled into one. "But you know my feelings on that."

"I do, indeed."

"And I can't say I've been overly sympathetic when you talk about what you sacrificed to be here, but it's been pointed out to me"—Gray's gaze moved from Abby to Ty, then back again—"repeatedly, that there's a possibility I'm being stubborn on that. Particularly now that

Ty and Hannah are looking to settle here, and it seems pretty clear that if we put the land up to a vote, you'd be outvoted."

"Seems that way," Brady agreed.

And made himself sound friendly and unbothered. It hurt.

Gray didn't look convinced. "The thing is, Brady, the last thing I want is to force you to do something you really don't want to do."

"The past year would suggest otherwise."

Ty laughed from beside him. Across the table, Gray's lips twitched, but his gaze remained stern.

"My honest belief was that if you stayed here and worked the land, if you got back in touch with the Everett legacy, you'd feel differently. Maybe I was kidding myself."

"Or maybe," Ty drawled, "you're not the only hard-headed, stubborn-for-stubborn's-sake Everett sitting around this table tonight."

"How come stubbornness is a virtue when it's you all?" Becca asked then. "But a problem when it's me?"

"Because you're a girl, sugar," Hannah drawled, a glint in her eyes. "And girls don't choose their virtues. Guess who does?"

Abby nodded sagely, flashing a similar glint from beside Gray. "Stubborn men like stubborn men, and pretty much only stubborn men."

"Because you're sixteen," Gray corrected them. "You have your entire adult life to be as hardheaded as you like. And about two more years to learn how to compromise."

"Is that what this is?" Brady asked. "Is there about to be a compromise? Llama lattes out in the barn?"

Gray didn't actually make a face, though he managed to convey his horror, even so. "We're going to carve off a piece of the land. You can do what you want with it. And I'm really hoping it's not llamas. Or lattes. Or whatever a *llama latte* might be."

After all the arguments, all the fights, all the months he'd spent hammering away at Gray for exactly this . . . Brady didn't know what to say. He hardly knew how to process it.

"I'm not going to lie," Ty drawled. "I was expecting more of a reaction."

"I'm waiting for the catch." Brady hoped he sounded less unsteady than he felt.

"Diversify your face off," Gray retorted. "That's what you said you wanted."

"It is."

It was. It always had been.

"You have what you want," Gray said again, and he pushed back from the table. And then there it was. That shrewd, considering, older brother look that put Brady's teeth on edge. "I won't fight you. Now you have to ask yourself, what do you plan to do without an enemy? Without anyone to blame?"

Brady felt that question with all the force of the blow Gray didn't throw.

"I don't need an enemy," he managed to say.

"Are you sure about that?" Gray didn't quite smile. "I guess we'll see."

13

When her buzzer rang, ten minutes after she turned out all her lights and climbed into bed, Amanda's weariness after a long day of shifts in both the coffeehouse and the bar disappeared in a flash.

Because she could think of only one person who would come calling at three in the morning.

She threw back her covers and catapulted herself out of bed. Then she raced across the length of the apartment to slam her fingers on the button that released the outside door at the top of the stairs.

Amanda fumbled with her lock, then opened her front door, and Brady was there.

Right there.

Like the dreams she'd been having since she moved in here, but better. Much better, because this time she knew she wasn't asleep.

He stalked down the short hallway toward her, scowling and male and beautiful. Far too beautiful for this hour. Especially as he brought the smell of rain with him from outside.

Like he was his own storm.

Amanda probably could have taken a moment or two

to do something about her own appearance. She was wearing a set of cozy plaid pajama bottoms, a tank top, and her hair was everywhere in what she imagined was probably a terrible snarl. But with Brady bearing down on her, it was hard to focus on anything else.

"You didn't ask who it was," he growled at her, not breaking his stride.

"I knew who it was."

"It could have been anyone."

He was *right there*. Amanda had gone to such trouble to give him her number, then basically dared him to call her, and he hadn't. She could have called him, of course, but she was the one who'd asked him to have sex with her. Not coyly either. She'd come right out and asked him.

Amanda had extended herself by any measure—and she'd been wondering how long she was supposed to wait. What sort of manners were involved in potential *sex arrangements* between people who weren't in any kind of relationship? Were there any? The internet had a lot of competing ideas, clearly based on the somewhat hair-raising dating habits of people who lived in places where there was both a huge selection and a whole lot of anonymity. People who were attempting to seduce strangers, not their older brother's best friend.

She'd thought a lot about the fact that Brady probably preferred strangers after all those years down in Denver. Not to mention his nights at the Coyote. Who knew what a man like him considered normal dating and/or sexual behavior?

It was possible he'd never call her at all. Or even talk to her again. She'd read about that too, and had almost made herself laugh trying to imagine what a day in Cold

River would be like if everyone avoided all the people who bothered them, for whatever reason. This valley was too small. A lot of miles, but too few people. It was far better to smile politely and keep a respectful distance than to make a bigger scene by trying to avoid another person when that was impossible.

But now Brady was here at her door, and that was much better than trying to puzzle out Denver dating conventions.

"I knew it was you," she told him. And she felt far giddier than anyone should after working a long shift in high heels. "And look at that. I was right."

Brady stared down her, something raw on his face, and hot intent in his gaze. Amanda's stomach flipped over. She felt as if she were doing cartwheels up and down the hallway when she knew she hadn't moved.

But he did. He hauled her into his arms, stepped through her apartment door, and kicked it shut behind him. All in a single, smooth sort of movement that made her feel like dancing for joy.

"Always ask who it is," he growled, right there against her mouth.

Amanda didn't know if she meant to promise him she would, or vow she wouldn't, because then he was kissing her.

She wrapped her arms around his neck and crossed her legs around his back, and let him worry about holding her up against him with those strong arms of his. And he did, while the world seemed to shimmer and spin around them. Then he turned, propping her against the wall inside the door, and pressing against her.

And he devoured her.

Or she devoured him.

It tasted like fire either way.

Everything was hot, wild. His hands were in her hair, hers were in his. His jaw was rough, and she loved the scrape of it against her palms, her cheek.

Then the long, deliriously slow sweep of his tongue against hers, until they both groaned.

He kissed her again and again, until she lost track of her own name, and when he pulled away, she wanted to punch him. So she did.

Her reward was his low, marvelously male laugh. It spun around inside her, filling her up and making her long for more, all at once.

"Settle down there, killer," he said. "I'm not going anywhere."

Brady shifted her against his body, and Amanda wanted to stop time and *marinate* in how strange and wondrous that felt. His chest was so hard. His jacket smelled good, like fall and the ranch, man and a hint of woodsmoke, and *he* was beneath it, smelling even better. His arms were around her, tough and sure. And her legs were tight around him, so it should have been awkward when he started to move—but it wasn't.

Amanda doubted there was an awkward bone in Brady's body.

He carried her farther into the apartment, then back toward the kitchen where he'd kissed her the first time. He propped her up on the counter on the kitchen island again, then he leaned in and got his mouth on her. He traced an impossible line of sensation down her neck, and she let her head fall back to give him better access.

Her breath left her on a kind of a sigh when he bent

lower still and found her breasts beneath her tank top. And then he rocked her through and through when he took one needy tip into his mouth.

As if the fabric of her tank top didn't matter at all.

He played with one, then the other, then he pulled himself back up. Amanda held her breath, there between his arms with her legs hooked over his hips. But he only leaned down and rested his forehead against hers.

For a long moment, there was only breath. Heat. That bright, wild need, so sharp that she was almost happy to take some space from it. To collect herself a little.

Just a little.

"Hi," Amanda whispered, unable to keep herself from grinning.

It was dark in her apartment. Still, she could tell when his mouth curved. "I was going to call. It's the polite thing to do."

"This is better. This way, I'll never be sure if it was a dream or not."

He moved then, dragging himself against that place where she ached the most, and she shuddered so hard, she thought she might break apart.

"Don't worry, Amanda," Brady said, his voice laced with promise and amusement in equal measure. "You'll know."

He took her mouth again, and for another long while there was only that slick, hot, wet glory. He buried his hands in her hair once more. And there was something about it that made every breath a shivering sweetness that threatened to tug her overboard. Those strong hands, rough and callused, holding her right where he wanted her. His strong jaw and wicked mouth. *Him*.

Amanda had never been truly drunk, but she had no

doubt whatsoever that alcohol would fade next to the intoxication that was Brady Everett kissing her silly in her own kitchen.

He pulled away again and dropped his head lower this time, as if he was fighting himself.

"I needed a taste of you," he said, in that low almost-growl that made her light up and hum inside. "But don't worry, that's all I'm going to take."

"I'm not sure that's up to you."

He lifted his head. And her eyes had adjusted sufficiently that she could see the expression there. He wasn't kidding. Really. He had every intention of walking out again.

But it was after three in the morning. And Amanda was fed up.

"I've had this dream a million times," she told him. "Appearances in the middle of the night. Wild kisses that build up to something, then go nowhere. It's time for a new dream, don't you think?"

"Amanda—" he began, and she could already hear it in his voice. The distance. That obnoxious *I know better* tone.

She was more fed up with *that* than she could articulate.

But there was something she could do that was much better than arguing. She reached down and grabbed the hem of her tank top, then peeled it up over her head. She tossed it aside and stared at the man in front of her to gauge his reaction.

It was epic.

If quiet.

Brady looked like he'd turned to stone.

Amanda kept going, pressing her advantage. She

rocked back on the counter so she could shove her pajama bottoms and her underwear off, then kicked them aside too.

She'd always wondered what it would be like to be naked in front of another person. She assumed that it would be . . . bizarre. She would feel embarrassed, surely. Overly exposed, because, of course, she would be. Literally.

In her head, she'd imagined it like someone walking in on her changing in a dressing room.

But it wasn't like that at all. It wasn't *mortifying*. It was magnificent.

Brady was staring at her, hunger and astonishment stamped all over him. And something else that if she didn't know any better, Amanda would have called almost . . . sacred.

She didn't feel diminished. She felt alive and deeply splendid, even brighter and hotter than before.

"Amanda, I already told you that I was going to be—"

"In control, yes." She waved a hand, noting how it made her breasts sway slightly. He noticed too.

"But you're blowing that off?"

"I'm tired of waiting, Brady."

He let out a sigh that didn't seem to make it into the rest of his body, so tense and hard and beautiful there before her. "You're too young to be tired of waiting. For anything."

"It's been twenty-two years." She was naked and that should have been the end of it. But this was Brady, so of course she had to mount a defense. She was close to him now, so close she could feel the heat coming off of him, and his taste was in her mouth. "Kissing you made me feel alive, and I like it. I want more of it. I don't want to waste another second waiting for my real life to start. I told you I wanted it to be you. I still do. And I want it to be now."

Amanda watched as different expressions rolled over him, through him. She felt humbled and exalted at once when he reached forward and took her face in his hands. Carefully, as if she was fragile.

Then he leaned in and pressed a kiss against her lips.

This time, it wasn't about the heat or the wildness. This time, it felt like a promise.

"You amaze me," he told her, gruff and low. "I don't deserve this gift."

"Maybe not," she said, and grinned. "But I do."

Then he kissed her again, but this time, it was less about gifts and vows, and more of that spiraling fire that burned its way into every part of her. He kissed her and he kissed her, and he let his hands roam up and down her naked back, compounding the sensation. Making her feel like silk. Making her *need*.

When he pulled back again, she didn't have time to protest, because he was lifting her into his arms. This time, he held her high against his chest as he turned. Then he made his way across her darkened living room into the bedroom.

Her heart was beating low and long. And hard enough that she thought it might have knocked her over if she'd been standing on her own two feet. Thank God she wasn't.

Brady laid her down on the bed, and she thought she ought to *do things*, but she couldn't seem to make herself move. Or do anything but stare at him—the *man* standing there *beside her bed* who also happened to be *Brady freaking Everett*—and wonder if all that clatter from inside her chest was maybe a heart attack. Not that she cared, because he was kicking off his boots and shrugging out of his jacket.

Then, even better, he was following her down.

"Why are you wearing clothes?" she demanded.

"Amanda." His voice was stern, but there was a light in his dark eyes that made her stomach flip-flop. "You decided when. I'll decide how."

"I guess that's fair."

"Thank you for throwing me that small bone," he said dryly.

She was naked on her bed with a man.

Naked. On her bed.

With Brady Everett.

That was impossible to take on board or even to keep in her head as a full thought, so she reached out instead. She brushed back that dark hair of his, marveling at how crisp and thick it was. How hot his skin was. She didn't think she'd ever been this close to anyone in her life. Ever.

And they were about to get a whole lot closer.

She'd read a whole lot about *that*, too, over the years. She'd also interrogated all her friends who'd crossed that threshold. None of it had answered her primary question to her satisfaction.

"Will it hurt?" she asked him.

Brady propped himself up on one arm and rested his other hand, strong and faintly rough from all the work he did, there on her belly. It made her jolt, then heat up. And it also steadied her. The warmth of his palm felt like he was teasing her and taking care of her, all at once.

"It might." He didn't look away when he said that, as if it, too, was a part of a vow he was making. "Sometimes it hurts a lot, from what I hear. But you have a couple of things going for you."

"I didn't realize I was supposed to have things going for me. Is that one more thing everybody knows that I don't?"

Her voice was too high and too quick, and she could almost hear Brady drawl *easy, killer,* though he didn't. All he did was smile. And the reassuring weight of his hand on her belly made it easier to breathe. And to smile back.

"There's no secret list of action items." His voice was solemn as he said that, his gaze serious. Amanda didn't realize until that moment how crucial that was. That if he'd laughed at her, she might have simply crumbled. "You've been riding horses your whole life. That's supposed to help. It could be you feel no pain at all. Just as many women do as don't."

"How many women's virginity have you . . . ?"

He moved his hand then, almost absently. Amanda caught her breath as Brady began to trace complicated, distracting patterns across her skin, leaving shivers of goose bumps in his wake.

"One. That I'm aware of. When we were both in high school."

Another time, she might have interrogated him about *which* high school girlfriend he meant. And if that was his first time too. But not tonight.

Amanda had bigger concerns. "Did she cry?"

"She certainly did not." And he was grinning, then. "I can't tell if you want it to hurt or you don't."

"I can't tell either." She heard herself giggle, and that struck her as absurd, especially when it happened again. "I always thought it was *supposed* to hurt. A full-on sacrifice upon an altar, or something. Like I'll be less than a real woman if there isn't blood and pain and maybe even screaming."

"You're always surprising, I'll give you that." Brady's drawl was still appropriately serious, though his eyes were bright. "As an alternative plan, we could also just see what happens."

"This is a major moment in a person's life, Brady. Whatever happens, screaming on an altar or something painless because of horses or whatever you said, I'm going to remember this night for the rest of my life." She realized she was frowning at him. "No pressure, though."

"Amanda." And the look on his face made her shudder again, this time in sheer delight. "Every night with me is memorable. Very few involve altars. I promise."

Then she was laughing, despite herself, as he rolled over and took her mouth again.

He kissed her, lazily and thoroughly, until she forgot that she might possibly be more anxious about this than she'd wanted to admit.

But she couldn't focus too much on that, because Brady proceeded to teach her everything she didn't know.

He kissed his way down the length of her body, taking his time and clearly enjoying the opportunity to explore. He worked his way back up, then settled himself between her legs—holding her thighs apart with his shoulders.

And he grinned when her eyes went wide.

"Trust me," Brady said.

She did.

He used his mouth until she fell apart, then he did it again, until she was making strange noises out of her throat, flushed hot and wild with it. Only then did he roll off the bed again, and finally—*finally*—take off his own clothes.

Amanda was too busy trying to come back together from all the millions of pieces he'd torn her into to appreciate him the way she wanted to do. Then it was all a kaleidoscope of physical sensations. The reality of an actual naked man—of *Brady*—who pulled her over him so she could wiggle all around, feeling parts of herself she'd never understood were erogenous zones pressed against parts of him.

His chest was roughened with hair where she was smooth. He was big with long, hard muscles where she was soft. He had planes, angles, and ridges where she had curves.

She was delirious. She was delighted.

She had imagined a lot of ultimate Brady moments, but this was better.

So much better, she thought she might cry, though she wasn't the least bit sad.

He turned her this way, then that. He used his mouth again, and his astonishing fingers. She made noises she would have sworn could never possibly come out of her. One time she clapped her hand over her mouth, not sure whether she should apologize or laugh, and Brady kissed her fingers away.

Then kissed her too.

"That's the good stuff," he murmured, there against her mouth. "You don't ever want to hide the good stuff."

Amanda had never thought of herself as a physical creature. Not really. The closest she got to it was when she was riding Cinnamon, the two of them fused together and made into one. She'd always loved the power of it, and how close she felt to flight.

But this was even better.

Brady fished a packet out of his jeans. And Amanda sprawled there, her heart thumping and her head spinning, watching him roll a condom onto himself.

There were too many new things to keep making lists, but she couldn't seem to stop herself. She'd never seen that part of a man. Now she felt it against her, and he let her touch him too, but only for a moment. And that was surprising as well. Satin on steel and yet still proudly male.

She loved it.

Brady stretched himself out on top of her, and she felt the tip of him notch there between her legs.

"Are you ready?" he asked.

She meant to laugh, but it came out as more of a gasping sound. "I don't know how to answer that."

"That's okay. You're not supposed to know."

"Is this like a count-of-three scenario?" Amanda's voice was perhaps overly bright. "I can count down, if you want."

"I got it." Brady was grinning again, and there was a light in his dark eyes that made her whole chest feel full and giddy. He settled himself against her and leaned forward, brushing her hair back from her face and then kissing her once again.

That same solemn, sweet kiss that struck her as a kind of vow. "Thank you," he said. "For deciding it should be me."

"You're welcome." She bit her lip, then stretched a bit, down to her toes, because she *felt things*, but she didn't know how to tell the difference between all the things she felt. "You haven't done it yet, have you? Because so far, Brady, there's a whole lot of talk but I'm *still* a v—"

He thrust forward then, his hard male flesh breaching her, then pushing in. Then farther in still.

Oh God, then even farther—

She felt him nudge up against something deep inside her, and he stopped, and maybe she was actually crying a little, and that was it.

Brady was inside her.

His grin took on a dangerous edge.

"No," he said. "You're not *still.*"

And then he . . . waited.

It took Amanda a shudderingly taut moment to realize that, too, was a gift he was giving her.

He waited, and she became aware again.

Of the fact that she'd tensed up, everywhere. That her back was arched and her fingers were clenched down, hard, on his arms. She took a breath, but all she could feel was that stretching inside. That almost unbearable fullness.

How had she never considered anything besides the potential for that initial tearing that she'd read so much about? Why did no one talk about *this*? The feeling of being crowded, intimately. Of being impossibly filled. Connected, shockingly, to another person who was *right there*. It all teetered just this side of too much.

Still he waited.

Brady smoothed her hair back again and studied her face, but he didn't move.

So she did, because there was something growing inside her, rolling, expanding, and she was terribly afraid that she would scream. Or sob. Push him off her—

But when Amanda moved, it eased a bit. Or changed.

She did it again, rocking her hips the way she had when she'd sat astride him in his truck. And that felt different, so she kept doing it.

There was something about the movement. About the drag when she pulled herself off him, then moved back close.

She was barely moving at all, and yet it felt momentous. Huge. And the more she did it, the more it seemed to shimmer, making her start to glow. There where they were connected, and everywhere else too.

The glowing led straight back into all that heat and longing.

That was when she was finally able to tell he'd been holding himself so rigidly this whole time. So still.

"You okay?" Brady asked, his voice husky and deep, like it cost him something to hold himself back like that.

Amanda wanted to say she *thought* she was okay. Or she hoped she was. She wanted to rattle off every last bit of sensation she was experiencing, and make him tell her what it meant. She wanted to slow it down and speed it up, take it apart and dive deeper into it.

So she nodded because she wasn't sure what would happen if she tried to speak.

Then she forgot that she'd wanted to in the first place, because Brady began to move.

All the other times he'd built her up and taught her how to shatter had been leading to this. All of that had been fun, but this—this was everything.

She could feel him inside her. Around her and above her. There was nothing in the world but him, her, this. There was the rhythm of it, the deep slide, and the wild, impossible fire that lit her up, inside and out.

Amanda surrendered to it, completely, and it didn't feel like surrender. It felt like flying.

It went on and on.

Brady kept going until she was sobbing out his name,

and only then did he reach between them and press down until she exploded. Far more intensely than all the times he'd tossed her over that edge before.

She felt him keep going, faster and wilder, until she heard him cry out too. Then bury himself deep within her, at last.

Her heart was a mad drum in her chest, and she could feel his too. Amanda had wanted this. She had gone after it, single-mindedly.

And she had finally lost her virginity, as planned.

But as she lay there in her bed, Brady stretched out on top of her and pressing her down deliciously into her mattress, her heart kept *kicking* at her.

Until she realized it wasn't the only thing that hurt.

Though *hurt* was much too small and sharp a word to describe how she felt. How *immense* it all was. How layered.

None of it was new.

Of course it was Brady, a voice in her said. *It was always going to be Brady. When you think of men, you think of him.*

Like no other men existed. Because they didn't. Not for her.

The truth rolled through her like thunder.

Until Amanda understood that she might have lost her innocence tonight, at last, but she'd lost her heart a long time ago.

Long before it had ever occurred to her that this could happen between them.

"Are you okay?" Brady asked again, his head near hers. He shifted, bringing her against his side as he turned.

"I'm good," Amanda assured him. Or maybe herself.

She sounded convincing too.

Then she slipped a hand over her heart, told herself sternly that she was absolutely *not* in love, and ordered herself to go to sleep. Now.

Before she ruined everything and told him.

14

Gray and Ty had given him land, and leave to do with it as he pleased.

Amanda had given him her virginity.

Brady should have been happy. Or content, at the very least. All of a sudden, he had everything he'd ever wanted and more than he'd dreamed possible.

Too bad it all sat a little funny.

Maybe he really was his own worst enemy.

He preferred to blame his dead father, or try to get into it with the old man's ghost. He'd much rather rail against his overbearing older brothers. Get a little bourbon in him, and he might even shout at the coming winter or throw stones at the moon.

But that all seemed a little foolish now.

October came in with an early snowstorm, then a fickle return to summerlike temperatures. Everybody roamed around muttering about the mountains, and out in the fields, ranchers took the warning for what it was and started getting ready for the inevitable winter.

Brady did too.

He sat with his brothers in the evenings, maps of their

property spread out before them across the dining room table where Becca and Abby sometimes gathered to do projects of one sort or another. He could have used the table in the kitchen, but he hated that thing. He refused to plan good things on the same refashioned barn door where his father had spent so many nights encoding his nastiness into that will of his.

"What kind of terrain do llamas prefer?" Gray asked one night as he looked over Brady's shoulder at the best, current map of Everett land, not precisely smirking.

"Llamas like to be close to the house, I hear," Ty replied, deadpan, from his other side.

"Keep it up," Brady drawled. "You might look out the window one morning and find a herd of them spitting at you."

He still had no particular interest in llamas, though part of him wanted to get a few for the sheer pleasure of messing with Gray. But that would be childish. That was the trouble with what Gray had done. Brady had what he'd always said he wanted. Now he had to figure out which of the many ideas Gray had shot down to run with—and it had to be the one that would work.

Because this was Brady's one shot to prove himself.

To any lingering ghosts as well as to his brothers.

And maybe to himself too.

But October hunkered down over Cold River, veering between winter and summer, making Brady feel better about how torn he felt. On every topic.

He'd made himself a lot of promises where Amanda was concerned. That night in her apartment had been a sweet, impossible madness, and part of him wanted to vow up and down that he would never do anything like that again.

Once was enough. Once was completing the bargain they'd made. Anything beyond that one time was . . . dangerous.

He assured himself he wasn't foolish enough to go back for more. He'd never been much for repeats anyway. Why start now?

"Really?" Amanda asked the next night he appeared at her door well after the bar closed, though her eyes gleamed. "I thought I already got my education."

"Education is a never-ending process, Amanda." Brady backed her inside and kicked the door shut behind them. "It can take whole lifetimes."

"We better get started." Amanda wrapped her arms around his neck, arching her body into his in a way that made them both sigh a little. "After all, you're very old. You could die any time."

He made her pay for that. Repeatedly.

For a while then, as the October weather waffled between snowstorms and callbacks to summer, but got colder every night—a lot like Brady, really—life was okay. More than okay. There was finally harmony between the Everett brothers. It wasn't as if they stopped poking at one another, but it all felt different when Brady knew they were taking him seriously at the same time. Or giving him space to fail spectacularly, anyway, which amounted to about the same thing.

He scoped out various parcels of land he might claim as his, trying to figure out which one he liked best. He started going back over the variety of different business plans he'd come up with over the years, trying to decide what would be the best tactic to take, now that he'd been here almost a full year and he was looking at diversification from the inside instead of from down in Denver.

One night, there was another big storm rattling around outside like October was trying to remind them all how intense the winters could get here. The family stayed in, gathered in the living room with a fire dancing in the grate and enough bright light to beat back the encroaching dark.

It was getting harder to remember how grim this house had been when Brady was growing up. Gray was pushing those memories back by the simple, revolutionary act of living here with his family and not being miserable.

Brady probably wouldn't have believed it if he didn't see it right there before his own eyes.

Baby Bart liked to be held, so Gray had him in the crook of his arm tonight while he watched the news. Abby and Becca sat on one of the couches together, fussing over a crochet pattern while trying to work out where they'd gone wrong in an afghan the two of them were making.

Ty and Hannah had taken Jack back out to their bunkhouse after dinner, because they liked to keep him to a strict bedtime—storm or no storm.

Mommy and Daddy like their evenings toddler-free, Hannah had said once, with that big laugh of hers. *And before your mind gets all dirty, we also like to talk to each other in big, old grown-up words every now and again.*

Whether they were talking to each other or communicating in other, more physical ways, that, too, was a far cry from the evenings Brady recalled when their father would shout at his current woman until she broke down and sobbed. Or started throwing things back at him. Or worse.

Brady was kicked back in the armchair by the fire with his laptop cracked open as he scanned through his business plans and proposals, aware that he was less creeped out by all this domesticity than he might have been before.

And *creeped out* wasn't the right term. It was more that all this congenial quiet usually made him restless. Edgy. He'd never been one for settling down—possibly because he was always braced for the telltale sounds of his father in the next room, muttering over that will. Or pushing his chair back from the only table he couldn't break when he flipped it, then swaggering drunkenly into the rest of the house to cause trouble and lasting damage.

"If you're heading in a dude ranch direction," Gray drawled when the newscast was over, "I know I promised I wouldn't get in your face about whatever you choose to do, but you might want to give me a heads-up. So I can be prepared."

"There's nothing wrong with a dude ranch." Brady smirked. "It brings in money and tourists all at once."

It was deeply entertaining to watch Gray fight to keep his expression blank, if not entirely judgment-free. "That's not the direction you're heading, is it?"

"It's not. Though I'm tempted to change my mind because you look so horrified at the thought."

Over on the couch, Becca and Abby exchanged a glance and laughed.

"I don't like random people on my land," Gray said, not looking at his wife or daughter. "I'm old school that way."

Brady laughed. "You're old school in every way, brother."

"Dad is so old school he doesn't know there's a new school," Becca chimed in.

"Careful, Abby," Gray warned his wife before she had a chance to join in too. Though his eyes gleamed as he gazed at her over the top of their baby's head. "Be very, very careful."

"I didn't know Gray in school," Abby said primly. "Any school, old or new."

Becca turned her laugh on her stepmother. "Good save."

It wasn't until later, when Brady was back in the bedroom that felt more like a tomb these days, that he allowed himself to admit the moment had been . . . nice. Truly nice, the way he'd always imagined families were supposed to be. The way the Everett family never had been.

You should be past all this, he chided himself.

But maybe that was the trouble. There was no getting past anything when you were still living in the middle of it.

He sat and called Amanda. He told himself it was a habit he'd gotten into because the weather was so iffy this time of year. He tried not to question why he sometimes called her on clear nights too.

Though he hadn't told her about the land. About what Gray and Ty had done. And he certainly hadn't told her he was staying. He couldn't have said why.

Nothing he did involving Amanda stood up to much scrutiny.

"I know, I know," she said when she picked up. "It's snowing out there, isn't it?"

"The pass might be open. It's not coming down that hard." He thought about Gray and Abby out there in the warm, cozy living room. "But it would be real hard to defend a decision to drive into town on a night like this."

She wasn't working tonight. He could hear her moving around as she talked to him and found himself trying to imagine where she was in her apartment. He knew it far too well, now.

He chose not to examine why he wanted to picture her there. Or why it felt like another step toward an intimacy he would have sworn he didn't want.

"That sounds perfectly sensible," Amanda said. "Also, that sucks."

"Yeah, it does."

Later, he knew, the fact that no alarms rang in him when he talked to her like this, or at all, was going to bother him the most. Because that was what always kept him up at night, staring at the same ceiling Amos had scowled up at, all those years.

The problem was, it was too easy to be with Amanda.

Brady liked too many things about her. Her cheerful practicality. Her sudden silliness. And God help him, her endless physical appetite and commitment to feeding it made him heat up even all these miles away from her.

He'd spent his entire adult life keeping his interactions with women on a casual level. On the rare occasions that he dated a woman for more than a night here or there, he usually went to great lengths to make sure there were no misunderstandings.

Brady had always told his friends that he liked to manage expectations early and often.

But when it came to Amanda Kittredge and the way she lit up when she looked at him, he couldn't bring himself to do it.

He understood it when he was actually, physically

with her. When he was moving inside her, losing himself in the little cries she made. Or marveling at how easily and eagerly she learned every last thing he taught her.

Maybe his Amanda problem was as simple as the fact that he was the youngest of three brothers. He'd had hand-me-downs all his life. Brady couldn't deny there was something in him that deeply liked that he'd finally found something that was only his.

He needed to tell her some hard truths on the phone, then, since he couldn't seem to do it in person. He glared at the ceiling. It didn't matter if it was awkward; he needed to set boundaries. Because there was something about the look she got on her face sometimes, so filled with wonder, that made him question exactly where her head was in all this.

Just freaking do it, he ordered himself.

"Tell me about your day," he said instead.

What?

"My day was a little weird, Brady. As a matter of fact."

She didn't know he was yelling at himself. She sounded the way she always did, sweet and right and funny, and he could never predict what his small-town girl might say next.

He could hear her sit down on her sofa. He could hear her breathe. Neither sound should have been *comforting,* for God's sake. There was also the distant sound of the relentless music from the Coyote's jukebox, and the funny thing was, Brady could hardly remember why he'd liked going there anymore. These days, if he made an appearance at all, he sat at a back table, brooded, and waited to see who he might have to kill if they strayed too close to Amanda.

He rubbed at his chest, irritably.

How could he *miss* Amanda when he saw her all the time?

"Do you remember the one and only Miss Martina Patrick?" she asked.

Brady laughed, despite himself, at the sheer randomness of that. "I don't want to remember Miss Patrick. I started trying to forget her while I was still high school. I haven't thought about her since, but now you mention it, why isn't she retired?"

"Because she's a whole thing and will never retire. My friend Kat does a killer impression of her dying in her office on school grounds, but part of me feels bad about that."

"Is it funny? It's hard to feel bad about something if it's funny."

"I think you'll find that's called a worrying lack of empathy."

"Miss Patrick once made me stand outside in the rain because she didn't like my 'tone.'" But Brady laughed, because even such indignities were funny now. "I have all kinds of empathy. For other people."

"Okay, sure, she can be harsh on students, but I've always assumed she's very sad and very lonely. Nothing but cats and an aging mother."

"And that enchanted gingerbread house in the woods with an oven she likes to push kids into."

"Today she came into the coffeehouse," Amanda said, her voice stern. Or trying to be stern. "I found that surprising all by itself, but the two kids who worked there assured me it wasn't. Apparently she comes in sometimes in the afternoons, I've just never seen her before. I watched them serve her, then do their own impressions. And I felt bad."

"Every kid who's graduated from Cold River High in the past forty years does impressions of Miss Patrick."

"Does that make it right?"

"Well, Amanda, it doesn't make it *wrong*."

He was still staring at the ceiling. But he caught himself grinning.

"I decided it was time to make up for my youthful callousness. I marched over to her table, plopped myself down, and gave her my friendliest smile."

Brady could picture that smile. Vividly. He liked imagining it in the coffee shop a whole lot more than he liked seeing it in the Coyote, where none of those degenerates deserved it. "I'm sure she melted."

Amanda laughed, and he liked the sound of it. He could feel it inside of him, kicking up a little fuss and making that grin on his face feel like it might be permanent.

Something else he could be pissed about later.

"She did not melt. She stared at me like I'd violated her."

"That's the Miss Patrick I remember."

"She makes me anxious. I found myself nervous-talking about how I never really got to know her while I was a student, but it was so much fun that she came to the coffeehouse now, because *the bond*. Or something. I hope I didn't really say *bond*, but I might have, it's all a big blur. But do you know what she said?"

Brady tucked an arm behind his head, stopped critiquing his own inability to stop grinning, and surrendered to the reality. Which was that he even liked *being on the phone* with this woman. Talking about nonsense.

That was probably a clue he should pay attention to. Instead, he concentrated on her.

"'Get thee behind me, Satan'?" he suggested.

Amanda laughed. "That was implied. She stared at me, for an uncomfortably long period of time, with that awful *face* she makes."

"I knew it well, many years ago."

"'Miss Kittredge,' she said, in exactly that *tone*." And Amanda pulled off Miss Patrick's chilly, unimpressed voice so perfectly that Brady found himself grinning like a fool again. "'I am perfectly comfortable with my own company. In fact, I prefer it.'"

"Oh, ouch."

"She said it exactly like that. Dripping with disdain."

Brady hadn't been kidding when he said he'd started forgetting about Miss Patrick while he'd still been in high school. He hadn't given the woman a single thought in all the years since, and now he could picture her so vividly, she might as well have been standing in the corner of the room. Glaring at him, as always.

"I hope you thought better of your attempt to befriend her and ran away," Brady said. "I can't prove it, but I'm pretty sure she can turn people into stone."

"I was stuck! I kept smiling at her, and *in desperation* I said something about how she was an inspiration. And it gets worse, Brady. *She laughed.*"

"What?" He was laughing, but he couldn't imagine the eternally bitter school secretary succumbing to hilarity of any kind. "*Miss Patrick?* Are you sure she laughed? You can't be remembering that right."

"She *laughed*. At me, to be clear. Then she stopped laughing and got serious." And Amanda's voice got more serious too. "'You think you pity me, Miss Kittredge,' she said. 'The truth is that you fear me. You don't know, yet, that lives are choices we make or that I am perfectly content with mine.'"

Amanda didn't laugh after she said that. Brady didn't either. And suddenly the ceiling up above him seemed a lot closer. A lot lower.

"I told her I was delighted with my choices," Amanda said, but she sounded different. Shaken, maybe. "That's the exact word I used. *Delighted.* And all she did was laugh again, and then shoo me away."

Suddenly Brady couldn't get past the reality that he was stretched out on the bed that had once been his father's. Staring at the bare and empty walls or the oppressive ceiling. And in the middle of an intense phone conversation with a woman he should never have been intimate with in the first place.

He sat up, ran a hand over his face, and told himself he was annoyed that she was telling him stories. That was why his chest felt so weird. "You can't let a bitter old woman like that get in your head."

"That's what's been bugging me all day," Amanda replied. She made a sound that could have been a laugh or a sigh. "What if she's not bitter at all?"

Brady shifted where he sat, ready to launch into his prepared speech. Because there was no time like the present to set appropriate boundaries. Or to keep ahead of any conversations about choosing which life to have or how to be content in it.

She was temporary and she needed to know that.

You need to know that, idiot, he growled at himself.

But as he opened his mouth to lay down the law, he caught a faint motion out of the corner of his eye. He looked over and found Becca standing there in the door he must have left cracked open.

Brady muttered that he had to go, then hung up. Like he was the teenager and Becca was a disapproving adult.

He stared at his niece, convinced he had guilt stamped all over his face. And the kick of temper he felt as he told himself there was no need for him to feel guilty about anything, even though he knew that was a lie, only made it worse.

"How long have you been standing there?" he asked.

Becca was looking at him much too shrewdly. "Who was that on the phone?"

"A friend." He stood, tossing his phone to one side. "Do you need something?"

"You were talking to a girl, weren't you?"

"What makes you think that?"

Becca studied him a moment. "It's that look on your face. Almost . . . gentle."

Brady tried not to openly scowl at his beloved niece. "Well, that's about the most horrifying thing you've ever said to me. I was talking to my broker. And the last thing he is, especially about brokerage accounts, is *gentle*."

Becca blinked. "And now you're lying. Why are you lying?"

"Did you need something?" he asked again, ignoring her question.

"Abby is making a late-night apple crumble. She thought you might want some." Becca sniffed. "But I'll go tell her you're too busy talking to girls and lying about it."

She didn't wait for him to respond. She pushed away from the door and stomped off down the hall.

There was no decent way to handle this situation. If he ran after her, issuing threats and shouting his head off, he would be protesting way too much. But if he said nothing, wasn't he tacitly confirming her take on things?

Brady wanted to lock himself away until he got over

this *thing* in him that kept putting Amanda in the middle of everything, when he knew better. Or he could jump in his truck and leave—though who was he kidding? If he got in his truck, snow or no snow, he'd end up at Amanda's.

Instead, he made himself walk casually down the hall toward the kitchen. When he reached the main room, he found Gray was now standing, rocking the baby while he fussed. And Gray didn't laugh when he looked at Brady, but that gaze of his sure did.

"I hear you have a girl."

"I can't wait to tell Riley Kittredge that Becca thinks he's a girl," Brady replied, sounding more flippant than he felt.

Another lie.

It made him feel dirty. Worse, it made him feel like his father.

There was no need for Amos's ghost, because here Brady was, standing in this house making the same messes. Keeping it all nice and toxic.

He wanted to confess immediately.

But he didn't.

It did the trick, because Gray returned his attention to the infant in his arms.

He should have been relieved. But when Brady looked over to the kitchen doorway, Becca was standing there, watching him. A speculative expression on her face.

Lives are choices we make, Miss Patrick said in his head, as chilly and disappointed in him as ever.

Lies were too.

He didn't apologize to Becca either. Or confess.

Instead, he congratulated himself on dodging a bullet.

And tried to drown anything else he might have been feeling—or hearing inside him, against his will—in too much sugar, butter, and cinnamon, the way God intended.

15

A few days later, Brady found himself in the Broken Wheel Saloon, surrounded by bottles of local Colorado IPAs, platters of cheeseburgers cooked to perfection, and his oldest friends.

There was a decent crowd there as dinner hours waned and tipped over toward more of a bar scene, with a local band tuning up to play a set. It was a gathering Brady would have enjoyed a lot more if he were only visiting Cold River, the way he'd thought he'd been a year ago when he'd come home for Amos's funeral. Now, he'd stayed long enough to cause real trouble instead of the fun kind.

That made everything a whole lot less comfortable.

"Where have you been?" Riley asked from beside him, where he was kicked back in a chair, toying with his beer. "You haven't been around in weeks."

"It hasn't been weeks."

But even as he said it, Brady realized he didn't know if it were true. October was galloping along and he wasn't ready. He wasn't prepared. He kept on spending more time with Amanda than he meant to, for one thing. And for another, Halloween was coming up fast.

And Halloween marked a full year since Amos's death.

Brady would have said that anniversaries didn't get to him. He couldn't remember when his mother had left, for example, only that she had. But somehow, this particular year felt significant.

Maybe because he couldn't quite kick his father's ghost, no matter how he tried. He was beginning to think there was no need to look for Amos's ghost, because the old man had taken up residence in him.

"Could be Brady found himself a lady at the Coyote," Jensen said from across the table. "Maybe he's gone and shacked up with her."

Everyone laughed. And Brady had to laugh too, because that should have been hilarious. People didn't *shack up* with folks they encountered in the dark, grim shadows of the Coyote. The Coyote was for furtive mistakes, beer-soaked regret, and enough whiskey to make it seem like trying it on all over again was a good idea.

"The only thing I've ever found in the Coyote is a headache," Brady drawled, because everyone was waiting for his reaction. "I don't take it home. I take a few aspirin."

That got an even bigger laugh, and he was tempted to relax, but then the crowd on the other side of the table shifted. Brady was still laughing as he looked up. And saw Amanda standing there, previously hidden by the two women standing behind Jensen.

Worse, she was staring straight at him.

He felt an ugly twist in his gut. There was no reason for it. But telling himself that didn't make it go away.

"You don't pick up anything at the Coyote," Jensen

said, craning his head around to squint up at his little sister. "Right, Amanda?"

"She shouldn't even touch the glasses," Riley added from beside Brady. "I've seen who drinks from them."

"Nothing but headaches," Amanda said lightly, and she even smiled, but Brady knew her better by now.

He could see the hurt in her eyes. Worse, he could see she was trying to hide it.

It didn't matter how many times he told himself he had no reason to feel guilty. That they weren't a public thing. That *of course* he hadn't announced he really had met someone in the Coyote.

Because it didn't work. He felt like a jerk.

Amanda spun back to the other group standing there, on what passed for the Broken Wheel's dance floor. He should have recognized them. And her.

Brady had to stay where he was, lounging in a chair with the remains of his dinner in front of him. He had to grin like he didn't have a care in the world, while all the time he was reading the tension in Amanda's spine. The particular way she stood. Brady couldn't believe everyone else wasn't able to see it as clearly as he could. It was blaring her irritation and bruised feelings to the entire saloon. More than that, to all of Cold River.

No one seemed to notice but him.

He told himself that was a good thing.

The conversation at the table turned to over-the-top lies about each man's hunting prowess, a favorite local game that could last for hours. Especially when Matias started making up stories about all the elk he could take down with little more than mind control.

"I stared him down and told him to kneel," he said, not cracking even the faintest smile as all around him, everyone hooted and about fell out of their chairs. "And he obliged."

"A 400-class bull elk." Jensen could barely speak he was laughing so hard. "*Knelt*."

Matias shrugged. "It's called prowess, friend."

"It's called fantasyland," Jensen retorted.

"You don't seem like yourself, is all," Riley said from beside Brady.

Brady took that as an opportunity to stop looking for signs of Amanda's mood on her freaking *back*. He turned toward his best friend instead.

"I can choose some land and diversify," Brady said with a grin. He did not ask himself why he told Riley so easily when he had yet to tell Amanda, who he'd actually been spending more time with lately. He didn't want to know the answer. "Gray gave me exactly what I want. Is there anything worse?"

Riley actually laughed. "It's the only thing worse than not getting what you want."

"Amen."

Riley toyed with his beer some more. "Thing is, though, you do want it. You've always wanted to see what you could do if you didn't have to be neck-deep in the usual Cold River cattle operation."

Brady wished his friend were less supportive. Particularly when he'd be anything *but* supportive if he knew where Brady's attention had been focused these past few weeks.

"I've already seen what I can do," he said. "We won the state championship twice. I got a full ride to college, and the only way to keep my scholarship was to get straight A's. So I did."

"Yes, Brady. You're like a god among us."

Brady made a show of scratching his jaw. With his middle finger. "Every single person in my family has always hated bankers. So I decided I might as well become one, more or less, to see what all the fuss was about. To demystify them."

"I didn't realize there was anything mystifying about banking in the first place."

"That's where you're wrong, Riley. Some people—my father, for example—always treated math like a list of suggestions. Suggestions he could shrug off whenever he didn't like the answers. Folks treat finances the same way."

"If you say so. Why are you lecturing me, again?"

"The fact of the matter is, I'm actually really good at almost anything I put my mind to."

To his horror, he started thinking about Amanda again. More precisely, sex with Amanda. All those glorious hours he spent tucked away in that apartment of hers, teaching her every last thing he'd ever known about pleasure.

Then letting her practice on him.

His temperature rose two degrees. Instantly.

Riley was right next to him. *Right there*.

"I'm not going to deny that you're good at things," Riley said, shifting to look at Brady directly—the last thing Brady wanted. "It's annoying, actually."

"I'm delighted to hear that."

His friend was clearly trying to say something serious, because he let that pass. "But being good at things isn't the same as doing something because you love it." Riley's dark gaze met Brady's for a moment, then dropped. "You're the one who told me that. A long time ago."

Brady remembered. It had been after Riley and Rae

had broken up, and Riley was down in Denver, trying to figure out what to do with his life now that it was no longer the one he'd had planned.

The memory only made him feel that same mix of guilt and temper all over again. How was he in this mess? And why hadn't he extricated himself already? What did he think was going to happen here?

"We've always been the same, you and me," Riley said quietly. "You love this land. You let Amos chase you away. You let Gray make you feel bad about coming back. But now you finally have a chance to do what you've always wanted to do. What I can't figure out is why you're dragging your feet."

Brady saw a flash of honey hair across the table. And the line of Amanda's pretty neck that he'd had his mouth on. Repeatedly.

He needed to get it together. Now. "I don't know."

"Don't you?" The corner of Riley's mouth kicked up. "Both your brothers faced their demons and came out happier for it. You have to be wondering what happens if you don't."

"Hey. Kittredge. Mind your own business." Brady laughed while he said that, but he wasn't sure he was kidding. "You want to sit here and talk about your problems?"

"I deal with my problems," Riley replied, something not quite a smile playing in the corner of his mouth. "I see my problems on the street all the time. There's no need to talk about my problems, because they're probably sitting at the next table, having a few beers."

"I don't know which is worse."

This time, Riley really did smile. But there was nothing nice in it. "I do."

Brady told himself he hadn't been watching, or waiting, but he noticed the second Amanda detached herself from her group of friends and headed toward the back of the saloon in the direction of the bathrooms. He should have let her go. He should have used it as an opportunity *not* to follow her. *Not* to invite speculation.

Brady waited maybe three seconds, then excused himself.

It was ridiculous. It was lunacy, in fact. He was begging for trouble—

But it didn't matter. The bathrooms of the saloon were in a small hallway in back, but the hallway then curved around toward the kitchen. A person could go around that corner and keep out of sight of anyone else who came back here.

Brady caught up to Amanda easily. Too easily. She had her hand on the door to the women's room, but he helped himself to a sturdy grip on her elbow.

She jolted as she looked up at him, but she didn't jerk away, so he propelled her farther along the hall. Then safely around the corner.

"Careful," she said, glaring up at him when he backed her into the wall. "I wouldn't want you to get a headache. I left my aspirin at home."

"What did you want me to say?" And like that, any lie he might have been telling himself about how he hadn't been primed for exactly this fight—since the moment he'd looked up and seen her—fled. "This is supposed to be a secret, remember?"

"I remember. Believe me, I remember."

"That's what we agreed, Amanda. Do we need to have a broader discussion about boundaries? Expectations?"

He knew they did. Why was he asking instead of telling her what she needed to know?

Because you think it will crush her, something in him said, very distinctly. *And that will crush you.*

"I don't know," she shot back at him. "Do we? Do you actually know what boundaries are?"

She wasn't cringing, there with her back against the wall. Not his Amanda. She glared. And then she surged forward and thumped a finger into his chest.

Because she had absolutely no fear of him. Something he thought he should probably celebrate, but not now. Not right now.

"You're the one who chased me back here, Brady. Why did you do that? Do you need me to break down how this thing between us works? You show up at my door. We pretend you don't. Sometimes we talk on the phone, but we don't admit that. And we *certainly* don't act like we know each other as anything more than distant family friends when we see each other in public." But the temper drained away somewhere in that last sentence. "That would be a disaster, obviously."

Brady wanted to hold her, soothe her, make it better—and that only made him angry.

"Two of your brothers are out there tonight, Amanda. I was sitting at a table with them. Did you miss that?"

"I'm not afraid of them. I thought you weren't either."

He wanted to punch a few holes in the wall. In case he needed reminders of whose son he was. "I'm not afraid of your brothers. The same way I'm not particularly afraid of elk or bears, but I wouldn't lie down and let them trample me or eat me for dinner either."

"I get it," Amanda said, in a small voice that announced

that she did not, in fact, get it. "Believe me, I get it. I'm fully aware this is what we agreed." The way she looked at him made his chest hurt. "I guess I wasn't prepared to watch you lie about it, that's all."

"I didn't lie about anything. Directly."

But as he said that, it dawned on him that he'd lied to Becca. And to Gray. Making this a third lie, and him a whole lot further down that slippery slope than he wanted to admit.

And Amanda knew it. How did she know it when he didn't?

"Oh, come on," she said, her eyes a bright gold while she looked straight through him. "Don't lie to *me*, Brady."

He was filled with things he didn't understand. Frustration. Need. A kind of fear. A very deep panic. And threaded through all of it, holding it together and making it hurt all the more was that particular intensity that he'd only ever felt about this one woman.

He couldn't name it.

He *refused* to name it.

Brady didn't know how long they stood there like that, entirely too close in a tiny spit of a hallway, only steps away from where most of their friends and too many members of her family waited.

He didn't know how long they stood like that, so close. So connected, though they were only *almost* touching.

It felt like a kiss, though his mouth wasn't on hers. It was that deep. That all-consuming. It was ripe with all the things that passed between them, that swirled around them. Knowledge and acceptance, resignation and something else. Something far more permanent than he was prepared to admit.

"Amanda . . ."

"Careful, Brady," she whispered, though her voice had a catch in it. "We're in public. Someone might hear. Someone might know. You might have to mean it."

Then she ducked under his arm and walked away, her back straight and tall.

He needed to let her go. He knew that.

But that didn't prevent him from driving across the river later that night. Or from hiding his truck a ways up the hill, deep in the trees, then picking his way back down to her building.

It didn't keep him from making her sob for him, or burying himself in her with a ferocity that bordered on sheer, dizzying panic.

He had to let her go.

Brady told himself that again and again as he watched her sleep hours later, curled up in a ball with her hands beneath her cheek, and a faint frown marring the perfection of her face.

He was betraying his friends. He was betraying himself. He was betraying her too, by making her sneak around. When any man in his right mind would be nothing but proud to let the whole world know he was with a woman like her.

You need to let her go, he growled at himself.

Because Amanda was the kind of woman a wise man married.

But Brady wasn't the marrying kind.

That was the beginning and the end of everything.

A few days later, he saddled up his favorite horse and rode out to the land he'd finally claimed as his. He rode the perimeter, explored the acreage, imagining the things he could do with it. He camped, out there in the cold rush of fall, between snowstorms. And when he looked up at the brooding mountains that kept him company out there, he didn't lie. He didn't pretend the land wasn't in him, deep.

Out there, there was nothing but wind and fields, and the Rockies standing tall, telling tales of endurance. Of stability. Of the profound beauty in simple survival.

He woke in the frigid mornings and coaxed the fire to life, then sat there as the sun poked its head over the eastern range. The rays of light danced over the valley, gilding all of it from field to cattle, river to ranch.

This land he'd been given at birth. This land he'd chosen now.

The cold sun made things clear. At last.

Amanda might not know her future, but Brady did. She was going to settle down. She was going to stay right here in Cold River, with that beautiful smile and those dreamy golden eyes, because this was where she belonged. The only reason she'd looked his way was because he'd decided years ago that he didn't belong here too. That he was better off in the city.

She'd chosen him to educate her because he was never meant to be anything but a fling. And better still, one with an expiration date, because everyone knew Brady Everett was going to keep his year-long promise to his brother, then leave again.

But now everything was different. Because now he was staying.

Which meant he needed to cut her loose.

Because if he didn't, if he held onto her when he knew better, sooner or later he was going to break her heart. Break her heart, crush her spirit, ruin her. He was already well on his way.

And if he knew all that and did it anyway? Then he really would be no better than his father.

He and his brothers all had a bit of Amos in them. They'd all been infected with that poison early on. But then, that was the Everett way. They lived out here, drowning in the elements, and it left them feral. More than a little mean. And very often horrifically drunk to boot. Accordingly, they often took it out on those closest to them. It was a tale as old as the pioneers who'd claimed these fields in the first place.

But he thought about what Riley had said in the Broken Wheel. That Gray and Ty had fought their demons and won.

Brady had every intention of doing the same thing.

He could live for the land like his ancestors always had, out here where loneliness was as much a part of the landscape as the snow in the mountains. He could find new ways to love, and he could love things that he couldn't wound. The land would never love him back, and that meant he couldn't poison it slowly, or bruise it, or destroy it. It would outlast him.

There was a freedom in that. A stark sort of joy.

He could do these things for Amanda, if not for himself. Brady vowed he would.

No matter how much it hurt.

16

Amanda woke up Halloween morning to find Brady still sprawled out in her bed.

That had never happened before.

She'd seen him almost every night this month, except when he'd been out camping, and he never, ever stayed over. That hadn't surprised her. She assured herself it was because he needed to get back home for that four thirty start of the typical ranch morning.

And maybe for other reasons, but that was the one she clung to.

Amanda sat up, her toes curling a little as the movement reminded her of the things they'd done in this bed last night. The things they'd done all over this apartment.

The things she would have done in the back hall of the Broken Wheel Saloon, even though her feelings had been hurt. And despite the fact her brothers and friends could easily have caught them.

Kat had asked her what had taken her so long, and Amanda had still been all riled up and reckless. She'd almost answered the question honestly. Almost.

But Amanda knew perfectly well that what happened

between Brady and her had to stay a secret. Or anyway, she'd agreed that it would.

What she knew and what she felt didn't necessarily match.

She'd accepted that.

Because she was in love with him, and she didn't know how to change that. She didn't *want* to change it.

Surely love made the wild pleasure that he could wring out of her, over and over again, that much better— whether she told him how she felt or not.

He made her blush. He made her sob. He made her wanton and wicked, and she loved it. She loved him.

But she still wasn't foolish enough to say it out loud.

This morning he was still here, so Amanda took the opportunity to study him as he lay there beside her, one arm tossed up over his head and his eyes shut tight. This never happened either. She didn't get the opportunity to stare at Brady as much as she liked, without him witnessing it. He'd kicked off the covers on his side of the bed, which suited her fine.

Because he was perfect.

She tried to resist, but gave in almost before the thought was fully formed in her head. Amanda reached over and carefully traced that mouth of his, stern and soft at once as he slept. His jaw was rough, darkened overnight, and it amazed her how much she liked the contrast.

Amanda trailed her fingers down his chest, liking the roughness mixed with the smooth. Liking everything about him. She wanted to shout her love for him to the whole world. She wanted to claim all this as hers.

She loved him so much, it actually hurt, and maybe

she liked the hurt too, because here she was. Still. And when he'd showed up at her door after that painful little scene in the saloon hallway, it hadn't occurred to her to do anything but let him in.

You can start yelling about how much you love him, she told herself, *or you can find another way to entertain yourself.*

Amanda chose the second option. Especially when looking at him already made her feel overheated and melty. She crawled over him, exulting in the heat he gave off and the small sound he made. Then she let her mouth follow the same trail her fingers had made, tasting him as she went.

Salt. Man.

Brady.

By the time she got to that fascinating *V* cut into his low abdomen that she liked to trace with her fingers— and now got to taste—she was shivering with her own excitement.

Especially when she saw that at least one part of him was already awake, and just as interested in what she was doing as she was.

He'd let her taste him there, but only a little. Only on the way to other things. And all those other things had made her dizzy with delight, so she had been happily distracted.

But there was light coming in her windows and he was still here. There was nothing to distract her now.

Amanda arranged herself there between his legs, her gaze on the most fascinating, most unapologetically male part of him. She flicked a glance up, and with a jolt, found him watching her.

His dark green eyes were at a lazy half-mast. He didn't tell her to stop. Instead, he grew harder as she watched.

So she did what she'd wanted to do since the first night. She tilted herself forward and took him deep in her mouth.

This was better. This was perfect. Because she could hardly cry out that she loved him when her mouth was full of him, could she?

Instead, she told him with her tongue.

Again and again, until she was shuddering, she liked the taste of him so much.

Slowly, with a deep groan she could feel as well as hear, he began to move with her. Lifting his hips, then dropping them at her pace, until she found it hard to tell the difference between them. What she was doing, what he was.

Only that it was all still so perfect.

His fingers sunk deep into the morning mess of her hair, and she liked that too. Even when he got more and more tense, and she thought he might try to pull her off of him. She didn't want that, so she wrapped her arms around his hips and held on.

And she felt it when Brady let go.

Then everything was the thrust, the heat. Her hands and her mouth. And when he surrendered completely, flooding her mouth with salt, she found herself shuddering straight over the edge too.

It felt like a magic trick.

"You're killing me," Brady growled.

The way he often did. Though he always lived.

He jackknifed up from the bed, pulling her behind him. Then he took her into her shower, made everything steamy, and taught her a few new tricks to match.

That was why it wasn't until she'd made them both coffee that she noticed there was a certain grim cast to his face when he looked at her. A kind of unnerving resolve.

"Are you okay?" she asked. Brady studied her for a moment, but didn't say anything, so she blundered ahead. "I know it's been a year since your father died. Today."

It shocked her how much time she could spend writhing around with him naked, shameless and filled with light and heat and joy, only to plummet straight back into awkwardness at moments like this.

"Yes," Brady said after a moment that seemed to drag on far too long, his face unreadable. "It's been a year."

"How did you hear that he was gone?"

He looked faintly startled. Then he frowned down at the coffee mug in his hands. And she didn't think he was going to tell her.

"It was a weird time for Gray to be calling me," Brady finally said, surprising her. "These days, he's in touch all the time about ranch things, but back then, he didn't really call me at all. The last time he had was when Ty got stomped by that bull. I guess I already knew something was wrong."

He blinked, and Amanda didn't think he'd keep going.

But he did. "It had been a normal morning. I'd gone to the gym for my usual five a.m. class. I'd checked in with one of my partners about a deal. I was looking forward to a few good hours alone in my office to work up a couple of proposals. And then everything changed."

Amanda made a soft noise of commiseration.

Brady shook his head. "He was dead. He'd gone out to the barn, and he hadn't come in. I got in my car and started driving. I don't think I really believed it, though.

Amos was always much larger and meaner than life. I'm not sure the reality hit me until I was actually driving down from the mountains into Cold River. Maybe not until his funeral."

Amanda didn't say anything. She reached across the counter and slid her hand over his.

"No one's ever asked me that before," he said.

She didn't think she was imagining the way he looked at her, as if she was precious to him. As if all of this was precious.

As if it was much, much more than a little education between friends.

Then again, maybe that was wishful thinking.

"I'm sorry to hear that." She toyed with each one of his fingers, tracing the lines between them, and ignoring the voices clamoring inside her. "I'm sorry you were alone."

"I wasn't alone. I came back as soon as I heard. Obviously Gray and Becca were already here, and Ty showed up not long after."

Amanda caught his gaze and held it. "That's not the kind of news you should get when you're alone."

Brady looked back at her, then, the way he had a thousand times now, but this time, everything changed.

They were still sitting at her counter. Her hands were still on his. But his gaze was dark green, and troubled, and something in her thudded.

Long. Low.

And she would have sworn the same thing drummed deep in him.

She couldn't recognize the look on his face when he drew his hand away. She didn't see the man she knew in the way he looked away briefly, swallowing hard.

Amanda suddenly felt cold, as if there were a draft in her walls and the frosty fall morning was getting in. Her bones ached, and a terrible sort of weight rolled through her—but she would not break down into sobs. Not here. Not now.

"Get dressed," Brady said, in a low voice that gave nothing away. "I want to show you something."

Amanda didn't know if it was foreboding or something else that kept her quiet, only that she couldn't seem to form the words to argue. Whatever it was, she went and dressed, then took a little extra time with her hair. She threw in a few extra curls, because she was never going to be Hannah, but that didn't mean she couldn't make an effort. Or an entrance, however small.

When she came back out of the bathroom, Brady was waiting there at the counter, every inch of him the cowboy he'd always been to her.

Oh sure, he'd spent those years down in Denver, but that didn't make him a city slicker. No matter how hard he tried.

He was too comfortable with that Stetson, and the look on his face was so familiar to her that it might as well be part of the view. A part of Cold River itself and the land that marked them all. It was there on his brow. In the line of his jaw.

She wondered if the world would always stop the way it did when he shifted that gaze to her.

"Ready?"

"As ready as I can be to go off on a secret excursion that doesn't seem to making you very happy."

"Have you always been this mouthy?" Brady asked, and she felt better, then. Because there was a hint of the heat she preferred in his gaze. And that curve to his lips. "Or is this a recent thing?"

"I've always been me, if that's what you mean. It's not my fault you've been walking around with blinders on for years."

"You mean when you were legitimately and legally underage? Those blinders?"

"I haven't been underage in years." She sniffed. "Though I do wonder why it is everybody is so afraid to get in a fight with my brothers when to my knowledge, they don't get in fights at all. With anyone. They talk about it, sure, but any actual fighting? Never."

"That's called being a man," Brady informed her, with great male arrogance. "If you run around getting in fights all the time, you're a punk. If you don't have to fight because you can intimidate other men into behaving themselves simply by standing there, you win."

"You could also try not standing around, exuding violence."

"You grew up on a ranch." Brady shook his head at her, though his mouth was still curved in one corner. "You know how male animals act. Don't be so surprised that humans are the same."

"I like to think humans are little bit better than farm animals, what with their big brains and stuff. Don't you?"

"I don't know." Brady's voice was darker, then. And the light in his eyes faded. "I'd like to believe that too, but there's not a lot of evidence for that, is there? Look around."

"I'm looking."

But she was staring straight at him, and she could tell he didn't like that. He pushed away from the counter and nodded toward the door. "Let's go."

You have to stop assuming that everything is on the brink of disaster, Amanda lectured herself as she followed him down the stairs outside into the shock of a bright Halloween morning, so cold that breathing in made her nose hurt.

But she was more focused on her heart. It was going a little crazy in her chest, and she was definitely holding her breath more than she should. And as much as she tried to tell herself it was because they were outside, in the daylight, daring anyone to happen by and notice them together here behind the Coyote, she was pretty sure her reaction had to do with the way Brady was holding himself. Tense and unhappy.

He never parked his truck out back because that would be as obvious as taking out an ad in the Longhorn Valley Tribune, so they had to hike it. Amanda was glad she hadn't gone with her first instinct and put on the heels she wore to tend bar. Because it was a steep walk. And when wearing appropriate shoes like the ones she had on now, Amanda loved hiking. She loved climbing up towering things and tough hills to see what she could see from on top. She liked the peaceful trails that wound through the woods, the comforting cover of the trees standing tall around her, and the long shadows that whispered secrets and solitude.

Even today.

She climbed into the passenger seat, belted herself in, and sat there in that charged silence as Brady navigated his way out of the woods, back down to the road.

"I don't understand why you didn't have to go back to the ranch this morning," she said when she couldn't take it any longer. "I thought that was the deal you made. Every morning, without fail. Or Gray wins."

"I told him I wouldn't be around this morning. It's fine."

"You say that like I don't know your brothers. But I do."

"They've backed off lately." He flicked a look at her, then returned his attention to the road. "It won't last, so I'm taking advantage of it while I can."

Amanda puzzled over that as he drove across the bridge into town. That didn't sound like the Everett brothers she knew. But she didn't have time to really parse it through because Brady wasn't heading toward any of the places she thought he might go. He didn't take her to Mary Jo's Diner. Or Cold River Coffee.

Instead, he turned down the street that led toward the courthouse. Then he kept going, winding around to a set of old barns and storage warehouses that had been used for a variety of different things over the past century or so, right there on the river. He pulled up in front of one and turned off his engine. It was a dark, weathered wood that looked inviting against the backdrop of trees that had been blazing gold earlier this fall.

Amanda had always loved these barns. They were a short walk from Main Street and had once been another bustling part of town. But she doubted very much that Brady would be so tense if he were taking her on a historic Cold River barn tour.

"This is beginning to feel like the opening of a horror movie," she pointed out, trying to keep her voice light. "Deserted barns in a lonely part of town on Halloween . . . Can homicidal maniacs be far behind?"

"Come on," Brady said, not responding to the horror movie crack. Which was worrisome. "I want to show you something."

"That doesn't make it better."

He was already climbing out of the truck, so she followed. He walked over and opened the door, then ushered her inside. It took her a minute to get her bearings. Because she'd always thought of the buildings down here as falling apart, or at least *historic* in the sense of being untouched for decades. But the shadowed interior they walked into didn't smell like dust or disuse.

Brady flicked on some lights, another surprise. It turned out the barn was spacious and clean, as someone had taken the trouble to convert it from whatever it had been before to a lovely open space. Those weren't holes in the roof up above, letting the light in. They were skylights. There were windows with darling shutters closed tight. And the great big barn doors on rollers that looked as if they'd been recently restored and finished.

Amanda forgot about how oddly Brady was behaving and took a few more steps inside. Barns made her happy. She liked them full of clever, spirited horses, but barring that, a repurposed barn got her all daydreamy. And this one didn't smell like hay or livestock. It didn't look like a lot of grubby work. It could so easily be something else. Something more in line with all those half-formed dreams of hers.

She sighed happily. "What is this place?"

"I've spent years thinking about what I would do if I ever had the opportunity to truly diversify Cold River Ranch," Brady said. She looked back over her shoulder, and he was still standing there by the door, but he wasn't looking around the barn. He was looking straight at her. "A few years ago, after Amos was a shade less hideous during Christmas than usual, I bought this place. I don't know what I thought I would do with it, but I liked the idea that I had an investment in the town. And over the past year, I've been very slowly refurbishing it."

"How could you do that without anyone knowing?"

"I didn't want anyone to know."

"You mean you didn't want Gray or Ty to know." But she couldn't get worked up about the level of subterfuge that must have required, or the fact he hadn't told her either. The space was too pretty. She smiled at him. "I'll be honest, I'm surprised you thought about Cold River or your ranch at all while you were in the city. I'm going to remember that in December when you go back again."

It cost her something to say that at all, much less in that cheerful way. The very idea made her want to double over and wail. But she did it.

Brady stared back at her. He did not smile in return.

"Gray and Ty have finally agreed to let me run wild and do whatever I want with a piece of the ranch," Brady said. Or really, threw down into the space between them. "I'm not leaving in December. If I'm going to make it work, I'll be here a good, long while."

There was too much noise in her head and her pulse was too fast and she didn't believe it. She couldn't have heard that right. It was too close to exactly what she wanted.

"You're diversifying the ranch into a barn in town?" she asked. Very carefully, because that didn't sound right and it was important she understand.

"It's yours."

That made even less sense. "Mine?"

Brady's gaze was darker than usual. Much darker. "You should open your farm stand, Amanda. Here."

"But . . ." She didn't know what she was protesting, so she stopped.

"You're wasting your time at the Coyote. And I don't think you want to spend the rest of your life at Cold River Coffee."

"I love Cold River Coffee."

"You have great ideas, and better still, you didn't come here from somewhere else to try to inflict them on people. You're a hometown girl, and people like that. You'll convince them to sell their things through you, and it will be everything you wanted it to be. A celebration of Cold River. Isn't that what you called it?"

Her pulse was still going wild and this didn't feel right, not when he was looking at her like they were at the scene of an accident. "Wait. You want to give me a barn? Because you don't like that I bartend?"

Brady blew out a breath, but the intensity of his stare didn't change at all.

"I'm giving you a barn because I want you to have the life you deserve. The life you dream about. You think you have to throw yourself into making mistakes for that happen. But you don't." And his voice got ragged, then. "You shouldn't waste yourself, Amanda."

There was sunlight beaming down from above, but it seemed far away. And all the sunshine in the world couldn't change the look on Brady's face. Or the way it ricocheted inside Amanda's chest. And hurt where it hit.

Her mouth was too dry. "This is starting to seem less about my desire to sell artisan jams made by my friend's mother and a little more about you."

The panicked dryness in her mouth turned into a matching tightness in her throat when he looked away. And a hard knot in her belly when he returned that dark gaze of his to her.

"You're the kind of woman a man dreams of marrying," Brady said, and he sounded . . . desolate. "If a man dreams of marrying, that is."

And she got it then.

Like a kick to the stomach.

"Let me guess." Her own voice sounded fuzzy, and she couldn't tell if she was hearing all that dryness or if the noise in her head was so loud, it was tricking her into thinking she sounded like that. Of course, none of that mattered. Not when her heart was breaking. "That's not you."

"That's never going to be me, Amanda." Brady didn't look away. He didn't relent. "I'm never going to be that man. I couldn't if I tried."

17

Amanda was holding herself very, very still. She felt brittle, like another blast of the air from outside might crack her into pieces. And she didn't know which hurt more, the tightness in her throat or the brick in her belly. Maybe neither one mattered.

Not when he was looking at her like that, his words still hanging there between them. With a finality that she was afraid might actually wreck her.

She tried to clear her throat. "Am I supposed to be distracted from the fact you're breaking up with me because you're dangling a barn over my head? Like a carrot?"

"I'm not breaking up with you. You can't break up with someone when you're not together." His gaze seemed even darker then, when that shouldn't have been possible. "You asked me to perform a service, and I did that. And now this has to end."

"Why now?" Her heart was beating so hard, it was alarming. She was afraid it would burst straight out of her chest. It took her a moment to realize that it wasn't a sob trapped in there this time. It was temper. "You don't suppose it has anything to do with it being the one-year anniversary of your father's death, do you?"

"Maybe it does."

That was a surprise. Brady crossed his arms and leaned back against the wall, though she hoped he didn't think he was fooling her into imagining that he was relaxed.

"I've had a lot of time to think about my old man and the actual legacy he left behind him." Brady's jaw worked, and it seemed like a lifetime ago that she'd sat in her bed and run her fingers over the breathtaking line of it, consumed with how best to love him. "It seemed like Gray and Ty worked it all out. But I'm not like them. I never have been. My father spent most of his time trying to beat them down, but he didn't waste his time on me. I know why, now. Some people are irredeemable. He was one. I'm another."

"I don't believe anyone is irredeemable, Brady. Especially not you."

"You're my best friend's little sister." Brady bit off the words like they were the kind of curse that led to the homicidal maniacs she'd mentioned earlier. "I was sitting at a table with him the other night, and all I could think about was you."

"You might think that's a bad thing, but I don't."

His eyes blazed. "It's only a matter of time before sneaking off in a crowded bar like we did at the Broken Wheel gets noticed. And then what?"

"I'm not the one who wants to sneak around, Brady. I don't care if they know."

"This can never last." His eyes blazed again, but it was a cold fire. "You need to understand that. You can't date me. Even if I dated, which I don't, it couldn't be you."

If she let it, that would knock her over. She concentrated on that kick of temper inside her instead. "Because you're obsessed with my brothers. I have to admit, I expected better from you. Like maybe you'd address the real issue."

"That is the real issue. Your family trusts me. And I betrayed them. I have to live with that."

"Which is it? First, it was that I'm the marrying kind, which is apparently a bad thing. Now, it's something to do with my family's trust. They can't both be true. Here's another possibility. You're afraid."

"You're not making this any easier." He jerked away from the wall then, slashing a hand through the air, like that could keep her quiet. "I'm trying to give you options, Amanda. You're a great—"

"If you say anything even remotely like 'you're a great kid, Amanda,' I won't be held responsible for my actions. I'm serious, Brady."

That seemed to reach him. He readjusted his hat, then ran the same hand over his jaw. She liked the notion that she wasn't the only unsteady one here.

He tried again. "You know as well as I do that people have to make their own way in a town like this. It's that or they leave. Because there are only so many jobs in this valley and most of them suck." Brady wasn't precisely frowning at her, but that sure wasn't a smile either. "I want to help you, that's all."

Amanda snorted. In a manner that would have horrified her mother. "Please. You want to buy me off. I guess you're lucky I'm the kind of girl who likes barns instead of sports cars. *That* would give the whole thing away. A sports car has *sugar daddy* written all over it."

He muttered something, not entirely beneath his breath.

She kept going. "But it's going to be hard to explain this too. Don't you think it's going to look a little weird that of all the girls in Cold River, you decided to give *me* a big old barn?"

"You're a friend of the family."

"Brady. They're all going to know." She waved her finger in a lazy sort of loop to encompass everything from the beams up high to the weathered wood floorboards at their feet. "You might as well paint *Brady Everett took Amanda Kittredge's virginity* on the side of the barn for the whole town to read."

His jaw was set hard enough to shatter. "That should never have happened."

"It did happen. It was a wonder. And you don't get to pretend otherwise just because you've had an attack of your overactive guilty conscience."

"If my conscience was involved, none of this would ever have happened."

"That seems awfully convenient," she threw at him. "Too bad you don't get to wave your magic wand and make it all go away."

"This was never supposed to be a thing, Amanda. We agreed."

She hated to admit that he was right. "We did."

"So maybe you can tell me why you're acting like I got you pregnant and tossed you out of a moving vehicle."

She knew better. She knew there was one thing he would want to hear even less than all of this. She'd been biting it back all month.

But he was staying.

He was staying, and he was ending things, and how was she supposed to handle that? Was she going to have to run away from him for the rest of her life? She had a vague memory of standing there at the homecoming game, talking blithely about walks of shame and awkward silences in grocery store lines.

She'd imagined it would be fun. Like the aftermath of a game of Cards Against Humanity.

Not the probability that she would watch Brady go out of his way to pretend he didn't see her. Or act like he'd never touched her.

Shame and awkwardness have never appealed to me, Kat had said then.

Why hadn't Amanda listened? Why didn't Amanda ever *listen*?

But imagining a hideously embarrassing grocery store line set something loose inside her in a terrible tidal wave. She was already losing everything. She was already going to have to live with that. He looked about as moveable as the mountains outside.

Why not put all her cards on the table? If he was rejecting her, he should know exactly what he was rejecting. Not only her body, but her heart.

"You're a smart guy," she managed to say, and part of her liked the way his scowl deepened at that. "You always have been. I'm sure it hasn't escaped your notice that I'm completely in love with you."

It was so quiet then, so still. Amanda was sure she could hear the river outside. At least it was moving, unlike Brady, who she was pretty sure had turned to stone.

"Head over heels in love," she clarified. "With you, Brady."

He looked grim. "Maybe you think you are."

"I know I am."

She hated the way he sighed, then. *Hated* it.

"This is part of the problem, Amanda," he said, and he sounded much too calm. Too removed and distant. "This is what happens when you decide to get rid of your virginity with a guy you hardly know."

"You're a friend of the family."

His dark green eyes narrowed at the echo of his own words, but he didn't back down. Instead, he shook his head. Sadly. Pityingly, even, and she wanted to kill him.

"You don't know any better. I get that. Sex isn't love."

"Of course I know better," she retorted, stung. "It's why I didn't have sex with anyone else."

His jaw was a rock again. "You didn't have sex with anybody else because your brothers would kill anyone dumb enough to go near you."

Amanda made a noise of pure frustration. "They would have to turn up at the house and ask me on a date in front of my entire family for my brothers to know they existed. And no high school kid is going to do something like that. But do you really think I couldn't have snuck off into the woods and dealt with things in the back of a pickup truck like everyone else does around here? I didn't want to. I chose not to." She leaned in a little closer to emphasize her point. "I picked *you*, Brady. And do you want to know why?"

"I absolutely do not."

"Because I've had a thing about you for as long as I can remember. Because you were always around. Because you were in my house, and *not* one of my brothers. Because you really are smart. Fascinating, even. And you didn't settle down into the family business out of obligation like a lot of people would have. You went to college. Now you're back and you still want to do things your own way. I like it."

He looked as if he wanted to say something, so she waited, but he didn't speak. Storms moved over his face, but he stayed where he was.

She'd already gone this far. Why not keep going?

"You were different then and you're different now," she told him. "Because while you certainly didn't notice me back then, you didn't tease me or mock me either. And every time you were nice to me, I called it a Brady moment."

He muttered something again that she was glad she couldn't hear.

"A Brady moment," he repeated, as if it *hurt* him. "Amanda—"

"But then one day, you looked at me like I was a woman. An actual woman. Because I was wearing a skimpy tank top and serving drinks in a sketchy bar. And I didn't want to go back from that." She lifted her hands but let them drop again, because she couldn't start begging. Not quite. Not yet. "So I chose you. And it was even better than I imagined."

"You have to stop."

"I'm not going to stop. You're the one who came back, Brady. You're the one who always came back. And not because you were broken, like Ty. Not because you didn't want any other path, like Gray. You *chose* to come home. You chose to subject yourself to your father. And when Gray asked, you chose to stay here all year and do what he wanted rather than what you wanted. I could love you for that alone."

"Says the girl who left the family ranch herself," Brady gritted out at her, as if he was fighting a mortal wound.

She couldn't help but hope he was. And that it matched hers.

"I wanted a taste of independence, sure. But I was never going to leave this valley. And not because I can't imagine a way out, because I can. I have. But because I love it here. And guess what, Brady? So do you."

He started a little, like he was waking up and was surprised to find himself here. She flattered herself that he looked even more unsteady than he had before when he scowled at her again.

"I knew you wouldn't take this well," he growled at her. "But I promised you when we started that I wouldn't disappear when this was done. I promised I would have this conversation."

"You love this town, Brady," Amanda said with a deep conviction she hadn't realized was in there, but wasn't surprised to hear come out of her like that. As if a part of her had always known. "You love your land, and you love your brothers, and you love my brothers too. And deep down, where you're too afraid to look, I think you love me too."

He stared back at her, and it was funny how what swelled inside her then wasn't insecurity. She didn't *wonder* if he loved her. She knew.

But it had never occurred to her that loving someone might not matter. That it might not be enough.

"I don't." And his voice was as stark as his gaze was dark, and it made her want to cry. "I can't."

"Why can't you?"

"Everything about you is bright, happy, new." And he moved then, closing the distance between them and pulling her into his arms with a rough sort of urgency. "But I know the darkness that's in me. I used to sit out there, all alone on that rock by the river, and wonder how it would come out in me. Would I beat my children? Would I lose myself in the bottle? Would I terrorize my wife? I made a promise to myself a long time ago that I would avoid having to answer those questions."

"You drink all the time," she pointed out, over the lump in her throat. "Somehow you've managed not to become a mean, bitter old drunk. Probably because you're not one."

Brady shook his head. "You weren't there when I tested that theory in college, Amanda. These days I don't *have* to drink. I like it every now and again. As long as I'm in control." His fingers pressed into her arms, and she liked it. She liked the connection. The heat. "But you're already too much for me."

She wanted to touch him too, but was afraid that would make him let go of her. "Is that a bad thing?"

"I think about you all the time. I want to be with you all the time. You make me forget promises I made to myself. I can't start down that road. I already know where it ends."

"Why are your brothers allowed to be happy, but you're not?"

"Don't act like they didn't pay the price. Gray's first wife almost destroyed him. Ty is lucky he can walk, much less remember anything that happened before that bull took him out." Brady's gaze was nearly black as it searched her face. "I'm not willing to sacrifice you. I'm not willing to see how badly you can be hurt because I can't bring myself to let you go the way I know I should."

"Why is that your decision? What about what I want?"

"Amanda. Take the barn. Make all your dreams come true. You say you love me? Love me that way."

"I want your heart, Brady. Not a barn."

"A barn is all I can give you," he said, and the darkness in his voice broke her heart all over again. "I didn't expect to stay here, Amanda. I never thought that Gray and Ty would agree to let me do my own thing. I assumed it would be all or nothing, because that's the way it always has been. I never would have started anything with you otherwise."

That was like a spike to the heart.

Even if, way back, she might have told herself the same thing. That he was a man who wouldn't stay and that made him an excellent set of training wheels.

She'd really believed that, hard as it was to imagine now.

"Is this you being noble?" she managed to ask, past the overwhelming urge to either break down into sobs or punch him. Preferably both. "I can have a farm stand, built on the ashes of this thing between us. Which for some reason can't continue because of your father. Your dead father. Is that about it?"

"I get that you're tired of everybody telling you that you don't know enough to make decisions about your own life," Brady began.

"You're right. I am."

"But I know me better than you do. And chemistry like ours is never going to lead to anything good."

Somehow, of all the blows today, that was the worst.

"Because you've had this kind of off-the-chart chemistry before? Is this always how it is for you?"

She could tell, as he stared down at her, that he wanted

to tell her that it was normal. That it was everyday. But a muscle flexed in his jaw. And his eyes burned.

"I go out of my way to make sure I don't let anything get this intense." He sounded furious. Oddly, that made her feel a little bit better. "It's too much, Amanda. It has to stop. Because you know what happens if it doesn't? Broken bottles. Broken furniture. Kids with black eyes. It's a disaster waiting to happen."

"I don't think it's a disaster at all," she whispered. "But even if it is . . . why can't we be a disaster together?"

"No."

That was when she really did cry, terrible, silent tears tracing down her cheeks, because he wasn't looking at her as if he didn't love her. As cruel as that might have been, it would have been easier. Instead, he looked tortured, and they were both hurting, and there was nothing she could do about any of it.

"I love you," she told him helplessly.

"You'll get over it." But he smoothed her hair back from her face as he said it. And he tried to wipe away her tears, but they kept coming. "You're going to meet a good guy. You're going to settle down, have a few kids, here in town or out on Bar K land somewhere. He's going to treat you right. You're going to have a nice life, I promise."

"You're making that sound about as appealing as ending up alone, with cats, like Harriet Barnett. Who will sooner or later turn into Miss Patrick, and you know it."

"Then I'm telling it wrong. You're going to be happy. That's what I'm trying to say. You and me? Sneaking around? Lying to your brothers? How's that going to end?" His thumbs moved beneath her eyes again and came away wet. And he might have sounded gentle, but there was steel in it. "I'll tell you how. Badly."

"Then we'll stop sneaking around. We'll tell them; they'll scream and yell the way they always do, and then it will be fine. Because it's always fine. Because they don't actually hate you, and they're going to have to accept that I'm a grown woman sooner or later—"

"But they don't have to accept that it's me." There was an awful finality in his voice. "It's never going to be me."

"It's only you," she retorted, desperate. "Only and ever you."

"I'm going to dance at your wedding, Amanda," he said, like he was making a vow. "I'm looking forward to it."

That was so ridiculous, so hurtful and hilarious at once, that she let out a sound that was as much a laugh as it was a sob. Or maybe it was a scream. And she couldn't help herself. She surged forward, kissing him like it was the last time.

Because he kept saying that it was.

And it was all that wild heat, and sweet too. It was all the promises he'd made her, and the sound of his laughter, and how stunned he always looked when she smiled at him.

It was his talented hands all over her body, and the things he did with his mouth.

He kissed her back, and it was a vow and it was a farewell, and she wasn't sure if she was going to survive it—

Brady pulled away and scowled down at her. Again.

"That's it." He sounded like he was telling himself. "We're done."

"You keep saying that," Amanda whispered. "But I don't think it's going to change anything."

"What the hell is going on here?"

Amanda blinked, then half turned to the familiar

voice—though it was louder and angrier than she'd heard it in a long time. Brady started to turn as well.

Because it was Riley.

Right there in the barn with them.

With murder all over his face.

"Why is my sister crying, Brady?" he demanded. "Why are you *touching* my sister?"

Brady dropped his hands. "I can explain—"

"Riley, wait—" Amanda began.

But it was too late.

Riley moved closer, and Amanda had never really paid attention to how *big* he was. She did now.

"Riley—" she tried again.

But it was happening too fast. Riley shoved Brady back away from Amanda, with a hard hand to his shoulder.

Then he slammed his other fist directly into Brady's face.

18

It was every bit as bad as Brady had anticipated.

Worse.

He'd never seen a look like that on his best friend's face. And certainly not aimed at him. Riley stood there, disgust and betrayal all over him as he scowled down at Brady. At Brady sprawled out on the floor, laid out but good.

It didn't occur to him to put up a fight.

All Brady could muster the energy to do was check to see if his nose was broken. It wasn't, though it hurt. And he could feel his eye getting puffy. He figured he'd have a shiner for the foreseeable future.

He couldn't help thinking he was getting off easy.

"Are you out of your mind?" Amanda yelled. She shoved at Riley's arm. "You just punched your best friend in the face!"

"Why were you kissing him?" Riley shouted right back. "How long have you been sneaking around with him? Is that why you moved out of Mom and Dad's house?"

The look he threw at Brady then was homicidal.

"No," Brady said, and took a moment to make sure

none of his teeth were loose. Brady hadn't expected he'd ever find himself in a position to confirm that yes, his possibly former best friend had a punch like a sledge-hammer, as rumored. "I had nothing to do with that."

"You don't have the right to ask either one of us those questions," Amanda snapped. She shoved at her brother again. Riley didn't move, but that didn't stop her. If anything, she went harder. "None of this is your business, Riley. When I want your advice about my romantic life, you'll know. Because I'll ask. Which will never happen, because it's not like *you* are in any position to be handing out advice, are you?"

"You have a romantic life?" Riley practically bellowed it. "With *him*?"

"For all you know, I have a romantic life with every single man in town!" Amanda threw at him. Not helping, to Brady's mind. He stood. Carefully. "It's still not your business."

"You're my little sister. Of course it's my business. And you're lucky all I did was hit him." Riley slid another filthy look Brady's way, making Brady all the happier about getting to his feet. "What do you think Zack's going to do?"

"Hopefully follow the law, which is his job," Amanda snapped. "And I think you'll find that means he can't be throwing random men in jail because he finds them kissing his sister."

"Then he can put me in jail for killing the random man myself," Riley growled. "Like a fox in a henhouse."

"I'm not a *hen*, you Neanderthal."

Brady checked out his jaw, because his whole face hurt, but wasn't foolish enough to take his eyes off his best friend.

"There's no point fighting about this," he managed to say. "It's over."

"You're damn right it's over," Riley snarled back at him. "I don't know why I didn't expect something like this. Of course you betrayed me. I trust someone, *boom*. They betray me. I should have known."

"News flash, Riley," Amanda snapped, clearly not as rocked straight through by that as Brady was. *He* felt it like a mortal blow. She looked like she might stop shoving and start swinging. "This isn't about you. If you want to talk about your broken heart and the mess of your marriage, I would be delighted. But this isn't the time. You've had years to talk about it."

If possible, Riley's scowl deepened. "I don't want to talk about it."

"Then don't talk about how betrayed you are. Go fix it. Or don't, I don't really care. But what you don't get to do is come barging in here, whaling on people."

Brady had never seen Amanda so fierce. And if he wasn't mistaken, protective. Of him.

He couldn't really take it in. He was too busy reeling from what had happened between them, even before Riley had appeared. And Riley glaring at him like he would hate Brady forever didn't help.

Brady was almost grateful for the pulse of pain that radiated out from the point of impact. Almost.

"I never meant to betray you," Brady said, very formally, to Riley. "I know you won't believe this, but it . . . just happened."

"She's my baby sister," Riley seethed at him, pushing against Amanda's grip like he was chomping at the bit to take another swing. And Brady would have to let him, wouldn't he? "You changed her *diaper*, man!"

Amanda made a frustrated noise. "I'm going to put you both in diapers in a minute.

Brady accepted the fury and betrayal on his best friend's face. He nodded and didn't offer up any further excuses or arguments. What was there to say? He'd known better, and he'd done it anyway.

He took one last look at Amanda, even more beautiful now lit up with indignation. Even more perfectly her, if that were possible, and everything in him was a deep, hard ache. But he'd made his choice before Riley had come in swinging. He wasn't going to change it now.

If he thought about it, getting punched in the face was a small price to pay for tasting her. He couldn't regret it.

"If you want to round up a good, old-fashioned Wild West posse of Kittredge boys to hunt me down, you know where to find me," Brady told Riley. Who growled back at him. "I'm not going to hide from you."

He cut his gaze to Amanda. But he couldn't think of anything to say. Or he could, but he couldn't bring himself to say it. All he could do was hold her gaze for another long, wrenching moment, basking in all that emotion-soaked gold.

Then he made himself leave.

He staggered out into the cold sunshine, the frigid breeze from the mountains cutting into him. He stood there a moment, unsteady on his feet, and wanted to blame the hit he'd taken.

But it wasn't Riley's fist that had knocked him off balance. If anything, getting sucker punched had cleared his head. At last.

It's only you, she'd said.

Brady couldn't let himself believe that. He couldn't

really let himself dwell on it. Or it would hurt him a whole lot more than the thudding pulse of pain in one side of his face.

He climbed into his truck, thinking he really should have hidden it again if he didn't want someone driving by and seeing it. The way he assumed Riley must have. Had he *wanted* someone to discover him with Amanda? Had he wanted to make sure he couldn't give in to temptation?

That a part of him still wanted to get out of his truck and go back inside—even if Riley jumped him again—well. That was the problem, wasn't it?

It didn't matter what he wanted. What mattered—finally, and too late—was what he did.

Or didn't do.

Brady meant to head out to the ranch and throw himself into work—where he could sweat out all this poison and emotion, he was sure—but he didn't. He drove over the hill and hated how beautiful the valley was today, with the sky so blue and the mountains so tall, the way they always were. He hated that his life could feel like this, broken irreparably and ugly straight through, but he'd never know it from the view.

That was what he loved about this land. It didn't care what happened to the men and women who broke themselves all over it. It didn't care if they lived or died.

At the moment, Brady felt almost . . . desperate. Like he didn't care much either.

Instead of heading back to Cold River Ranch, he headed out toward the rock where he'd taken Amanda. Once he made it through the fields and down to the river, he grabbed an old T-shirt he'd tossed in the back seat and forgotten about. He dunked it in the surging water of the cold river, then held it to his eye as he sat there.

"Ouch," he muttered. Freaking Riley.

Not that he blamed his friend.

No matter how much the side of his face throbbed.

He sat there for a long time, reapplying the cold water to his face. He waited and waited, but the riot inside him didn't ease.

If anything, it got worse. Darker, thicker, and more painful.

At some point, he accepted the fact that he might just have to live with this. With what he'd done and the fall-out from it. That this was simply . . . how things would be now.

Riley hated him. Brady had done that all by himself. And Amanda might think she loved him now, but he knew that would turn around. She would end up hating him too. She would meet that nice guy and wish she hadn't thrown her innocence away. He would be her big regret.

The inevitability of that shouldn't have stung as much as it did. Almost worse than his eye.

But he could see it as if it had already happened. He could see her, round and pregnant and glowing—with another man's baby. He could see her pretending she hardly knew him.

He could see himself dancing at her wedding, all right, with one of the elderly widows who always liked a handsome young dance partner—all while avoiding making eye contact with the bride or any of her family.

It made him feel vaguely ill.

But then, that was nothing new. After all, he was the

kid who'd made his own mother leave. Bettina had stuck it out through Gray and Ty, but Brady was the one who'd turned the tide. He was the bridge too far, the straw that broke the camel's back, whatever you wanted to call it.

He deserved to be alone, he'd always thought, and he'd tried to be. He'd never seen Amanda coming.

But thanks to her, Brady was right on track to making himself into Amos, once and for all.

What he couldn't get away from was the idea that this had all been a self-fulfilling prophecy from the start. He'd meant what he told Amanda. The more he thought about his brothers and their demons and the way they'd fought their way to a kind of happiness none of them had ever seen play out on the ranch, it was hard not to read Amos's response to his youngest as deliberate condemnation.

The more he thought about it, the more Brady was convinced Amos had known the truth about him all along. And soon everyone else in the Longhorn Valley would too.

Word would get out. It likely already had. And Brady knew better than to think that folks would take his side in this. *He* wasn't even on his side. The whole town would choose, and it wouldn't be the city slicker, college-educated Everett boy, who should have known better than to put his hands on that sweet little Kittredge girl.

He'd known that going in too.

Maybe some part of him had always known he'd end up here. On the land and of it, but connected to nothing and no one. The only difference between him and his father was the booze.

And Lord knew he could remedy that any time he chose.

Was this what had happened to Amos? Had he tried to be a good man once? Because Brady understood now, the great gulf between the things a man told himself about who he was and the reality of his actions, and how that could get into a person's bones. How it could warp them. He understood how much easier it would be to dive headfirst into the slick embrace of alcohol.

Getting drunk and mean with it meant Amos had never had to face this . . . emptiness. If he drank enough, the drinking caused its own problems, and the real problems never needed to be addressed. They could fester there. They could sink in deep.

Maybe it had been easier for Amos to give in. To allow himself to go dark and stay dark, because the light hurt too much.

Of all the things Brady might have imagined the year anniversary of his father's death might kick up in him, it wasn't this. It wasn't . . . *sympathy*.

It sat strangely on him. Like another blow to the face.

Brady made his way back to his truck. Then he wheeled around and headed for the ranch. He was stiff and cold, and he saw he'd been sitting out there a long, long time. The day was still bright around him, but there were clouds up over the mountains, hinting at the storms to come. He rubbed a hand over his heart as he drove, trying to piece together all the strands of the heavy things that sat on him.

But all he felt was the weight.

When he got back to the ranch house, it looked like Abby was home, but Gray and Ty were still out in the fields. And maybe it made him a coward—or more of one—but the longer Brady could put off discussing the state of his face and how he'd come by a fist print there, the better. He parked in the yard, then headed for the entrance on the back of the house that led directly to his room.

To Amos's room. Where Brady had marinated for almost a year, and had turned out to be no better than the man he'd been so sure he'd done everything to avoid becoming.

He wasn't *hiding*, he assured himself as he went inside and got his first decent look at his face in his bathroom mirror. He winced, because it looked like what it was. A very hard, very deliberate blow. *Ouch*.

"I'm not hiding from anything," he muttered as he turned away from the mirror. "I'm waiting."

Because there was no need to dive headfirst into something he knew was going to be unpleasant, like his family's reaction to his face. And their further reactions when they found out about Amanda, the way he knew they would.

Amanda might tell them herself, for all he knew. The mood she'd been in, she might do anything.

That should probably not have made him smile.

He cracked open his laptop and immersed himself in the financial world he'd left behind him in Denver. He'd always been good at numbers, and he still was. And more, he knew exactly who to contact to start putting the wheels in motion for his diversification project. He thought it would pay off in spades, but even if he was wrong—and he hadn't been wrong about a money-making venture in quite some time—the beauty of it was, he would preserve the land.

That was the lesson of all of this, wasn't it? No matter what happened, an Everett preserved the land.

No matter what he sacrificed. No matter what he lost. No matter what he gave up along the way, none of that mattered as much as the land. That view he'd hated and loved in equal measure when he'd come over the hill today.

Whatever else Brady was, he'd finally come to understand that above all else, he was an Everett.

That probably should have felt like more of a victory.

Instead, what he felt was that same heaviness, so he ignored it and started reaching out to colleagues and friends.

When the commotion started in the main part of the house, he ignored that too. There were a lot of people living in and around this house these days, and no need for him to go sticking his nose in every time he heard a noise.

But the second time he heard a particular voice, he couldn't ignore it. Because it sounded a whole lot like Amanda.

Even though that should have been impossible. Hadn't Riley locked her up by now? Built her a tower and thrown away the key, or something equally dramatic?

He slid his laptop off to the side, then headed out of the back room. But Becca was there in the hallway again.

"Why are you lurking out here?"

She gasped. "What happened to your *face*?"

"I walked into a door. And that still doesn't tell me what you're doing back here, clearly up to no good."

Becca looked wounded. "I was looking for you."

"You could have knocked." He wanted to look away from her dark, too-clever gaze, but didn't.

"Why is Amanda Kittredge here?"

"She's your neighbor, Becca."

"She didn't come by with brownies or a pot roast, Uncle Brady. She came to see you."

"That's ridiculous," he muttered.

But Becca was studying him, that considering look on her face that he both recognized and intensely disliked.

"Is Amanda the girl you were talking to the other night? When you lied?" And she reminded him a little too much of her father just then. "*Twice?*"

"I marched in your parade, Becca. Surely that should buy me fewer questions."

Becca rolled her eyes, but she stepped aside. And Brady moved past her, aware that he was walking like his bones might give way. Like he'd been on a bender. It annoyed him.

He moved faster, out into the living room where, sure enough, Amanda was standing in that archway that connected the big room to the kitchen.

Amanda.

Looking stubborn and furious and so beautiful it made his ribs feel a little precarious inside his chest.

She was saying something to whoever was still in the kitchen, hidden by the wall, but stopped when she saw him.

"Brady . . . ," she breathed, and his curse was that he loved the way she said his name. It got into him like heat. It warmed him up and made that weight ease a little too—and that was a problem. *She* was a problem. "Your face . . ."

He glared at her. "You shouldn't be here. And I'm fine."

"You're not fine. Your face is swollen and you already have a black eye." Her hands twitched, as if she'd started to reach for him and then thought better of it, and Brady didn't know why that hurt even worse than the rest. "It's probably going to turn colors before it's done."

"I said I'm fine."

It had been hard enough to do this once already today. Almost impossible, *before* Riley had turned up swinging. He didn't think he could go through it again.

Why couldn't she understand that he was trying to do the right thing here?

Brady opened his mouth to ask her that, when he remembered they weren't alone this time. Because Abby moved from deeper in the kitchen to stand behind Amanda, a dumbstruck look on her face and Bart strapped to her front. She was cradling the baby's head with one hand, but she didn't take that scandalized gaze off Brady.

"What on earth is going on?" she asked.

"I told you he had a girl," Becca said from behind him, sounding far too satisfied.

He decided she'd won herself a spot as his least favorite niece, then and there. But he couldn't tell her that, because Abby was still staring at him. The same way Riley had earlier.

Like the monster Brady had always suspected he was.

He wasn't going to fight it anymore. What would be the point? He lifted his chin and met his sister-in-law's appalled gaze.

"Are you . . . ? Are you and *Amanda* . . . ? No, that's impossible. Tell me that's impossible."

It was like a nightmare. A nightmare he'd had quite a few times over the past month. Because it wasn't enough that Abby was here, looking at him like he'd killed someone. Worse, everyone else crowded in right behind her.

Gray, clearly straight from the fields. Ty right behind

him. And a split second later, Hannah too. She was tot-
ing Jack, all kitted out in a Halloween costume that made
him look like the cutest bear cub Brady had ever seen.

"Hey, Amanda—" Hannah began happily, but then
stopped when the tension in the room got to her.

Or when she got a good look at Amanda's reddened
eyes and Brady's busted-up face. It was hard to tell.

For a long moment, no one said a word. Even Jack and
the baby were quiet.

They all stared.

Brady stared back, but he couldn't bring himself to
care about his family's reaction the way he probably
should have. Not when Amanda was there, with curls in
her hair and swollen eyes and all that hurt and hope in
her expression that told him she hadn't gotten around to
hating him yet.

He wanted this part to be over.

He wanted to fast-forward straight into getting his
Amos on.

"Take a good look," he growled, his chin still lifted.
"Amanda and I had a thing. It's over. Riley took exception and punched me in the face. That brings everyone
up to speed. No need to discuss it further."

There was another long beat of silence.

Then everyone reacted all at once.

Ty laughed. Because of course he did. Hannah didn't actually laugh out loud, but she didn't look particularly scandalized either. Gray looked like a thundercloud, as ever.

But Abby, on the other hand, still looked stunned.

And worse, horrified.

Amanda was staring at all of them, then turning to
look at him, back and forth like she couldn't decide who

she was angriest with. Becca stayed where she was, standing in the entrance to the hallway behind him, her hands over her mouth and her eyes wide.

Brady had the deeply ungallant and cowardly thought that if he really wanted, he could dive out one of the front windows and be done with this. He could ride off into the fields and let the land have its say as fall rolled in hard behind him and swallowed him whole.

If Amanda hadn't been here, he might have.

But she was, and he couldn't leave her to deal with the fallout on her own, so he stood there. And took it.

Because he always took it. Because Gray brooded, Ty laughed, and it never much mattered what Brady felt about anything.

He'd been sick of that all year. Today, he found it intolerable.

He was working his way up to announcing that, no matter how disappointed Gray and Abby looked, when Amanda jumped in.

"What is the matter with you?" she demanded, and Brady was surprised to note that she was directing her ire toward the kitchen, not toward him. And her voice was loud and clear, no doubt honed from two months of shouting down the drunken masses at the Coyote. "That's your *brother*. You'd treat a random stranger off the street better than this. Can't you see he's hurting?"

"Amanda," Abby said, sounding . . . careful. Too careful. "I don't think you understand—"

"Of course I understand, Abby. I'm in love with him."

"Are you knocked up?" asked Ty, still laughing.

Or at least, until Hannah punched him in the arm, at which point he stopped laughing and scowled at his wife instead.

"No, I am not pregnant." Amanda's voice shook a little, but not with any kind of weakness. That was clear. "Not that there would be anything wrong with it if I were. Given that neither Brady nor I are children ourselves."

Brady might have been amused at the way they all looked at one another then, like that was a confronting thought. If things had been different, that was. If he hadn't actually *defiled an innocent*, the way they all thought he had. It was hard to work up any righteous indignation.

"I have to hand it to you," Gray said, in that leathery, well-worn way of his that made Brady want to curl up inside and die. The way it always had. "I didn't think that when you talked about diversification, you meant . . . the Kittredge family."

Brady wanted to punch something, but he didn't particularly want his knuckles to hurt as much as the side of his face did. "Very funny."

"I'm not surprised Riley took a swing at you," Gray continued, and there it was. That patented Gray Everett disapproval. "I'd have similarly murderous thoughts if some man ten years older was panting after Becca."

Brady reconsidered taking that swing at his older brother, then, but he was already too much like Amos. That would make it even worse. He bit back the angry words that crowded his tongue, and if that was how it tasted to be so small a man, no wonder Amos had chased it down with whiskey.

But Amanda was glaring at Gray, and she didn't appear similarly afflicted.

"You should be ashamed of yourself," she snapped.

To Gray.

It shocked him and the rest of the Everett family into silence.

"Maybe instead of standing around, congratulating yourself on your own virtue, you could spend one second taking care of Brady," she said, every word like a bullet. A hail of bullets.

Brady didn't know where to look. At his brothers? At their astonished wives? Or at fearless, impetuous Amanda—who was standing up for him . . . again?

"My brothers treat me like a child," she continued in the same fierce, furious tone. "They make me want to tear my hair out regularly, but when my older brother thought something was going on with me that shouldn't have been, he took a swing at the problem. But not you, Gray."

For the first time that Brady could recall, a person who was not Ty or Brady himself was actually looking at Gray in grave disappointment. It was certainly new. He hardly knew where to put it.

"You'd rather take a swing at Brady," Amanda was saying, shaking her head. "Does that make you feel better about the fact that you could have stepped in years ago and *helped* instead? He's been looking up to you his whole life. Would it kill you to be nice to him for a change?"

There was another stunned silence, and Brady thought that someday he might look back on this moment and find it amusing. He didn't think he'd ever seen Gray look so . . . *thunderstruck*.

But at the moment, he didn't really see how he'd ever find anything amusing again.

"Amanda," he said in a low voice, as if her name didn't hurt. When it did. "You need to tone it down, killer."

The only sound from the kitchen was Ty, laughing again.

Amanda glared at him, then. Because she was apparently the only person in Cold River unfazed by Ty Everett, the rodeo star. "I'm glad you think it's so funny. Meanwhile, your younger brother is so tied up in knots, he thinks that of all the people standing in this room, he's the most like your father."

"None of the people standing in this room are anything like Amos, Amanda," Abby said then, and it was about the closest to a temper that Brady had ever seen on her.

"Grandpa always yelled a whole lot more," Becca said from the hallway, her voice matter-of-fact, and wasn't that another kick in the gut? "And he used way more bad words. Amanda just thinks you all should be nicer to Uncle Brady." She sniffed. "I agree. You should."

"I'm nice to everyone," Ty drawled, but there was an arrested sort of light in his gaze. "It's part of my charm. Ask around, peanut."

"And while you're at it, maybe you could all stop confusing Becca and me," Amanda said, in a dangerous sort of tone.

Brady didn't know what the danger was, precisely, but he could feel it ignite. As if she'd lit a match too close to him and the hairs on the back of his neck were standing up in protest. He started toward her, determined to contain the damage, at the very least.

Though he wasn't sure, at this point, if he was protecting her from his family or if it was the other way around.

"I love Becca myself," Amanda said. "But she's your daughter, Gray. She's an honest-to-God teenager. I'm not.

You're aware of that, right? If I recall correctly, I'm the same age Becca's mother was when you married her."

"Seriously, Dad," Becca chimed in.

"Okay," Gray said then, his voice stern and his eyes on Amanda. "You've said your piece."

"I'm just getting started," she replied hotly.

Brady reached her then and snaked an arm around her waist, pulling her up against him because he wasn't entirely sure she wouldn't launch herself across the room at one or both of his brothers. She was a Kittredge, after all. They weren't afraid to swing first and ask questions later.

"What's gotten into you, Amanda?" Abby asked quietly, then, one hand on little Bart in his carrier and another on Gray's arm.

She looked a lot as if she was the one who'd gotten sucker punched. And by Amanda.

"I think it's real clear what got into her, Abby," Ty drawled. "He's standing right there."

That got him another punch from his wife.

Everyone started talking at once. At Brady, at Amanda, at one another. Amanda shook Brady's arm off and stepped forward, obviously perfectly happy to dive straight into the fray.

But all Brady could think was how happy this would have made his father. How delighted Amos would have been to see them all at one another's throats. And if he looked through the archway into the kitchen, he could see that damned table sitting there. The barn door they'd put into place because they were so tired of picking up the splinters every time Amos broke it.

If he squinted, he could see the old man sitting there the way he always had. A half-drunk bottle of whiskey at his elbow and that bitter scowl in place, muttering to himself—but loud enough to be heard—about who he was adding to his will and who he was crossing out. If he listened, he could hear the sound of the whiskey bottle *thunking* against the table top, and worse, the sound of Amos's angry scribbling.

Amos would have *loved* to know that a year later, there was still all this animosity. He would have fed on it.

Brady made a decision then. He ignored all the sniping and headed for the door at the back of the kitchen.

"What a surprise," Gray growled as he moved. "You talk a big game, Denver, but anytime it gets hard, you're out the door."

"Why would he stay here when you think so little of him?" Amanda demanded, surprising Brady once again with her *fierceness*. Like she would fight Gray all night if she had to. For him. And something shifted in him at that, but he didn't stop. Neither did she. "I'm not at all surprised that he left for college and had no intention of coming back here. The only thing that surprises me is that he actually did come back anyway. And spent a year here because you asked him to."

"I'm not going to have an argument with you," Gray gritted out.

"What could you possibly argue? That when you call Brady names and say snide things you're somehow supporting him?" Amanda made a noise. "Because you're not."

"She's got you there, big brother," Ty drawled, sounding like that laughter of his was brewing right beneath the surface.

"Like you're any better," Hannah said then, surprising Brady enough that he stopped by the door. And stared. Everyone else did too, if that astonished silence was any guide. "The two of you are relentless. It was clear to me the day I arrived here that Brady is a powerful man in his own right who locks it up around the two of you because you refuse to see it. And don't think it's not perfectly clear that you two letting him do what he likes with his diversification idea is because you think he's going to fall on his face." She smiled then, big and bright, which was Hannah at her most lethal. "Meanwhile, sugar, you know I love you, but there are other forms of success besides the rodeo and a herd of Angus."

"Way to knife me in the back, Hannah Leigh." Ty didn't look angry, though there was an edge to his usually lazy voice. "You can't resist a crowd, can you?"

"Never have," Hannah said softly. "Never will."

Brady couldn't take any more of this. Next Abby would turn on Gray and that would mean the world was ending. He wanted no part of this. He pushed out through the door.

It took him two steps out the back to the woodpile, where he ignored the carefully stacked wood, most of which he'd put there himself, and grabbed the axe. Then he wheeled around and came back inside the kitchen.

"Whoa now, little brother," Ty said, turning that edgy drawl on him. "No need to introduce a weapon. Everetts have always been capable of grievous bodily harm with their words alone."

Brady ignored him. He ignored all of them and stalked directly toward that damn barn-door table.

Then he swung the axe down, hard.

Because it was his turn to make a table into splinters, and he was going to do it right.

He chopped and he chopped, glad he'd spent so much time contributing to that woodpile out back. Because each time the blade met wood, it was satisfying. It was right.

And he said goodbye to Amos and his poison with every swing.

Enough of the lies. Enough of his nasty, insinuating stories about each and every one of them. Enough of Gray, the martyr. Ty, the drunk.

And Brady, the smart ass, unwanted kid.

Enough.

He was sweating like a wild man, the whole side of his face ached, and Brady didn't care at all.

In fact, he wasn't sure he'd ever felt more free.

Only when that old barn door was completely reduced to splinters that no one could ever put back together did he lay down the axe. And only then did he turn to face his family once again.

His family and Amanda. His beautiful, fierce, and innocent Amanda. She was covering her mouth with her hands. Tears flowed freely down her cheeks.

But still Brady looked at her and saw nothing but sunshine.

He understood, finally, the ache in his bones. The pressure in his chest. The panic and fear that had been riding him this whole time.

Brady was going to have to bronze that tank top. Because without it, he might never have truly seen her. And if he'd never seen her, none of this would have happened.

He couldn't think of anything worse.

But this wasn't the time to get into all that. Brady met Gray's gaze. Then Ty's. He looked at each one of his sisters-in-law, and then at Becca.

He made sure he had everyone's attention.

"Dad has been dead for a year," he said, and he'd meant to speak quietly, the way he always did around his brothers. But instead, he sounded a lot more like the other version of himself. The one who commanded board rooms and led high-powered meetings without thinking twice. "But he never really dies."

Hannah had met this version of him before. She didn't look as surprised as Abby and Becca did. He saw Gray and Ty exchange a longer look.

But Amanda only smiled.

"And he never goes anywhere." Brady wiped his face with his sleeve, then nodded toward the pile of wood chips he'd made. "Because we all keep carrying him around. And every night we come into this house and we sit at that table where he spent years upon years scratching his poison into that will of his."

He could still see Amos there. Maybe he always would. But Brady didn't need to keep taking part in this sick little vigil.

"All the games he played, with all of us. All his schemes, all his lies." Brady shook his head. "He poured them into that table and we eat off it. We keep it here like a monument to a dead man every one of us is afraid of becoming. I don't want to become him. I'm afraid I already am him, if I'm honest. I'm staying on this ranch, and I guess that means I have to face up to what it means to be an Everett. I can handle that. But I'm not sitting down at that table ever again."

Brady waited for someone to speak. But everyone was staring back at him, and he wasn't sure he wanted to see if he could make sense of their various expressions.

"I want to start something new," he said in the same tone, the one that sounded like he *expected* agreement and approval, which typically led straight to it. He'd always been a closer—everywhere but here. "We tried it Gray's way. It's kept this ranch going all this time. But the future can't be surrendering to the past."

Someone made a noise, though he didn't look to see who. He forged ahead, words pouring out of him that he hadn't known were in there.

"It can't be pretending to get along until something happens, one tiny little thing, and then it's back to name-calling and sandbagging one another. If we're not Dad, we need to stop acting like him."

"Agreed," Ty said.

With remarkably little rodeo drawl.

"It's not even the three of us anymore," Brady said, looking around at all of them. The crowd they made, here at the end of this long, strange year. "It's all of us. We're all Everetts. We're all a part of this land. We've all committed ourselves to it in one way or another. But we get to decide how we do that. And we get to decide what it takes from us in return."

Gray was staring back at him, a look Brady couldn't decipher on his face.

It took him another moment to understand it was respect. And still another moment to know that Amanda had been right about this too. Amos was the demon on all their backs. Gray had been more of a father to Brady than Amos ever had.

He'd never imagined that Gray might respect him in return. And he'd never understood fully, not until today, how deeply he'd craved it.

"This is a new dawn of a new day," Brady said, and he believed it. He truly did. His brothers were already further along this road than he was, but it was going to take all of them to stay on course. It was going to take them all working together. It was going to take . . . a family. And for once, he found he liked that word. "The beginning of a brand new year. Dad is gone. I have to hope all that darkness is gone with him, for good. And I don't know about you all, but I'm ready for some light."

19

Everything in the Everett ranch house was silent. Even Bart and Jack, who'd made some noise during the destruction of the table, were quiet now.

Amanda held her breath, not sure if it was tension before another explosion, or—

"Well, Denver," Gray said, his face like granite. "Trouble is, we're running out of barn doors."

Amanda was so primed for battle that she almost leapt at him, then, physically, not caring at all that this was Brady's older brother. The one she knew he loved and looked up to, as she'd yelled like a banshee not long ago. And not caring that she had liked Gray Everett fine until today. Well, maybe not *today*. She'd been fine with him until she started thinking about how he could have helped Brady at any point, and hadn't.

She was so tired of everyone dumping all over Brady that she actually felt sick with it, and she opened her mouth to yell about it some more—

But everybody laughed.

Including Brady.

They laughed and they laughed, and even Gray smiled. Amanda realized belatedly that there'd been a storm all right, and she'd been standing in the middle of it, but it was past now. Over.

She didn't know if she wanted to laugh along with the rest of the Everetts or slink off in shame. Because the truth of the matter was that she wasn't family. The lovely words Brady had said weren't for her. He'd broken things off with her very decisively this morning, which likely meant she was a part of the darkness he wanted to leave behind.

She could feel the sting of tears again, then. There at the back of her eyes. And all the righteous indignation that had carried her along all day—that had allowed her to deal with her own family and then drive out this way to argue her case—drained away.

All the things she'd felt in that barn flooded back to her. All the things she'd shoved aside when Riley had appeared and given her something to fight.

Like the fact she'd told Brady she loved him and that hadn't mattered.

Why exactly are you here, again? she asked herself sharply. *You may have helped the Everett family bond, but you're only making a fool of yourself.*

But before she could make a break for it, she found Brady's tough, hard hand wrapped around her elbow.

Her curse was she liked it when he got bossy.

"I'm going to find you an actual kitchen table," Brady told Gray. And maybe everyone else too. "And I'll clean this one up. But first, I have some business to attend to."

He looked down at Amanda, and she loved him more than was probably wise, but that didn't mean he couldn't intimidate her with his dark, unreadable gaze. It just meant that her little shiver was only half intimidation. The rest was desire.

Ty stepped forward then, clapping Brady on the shoulder without that trademark grin of his. His gaze was direct and not the slightest bit lazy.

It occurred to Amanda that the Everett brothers really did all look alike. Especially when they were stern.

"That table had to go," Ty told Brady gruffly. "I have a mind to burn what's left into ash, in fact."

"I'll help," Becca said hotly.

"And I," Abby said in her usual quiet, capable way, handing the baby over to Gray, "will serve dinner on the dining room table for a change. You all do what you have to do."

When her gaze met Amanda's, it was clear. Faintly apologetic. And wholly lacking the condemnation Amanda had seen there before.

Of all things, that was what put a lump back in Amanda's throat.

She had to blink, hard, to keep from collapsing into sobs.

Then Brady was ushering her outside. Straight out the back door and toward the car she'd driven out here on a mission, filled to bursting with all the things she felt.

Now she felt a little sick from it all, like she was teetering on the edge of one of those hangovers she'd heard a lot about, but had never personally experienced. If this was any indication, they were to be avoided at all costs.

Brady was walking her out pretty quickly, which couldn't possibly bode well. And there was a limit to what her heart could take.

You have to love hard, her mother had told her.

She was sure there had to be a limit.

"You didn't have to leave the barn like that," she said as they walked across the cold yard. "I wanted to kill Riley, and believe me, he got an earful."

"I believe you."

That made her flush, but it didn't make him stop, and her car was getting closer with every one of his long strides. She was sure it made her pathetic that she still didn't want to leave him. Even if *he* wanted her to.

"I refuse to apologize for defending you," she said, with all the urgency she could feel sloshing around inside her. "Though I'm sorry if it made you uncomfortable. I know I overstepped my bounds. And I know you broke up with me, even though you claim we weren't dating in the first place. I didn't forget. I just don't—"

"Amanda. Take a breath."

She took his advice. Reluctantly.

"I came to see if you were okay," she said, more quietly. "I actually didn't mean to tell your whole family our business. Or yell at them. It all just kind of . . . blew up."

They reached her hatchback then, still parked haphazardly near the corral. She'd driven out here after she'd finished her knock-down, drag-out fight with Riley. After he'd told her that he would drive her back to her apartment, and had taken her to the sheriff's department instead.

Where he and Zack had gotten into their own little scuffle over whether or not Zack could lock her up, arrest Brady, or any combination of the above.

Amanda's response had not been *appropriate* in any way, and she didn't care if her mother heard about it. Or was appalled.

She had been sick to death of her brothers by the time she left town—even more than usual—and she'd taken the mountain pass with more temper than sense. Something no one who'd been born and raised here should have been dumb enough to risk—and she was lucky the weather was cold tonight, but not actively dangerous. She'd promised herself that when she got to Cold River Ranch, sanity would return. She would be reasonable. Understanding. Quiet and elegant, like the woman she imagined she was sometimes.

Like her mother.

But Brady's face was bruised, his brothers were idiots too, and she'd lost it.

Completely.

Sorry, Mom, she thought.

Now they were standing outside as the last of the October sun put on a little show to the west, on its way toward the gleaming white mountaintops. The temperature was plummeting. Her hopes went right along with it.

Amanda wouldn't take anything back, but that didn't mean she felt good about any of this either. Especially not when Brady was looking at her the way he was now. Like he didn't know what to do with her.

When she knew exactly what she wanted to do with him.

"I'm not going to stop being in love with you," she threw at him, feeling helpless and defiant. And once again, unable to stop herself. Brady was bad for her self-control, that was the only conclusion she could reach. "I don't think it works that way, no matter how much you might wish it did."

"No one's ever defended me like that," Brady said quietly. She stood at the door to her car. He stood in front of her, not quite trapping her there. She wished he would. "Or at all, I guess. Especially not in this house."

"Maybe that will change now."

"Maybe it will. If it does, I know who to thank."

She searched his face and couldn't read anything there, in the shadows. But she could feel her hope rolling back in, like the tide. "You chopped up that table. I think Ty really will throw it in a fire."

"I have no doubt."

"And maybe that's how you exorcise a ghost," she said, trying not to smile at him with all that foolish hope on her face. She could feel it all over her, like a sudden October sunburn. "You take the whole year, let it haunt you. And then you throw what's left on a bonfire, and let it go."

Brady's expression was intense. And filled with something like wonder, then, there in the yard as the last night of his haunted year fell around them. He reached over and carefully, almost reverently, ran his finger down the line of her jaw.

"My father was a liar," he told her, his voice as quiet as his gaze was fierce. "He never saw the back of a person without sticking a knife in. Deep. It was a game to him. The more harm he could cause, the better."

"You're not your father." And she could hear how serious she sounded. How determined. "There's not one part of you that's like him."

"That's what I want to believe. But there's no denying I've been sneaking around with my best friend's little sister, is there? Riley wasn't wrong about that."

"Keeping something private isn't the same as sneaking around."

"I agree. But that's not what we were doing, baby, and you know it."

She wanted to shout at him, argue, *convince* him—but instead, she melted. "You called me baby."

Brady didn't smile, but his eyes seemed lighter. "I'm not going to stand here with that table in pieces, your brother's fist imprinted on my face, a month of lies behind us, and make you any promises. I'm not going to tell you that I love you."

"You're not?" She scowled at him, even as her heart kicked at her, because what did that mean? "Why not?"

"Because, Amanda, I'm going to do it right. I'm going to earn it."

"What are you talking about?" She reached up and took his face in her hands for a change—but carefully, because she didn't want to hurt him. "There's not one part of you that needs to change. I love *you*, Brady. Not some idea of who you might become, in time, if you do something right. There's nothing wrong with you."

He turned his unhurt cheek and pressed his mouth against one of her palms. He took the other and put it near his heart. She could feel it beat, deep and strong, like him.

"Down in the city, I was a different man. I thought I had to be. And I behaved in ways that made sense for that man. But you deserve the real me, Amanda. And that's not a man who would take the gift you gave me and pretend it was a casual thing."

She didn't try to fool herself into thinking he was talking about something other than her virginity. And she tried not to flush too.

"It was my gift to give," she said stoutly. "And between you and me, Brady, I never thought it was all that casual."

He smiled at that. "I'm looking at this like I'm playing a long game."

"I know you were the quarterback and all, but I liked horses in high school. Not football."

Brady smiled, then. A real smile.

He looked like a fantasy to her, even though she could feel that he was solid and real. All cowboy. All man. And this time, she didn't get the sense that whatever noble impulse he was talking about was coming from fear.

Not when he was looking at her as if, finally, there was hope.

"Buckle up, killer," he drawled. "Because I'm about to do what no man in Cold River ever has."

Amanda didn't know whether to be horrified or delighted. "You don't mean—"

"Yes, ma'am," he said, his eyes gleaming bright and his drawl like one the Wild West. "I'm not afraid of your brothers. Not even while I'm sporting this shiner, and I'll prove it. I'm going to court you."

Amanda could have waited for Sunday dinner to have a long overdue talk with her family, but she was too fired up after her discussion about *courting* with Brady to wait any longer.

She also knew her brothers. Given enough time, they'd all band together the way they had when she was younger and who knew? They really might lock her up again.

After Brady waved her off in her car, she had to ask herself why she was all right with confronting his family but not hers.

Maybe it was time the Kittredges buckled up.

So instead of going back to her apartment and letting

Riley and Zack stir everyone up in her absence, she took matters into her own hands and called her mother.

"Can you ask everyone to come to dinner?" she asked. "Tonight?"

Ellie was silent a moment, and Amanda froze there where her car stopped at the end of the dirt road that led to the Everett ranch house. Because her family didn't normally gather as a family in the middle of the week. And Amanda had never *requested* that everyone show up.

"Zack's already here," Ellie said. Neutrally.

Amanda squeezed her eyes shut, waiting for her mother to lecture her on her behavior in the sheriff's office today. To tell her how appalled she was that Amanda had made a spectacle of herself, shamed the family, and embarrassed Zack.

"He's always the hardest to wrangle," Ellie said instead. Placidly. "It shouldn't be too difficult to get the rest of them to come over. When can we expect you?"

"I'm coming from Cold River Ranch."

There was another pause.

"Don't take the back way through the high pasture," Ellie said, with no discernible change in tone. "Your father says there's too much water on the road for your car."

Amanda was jittery, though she couldn't tell if it was leftover adrenaline from what had happened with the Everetts, or the very idea of *courting*. It could have been that there was water on the road, which meant one of the creeks had swelled in the last rainstorm a few nights back. Then again, maybe she was getting ready to have it out with her brothers at last.

Stay calm, killer, she told herself.

But then she remembered that Brady had called her *baby,* and that had her smiling giddily for the rest of the drive.

When she finally made it to the Bar K, she went into the house and found her whole family waiting for her. They were all packed into the kitchen. And silent.

Meaning they'd seen her car pull in and had stopped whatever conversation they were having about her so they could all loom around and glare at her as she walked in.

All except her father, who was hiding behind his newspaper.

She had the most absurd urge to laugh. Especially when she saw her mother over by the stove with an aggressively neutral expression on her face that matched the tone she'd used on the phone. Ellie was a mystery, always, but Amanda thought it was possible she was on her daughter's side tonight.

"I'm so glad you could all come," Amanda said sweetly.

Because she thought it would annoy them, and it clearly did. Connor and Jensen muttered something back and forth.

Riley scowled at her like he was *this close* to shouting and punching things again.

"Did you come here to apologize?" Zack demanded. He was standing in the kitchen with his back to the sink, looking about as furious as he had when she'd expressed her sentiments on his controlling ways back in the sheriff's office. "I'm going to have to hear about how my kid sister tried to have one of my deputies arrest me for abuse of power for, oh, I don't know, the rest of my career. Thanks for that."

"I wasn't joking," Amanda said. She made sure her smile was as sweet as her voice. "And you're welcome."

"Nice attitude," Jensen rumbled.

It was different to defend herself than it had been to defend Brady. She'd been filled with righteous indignation when she'd looked at Brady's brothers. Yet when she looked around at her own, there was part of her that would always feel like the little girl they thought she was. She told herself to ignore it because there was no changing it.

"I've put up with all of the overbearing nonsense for years," Amanda announced. "But I'm officially done."

"Is this what happens when you spend time with Brady?" Connor demanded. "This is what he brings out in you?"

"Brady is a good man," Amanda said. She wanted to start screaming, but she held it in. She knew they wanted to see her freak out. It would prove their point. "And I know that because of all of you idiots have been best friends with him since birth. Not my birth. Riley's."

Ellie made a small, disapproving noise. "Do not call your brothers idiots, Amanda. Even if that's accurate."

Everybody protested, or rather, all her brothers who were currently verbal complained. But when Amanda looked at her mother, she saw Ellie's small smile in return.

Her mother's blessing, she was pretty sure.

"He's a good man," Amanda said again, when the complaints died down. "And every single one of you thinks so too, or you wouldn't have all spent all these years hanging out with him. Especially after he moved to Denver."

Jensen muttered the word *Denver* like it was a filthy curse, as if he hadn't spent time there himself.

"I'm going to have to rethink a friendship with a man who would sneak around with my baby sister," Riley growled. "That's not much of a man, Amanda. Maybe you're too young and infatuated to see it."

The jitters she'd been fighting off turned into temper, pulsing in an alarming way behind her eyes. But Amanda didn't have the luxury to give into it. No whaling on people or shouting for her.

"Weirdly, Riley, he was afraid you might have a bad reaction." Her voice was scathing. "And it turns out he was correct. He didn't tell you something. You attacked him. Which one of you is a worse friend?"

"He is," Riley retorted.

"Everett, one hundred percent," Jensen growled.

Zack nodded. "Agreed."

"That's a cosign from me too," Connor chimed in. "There's a code, Amanda. There's a freaking *code*."

"I never agreed to your code, sorry," she replied.

"It's not for you to agree or disagree," Riley snapped. "Brady knows what he did."

Amanda wanted to snap right back at him, but she wasn't here to squabble. Squabbling suggested she was open to their interference, and she wasn't. It had to end. She looked around the room.

"I hope you've all had a lot of fun intimidating any boy who ever thought about looking at me twice. But that's over now." She lifted a hand when Connor started to object. "I know you love me. I know you think you're helping me. But I want you all to really think about the fact that I had to move out and get a job in the sleaziest bar in the Longhorn Valley to get away from all that love. You need to dial it back to a dull roar. All of you."

Her brothers exchanged those looks that had always

driven her crazy, because they were designed to communicate while excluding her. Tonight was no different. But again, she kept it to herself.

"Amanda," Zack began, in that voice he used to disperse crowds.

"I don't need to be placated," Amanda said, trying to channel her mother's calm. "I need to be heard. I've met a man. I like him." She loved him, but there was no point throwing that bomb into the middle of this gathering. Not yet. "The good news is, I know and you know that you already like him. A lot."

Connor snorted. "I've never liked him that much."

"What are his intentions?" Zack demanded.

Amanda rolled her eyes. "You're not Dad, Zack. Nice try, though."

They all looked at the newspaper at the end of the table, but Donovan Kittredge clearly had no intention of weighing in.

"Typical," Jensen muttered.

"I have no idea what's going to happen with Brady and me," Amanda said quickly, before this whole thing turned into another rendition of all the ways her brothers felt their father was a disappointment. Another conversation Donovan would refuse to participate in, but that never stopped them. "And even if I did know, I wouldn't tell you until I was ready. Because it's my relationship, not yours. None of you get a say. Do you understand that?"

"What do you think is going to happen here, monkey?" Connor asked. "This is Brady Everett we're talking about."

"He's going to court me," Amanda said, and she must have had a terrifying look on her face because none of them laughed. At her, anyway. "And you're going to let him. In fact, you're going to enthusiastically support him."

"Yeah, pass," Riley growled. "You know this is a joke, don't you? It will never last. *Never.*"

That was her worst fear, and she felt her stomach cramp up a little, but something else gripped her at the same time. A kind of relief, maybe, because it was said. It was out there.

She already knew what it felt like for Brady to break her heart. She could still feel the sharp, jagged edges inside her. It wasn't as if she could pretend everything was perfect. Brady hadn't said he loved her. She had no idea if he ever would.

But maybe that was the point. She had to do it on her own, and without hiding it away from the rest of her life, or how would she ever know if what she felt was real?

And Lord help her, but she wanted this to be real. She wanted it so much, it made her teeth ache.

"Then it doesn't last," she said quietly. To Riley. To all of them. Even her father behind his newspaper. "Isn't that the point? Some things last. Some things don't. But I don't need a committee to make decisions. And I need to know I can walk around with Brady in public without risking attacks."

"I can't promise you that," Riley threw right back at her.

Amanda shrugged. She matched him glare for glare. "Do your worst, Riley. Brady can handle himself. This is happening whether you have a tantrum about it or not."

Then she turned around and walked back out into the night before they could launch another offensive. She cried all the way back to her apartment, hoping against hope that Brady had meant what he'd said. That all this would be worth it.

And that somewhere along the way she could make him love her too.

20

The entire town of Cold River seemed to know all about Amanda and Brady almost before Amanda left the Bar K Halloween night.

"Did Riley really give him a black eye?" Noah Connelly asked the next day, taking time out of his usual surly morning routine of slamming pots and pans around while cooking spiteful platters of breakfast food for the ungrateful masses.

"Brady *let* him land that punch," Amanda replied. Maybe a little too testily, if Noah's expression was any guide.

She reminded herself that Noah was the owner of Cold River Coffee and more importantly, her boss. Not one of her annoying older brothers. *You don't actually have to yell at everyone*, she cautioned herself.

But it was hard to keep a civil tongue in her head when Noah paused for a moment and *looked* at her. In a way he never had before. A way that reminded her of Brady's reaction when she'd offhandedly called Noah attractive.

Almost as if he'd never actually seen her until today.

Then he shook his head and turned back to his cooking. With even more slamming of heavy pots than before.

Amanda would have forgotten the weird moment during the morning rush, but it kept happening. She noticed it first with men she'd known her whole life. It wasn't that anyone leered or made inappropriate remarks. In Amanda's experience, it was usually the women in small towns who made remarks, not the men. She'd braced herself for pointed prayers and inquiries about her mother. Or if the women were playing hardball, her grandmother. Just to help Amanda remember her morals and how she was raised.

But today, there were *pauses*. An extra moment or two of a little too much *focus* from men who had, yesterday, looked straight through her like she was a lamp or part of the counter.

When her shift ended, she walked through the coffeehouse toward the back, passing by a table full of young moms she knew. She smiled and they all smiled back, but then there was that moment again. An extra beat—and with these women she'd known forever, she could identify it.

It was speculation, sure. But it was also recognition.

Cold River had finally noticed that little Amanda Kittredge had grown up.

Amanda had spent her entire life bemoaning the fact that no one ever *saw* her, until Brady. They saw the Kittredge boys' baby sister. Her parents' daughter, and some might like to whisper that Amanda had come around to save the marriage, but they were really talking about Ellie and Donovan. Her respected grandparents' only granddaughter, which some older folks seemed to think came with requirements for a certain way of behaving. They saw the girl who worked in the coffee shop all the time, the one who wasn't Abby. These days, there were perhaps some sideways looks about her bartending stint at the Coyote—but all of that within the context of all the rest of the ways she was known but never seen.

But the day after Halloween, *everyone* saw her.

And took a minute to really *look* at her.

Two weeks later, it hadn't let up.

"I'm trying to adjust to being in the middle of all this endless scandal," Kat said one afternoon.

They were halfway down an aisle in the little local market near the courthouse that served as a great spot to pick up a few things when a person didn't have the time or energy to drive all the way to the big supermarket halfway to Aspen. Amanda and Kat had gotten together to spend the afternoon watching the newest episodes of their favorite shows, eating unquestionably atrocious food, and aggressively lounging. A practice they'd started when they were in high school on those nights Amanda had stayed over in town, and had carried on most recently at Amanda's apartment.

Amanda nodded. "I'm a scarlet woman. I'm practically Kathleen Gillespie or Tracie Jakes."

"I don't think you're *that* scarlet. You're more of a pale magenta." Kat leaned in closer. "Don't look now, but Genna Dawson is giving you speculative looks from behind the produce bin."

"That's just her face, Kat."

"It is not her face. She has that look."

Amanda was very familiar with *the look* by now. Sometimes it was about her. Other times it varied, depending on how the person in question felt about Brady.

Or Amanda's brothers. Or any member of either of their families.

Once upon a time, Amanda had dreamed of blowing up the image the town had of her. She'd fantasized about it. But now it had happened, and it wasn't quite how she'd imagined. Because while she kind of liked being an unknown quantity, a woman at last, she still didn't know how things were going to go with Brady.

And she wasn't looking forward to the way all the looks would change if it didn't work out.

The very idea made her feel a little sick.

That was the part she hadn't counted on. The public side of heartbreak. She felt a deep, retroactive sort of sympathy for all the people whose lives had imploded in Cold River—and then they'd stayed here. Keeping their heads up while everyone around them discussed the most painful episodes in their lives.

Amanda had been so desperate to have something—anything—happen in her life that she hadn't stopped to consider the fallout. Because even a polite, well-meaning sort of fallout was still fallout.

There was no hiding from a scandal in a small town. It showed up in the produce aisle of the local market. It smiled thinly in the checkout line. It called your mother to report on your whereabouts, and it agreed with your grandmother that you should make more time for church.

It had been a strange two weeks. Riley didn't take another swing at Brady, but he didn't relent either. Neither did anyone else.

You don't really think that you're ever going to get their blessing, do you? Amanda had asked Brady in exasperation one night. She'd put their continuing phone conversations in the column of positive things. Reasons to hope. *You know what they're like. They'll hold out forever, just to be stubborn.*

Let them be stubborn, Brady had drawled in reply, and that drawl was definitely a positive thing. It curled around her and made her cheeks feel warm. *There's no time limit. I'm not going anywhere. Are you?*

Not at the moment, she'd said. Grumpily.

The only place Amanda was going was crazy. Because Brady refused to resume their relationship as it was before. No sneaking around, to his mind, meant no private time of any kind until said blessings were received.

And he could not be moved on that point. No matter how she tried.

"I like it," Kat said later that same night on Amanda's couch, when Amanda complained. "What's better than a man who knows his own mind, respects you, and is willing to put his money where his mouth is?"

"I prefer where his mouth used to be," Amanda grumbled.

"Of course you do." Kat rolled her eyes and rummaged around for more popcorn. "And don't think it's escaped my notice that you're the only person I've ever heard of who set out to have a one-night stand but ended up with a stubborn cowboy who would prefer to court you, thank you very much. And is going to go right ahead and do that whether you want him to or not."

"When you put it that way, it sounds like a lot more fun than it is."

"Amanda, you would have *died* a few months back if Brady even glanced in your direction."

"I did die, I think. Remember? At Ty and Hannah's wedding?"

"This is better than dying," Kat said gently. Then she

laughed. "This is the good stuff! You're supposed to enjoy it."

Amanda took the bowl of popcorn from her friend. "You're only saying that because you have Brandon, and you know how it all ends. You've completely forgotten that it all might *not* work out and probably won't."

"Is that what you think? That after all this stuff with your family and his, it won't happen?"

Amanda didn't like hearing that said out loud. It was worse than when she said it in her head. She tried to smile. "It's not happening now."

"Yes, it is. It's happening the right way, that's all."

"I liked the way it was happening before!" She saw the look on Kat's face, then. "I'm not you, Kat. I never wanted to wait. If I'd had a Brandon in high school, I would have happily stopped waiting at any point."

"You were always waiting, Amanda," Kat replied calmly, which was not the reaction Amanda wanted. "I think you know you were always waiting for Brady. Now *he's* waiting because it's serious. That's not a bad thing."

"As long as this is him waiting," Amanda whispered, horrified that her voice cracked—but not enough to stop. "And not him changing his mind."

Kat reached over and wrapped an arm around Amanda's shoulders.

"He's not," she said fiercely. "And if he is, your brothers will be the least of his worries."

The idea of Kat swinging at Brady made Amanda laugh. But it didn't ease that panicked thing inside her. She wanted nothing more than to be stretched out on her bed with Brady, right now, held so tight in his arms, they felt like a single person instead of two.

She wanted to taste his intentions, not analyze them.

That Sunday, Brady turned up at the Bar K after church and smiled blandly when Connor opened the door, Amanda at his heels. Connor scowled, but Brady went off into Donovan's study with him anyway. A little while later, Donovan had called for Ellie to join them.

"Really?" Connor glared at Amanda as if she was personally attacking him, standing there in the hall. "What do you think this is going to accomplish?"

"I already told you," Amanda replied. She smiled as if she'd never been more serene. "Did you think I was kidding?"

"I think Brady deliberately planned his visit when Riley and Jensen weren't here. Did you tell him they were delivering stock this weekend?"

She hadn't, but only because he'd already known. She gave Connor her most enigmatic look in reply.

"This is stupid, monkey," he growled at her. "You know there's no way out of this where you don't get hurt, right?"

Amanda kept smiling, because it was that or admit that she was already hurt. And that she was afraid there was a lot more where that came from.

When Brady was done, he came out, smiled at her, and proceeded to be frustratingly non-forthcoming when she walked him back out to his truck.

"Are you really not going to tell me what they said?" she demanded, angrily standing a foot away from him with her arms crossed, wishing she'd worn a coat.

"Your parents aren't the problem. They know I'll make an honest woman out of you or get run out of this town forever."

He grinned when he said that. Amanda should have grinned too. He told her they had to wait, and that suggested they were waiting for something. He was talking about *making an honest woman out of her.* About *courting* her, not dating her or sneaking around with her in the middle of the night, and he was doing it. It all seemed headed in the right direction . . . but this wasn't how she'd imagined it.

Amanda had always figured there would be way more giddiness and heat, way more time alone with each other, and a whole lot less involvement with her family.

She blew out a breath and let the cold seep into her. The brooding sky matched her mood, and the brisk slap of the wind helped it along. But she sighed when Brady reached over and rubbed his palms over her arms, warming her up.

"You should stay for Sunday dinner," she said quietly.

She meant, *Stay with me. Stay forever.*

"We'll get there," Brady said, and his dark green eyes gleamed so bright, she could have sworn she'd said those things out loud.

Better yet, that he'd heard her.

She was still thinking about it when Brady picked her up after her next shift at Cold River Coffee and announced they were going on a walk.

"A walk," she repeated. Flatly. "In November. After I spent all these hours on my feet."

"A walk, Amanda," Brady drawled, with a grin, "is the perfect thing after a long day of work. I know you'll agree."

"This had better be a euphemism," Amanda grumbled, zipping herself into her coat and following him outside into the wet and cold.

It was not.

They literally walked. Up and down Main Street. In a

big, lazy loops, while keeping their hands to themselves—
and not because of the weather.

When they'd completed a loop or two, he deposited
her at her car. And left.

Also without involving his hands.

She went home, screamed in her shower, then got
ready for her shift at the Coyote.

But he showed up again the next day. And the next.

Now it was three weeks past Halloween, to the day,
and they were doing nothing but tramping around Cold
River while November kicked up a fuss in the mountains
and the rain flirted with hail and snow, depending on its
mood.

"Maybe I don't like walking," she said, not doing a
great job of keeping a smile welded to her face.

They were trudging past the Flower Pot, the Trujillo
family's floral shop that was one of the few businesses
on Main Street that stayed open year-round. Though
there were more all the time, as Cold River became more
and more of a tourist destination. Something Amanda
couldn't care about the way she probably should have
when all she was doing these days was collecting *looks*
and *walking*.

"I don't know why you think we need to parade
around like this," she said, glaring up at him. It was unfair that he looked as good as he did, even in the cold
clutch of a fall afternoon that promised snow. Every inch
of him a cowboy, impervious to the weather and able to
make her knees quake with a single curve of his mouth.
"And I really don't know why the parading means there
can't be any kissing."

"I told you there was going to be no more sneaking
around," Brady said, sounding reasonable and friendly.

She wanted to strangle him. "There's not a whole lot less sneaky than taking walks up and down Main Street in full view of the entire town."

"I don't remember being consulted. Because if I had been, the *no sex* part would have been an immediate no for me."

The smile Brady slanted down at her reminded her of when he'd been inside her, and it took her breath away, here on the street, the same way it had in her bed. Her heart stuttered in her chest.

"You didn't have sex at all," he reminded her. "For years. You're good at waiting, remember?"

"I *was* good at waiting. Then I stopped waiting. Now I don't want to wait anymore."

"Too bad, killer," Brady drawled. "You have to respect my boundaries anyway." And he laughed at the expression on her face. "Why don't you tell me what you're going to do with your barn?"

Amanda made a noise of protest. "I didn't agree to no sex or touching. And I didn't agree to your breakup barn either."

"Maybe you should start agreeing to things," Brady suggested. "Who knows what might happen?"

Amanda hadn't planned to go anywhere near that barn. A girl had to draw a line in the sand somewhere, surely, and the barn he'd tried to give her as a token of their breakup seemed like the perfect place to start. But he'd given her the keys a few days after Halloween, and despite herself, she'd found herself down there more and more.

As November rolled in and settled down hard on Cold River, she'd found herself making lists of all the things she would need to do to transform the space into that dream she'd had. And the more lists she made, the more she found herself talking about the farm stand. With the people who came into the coffeehouse, many of whom were exactly the sort of people she wanted to incorporate into the shop. Artists and farmers. The sisters with the new creamery. The brothers from the far hills who could build pretty much anything out of wood and make it art.

It was a great way to stop people from giving her *that look*, in fact.

If they were going to think of her as something other than *that little Kittredge girl*, they might as well think of her as the grown-up Kittredge who wanted to sell their stuff to a wider audience. And not whatever she was—or wasn't—to Brady.

"I don't know how you maneuvered me into this situation," she said a few nights later, her hands shoved down deep into the pockets of her coat as she and Brady walked outside in the fog, skirting around a group of people standing outside Capricorn Books. "I'm pretty sure that none of this is really what I wanted, and yet here I am, doing it anyway."

"Weird," Brady replied. "That's how I felt when my best friend's baby sister propositioned me. I dealt with it."

She rolled her eyes. But then looked away, because it was even less entertaining when the subject of Riley came up. Amanda had personally handled Connor herself this week, threatening him until he grudgingly gave his blessing, promised to only call her "monkey" in private, and texted said blessing to Brady so he couldn't rescind it. Buoyed by that success, she'd gone toe-to-toe with Zack again. In his office, where he'd given up purely so she would be quiet. Or so he claimed. But she made him record a voice message all the same.

Go ahead and date my sister, if you're that masochistic, Zack had said, glaring at Amanda while she smiled and held her phone out between them. *It's your funeral.*

Thank you, big brother, she'd said when he finished. *I love you too.*

She'd driven by the barn the other morning and found Jensen there, putting in the lighting she'd wanted.

Wow, she'd said when he'd scowled down at her from his ladder. *This could definitely be interpreted as you giving me your blessing.*

Don't get ahead of yourself, he'd growled. *Lights are just lights, Amanda.*

But later that day Brady came into the coffee shop and announced that Jensen had gone ahead and given his okay after all.

She'd been so excited, she'd leaned over the counter and kissed him, then had nearly forgotten herself while the punch of heat and longing walloped her.

How are male blessings on topics that don't concern them given, anyway? she'd asked, breathlessly, when she'd pulled back. Because there was a line, not because she wanted to. *Is there a ritual? A ceremony? Bloodletting of some kind?*

Brady had stared at her. *We had a beer.*

But Riley was a different story. Riley wasn't speaking to Brady at all, and he didn't have much more to say to Amanda either. He'd spent the better part of November making deliveries that the family normally entrusted to employees—because he wanted to stay out of town and away from this mess, Amanda knew. He wanted to make it hard. The jerk.

Brady reached over now and took her hand, squeezing it tight while the fog made the street seem eerie. Too close when the two of them were walking and talking, but too far apart.

"Riley's my problem" he said. "I'll handle him."

"We'll get there," she told him, then, repeating his words back to him like a prayer. Because she needed to hear it herself.

Brady might know where they were headed, but she wanted to get there because they both wanted to get there—because they wanted nothing more than to get there and stay there—not because Riley had caught them together.

But she didn't know how to say that.

She still didn't know how to say that, not now that everything was so public and there was the barn and he'd talked to her *parents*.

Amanda took a deep breath, but she still couldn't do it. She was too afraid of what would happen. And his fingers were threaded with hers, warm and strong, and she didn't have it in her to throw that away. No matter what that made her.

Pathetic. Weak. Silly.

"I know we will," she said instead, holding tight to Brady's hand, and letting him lead her deeper into the cold, wet night.

21

It was the night before Thanksgiving when Brady and his brothers finally held their bonfire.

They'd batted around several different ideas about how best to burn what was left of the table that had been such a symbol of the stranglehold Amos held over all of them. Every night at dinner, first in the dining room and then around the new table that Brady delivered one day from the shop of a local woodworker, they talked about what to do with all that kindling.

Brady figured it was another way to talk about how much brighter and happier things were without that last remnant of Amos here in the house with them. Even his bedroom seemed free of ghosts these days.

He was tempted to believe he might be getting there too.

"We should do it out by his grave," Gray said that afternoon. They'd been out in one of the pastures, all of them saddled up on horseback as they'd rounded up the herd and looked for stragglers. "Seems fitting."

They would all end up out by the river, where the family plot waited for them. That was a given. But Brady no longer viewed that as a kind of prison sentence.

Instead, it seemed more and more like a fitting end to every Everett story. The land gave and the land took, season after season, but one day, they would all rest in it.

It was practically a lullaby.

"Too morbid," Ty drawled, managing to look like he was lounging while on a horse. A rodeo trick, no doubt. "We'll all be there ourselves soon enough. Why rush into it?"

"Because that's less morbid," Gray said with that laugh of his that still surprised Brady, though he heard it a whole lot more these days.

"I'm not sure I want to give the old man another somber, serious occasion." Ty shrugged. "We had that at his funeral."

"You were drunk at his funeral," Brady pointed out.

Ty nodded. "I'm not sure he deserves a moment of clear-headed reflection from me."

"Maybe a moment," Gray said, his gaze on the horizon. "If it's the last moment."

"Doesn't sit right with me." Ty switched direction in that elegant way of his, barely seeming to move as he controlled his horse with ease. "I'm ready to move on. I have no idea if Dad can rest in peace, but it's time to leave that to him. We have lives to live."

Brady kept pace with them, the way he had so many times he could have counted for a year and still not made a dent. They'd spent their lives on the backs of horses. They'd spent even more time running cattle, fixing fences, and tending to the thousand and one things that could crop up in the course of a day on a ranch. His brothers looked like cowboys through and through, riding out to the fields in the cold. He guessed that made him one too, with the cold November wind in his face. There was the crisp, clean scent of snow in the air, clouds over the mountains, and the gift of bright autumn sun while they worked.

"What do you want to do?" Gray asked Brady.

Because that was what had changed the most since Halloween. They asked him now.

They didn't necessarily do what he wanted to do, or how he thought they ought to do it, but they asked.

It seemed like such a little thing.

But it was enough.

That was how they ended up out in the yard later that night. Not just Gray, Ty, and Brady, but the whole family. Everyone was bundled up against the cold while Ty started a fire in the portable fire pit they usually used only in summer. They went out after dinner and gathered around it as if it weren't a cold, damp November night too close to the end of the year.

"No one wants to make this sad," Brady said when the flames were jumping. "Because it shouldn't be. Not anymore."

He took a moment to look around at his family, gathered there in the dark with the Colorado stars stretched out high and bright above them.

There was Gray with his arms wrapped around Abby, a few days out from their one-year anniversary. Abby leaned back against her husband's chest, baby Bart snuggling in her arms, and if the only thing the year had brought was the way Gray smiled down at them, that would have been enough. But next to them was Hannah, holding hands with Ty like they were loved-up teenagers. And rounding out the Everett clan was Becca, no longer overly serious and old before her time. She held Jack on her hip, singing little songs to him while he laughed at the flames.

"I would have thought a good way to not make it sad was to avoid speeches," Gray said, not looking up from his wife and child.

"If it were up to you, there would never be any speeches, ever," Brady pointed out. "Or unnecessary sentences of any kind."

Gray laughed. Another actual laugh, not just a curve in the corner of his mouth that was open to interpretation, which was itself such a shock still. "Fair."

"I meant what I said on Halloween," Brady continued. "I'm looking forward to what we build, and I'm happy to put Dad behind us."

"Hear, hear," Ty drawled, and everyone raised what they were drinking.

Which for Jack was a sippy cup. That Becca had to grab before he threw it in the fire. Or did the same with her Coke.

"I hereby declare this Everett night," Brady intoned, while everyone's drinks were still in the air. "A night of merriment, out with the old and in with the new. Tonight, we will burn the bits and pieces of that table, and tomorrow, we'll eat too much and give thanks. Next year, who knows? We'll burn what doesn't fit anymore to make way for better things."

Everybody cheered at that, even Gray.

Brady pulled out his phone and put on some music. Not a mournful, funereal dirge, but some solid country to remind them where they were. Out here on the ranch that had been handed down to them, but required all of their hands, linked together, to keep going.

They all took turns taking handfuls of splinters from the wheelbarrow they'd set up earlier, then throwing them into the fire.

Becca danced with Jack. Hannah taught them all how to do her favorite two-step. Abby went inside at one point, then came back out with blankets to swaddle themselves in and the makings for s'mores.

And they all sat around and talked. Not about Amos, but about life. The here and the now and finally, without any fighting or sniping, the future.

"Think of it like a state park," Brady said, sitting with his brothers as the splinters dwindled, and the bonfire kept going. "Except it will be private. And we'll make money on it. There will be camping. Access to the river. And a more high-end tourist option as well, because like it or not, the tourists have found Cold River."

"He's trying not to say *glamping*," Ty told Gray lazily. "Because he doesn't want you to say—"

"What? *Glamping?* That's not a word."

"—that, Gray." Ty laughed. "Brady doesn't want you to say exactly that."

"It's glamorous camping, Dad," Becca said, rolling her eyes like a proper sixteen-year-old, disgusted to death by her parent. It made Brady's chest tight. "For people who want to camp, but without all the gross stuff."

"Like nature," Hannah chimed in. "And dirt."

"There's nothing gross about nature," Gray said. "It's nature. Dirt is the point."

"Gray is not going to come around on the glamorous camping thing," Abby said, looking like she was trying not to burst out laughing.

"You'll like what they pay to do it," Brady said idly. He named some competitive rates. And when Gray nodded instead of muttering darkly about real ranching and the problem with college degrees, that wasn't just *progress*. It was a miracle. "I'm going to build a little lodge. More of a visitor center than a hotel, but you never know. We'll see how things go. Maybe down the road, a hotel wouldn't be out of the question."

Gray made a face at that. "Seems like a slippery slope to me. One minute it's a hotel, and the next it's a dude ranch. Filled with the kind of people who would pay money to go to something called a dude ranch." He blew out a breath. "Can llamas be far behind?"

"Obviously I'm planning the llama farm too," Brady said. "But that's phase two."

"Everyone loves llamas," Ty drawled.

"I'm looking forward to it," Gray replied. He grinned. "Can you train them to actually serve the lavender hemp lattes?"

And there, while the fire danced and the table burned, Brady believed he could. He believed he could do anything. That together, he and his brothers—he and his family—could rearrange the mountains.

He thought that finally, after all this time, Cold River Ranch was really a home. His home. He had everything he'd ever wanted but had figured he wouldn't get to have. His brothers, treating him like a friend. Their beautiful wives, funny and fascinating. And three remarkable members of the next generation too, growing up here with the land all around and a whole lot less Everett family turmoil. Relatively speaking. Who knew what they'd accomplish?

If Brady did nothing else in his life but bask in this, he would be perfectly content.

But he wanted to be more than simply content.

Brady had his heart set on happy.

"Is it safe to talk about Amanda Kittredge?" Ty asked sometime later. "Or will there be more destruction of property?"

Gray whistled, long and low, but didn't contribute a comment. Likely because that was his comment. Brady looked back and forth between them.

"That depends what you have to say about Amanda Kittredge," he said. "I can't rule anything out."

"An observation, that's all," Ty replied. Innocently.

He was kicked back in one of the camp chairs some-one had found in the barn, because heaven forbid Ty didn't look as lazy as possible at all times. Even when he had Jack sprawled out over him, unconscious in the wake of his s'mores-induced sugar crash.

Brady sighed. And braced himself. "Hit me."

Ty grinned. "There are a lot of women out there that a man might get in a fight about, circumstances being what they are."

"I'll want an accounting of those circumstances later, sugar," Hannah said from beside him.

Ty glanced at Hannah with laughter in his gaze, but his expression was serious when he looked back at Brady. "But a woman prepared to burn down the house for you? A woman who doesn't pull her punches, even in the middle of some ugly family stuff? That's gold, in my opinion."

"You need to lock that down, college boy," Gray drawled, and this time, Brady knew exactly what that curve in his oldest brother's mouth meant. "No more walks in town. Whatever that is. Get it done."

Brady knew Gray hadn't been hanging around gos-siping about his younger brother. Gray hardly bothered going into town at all if he could avoid it. But Abby went in all the time. So did Hannah. And Becca. All three of them smiled at him, which was as good as an admission of guilt.

There was a time not so long ago that he would have found these small-town games of Telephone suffocating. He would have longed for the anonymity of Denver. Tonight, however, it felt good to have so many people this invested in him. In his happiness.

Maybe that was what family was. What it was supposed to be.

"Not to mention," Gray said, "making an honest woman out of her might take that Kittredge bounty off your head."

"There's no bounty on my head." Brady didn't think there was. But who knew with Riley. "I'd like to see them try."

Ty laughed. "Look who's full of himself now that his shiner's faded."

"I appreciate the concern," Brady said, and he incorporated the whole family in that. With a smirk. "But don't you worry. I know exactly what I'm doing with Amanda."

Because he hadn't been kidding when he'd said that he wanted this night to be an annual thing for his family.

And it was past time Amanda was a member of his family. Officially.

Which meant Brady needed to handle the last holdout from hers.

The next morning was Thanksgiving, so he finished his usual chores and then skipped breakfast, because it was time to hash things out with Riley.

Because even Riley Kittredge, one of the most stubborn men alive, couldn't pretend to have urgent business somewhere outside Longhorn County on Thanksgiving. Not while his mother drew breath.

Brady knew he'd be home.

Riley's cabin sat at the end of a dirt road on the edge of the forest, almost all the way out into the foothills. Brady had helped build this house. The summer before college, he and every other able-bodied member of the Cold River High School Cowboys had come out here and helped. And Riley had added to it over the years, broadening his windows to better take in the view. Adding a shop and his own barn.

Brady hadn't envied his friend the life of domesticity he was settling into back then. Not when Brady had been all set to take off to a better life. He'd wanted to see exactly how wide and how far he could sow his wild oats, and he had.

But here, now, everything was different. And he understood far better why a man might take a deep pleasure in owning a piece of land, building a house with his own hands, and settling into the life he'd made.

Maybe he understood better than Riley did these days, because last night he'd done his best to burn out what ghosts remained. He'd burned away what kept him bitter, and Brady wanted what came next. He was ready.

He knew that wasn't true for his friend. Not with his ghost alive and well and often popping up in the same room.

Brady parked his truck out front, then climbed out into the still, cold morning. He could see smoke coming from Riley's chimney, but he didn't bother to look for his friend inside the house. Not at this time of day. He made his way over toward the barn, his feet crunching into the frigid ground with every step.

He wasn't surprised to look up before he got near the barn door to find Riley standing there, watching him approach.

Without a single sign that they'd ever been friends on his face. Much less best friends. Best friends who would even have called themselves brothers not too long ago.

Riley was acting like none of that had ever happened. Like Brady was nothing more than *some guy*.

Brady knew that Amanda thought he was sad about what had gone down between him and Riley. But he wasn't. Maybe on the day. But not now, weeks later.

Now he was pissed.

"You took a shot at me already," Brady tossed out into the frigid space between them, as much of it coming from Riley as the blasts of cold air when the wind picked up. "You punched me in the face. And I let you because I deserved it. That was almost a month ago, so why are you still sulking?"

"This isn't a high school football game, Brady. I'm not impressed by your offense. I asked you to *protect* my sister from men like you, not to go ahead and—"

"I want to marry her." Brady threw that out, and it wasn't to placate his friend. It came out a whole lot more like a weapon he thought he could use here. "I love her. I'm *going* to marry her. And I don't need your permission or your blessing, but I would like it."

Riley laughed, his gaze much too dark. "Over my dead body."

"That can be arranged."

Another laugh. "You don't want to fight me."

"You're right. I don't. But not because I'm afraid. You

and I both know that people started calling you the most dangerous of the Kittredges because you pushed Stephen Crow into a locker in seventh grade."

"He would be the first person to tell you he had that coming."

"The point is, it's not because you moonlight as a ninja." Brady opened his arms wide, the universal sign for *come at me*. "We can fight if you want. I already took the hit that was coming to me, but sure. Let's make it worse."

"Do you think this is a joke?" Riley demanded, taking another step out of the barn into the cold, gray morning.

"I don't think it's a joke at all," Brady replied. "But I also don't think it's really about me."

Riley scowled. "Are there other two-faced liars who've been messing with my sister? Because I'll handle them too. But then Amanda and I are going to sit and have a talk about what people call—"

"I love you like a brother, man," Brady said with a quiet ferocity. "But you do not want to finish that sentence."

They stared at each other, both of them a little too hot in the frigid morning. Brady could see their breath like clouds. Evidence of the temper they were both clearly fighting to keep at bay.

Riley's chest heaved and his scowl deepened, but he didn't finish what he was saying.

"There's something you need to know," Brady said, holding his friend's gaze. "I would never have gone behind your back if it was a casual thing. I would never risk a lifetime of friendship for a simple roll in the hay."

"Good to know you save your deception for big-ticket items. That's a real comfort."

That stung, but Brady kept going. "I shouldn't have done it either way. I regret that you walked in on us like that. I really hope you know how sorry I am. And how much I wish I'd handled things better."

Riley studied him for a moment, not bending an inch. "But you're not sorry you put your hands on her."

"No." Brady kept his gaze steady. "I'm not sorry about that part at all."

Riley swallowed hard, then looked away. Away from the house and the mountains that rose up severely behind it, out toward that view of his. That rolling view over the whole of the far valley, where their families had feuded, tended the land, raised up herds and horses, and kept on keeping on without killing each other outright. For generations now.

"The Kittredges and the Everetts have had feuds before," Brady pointed out. "We can have ourselves another twenty-year standoff, if you like. But I'll remind you, Amanda's younger than the both of us. She'll wait twenty years, and then she'll knock you upside your head when you're too old and feeble to do anything about it."

Riley shook his head, still staring out at the valley. "I don't really think you should be reminding me how much younger my sister is than you."

"Fine. A twenty-year feud it is. Good times. I'll use Thanksgiving to notify the rest of my kin. Isn't that how it's done?" He rolled his eyes. "Or we could fast-forward to the part where we ride off into the mountains as enemies, but come down as friends."

"You don't need my input one way or another," Riley muttered, still staring off into the distance. "I got an earful from my mother about how respectful you've been.

How you've asked not only her and my father, but each and every one of us—and my grandparents—to give you the green light. She just can't stop talking about what a forthright, trustworthy *gentleman* you are, Brady."

Ouch. "Riley—"

"But you and I both know that's not the case." Riley turned back then, his dark gaze flat. "Because you and I also know that I didn't walk in on you giving her a peck on the cheek. That wasn't a sweet little kiss. It was the kind of kiss a man gives a woman he—"

He didn't finish that sentence either.

Brady stared back at him, refusing to give an inch. "I kissed her like a man who has every intention of marrying her. But Riley. Come on. Do you really want to stand around talking about *how I kissed* Amanda?"

"I do not."

"What's it going to take?" Brady demanded. "You already hit me. I don't think you really want to talk about it anymore. The good news is, I have good intentions. I'm guessing from your perspective, that's also the bad news. But I'm running out of patience."

"Patience?" Riley belted out one of those laughs. "I would not describe anything you've done since you got your hands on my sister as *patient*."

It was Brady's turn to laugh, suicidal as it might have been. "You have no idea what you're talking about."

Riley ran a hand over his face, clearly thinking about what that might mean. And just as clearly wishing he hadn't. Then he met Brady's gaze again.

Two old friends. Possibly bitter enemies.

"Don't ever lie to me again," Riley said, his voice dark.

"I swear on everything and anything holy, I won't."

Another moment dragged by. Riley's jaw worked. But nothing else moved.

Finally, he blew out a breath. "I guess this was always going to happen. And I guess it could have been worse. She could have had a teenage rebellion."

"She could have behaved like we did in high school," Brady said dryly. "Imagine that."

Riley grunted. "I'll pass."

Brady waited.

"Given that it was inevitable," Riley muttered, "I'm glad it's you."

"Why, thank you, old friend." He didn't actually laugh, but it was close. "I believe that's the kindest thing you've ever said to me."

Riley glared at him, which was better than the flatness. "You ever make her cry like that again, and I'll take your head off. Let's be real clear about that. You're my best friend, but she's my sister. If there's a side to take, assume I'm on hers."

"I would expect nothing less."

The morning was still cold and gray and raw enough to be called bitter. But when Riley looked at him, Brady was relieved to see that the worst of the darkness had lifted. If he wasn't mistaken, that was a smile he saw lurking around in there.

"If you're marrying her, I guess that means you're part of the family," Riley said. Grudgingly. "It was one thing, you being only an Everett. You're going to have to step it up if you want to be one of the Kittredge boys."

"I don't want that. I don't want any part of that."

For the first time since he'd walked into that barn on

Halloween and started swinging, Riley looked down-right cheerful.

"We'll train you up right." He closed the distance be-tween them and slapped Brady on the back. Harder than necessary. Much harder than necessary. "We'll get you there."

"Happy Thanksgiving to you too, brother," Brady re-plied.

He and Riley talked a bit more, had a cup of coffee to mark the occasion, and then Brady got back in his truck.

And that was that. He'd done it.

There were nothing but green lights and blessings as he set off down Riley's dirt road, toward the rest of the valley and the start of Thanksgiving Day.

Brady had spent the past month paying a kind of pen-ance, fighting every minute of the day to keep his hands to himself. He'd wanted to do it, but it had been sheer torture.

Near impossible, some days.

He'd kept reminding himself that Amanda deserved to be treated well. Respectfully. And Brady really had known her since she was in diapers. She never had been a roll in the hay, and he never should have treated her like one.

But he was tired of it. He was tired of chaste walks down Main Street. He was tired of that clawing need in-side him that he was sure was tearing him up. And above all, he was sick and tired of not being able to call her his.

And then act accordingly.

He'd had vague plans to wait until after the holidays, but as he left Riley's, he decided that he'd waited long enough. He'd spent this whole year waiting, period.

For the time to pass. For his brothers to magically come around to his way of thinking. For his fury at his dead father to go away.

He been waiting and he'd been waiting. He'd come here thinking his life was on hold for a while, not that it would have to change completely. That was why he hadn't changed it. He'd been here in body, but not in spirit.

Just as Gray had always accused him.

Then in the course of two months, everything had changed. *She* had changed him. Everything was different now. Brady most of all.

He could barely remember who he'd been even back at Ty and Hannah's wedding at the end of August, when little Amanda Kittredge had worn a dress he'd tried his best not to look at too closely, out there in the sweet grass behind the Everett ranch house.

He'd been waiting his whole life. He was tired of waiting.

He was ready for his real life to start.

Right now.

22

Amanda woke bright and early on Thanksgiving morning, agitated.

Her mother didn't expect her until around eleven, so the bright-and-early part meant only that she was wide awake and all alone, staring up at her ceiling with nothing to do but stew in her agitation.

It wasn't fun.

She stayed in bed as long as possible, first trying to sleep again. Then thrashing angrily around. Then lying there, furiously staring at her ceiling.

After the joy of all that wore off, she got up and took a long shower until even that became too much. Or maybe it was that the water went cold.

But then, dressed hours too early and sitting there, fuming, in the living room that felt a lot less cozy and cute now that she kept seeing Brady all over it, Amanda decided she'd had enough.

"Enough," she kept saying, out loud. And not under her breath.

She stomped down the icy stairs outside—but she respected the ice, so she stomped slowly and with precision—and she jumped into her car. Then she headed out over the hill. She didn't see a soul as she drove over the cold roads, and that somehow made the restless thing inside her worse. More acute.

As she crested the hill, it was like looking out over the history of her family. Brady's family too. And that made her even madder.

So many lifetimes were tangled up in these fields, and yet here they still stood. Her life was minor in comparison. She hadn't set out in a covered wagon to an unfamiliar land. She hadn't homesteaded through a Colorado winter. Her ancestors had made things work. Even her parents' marriage, the one her brothers still complained about, had worked out in the end. They'd *made* it work.

Why couldn't she?

Amanda was halfway down the county road toward the turnoff for Cold River Ranch when she remembered that the last time she'd visited the ranch, it had been Halloween.

You can't do that again, she told herself firmly. *Especially if this time, you're the one attacking Brady.*

She pulled over and sat there by the side of the road for a moment. Then she turned her car around. Maybe the best thing here was not to go in guns blazing, making a big deal out of everything, and essentially announcing to the entire Everett family that she was very much the overemotional, overdramatic teenage girl they all probably still thought she was, anyway.

Maybe the best thing here was to take a breath. To regroup.

Amanda took one of the dirt roads. This one skirted around what had once been Abby's family's farm, headed up into Everett land, then led into one of the lower Kittredge pastures. When she got to the pasture, she took a different dirt road, this one more of a scenic route. It wound around and would eventually drop her on the county road that led to her parents' house.

When she saw the truck in the distance, still out in the network of dirt lanes, she sighed. Because it was inevitably going to be one of her brothers, and she didn't want to deal with any of them. And because she couldn't think who else could be driving around out here on private property, early in the morning on a national holiday.

But as the truck drew closer, she saw that it was Brady.

Her foolish heart thumped. Hard.

Custom dictated that since she had the smaller, more maneuverable car, she should pull off to the grassy bit on the side to let his much bigger truck go through. Instead, Amanda slammed on her brakes and stopped. She threw her car into park, switched off the engine, and then climbed out.

She wasn't surprised when Brady did the same.

She walked toward him, keeping her eyes on him, not the vast sky overhead, heavy with the threat of snow. She didn't look at the land all around them, rolling winter fields giving way to the forest land, then the evergreen march up the slopes of the steep mountains.

It was hard to get more private than out here in the middle of nowhere, with no one around for miles and miles.

"I'm done," she told him, when they were a few feet apart.

And Brady laughed.

That felt unduly aggressive. Amanda scowled at him until he stopped.

"I'm tired of this," she threw at him. "I don't want to not hold hands, and talk on the phone, and then sit around hoping that my stupid brothers behave for once when they won't. I don't know why they're a part of this discussion at all. I liked things the way they were before. I don't understand why you got punched in the face and turned into some . . . Victorian."

"I'm not a Victorian."

"Do you have a concussion?"

"If I did, it probably would have gone away by now. Or killed me."

"That's not comforting, Brady."

"I told you I didn't want to sneak around anymore," he said. "And I think you're forgetting this, but neither did you."

Amanda made a frustrated noise. "Surely there's a middle ground between the naked late nights after the Coyote and supervised strolls that would make every pastor in the Longhorn Valley proud."

"I can think of a decent compromise."

But Amanda wasn't done. "I don't like you making decisions that you expect me to go along with when you can't be bothered to talk them over with me. I don't think you'd like it much if I did it to you."

He started to answer, but she cut him off.

"And we can talk about the breakup barn like it's funny, but you really were ending things with me. The only reason you didn't is because I drove out to your house like a psycho, invaded your family's home, and started yelling at everyone. Then you muttered something about courting me, and we never addressed the subject again."

Brady was staring at her like she had a selection of heads, and that only made her more agitated.

"We address the subject all the time," he said. "What exactly do you think we've been waiting for?"

Amanda flung open her arms because the only witness was the Colorado sky. She had a big mood on. "*I don't know!*"

"I needed every single one of your brothers to get on board because you think they're a barrier to the life you want to lead," Brady said. With exaggerated patience. "Now they're not. You're welcome."

"I already decided they had no say over my life. I was demonstrating it. I didn't need you to drag us through the whole thing all over again."

"It had to be done."

"You keep saying that, but you won't say why." She shook her head at him and felt the cold wind pick up, slicing into her. "I think you didn't like the fact that for once, the golden child quarterback of the high school football team wasn't universally beloved. You didn't like the fact that this time, your education and your charm and all your usual weapons couldn't do you any good."

"Wrong again, killer," Brady drawled, though his gaze on hers was hard. "First of all, if my usual weapons worked out here, Gray would have sold the ranch a year ago. Second, I work with numbers. I'm methodical. When I close a deal, I like to make sure there are no loopholes. Do you understand what I'm saying to you?"

She told herself it was the cold that was making her fidget, and making her throat feel tight. "Right. Closing a deal. That's very romantic."

He looked almost surprised.

The agitation in her seemed to swell, expanding like a wave, until Amanda had to face the fact that she wasn't *agitated.* That was fear threatening to knock her sideways. She'd been avoiding this conversation for weeks, and now she'd forced it.

But it might kill her to drag herself through another day, not knowing.

She was still afraid of what she might hear. But she reminded herself that she'd grown up on horses. Which was to say, falling off horses. Amanda had been practicing falling on her face and eating dirt her whole life. Getting up again hurt sometimes, but she'd always done it. She would again.

Even if Brady flattened her, she'd find her feet. One way or another.

What she couldn't do was stay stuck in this limbo any longer.

"You used the word *courting.*" It also might kill her to actually say this out loud. At least then she wouldn't have to worry about falling or climbing back up. There was that. "You've made the whole town think you mean marriage. But you can be honest now. Here. Is that what you really want?"

She didn't want to ask that. Because she still didn't want to know the answer.

Brady looked even more shocked. "What?"

Amanda ignored her own queasiness. "You wanted to end things. Then Riley walked in, and you had to make it right. He caught you, so your intentions had to be good. It's like a shotgun wedding, but I'm not even pregnant."

"Is that what you think?"

"I told you that I loved you, Brady." And the bravado and agitation that had got her here deserted her. It all blew away on a gust of cold air, and all that was left was her growing, painful awareness of her own vulnerability. She didn't like exposing herself like this. But what else did she have? "And I told you that I was pretty sure you loved me too. And neither of those things mattered. You were saying goodbye."

The way he looked at her made her feel light-headed. "What I remember doing was kissing you when I shouldn't have."

Amanda felt so many things then that she couldn't have picked them apart if her life depended on it. It was all a big, messy snarl. And yet, somehow, she finally understood.

He'd been so determined this past month to set things right. To take their scandal and make it a sweet story. She understood in a flash, then, that he'd been doing that for her. So what people remembered wasn't Brady's black eye, but those walks. Folks could speculate about what happened behind closed doors, but he'd balanced that out with what they'd seen. He'd created a counterargument.

It was so sweet, she wanted to cry. Maybe she was crying.

"I don't think I love you because I was a virgin and I don't know any better," she told him now, because she was already too wide open. She felt like the sky, endless in all directions and gray straight through. "I loved you while we were having sex, and I love you even now that we're not. It's not going away. But, Brady." And her voice cracked a little, because she wasn't the sky after all. "I don't think one person can do all the loving. I don't think it works that way."

He took another step toward her, but she put up her hands. And somehow, they got tangled in his. Amanda thought that later, maybe, she would marvel that the cold made her shiver, but the heat of his fingers made her shake twice as hard.

"It's okay if you don't love me," she told him, and she wanted that to be true. She really did. "I mean, to be clear, I'll probably hate you for it, but it's *okay*. I would never want you to feel trapped. There's no shotgun, and you don't owe me anything. I'm the one who propositioned you."

"Amanda—"

She tried to pull her hands away, but he didn't let her. "I don't think this is what you want. We should end it. For real this time."

"That's not going to work," Brady drawled, the look in his dark green eyes so intense, she forgot to feel queasy and exposed. Or to breathe. "You're not the only one in love here. You never were. I'm completely, totally, head-over-heels in love with you, Amanda. I think you're going to have to stay with me."

Then Amanda couldn't tell anymore if she was the one who couldn't breathe or if the world had collapsed all around them.

She also didn't care.

"I've spent years going out of my way to not notice you," Brady said, low and fierce. He pulled her even closer. "It was obviously a defense mechanism, because all it took was one glimpse of you where I wasn't expecting you. One look at that freaking tank top, and I was done for. There was no pretending you were still a little girl anymore. And once I really saw you? That was it. I fell that fast, that hard."

"Brady . . ."

"There is not a single thing on this earth that could

make me go back on my word to your brother," Brady said, urgent and intense. "Except you."

"But ever since Halloween . . ."

"Listen to me, baby." And she didn't know which one of them moved, but she was in his arms again, and nothing else mattered. "You really are young. That's not an insult, it's a fact. You should go out there in your tight little tank tops and see what kind of trouble you can get into. That was what you wanted, isn't it?"

"I don't know what I wanted."

"Yes, you do. And those are perfectly reasonable things to want. All those regrets and mistakes. All those adventures. You have all of that before you."

She wanted to scream at him that she knew what she wanted *now,* and that was what mattered. That she'd found herself the best adventure, and she didn't need to sample others to know that. Amanda knew quality when she found it. She knew what suited her.

But she couldn't make her mouth work the way it should.

And Brady was still talking, in that same fierce way. "But it turns out, I really am a selfish man. I want you to do every little thing that your heart desires, Amanda. But I want you to do them with me."

She couldn't tell if she was sobbing or laughing, breathing, or maybe even dreaming. But his eyes were dark and green, and when he looked at her, the mountains moved. And the sky felt blue, even when, like today, it was a sullen snowstorm waiting to happen.

Then he made the summer sun appear because he sank down before her on one knee.

Amanda stopped worrying whether she was breathing or not. Maybe she said his name. Maybe she screamed it.

It didn't matter because he reached into the pocket of his coat and he pulled out a ring.

Her heart, already working overtime, kicked into higher gear.

Because she recognized it.

"I went and saw your grandmother," he told her, gazing up at her as if she were the sky. "We sat with her Bible and we looked through that family tree, looking for evidence that there had ever been an Everett and Kittredge match before. But no matter how we looked, we couldn't find one. She figured old, founding families learned how to keep proper distances. I told her I had a better idea."

Until this moment, Amanda hadn't realized that a person could be laughing and crying at the same time. The human version of a fox's wedding, like her grandmother always said.

"And she told me that regretfully, she didn't think a whole lot of my father," Brady continued. Almost gravely. "But she'd known my grandfather Silas, and a finer, more upstanding man had been hard to find around these parts. She wondered if I thought I took more after him."

"She did like your grandfather. She's always said that."

"I said I expected that was a bit of a trick question. A man like my father would claim that, of course, he was like my grandfather. While men like my grandfather would be too humble. I'd have to settle for hoping I took the best of each man."

"You're the best of all men," Amanda whispered fiercely. "And you don't have to keep proving yourself to my family."

"Don't you understand, baby? I'm not proving myself to your family. I love your family, but it won't keep me up at night if I'm not their favorite person every minute of the day." Brady kept his gaze trained on her. "But you're a different story. You might have moved out. You might have defied them by working at the Coyote. You might like to poke at them, whenever possible. But you love them."

"Sometimes more than other times. And lately not at all."

He didn't smile, but still, the way he looked at her warmed her. "You could never be happy with a man who didn't take the time to make sure they approved. Not for me, but for you. It matters to you what they think, or you would have dated someone just to date them. Years ago."

He held the ring out between them. "Your grandmother told me this was a ring that had been passed down in your family for a long while. And that if you didn't like it, I could go do what young men did and try to express myself in carats."

He took her hand and slid the ring onto her finger. It was an old gold with a pretty ruby in the center. And she knew without having to ask that this was the ring she'd seen on her grandmother's hand when she was younger. The one that the original Kittredges had made out of gold from the California rush and a ruby from the old country.

"It's perfect," she whispered. "You're perfect."

"I never want you to forget where you came from," Brady told her. "Where we came from. This valley and these fields and all the people who came before us and made us who we are. Including your brothers. That's what this ring is."

"I love it, Brady. I love you."

"But we also have a future," Brady said, then. "And the future is all ours. I want so many things from you, Amanda. I want love. I want more mornings waking up with you next to me. I want a house on our own land, with a beautiful view and the sound of our kids rough-housing from the other side of a firmly locked door."

They both smiled at that, but he kept going.

"I want that barn of yours to take off. I want my park project to bring in every single tourist from Denver and beyond. I want to take all that we've been given, put our spin on it, and hand it on to the next generation. I want to teach our children that it's always okay to go out there and see what the world has to offer, but that this is their home, and they can always come back here. And that we hope they will."

To her surprise, he pulled out another ring. And as he slid it onto her finger, moving it into place with the first ring, she understood that this was the kind of methodical he meant. That he'd planned for these two rings to sit there, side by side. One, the old, historical Kittredge ruby. And the other, a gleaming diamond she knew he must have chosen himself, set in a delicate rose gold that played off the ruby, then somehow, together, made one. Better than before.

Just like them.

"Brady," she tried to say, though she was sobbing and laughing and wasn't sure she'd ever stop. "It's so beauti-ful. They're both so beautiful. You're so beautiful."

"Amanda," he said, still there on one knee, though he was smiling now. "Will you marry me? I want you to—"

"Yes," she said, too fast and too wild. She sank down, so they were both kneeling there on the cold ground, but she couldn't even feel it. There was only him. There was only this. "Yes and yes and yes, to everything. I love you."

His mouth was on hers, then, and his hands were in her hair. And she was pressing herself against him, desperate and giddy. There was water on her face, but his mouth was so hot, she didn't care.

Then Brady pulled back and hauled her to her feet.

"I love you, Amanda," he said, very seriously, as if these were their vows. "I will spend the rest of my life making up for that morning in the barn."

"You don't have to do that," she said in the same tone. "Because I love you too. And we're going to have those babies, and a lock on our door to make more whenever we like. And every other good thing under the sun because it's Thanksgiving. And you love me. And that's the only thing in the world I can think of that's better than my grandma's sweet potatoes."

"You humble me." And there was laughter in his voice, but Brady's gaze was serious.

"While you make me feel like I can fly," Amanda whispered. "From one perfect Brady moment to the next. And I can think of a way you could make us both fly pretty high, right now."

She braced herself for him to decline. To talk to her some more about the virtues of waiting.

But instead, Brady smiled.

"You do have my rings on her finger," he drawled.

"I do, indeed."

"And if I'm not mistaken," he said, drawing her with him as he moved backward, heading toward his truck, "your education when it comes to the joys of pickup trucks in remote fields is patchy. At best."

"I've probably forgotten everything you've taught

me," she said solemnly, then laughed as he picked her up. He tossed her through the open front door into his truck. Then crawled in after her. He slammed his door, turned on the ignition, and then jacked up his heater.

Then he turned to her on that bench seat with pure wickedness in his eyes again.

At last.

And it was truly the most beautiful thing she'd ever seen.

"I'm not afraid to do a little remedial work with you, Amanda," he told her solemnly. "That's how much I love you."

She was smiling so wide, it hurt. "I appreciate your sacrifice. To education."

And as if the land wanted to celebrate with them, it started to snow.

Then, out there in the fields, beneath a sky that couldn't begin to contain how much they loved each other, Amanda and Brady stopped worrying about the past and started working on their future.

Together.

In the best way they knew how.

23

It was the best Thanksgiving Brady had ever had.

Possibly because he'd never had so many thanks to give.

That Saturday, his family gathered to celebrate Abby and Gray's first year of marriage. And this time, Amanda was by his side with his rings on her finger, right where she belonged.

"I'm proud of you," Abby told her when she arrived, giving her a hug. "I've been meaning to tell you that all month."

"That wasn't an entrance," Hannah drawled, grinning wide. "That was a whole stinking show!"

Amanda was flushed with happiness, there with the women who would be the sisters she'd never had, so Brady didn't ask what that meant. Not then.

But later, stretched out in that bed above the Coyote, he learned all about what it meant to make an entrance, Hannah-style.

"I think you have it covered, baby," he told her, his voice a little rough after all that making up for lost time they'd been doing. "When you walk in a room, there's nobody else there as far as I'm concerned."

Then he showed her what he meant.

Again.

Amanda worked that Sunday, but then went ahead and quit the Coyote the following week. "Not because you don't like me working there. But because *I* don't like working there enough to keep doing it."

"Noted, killer," he drawled.

Then he thanked her at some length, out in the woods. In the back of his pickup with a whole lot of blankets and nothing around for miles but the wind.

In furtherance of her education, of course.

Brady went with her to give her notice that first week of December and wasn't surprised when Harry did nothing more than roll his eyes.

"Can't say I'm shocked," the grizzled old man said. "Though I thought it would be her brothers in here with her, telling her to quit. Not you."

Brady shrugged. "Life is full of surprises."

Harry cracked a smile. "Ain't that the truth." He shifted his gaze to Amanda. "You can have the apartment until the end of the year. But then I'm going to have to get a new bartender, and that apartment's pretty much the only draw."

"I understand," Amanda assured him.

But later, she confessed that she really didn't want to move back home with her parents.

"It was one thing before, when I didn't know any better," she said. "But now? It would feel like backsliding."

Brady thought of that bedroom in the ranch house, empty of everything but Amos's ghost. And agreed.

It only made him work that much harder on her barn. And the carriage house out back.

One cold December evening, when he'd come back

into town to do some more work while Amanda had one of her movie nights with Kat, he looked up from his hammering to find all four Kittredge brothers there. Coming toward him.

"If this is a hazing ritual, is it okay we put it off?" He smiled lazily. "I'm meeting your sister in a little while, and you know how she gets when you rough me up. She likes my face pretty."

They all glared at him in unison.

Until Riley grinned. "Idiot."

Zack did not grin. "Amanda seems to think she's moving home when her lease is up. I'm betting you have other ideas about where my baby sister should live."

Brady reminded himself that he wasn't afraid of these men he'd called friends his whole life. But there *were* four of them. And they were big.

Still, a man had to stand tall in his own space. "I do, indeed."

"Let's get to it, then," Jensen said darkly. Then ruined it by laughing. "I don't want to hear about your face, pretty or otherwise, ever again."

"Amen," Connor agreed.

Which was how, come Christmas Eve, he took his beautiful fiancée to the carriage house off the back of the barn that he and her brothers had fixed up. They'd made a sweet little home for two people just starting out, far away from meddling family members or too many small-town eyes.

Better yet, no one had gotten a black eye out of it.

"Brady . . ." Amanda turned in a circle in the cozy front room where he'd even put up a Christmas tree. "How did you do all this? It's *perfect*."

"How do you think?" He grinned at her. "Magic, obviously. And four big, strong elves. It's Christmas Eve."

Her eyes gleamed that gold he loved so much. She came into his arms and she tipped her head up, and he wished he'd known that it was possible to love like this. He wished he'd had the slightest idea.

Because he would have found her earlier, if he'd known. He would have moved heaven and earth.

"It's Christmas Eve," she said very solemnly. "That means it's been the full year you promised Gray. What do you think? Are you going to stay?"

He dropped his head to hers and tasted her. Then pulled back to get another hit of that smile. "You couldn't make me leave."

Amanda's smile got even bigger. "Every time I think we've hit the best Brady moment ever, there's another one."

"There always will be," he promised her.

That night, they lay in bed in their first home together while the snow fell outside. They talked about getting married in the spring, because neither one of them wanted to wait.

"Ever again," Amanda said, so vehemently it made him laugh.

They decided they'd do it down on that rock by the river that had always been Brady's favorite place in the valley.

"Because," Amanda said, propping herself up on his chest to gaze down at him, "that's where it started, really."

Someday, they would build there, Brady thought, and make his first refuge a part of their forever home.

But first they lost themselves in each other in the cozy little cottage behind the barn he'd tried to give her as a goodbye.

And that very same night—a year to the day Brady had promised his brother he'd give Cold River a chance, but had never expected he'd stay—they started planning their own family. Their own future.

It started with their wedding. That was absolutely not a shotgun wedding, because the Kittredge brothers—his brothers, now, by marriage—really would kill him for the disrespect after all that courting.

But it wasn't the ceremony that Brady cared about, as beautiful as it was to see Amanda in her pretty dress, her hair like honey and the gold in her gaze all for him. Or how much fun it was to dance with her at her wedding the way he'd promised her he would.

Back when he'd truly believed he wouldn't be the groom.

The marriage was what he was truly excited about.

It started with *I do*, and carried on forever, one kept promise after another. His successes and hers. Their failures and sorrows. Their joys. What they learned, what they threw aside, and who they became when they were together.

As time went on, Brady often had to stop to marvel at his good fortune. His life was brighter than he ever could have imagined in the darkness of his childhood. And thanks to that little Kittredge girl he'd first made his wife, then the mother of his babies, about as close to perfect as a man could get. It was far more than he deserved.

"You're a good man," Amanda would tell him as the years rolled on by, her eyes shining and her voice fierce. "You deserve everything."

The more she believed in him, the less room there was inside him for ghosts.

Eventually, if he thought about his father and all the

old man had missed out on, it made him sad. For a moment.

But only a moment.

Brady and his brothers were better husbands than Amos ever had been, because they worked at it. They were better fathers, and they did their level best to be better men. And their lives were filled with the love they gave and the love they got back.

And all the complicated, beautiful, maddening, and magical gifts love gave to them, they called family.

Because life went on until the land called them home. That was the Everett tradition.

But a man didn't have to go to his place by the river broken and bitter, mean and alone. That was a choice.

Brady chose love.

Day after day, one season into the next, he chose love.

"Love chooses you right back," Amanda liked to tell him, honey and gold.

Year after year, behind their locked door in a house more loud with laughter than pain, she was always more than happy to prove it.